No Quie

by

Philip W Lawrence

Book 4 Detective Toni Webb

To From Mike
+ Callum

For your kindness
through a difficult
time.

Philip

With thanks to my family and friends for their comments and the time they gave to read my work.

To Sanjay Gupta who inspired me to write, although I did not realize how much time it took, not the writing, that came fairly quickly, but in my personal editing and the constant adjustments needed to make everything fit together, which it never really does.

To Daisy for the arduous task of editing.

I like spell-checking software; my dyslexic fingers never match my thought's, or it is the other way around?

To my lovely Margaret who allowed me the space and time, when time is now so precious.

All the locations in this story are based on real places I know. Sometimes I changed the names sometimes I did not. The characters and plot in this tale however are fictional; any similarity to real persons or events is purely coincidental.

I do not believe in coincidences, except sometimes.

No Quiet Find

For my grand children
and their children

Sonnet Number 27

Weary with toil, I haste me to my bed,
The dear repose for limbs with travel tired;
But then begins a journey in my head,
To work my mind, when body's work's expired:
For then my thoughts, far from where I abide,
Intend a zealous pilgrimage to thee,
And keep my drooping eyelids open wide,
Looking on darkness which the blind do see:
Save that my soul's imaginary sight,
Presents thy shadow to my sightless view
Which like a jewel hung in ghastly night;
Makes black night beauteous, and her old face new.
Lo thus by day my limbs, by night my mind
For thee, and for myself, <u>NO QUIET FIND</u>.

William Shakespeare

Prologue

Running was not something she was good at but running had kept her ahead of him. Her breathing came in gasps, she paused for a few seconds, leant forward resting her hands on her knees as her chest heaved satisfying her body's demand for oxygen. She ran on again, fuelled by fear induced adrenalin, until the silver ribbon of the river that snaked through the woodland, blocked her way.

She couldn't swim she hated the water; in fact she was terrified. She looked down at the expanse in front of her, shrinking back in dread from its swirling deep blackness; inviting her to escape in its murky waters but offering no comfort; the only way to elude him was by crossing to the other side of the river; if she was a swimmer it would've been only a few moments and she would be free but to her, at this very time, it might as well have been an ocean.

'What can I do'? She thought. 'Not my lucky day'!

Chapter 1

Earlier in the afternoon she had been sitting on one of the benches outside the Hillview restaurant in the lane behind Queen Mary's; relaxed, warming herself in the early Spring sun, waiting for Charlie. They often met there after she had finished school, or as it is now known, the sixth form at Queen Mary's, the local young adult college where she was soon to take her 'A' levels. An enjoyable brief moment for them to be together during the late afternoon break between the restaurant's lunch-time trade and his preparations for evening service. Charlie was a trainee chef where the restaurant manager, and owner, gave him day release to attend cooking classes at college on Wednesdays; otherwise he was always here. Today Monday they did not open for lunch but preparations for the evening were always busy; he was late; later than usual but she waited anyway. After half an hour she went inside to look for him; Dawn Westcott was a familiar sight to the staff as she and Charlie had been going out for more than six months and she called by to see him most weekdays. The dining room was empty, the last of the lunchtime diners having long gone, the tables were already laid for the evening.

"Hello Dawn, looking for Charlie"?

She turned to see Gavin, one of the waiters she'd often met before, standing in the doorway to the kitchen.

"Hello Gavin, yes, is he busy"?

"Sorry luv he didn't come in today, phoned in sick I believe".

"Oh, I didn't know".

She said pulling her mobile from the side pocket of her bag, she stared unbelieving at the black screen.

"Guess what my bloody phones been off all day; we're not allowed phones in class you see and I forgot to tun it back on, dam, dam, he's probably been trying to get me".

Gavin tried to mollify her obvious distress offering an explanation even though he had none.

"I don't know what's wrong with Charlie though, I didn't speak to him, no one said it was serious, just a bug of some kind I expect; he's probably at home in bed".

"Thanks Gavin I'll give him a call".

She turned and left, switching on her phone as she went, walking impatiently during the few, seemingly over-long, seconds it took for the phone to come alive. She stopped; scanned through her missed calls, her Mum twice and Joan her friend but none from Charlie. She then opened her text messages, again nothing from Charlie. She was thinking he must be quite ill if he didn't phone me or anything. She hadn't seen him Sunday as the restaurant was always full for Sunday lunches and she had a project to finish to hand in this morning. She called him on speed-dial; it went straight to message centre. "Bugger he's switched it off or let his dam battery go flat" she said aloud to herself in frustration and left a message for him to call back, added as an afterthought, a sorry for him being ill, but annoyed he hadn't told her. She then felt guilty in case he was so sick that he couldn't; so another text message this time to salve her conscience and say she loved him and was on her way round.

Charlie Brady's home was out of town in a small detached cottage that he shared with his Mum in the area known as Wildmoore; Dawn lived some distance from him, with her parents in Basingstoke on the Popley estate. She had two choices, go home first and take her bike or walk down the hill and take the bus to Shenfield and walk back to Wildmoore. She decided It was quicker to take her bike as the bus was unreliable, and the walk would take too long. She left a note for her Mum, changed clothes and set off for the five mile ride. Wildmoore was no more than a hamlet off the A33 on the road towards Reading; there were few houses spread out along a horseshoe shaped lane; the first entry into the lane enclosing Wildmoore was off from the main road to the right some four miles after leaving Basingstoke; it extended over a mile before looping round returning back to the A33 another mile further on. The houses were mostly on the outside of the loop with Charlie's well over half a mile along on the right. The inside of the horseshoe shaped lane used to be a privately owned protected woodland area but a large part had been converted, after much protest from the residents, to a golf course although it was so well hidden you couldn't see any part of it from the road; a condition in the planning consent imposed by the Council to appease the irate local homeowners; you would only know the golf course existed if you noticed a small sign by its entrance sited well away from any houses.

Dawn arrived at Bright Cottage, Charlie's house, a little breathless. She was so worried that she had ridden as hard as she could in order to arrive there quickly. Her knocking on the door several times produced no reply; his Mum was normally home at this time of day, to Dawn's concern her car was not in its usual place on the small drive; perhaps he was in bed and couldn't answer. She went round the side and peered into the kitchen; all was in darkness; the rear conservatory was also unlit and she could see clearly through into the empty lounge. Returning to the front she shouted through the letter box to no avail; she was now sure no one was in. She tried her mobile again with the same negative result; its flashing 'low battery' icon was a problem she would lose communication soon; nothing for it she would have to go home and wait there. She would keep phoning he was bound to answer or call her as soon as he could.

When she came back to the front of the cottage her bicycle and helmet had gone, astonished at first she had to look twice at where she left them before the loss registered; she then thought it must be Charlie and he was playing a trick on her; he was here after all; she'd give him a big 'what for' the silly sod. Annoyed at his thoughtless prank she cupped her hands and yelled.

"Come on Charlie where are you; you bugger"?

Nothing; no reply just silence.

"Stop messing about you're frightening me".

Again nothing. She looked both ways up the lane. She could see the way she had come in, all the way back to the distant A33 with no sign of anyone or her bike, the other way was obscured as the bend in the road began less than a hundred yards from Charlies house. She jogged along the lane following the bend expecting to see him hiding somewhere waiting to jump out. The bend went on for some considerable distance with no sign of anyone. She came to the conclusion her bike had really been stolen after all; Charlie would not have carried on this stupid game for so long. Her anger rose; this time against the unknown thief; who out here would pinch her bike and on the spur of the moment like that? She had no choice but to walk. Having reached the mid-point of the lane she slowed from her jog to a more sedate pace deciding to continue the way she was going towards the main road and the village of Shenfield-on-Bolden; there she could take a bus back to town. She looked at her phone nothing, her battery was almost flat now, so soon she wouldn't be able to receive anything. Why didn't he phone her? He'd run out of credit; that's it! He was always forgetting to top up, but where was he?

She passed the entrance driveway that led to the golf course on her left, this purposely twisting drive hid what lay beyond, maintaining the privacy this exclusive club demanded, no sign of her bike there either; whoever had taken it was long gone.

She was feeling tired and frustrated walking was not something she did from choice; apart from an enforced daily trudge to college and back; her bike, local buses and her parents' cars were her chosen methods of transport.

The bend in the lane eventually straightened with the main road a welcome view in the distance not much further now. A few yards in front the man stepped from a gap in the hedge her bicycle held off the ground in one hand the other pointing directly at her.

"Looking for this are we"?

She froze holding her breath unable to answer or move, the situation not registering at first.

"My bike"!

Was all she could muster in a weak voice, fear creeping into her body knowing from his stare this man had not stolen her bike for a joke. His intentions were different.

"If you want it back come and get it".

He said, holding it even higher stepping forward so he and the bike seemed to tower over her.

She turned and ran, going back the way she had been walking; she glanced behind her as she ran, saw him toss her bike into the hedge and start after her. There were no houses near and the golf course was now too far; a small but overgrown gap in the hedge to her left appeared which she jumped blindly through, the branches and thorns grabbed at her as she pushed against the restricting shrubbery with adrenalin fuelled force tumbling into part of the old woodland. Her cycling clothes gave her body some protection from the brambles but her exposed hands and ankles were stinging from the barbs that had bit in as she passed through. Now in the clear she ran straight and fast dodging the larger trees and bounding over the lower obstructions, not knowing exactly where she was going but hoping to end up close to the village of Shenfield with houses and people. She heard the man curse out loud as the spikey bushes bit into him, hoping the natural barrier would delay him long enough for her to get away. Her young body, more agile than the bigger and older man, was moving rapidly gaining for Dawn a good distance ahead of her pursuer; she would come across a road soon and the safety of Shenfield. She stopped suddenly a few paces from disaster, she'd forgotten about the River Bolden stretching before her in both directions. If she ran to the right there were no crossing points for miles and it would take her far from any help, to the left the old mill close to the village and safety. The ground to the left was so open he was bound to see her and without the restriction of the woods and bushes he would catch her long before she reached the mill, the only crossing near the village.

She was trapped and couldn't turn back he was somewhere behind not knowing exactly where, moving undeterred towards where she stood. Standing here was stupid, she had to do something. Dawn removed her reflective jacket, threw it into the water trampling the plants near the edge flat. He must have seen her ahead and would be looking for the flashing of her bright yellow top as she ran; she hoped the disturbance here would distract him. She moved carefully from the bank back towards the trees trying not to disturb the plant life as she went. Fifty yards back she was amongst the shrubs and bushes at the edge of the heavily coppiced trees, she moved as far from the river as she could where there was still cover, crouching down in the densest patch of greenery she could find. She heard his laboured footsteps getting closer and closer; perhaps if she lay still in the tall grass he would miss her and see her yellow jacket in the water, if it hadn't floated away. Would he believe she had jumped in and crossed over to the other side of the river? She hoped he'd give up as she pulled the reed like fronds around her small frame. Holding her breath, eyes closed like a child praying 'can't see, can't be seen'. He passed noisily by a few yards from her hiding place followed by silence for a moment when he stopped probably arriving at the river's edge; his cursing her aloud froze her in fear. She thought he must have reached the bank by the trampled area but had no idea where he was now, she could hear movement sometimes it came closer sometimes moved away, she lay unable to move willing him leave. Evaporating sweat from her earlier exertion rapidly draining the heat from her slender frame, she was becoming very cold and tired but could not summon up the courage to quit her hiding place, for all she knew he may be very close silently waiting for her to appear. She lay a long while, drifting in and out of awareness almost sleeping, willingly falling into an unconscious dreamlike warm safe place; unaware of the passage time. Not her lucky day!

Chapter 2

Much as she liked her own space Toni Webb missed her Larry. They had been divorced a long time but he called her every now and then 'just to make sure you are alright' he would say. They would chat for a few minutes; inconsequential stuff really; the weather, how her work was going, her house and garden. It seemed as soon as he had called he wanted to hang up. When he said his goodbye it left her deflated; empty somehow. She recovered slowly each time he disconnected, leaving her thinking of lost friends. Those of today are almost all work related, silently thanking them for being there and for her work, it kept her occupied and sane. The friends of her childhood and at college in London had faded into obscurity; when new acquaintances became her's and Larry's together, they became friends of a marriage around which their social life revolved. They all lived near to their home in Southampton, when she left and moved to Basingstoke they gradually absented from her life with each passing week until the calls stopped altogether.

Her neighbours, who lived two doors along, Josephine and her brother Nathaniel; they had helped her when she first moved in and were now firm friends. She and Jo were well matched in their ideas, likes and dislikes, so had taken to being together socially from the outset. She often went for a meal or a drink with Jo and Nathan came along occasionally. Recently she and Nathan had been for a curry a couple of times as a couple, she liked him a lot and was attracted to him in a way she had not felt for years. Larry's pull was smothering but of late she felt willing to let go and move on. Nathan was maybe the first person to offer a passage to free her from the emotional bondage that her failed marriage still had a hold on her. Today was special she would have liked him be there but knew it would open the door to questions and a little ribbing at work she was not yet ready to handle, so held back her intended invitation.

Today was the seventh anniversary of her arrival at Basingstoke, Larry's latest phone call, not forgotten but put to one side, was not going to spoil the occasion; she was going to celebrate with her team in the 'Shoes' tonight. The doorbell rang; her taxi had arrived. She pulled on her coat and left determined to make the most of the next few hours.

"Colin glad you could make it; I've ordered a bucket of spiced chicken wings just for you".

Colin Dale was a former Detective inspector at Basingstoke who had moved to London; his old stomping ground. Now a Chief Inspector, they had worked several cases together and had become more than just colleagues. Toni was already seated in her favourite corner; she came early needing to unwind a little before everyone arrived; her first pint of ale, almost supped, had mellowed her mood, making her extra friendly towards him. She was more than pleased that he had made the effort to drive down from London so the normal banter between them, about his never paying for a drink if he could get away with it, was forgotten for tonight.

"And a pint of Doombar I hope".

"Of course; lovely to see you Colin how's the family"?

"Glad to see you too; they are fine; Sonia's given me the night off so Jonesy has made me up a room, I'm staying here tonight".

"You are a lucky bugger with her you know".

"Don't I know it; Sonia loves you too and wouldn't want me to miss this".

The Four Horseshoes is a pub in the village near where Toni lives and where Colin used to drink before he moved from Basingstoke station back to London. An old coaching inn that had not been spoilt by over modernisation. The original timbers, low ceilings and ancient fireplaces provided an intimacy for whoever entered its comforting ambience. It became her favourite place to eat and relax and on occasion a meeting place where she and DCI Colin Dale would help each other in times of crisis. Many a difficult case had been ironed out over a pint or two and a plate of hot chicken wings.

Soon after Colin settled in his usual chair with his first pint of Doombar, half the station arrived 'en masse'; the greetings and good lucks abounded with Jonesy busying himself serving as fast as he could, the initial noise level, with everyone talking at once, settling to a gentle buzz. Detective Inspectors, Sergeants and Constables together, this time, as a team, bent on consuming as much of Toni's liquid hospitality a possible. Constable Compton Busion had drawn the short straw and was designated driver of the mini-bus, she didn't drink much anyway so was pleased to assist her colleagues in letting their hair down. There was never much joy in police work, sometimes a job well done would bring closure to a family, but more often it was quite depressing; days like this were few and far between so she was happy to be designated as the non-drinking driver. She would enjoy the inevitable change that came over her friends and colleagues as they gradually lost their inhibitions. The rubbish chat and wildly exaggerated stories abounded, becoming more comical as the night wore on with none of them remembering what they had said the following day. Wonderful ammunition for Compton to use with leg-pulls later.

Closing time approached with every scrap of the finger food consumed and the bar drunk almost dry, the party goers had said their good nights and left in the bus singing and laughing under the benevolent control of officer Busion. Toni finished the last dregs of her beer, paid Jonesy his large but well discounted bill and left Colin, with a farewell hug, to finish his nightcap. Her taxi ride home found her reflecting on what a good team she had and her hopes that a quiet Spring and Summer would follow for them all.

She closed the door of her small house nestled in the wooded close; needing a coffee and some water, lots of water, before she settled down for the night. Toni moved into her compact kitchen realising how small her world had become. Although, outside her nest, the green expanded all around, the home she loved confined her and concentrated her thoughts inward. Depression, an ever present danger she managed well, loomed again this night; the party had lifted her temporarily but the dark now reared its ugly head. The initial effect of the alcohol wearing off, the earlier call from Larry and the memory of her lost baby pushed her closer to the edge of blackness; she would exercise; a little light yoga always helped lift her spirits. She would phone Nathan tomorrow he would make her feel less morose. Sleep came eventually.

The morning brought a new purpose; the early sun looked promising; the loneliness and introspection of the night before gone. Coffee and toast, prepared in her tiny barely functional kitchen, gave her the energy to shower, and dress her mind on the day to come. From her usual sombre coloured clothes; today she chose a grey skirt beige blouse and green cashmere jacket. She looked in the mirror and thought she may buy something a little brighter next time. For now she applied lipstick, which she seldom did, for a splash of colour against her dull ensemble; pulled her tight curly hair back away from her face and tied it with a matching green ribbon. Trainer like shoes were slipped on just before she left. It was six thirty exactly.

She nearly always arrived before her officers, sometimes chatted with the scant night crew, if any remained that is, then went down to say a quick good morning to Compton Busion, who was always in earlier than anyone, before she went to her office. Her first act was to switch on her coffee machine followed by the desktop computer.

The understaffed officer numbers in Basingstoke had remained almost static for nearly a year, luckily no one had left the only newcomers being two trainee PCs, youngsters fresh out of Hendon Police College. It would take a while before they were able to operate unsupervised and contribute positively to their force. She hoped they were bright and their break in period would not be too long. Although overstretched at times she liked that all her officers were amicable, no real rivalry, although her two Inspectors did not always agree. They all had their quirks of course and some officers worked harder than others, the station banter was mostly friendly even if near the mark on occasion. Her boss Superintendent Walter Munroe was not a hands on guy and hardly interfered during cases, he left her to run the CID and the day to day business of her department; his main concern was dealing with the politics from above and supervision of the uniform branches. He had considerable influence with the top brass which helped a lot when things were difficult. He supported her and she trusted him.

The coffee poured and half consumed saw Toni perusing the reports from the evening and night before. The usual town disturbances, one arrest, a DUI sleeping it off in the cells, a repeat offender; will they never learn; he will probably do it again too; was there a real solution to the problem of drink drivers? She thought not. She went down to the squad room to find many officers at their desks, the remaining night crew having handed over and departed. Detective Inspector Jonny Musgrove looked up as did everyone; silence for a brief second; 'good morning Ma'am' from all abounded, then the hubbub of fingers clicking on keys and chatter between officers continued. Jonny Musgrove rose to greet her. He was tall, on the thin side with mousey hair, neatly combed in the morning but all over the place an hour later. Always smart in his clothes which he changed often; not like Harrold Davis who was considerably shorter, balding greyish hair and always wore a dark suit and tie, whether he changed them or not didn't matter they all looked the same. Today Jonny was in pale blue chinos with a darker blue cashmere sports jacket.

"Good morning Jonny".

"Morning Ma'am, a good do last night wasn't it"?

"Oh yes, not often we all get together like that eh. Anything going on with you at the moment".

"Nothing new, just tidying up the case against the young lads we caught last month; you may recall a charge of car theft; the Crown Prosecution Service want to proceed against all of them but in my opinion it was just one bad egg influencing the others. A warning in most cases would be more appropriate".

"Let me have the details, I will speak to the Super he will have a word with the prosecutor. Where are Mel Frazer and Keith Crane"?

They've gone down to Constable Busion, she has been digging up some background on the kids for me just to make sure we haven't missed anything before we proceed with the CPS and formal charges.

"Good, I'll let you know what the Super says; that's all then, thanks".

Her next stop was at the desk of Harrold Davis who was talking to sergeant Peter Andrews and constable June Owen; all three looked up as she approached.

"Good morning what's cooking Harrold"?

"Morning Ma'am, don't know yet maybe nothing; we're looking at a missing person report that's just come in. A young girl did not come home from college yesterday, the parents were worried so called it in last night. She's nearly eighteen and apparently has an older boyfriend whom she sometimes stayed out late with, they said she had exams coming up soon and thought she would want to study and not stay out. They were told by the night crew to call back if they could not locate her by this morning. They are downstairs now talking to uniforms and are saying she didn't come home and could not locate her at any of her friends houses. She and her boyfriend's mobiles go straight to answerphone. We were debating whether to become involved or leave it to uniform".

"Probably just a night of passion somewhere private, if you're not busy and to be on the safe side go and question them, see if you can locate her and her young fellow".

"My thoughts too, Ma'am".

Harrold glanced towards Peter with a positive nod of his head; Peter Andrews understood and left at once. Toni smiled and moved on through the room with appropriate good mornings to the uniformed officers as she went. Back in her office, one floor up, she looked wearily at the mound of files that had appeared in her in-tray, grown considerably since she last tackled the inevitable paper mountain modern policing required; being a Chief Inspector had its drawbacks.

Before she cracked on with reading the never ending reports and forms that needed signing off, she decided to give Nathan a call. Her and Nathan's backgrounds could not be more different however just like with his sister Jo, they seemed to click from the first time they met. Toni a full blooded Igbo from Nigeria who had come to England as a child, with her parents, to escape war torn Biafra; he of mixed English and West Indian decent Nathan Penryn's mother came to England with her Jamaican parents, in the fifties, she married his father, a Cornish fisherman, as a teenager, in her eyes a great combination. Nathan was a handsome man with darkish skin and bright brown eyes, fair hair like his father but with a curl inherited from his mother his accent a delightful mix of Cornish and creole. He had married very young and split from his wife after just one year, now divorced. He went to Bristol University studying biology followed by several years researching tropical disease in hospitals at home and abroad; his current position being a senior scientist working at Beecham laboratories. Sister Jo was a primary

19

schoolteacher always pulling his leg by calling him, 'my little pill maker'. She went on to jokingly that he made pills to cure the side effects of other pills made by his colleagues with the sole objective of making money from a gullible public. He always retorted 'why not, my little pill popper if it keeps you in curry and wine'. A press on speed dial 3 was answered almost at once.

"Nathan its' Toni, are you free this evening"?

"Hello oh, yes why"?

"I'm having one of those 'drive you mad' days at work and need a few hours of normality; fancy a pint or a curry or both if you want, my treat"?

"Well I'm not sure a pint will persuade me I'm not even sure a curry is enough, both I will accept on two conditions".

"What conditions"?

"Not the 'Four Horseshoes'".

"And the second"?

"I don't know yet but I'll think of something; I'll call a cab and knock on your door at eight okay"?

"Lovely; bye Nathan".

She felt better at once, already looking forward to her evening. 'Paperwork here I come'.

Chapter 3

"Mr. and Mrs. Westcott I believe. I am Detective Sergeant Andrews please follow me we will go somewhere more private so I can ask you a few questions which may help us find your daughter".

Mrs. Westcott started to speak but Peter ignored her and turned quickly for them to follow, so she held back her intended question. Peter wanted to be in control and a distraught mother demanding answers from him in a corridor was not on. He arrived at interview room one; a room pleasantly decorated with comfortable chairs, unlike the much more brutal looking interrogation rooms two and three. He ushered them in pointing to the two seats in front of a small coffee table he sat in the chair opposite took out his notebook and smiled.

"This is better we don't want everyone listening in do we. Your daughter's name is Dawn I believe"?

Mrs. Westcott accepted the situation and answered calmly.

"Yes, she didn't come home last night and that's not like her; she's supposed to be taking her exams in a few weeks and was going to revise last evening; I know she wouldn't want to want to stay out, these exams were too important to her; she's been studying for two years you know".

Mrs. Westcott broke down and started to cry; her husband leaned over put his arm on her shoulder and he continued where she couldn't speak.

"Dawn would always go and meet Charlie; that's Charlie Brady her boyfriend; he works at the restaurant quite near the college. She sees him when she's finished school usually for just half an hour or so then comes home; we tried to get hold of Charlie he's not answering his mobile and there is no one at his house, we tried; none of her friends seem to know where she is and I know she left school because they saw her heading towards the restaurant as always. We went to the restaurant but by then it was so late it had closed. That's when we phoned you. We waited like you said, we've been up all night but she never came home".

"Hold it there a moment please. First of all where does Charlie live"?

"Charlie Brady lives at Wildmoore off the Reading road, Bright Cottage it's called, I've just been there but no one's in".

"Okay the restaurant next"?

"Hillview, I don't know the address, its behind Queen Mary's".

"That's okay I know it. Would you give me Dawn and Charlie's mobile numbers please"?

Peter offered him his notepad and pen for Mr. Westcott to comply. He opened his phone to retrieve the numbers and wrote them down with a shaking hand. Andrew knew they were suffering and wanted to terminate the questions soon, he could come back later but he had to ask one more just in case.

"Anything else you can tell me"?

"No I don't think so".

Mrs. Westcott then spoke.

"She must have come back home sometime and taken her bike, anyway its missing and she left a note".

Mr. Westcott looked at her angrily.

"A note and her bike gone, why on earth didn't you tell me; what did it say"?

"Just 'Mum, won't be late. love you Dawn'. I'm sorry I forgot".

Mrs. Westcott's began to sob again; her husband comforted her again; his sudden anger forgotten on seeing her obvious distress.

"Don't fret my love it's alright, the police will find her".

"By the way how old is Dawn and Charlie for that matter"?

"She's seventeen now her birthday is next month; he's nineteen I think, they met at school; been going out regular a few months now he's a nice boy; hard working too, he wouldn't go off with her if that's what you're thinking".

"I'm sure you're right; I know it's hard but try not to worry we will find them or they will just turn up, sorry for the trouble they've caused. You go home now we'll be in touch soon. I'll send an officer round for a photo and a description of what she might be wearing".

"If she was on her bike she would have changed; it would have been her cycling stuff, long black lycra slacks, a yellow reflecting jacket over a blue top, oh and a white striped helmet. I'll check they are gone when we get home".

"Fine thankyou Mr. Westcott; Mrs. Westcott, I'll be in touch".

Peter saw them to the exit and arranged for a car to take them home when he discovered they'd walked here. After they'd gone he hurried up to the squad room, he was very concerned, he'd a bad feeling, it did not sound like this was a couple of teenagers who'd gone off for some fun, not caring about their parents. He didn't know about Charlie but the note to her Mum told him a lot about Dawn Westcott, she wouldn't leave without contacting her family.

"Harrold, Sir I think we should have a look at this".

Peter then went on to reiterate his interview with the Westcotts and his disquiet.

"I agree, Peter you go round to the restaurant, June go to the Westcott home have a look in the girl's room, check on her clothes, you know what to do, a recent picture if you can and find out what type of bike. I'll go down to Compton's, put a trace on those mobiles; call me soonest.

The restaurant doors were locked. A closed sign with the opening hours was displayed on a board set up outside. Peter could see activity inside so knocked on the frame holding up his warrant card to one of the bevelled glass windows. A young girl

23

all in black came to the door looked at his card, smiled at him through the glass and nodded. She reached up on tip toes to release the top bolt and then down to the floor likewise. She pulled one of the doors inwards, pushed it to the inside wall where it automatically stayed fully open.

"How can we help, Sergeant, I didn't quite see the name; were not open yet"?

"Sergeant Andrews and you are"?

"Wendy sir, I'm just a waitress here. I expect you want to see the boss"?

"Well maybe, I'm really looking for Charles Brady".

"Oh poor old Charlie he's in hospital, was carted off yesterday or the day before, anyway middle of the night. His appendix popped on him they said. I'll see if Mr. Jarvis is in he knows a bit more, he went to see him last night".

"No wait a moment, I'm also looking for Dawn Westcott do you know where she might be"?

"Dawn, no I don't. Isn't she with Charlie at the hospital"?

Peter felt relieved a drama but not a crisis, the girl never called her Mum for some reason, her phone not working maybe; he was happier now. In the meantime Wendy had disappeared into the back returning with whom he assumed was the manager Jarvis.

"I'm Gavin young man Mr Jarvis is not here at the moment, I'm his number two if you like".

"Hello, I understand Charlie is in hospital but I am also trying to locate his girlfriend Dawn, Wendy here seems to think she is at the hospital".

"I doubt that. She came here yesterday afternoon as she always does, I told her Charlie was ill but at that time I had no idea he was in hospital. Her phone was switched off so she couldn't have known either. She was going to look for him so I expect she went to his house first".

"Thank you Gavin, Wendy, I'll come back if I need ".

"What's up why are you looking for Charlie and Dawn, what have they done"?

"Nothing, they have done nothing its just Dawn is missing; I'm sure she will be at the Hospital".

Peter did not even wait to listen to the next question that was being formed by Wendy, he wanted to go to the Hospital at once.

Peter was sitting at the bedside of Charlie Brady; the young man was propped up in bed groggy but awake.

"You say you have not seen Dawn since the day before yesterday and she hasn't been to see you in here, at least as far as you know".

"I was whisked off early hours and have only just woke up, my Mum has been with me a lot of the time, she's gone for a cup of tea five minutes ago, she'll be back soon; Mum never mentioned Dawn coming. She probably doesn't even know I'm here; I've not had my phone with me it was left at home when they brought me in, so no chance to call her until a little while ago; her mobile's switched off or the battery's gone flat. My Mum never realised she didn't know I was in here so she never called her either; too busy worrying about me I suppose; Mum did say my boss came when I was asleep but he didn't stay. Someone should go round Dawn's house and tell her; she would have missed me at work yesterday and will be wondering where I've been".

Peter was having that nasty feeling again; Dawn Westcott was missing after all; no one had seen her since she left the restaurant for her house yesterday afternoon presumably going to collect her bicycle to ride to Wildmoore looking for her boyfriend. He would not tell Charlie she had not been home, not yet anyway.

"I'll try and find her for you Charlie, you get well soon".

Peter called Harrold with his disturbing news; time was of the essence now; she had been missing too long already with no one really looking for her; he wanted Harrold to send a team round to Wildmoore and do a house to house. Harrold Davis was on it even before Peter had finished, tasking Compton to scan the town and surrounding areas CCTV to see if she could trace Dawn's movements. Harrold said he would go to Wildmoore and that Peter should come back to the station to follow up on anything Compton might find.

It seemed an age before Peter arrived at the station, he went straight to Compton Busion's office.

"Hi Peter, you took your time".

"Bloody traffic in the town is impossible some days, have you found anything yet"?

"June's with the parents now; she sent me a photo and a description of her clothes; I'm just going through the town centre CCTV now haven't seen her yet; ah, there she is look, running just coming off the camera going towards Popley. There she is again on her bike this time with a change of clothes; likely she is on her way out to the Reading road. I'll download the other cameras and see where she went, I'll also widen the time slot".

Peter put his hand on her shoulder stopping the unnecessary haste.

"No need to rush things; I know where she was going; Wildmoore her boyfriend's house".

"No CCTV anywhere near there except maybe at the golf course; I don't have access to that, you'd have to go and ask for it".

"Can you go through it all again this time slowly; look for anyone following, in a car maybe, I'm going out to Wildmoore; let me know if you find anything".

Peter arrived at Bright Cottage where three police cars were parked along the lane. One officer was standing by the gate everyone else was out of sight. Peter parked and approached the lone PC.

"Where is everyone".

"They've all gone along the lane sir, door to door and searching. The boss too; there's no one in here". He said, indicating the Brady's cottage.

Peter nodded his thanks and jogged along the road looking right and left he followed the curve and saw several officers ahead as he came level with the golf course entrance. There was a shout from a uniformed officer as he stepped from the bushes a hundred and fifty yards ahead. Everyone stopped, several officers appeared from the verges or front gardens of the three houses behind him that were the only dwellings along this section of road. Harrold Davis came running back; he had been much further ahead on the other side of the road. He and Peter arrived at the same time.

"What is it what have you found"?

"A cyclist helmet Sir; look it is caught in the bush there".

Harrold pulled on some neoprene gloves; ignored the brambles, reached for the helmet and pulled it free. He held it up hoping that he had not smudged any prints, looking for someone to bring him a big enough bag. Within a few seconds he had the offer of three. The helmet was safely stowed.

"Right listen up everyone we need to go over this area again carefully and slowly, if you see anything call out don't touch. We are looking for signs of broken branches trodden grass you know what I mean, oh and a bicycle. Peter call in a SOCO team and an ambulance on standby; this girl is around here somewhere or was abducted from nearby".

"Sir. Do we have a map"?

"Satnav picture on my phone, it's a bit squashed but gives you an idea".

Peter opened his phone loaded the same image; he could see the curve in the road the woods and field beyond the hedgerow with the river winding its way towards Shenfield.

"This is a large areas Sir shall I call in some more uniforms"?

"Not yet Peter let's go with what we have for now. If nothing turns up in the next hour we'll do a full scale with dogs, okay"?

Harrold was not experienced in this type of police work; having been in London dealing with fraud most of the time he felt a little out of his depth, confirmation from Andrews that he was making the right call was what he wanted.

"Sounds fine to me, I'll call them to be on standby just in case if you like"?

"Yes do that Peter, good idea it will save time if we need to use them. Right everyone listen; let's go back to the cottage and start from there, two of you go back the way we came in, the rest cover what we have already looked at but be on your guard, any little thing may be significant".

Fifty minutes later and at a much slower pace each man was painstakingly searching the ground and hedges along the road. They were well past the houses and the golf course entrance when two shouts at almost the same time made everyone stop and look to where they came from. Harrold was behind his men this time, close to the officer on his left with his hand held high. The other was just behind him on the other side of the road. He pointed at the officer ahead.

"What"?

"A bike sir it is way back behind the hedge I can see a wheel".

He turned to the other officer.

"What do you have"?

"The hedge has been broken down here sir someone has pushed through recently, there are footprints in the mud on the other side".

Harrold stood for a moment deciding what to do.

"Peter check the bike with the officer who found it, you three follow me; the rest of you keep searching".

Harrold went back to the break in the hedge with the three selected officers behind him. The gap was not obvious at first glance so he understood why it had been missed first time round, he pushed through taking care not to tread in the footprints. The gap was very overgrown and difficult to push through. He tapped the officer, who had found the gap, on his shoulder.

"Well done constable this looks promising. Right follow me; be careful not to tread in the footprints and keep clear of any tracks you may find on the other side".

When all were through it the gap was considerably wider; it was easy to see where Dawn and her pursuer had crossed the ground, although at this time they were only guessing it was Dawn who had made the original trail. There were short narrow footprints and large tread boot-type marks following the same direction. All five walked either side of the trodden ground eyes scanning left and right looking for any sign of their quarry. The wooded area was sparse with the occasional bush and lots of bramble, it thickened the further they went and the ground became more solid till the marks they were following disappeared. They kept walking eyes down till they came to the rivers edge.

"The village is to the left on the other side of the river across open ground, the bank to the right offers more cover. You three go towards the village spread out one on the bank one twenty yards in and the other follow the tree line about fifty yards back. You follow me, I'll keep to the edge you follow parallel about fifty yards from the bank, call if you see anything".

29

They had only moved along for a few minutes when the officer following the bank called out. They were still in earshot so he shouted to Harrold that someone had entered the water at the spot where he was standing. They all returned to where he was waiting. Footprints of both types were visible in the softer ground by the river, with broken shrubs and well-trodden grass showing activity right up to the edge.

"It certainly looks like something happened here".

He bent to the ground examining the footprints.

"Look, all the smaller prints are covered by the heavy boot impressions none of the large prints are under. If they had been here at the same time surely some of the small ones would be on top. If it is Dawn it seems she arrived first and the guy arrived after, I wonder did she jump to escape, it doesn't look very inviting does it, I'm not so sure she did? Go back to where you were and keep looking".

Peter and the constable who found the bike had managed to recover it by climbing through the hedge further along the road and approaching it from the rear. The brambles had made a mess of both their hands the neoprene glove affording them little protection. Peter told the officer to wait with the bike until the forensic team arrived, he was going to follow the Inspector. He ran to the gap in the hedge wiping his hands in this handkerchief as he went. Once through he followed the same path as the others, eventually coming to the river and the disturbed area by the bank. He called the DI's mobile but there was no signal, so moved from the bank towards the bushes and long grass. He worked his way slowly heading away from the village unlike the others; he was trying to think like her. The open ground he could see in that direction was not a way he would go if being chased, he would find the heaviest cover to hide his escape. If she had jumped in the river as it seemed she might, she would have either swam to the other side and escaped to the village or gone down stream towards the mill and safety. Would the chaser have done the same? He doubted it. If she had swam she would have reached the village or the mill; she would almost certainly have been found before now. The thought that she may have drowned and still be in the water somewhere, crossed his mind fleetingly. What to do? Just keep looking in all the bushes. She would have hidden somewhere or been caught, either way she was nearby he could feel it. He walked slowly examining the densest places calling her name. He heard the odd animal and bird escape from the undergrowth as he approached. Harrold and his officers who had searched right up to the mill and the road beyond were now returning the way they had come; disappointed and tired. Peter heard their feint conversation as they drew near to the original path. He continued his search, not wanting to give up just yet. Soon the others caught up with him.

"Hello Sir, we found the bike it will be with SOCO now. I tried to call you but no signal here. I think she may have hidden somewhere from the village; I don't believe she took the plunge you know, that river is pretty uninviting".

"Maybe, I'm not sure; we've covered all the ground right up to the mill and the road, she's not there, I think he may have taken her; When SOCO have finished with the bike and the area along the road they can cover the ground here to try and find out exactly what happened, we might have to search the river".

"I'm going to go a bit father if you don't mind"?

"That's okay Peter take one of these guys with you, we'll go back and organise SOCO to check all the footprints and the area near the riverbank too".

Peter and the uniform sergeant walked side by side a few yards apart pushing their way into the tall grass and bushes as they went. The brambles bit every now and then with the odd curse as they pushed on. Time was passing, and they were coming to the end of the wood with open ground in front. Was there any point to this, still they went ahead one step at a time?

"Hey what's this"?

A yell from the sergeant brought Peter to an abrupt halt.

"You found something"?

"Yes, yes it's her I think".

Peters heart sank as he pushed through the reedy grass to where the still form lay covered in twigs and grass. They both knelt down beside the curled up body saw it was a young girl, he knew instinctively it was Dawn. Touching her face, made him fear the worse; it was cold; he felt he neck for a pulse nothing, but the skin here was warmer. He lifted her arm and grabbed her wrist feeling for the pulse, the sweet spot. Did he feel a beat? He wasn't sure. He leant forward rolled her over onto her back place his ear to her breast, there it was a feint drum, drum, drum. Relief swept through him like the wave of emotion when you hear a magical piece of music; she was alive. Cold and unconscious, the thin lycra cyclist material, designed to keep her cool when riding hard, was useless in the low temperatures of the night just gone; hypothermia a real problem now.

"Sergeant, run like hell, get to where you have a signal, call an ambulance here pronto, she's still alive but only just".

The Sergeant didn't hesitate he was up and running even before Peter had finished speaking. Peter removed his jacket and sat beside Dawn lifted her into his arms her cold body pressed close to his; he wrapped his coat around her massaging each arm one at a time trying and instil some warmth from him to her. Her shallow breath was hardly discernible, he didn't know what else to do so hugged her closer acutely aware of her chilled unresponsive body and prayed. He rocked her like a baby speaking gently, soft words of encouragement wishing the medics would arrive soon.

Peter was back at Bright cottage; Dawn having been whisked into an ambulance within twenty minutes of him finding her. The medics would not commit themselves but said although her body temperature was very low it had not reached a critical point, she had a every chance of recovery. He called June with the news and asked her to ferry the parents to the hospital. He and the search officers returned to the station leaving Harrold Davis with the SOCO team to gather what they could. Although Dawn was safe, someone had separated her from her cycle and caused her to run through the woods towards the river in a panic. Evidence of a man in pursuit was clear, her being able to hide had saved her; but from what? She would have died had she not been found in time. A crime probably, but how to know which? They would have to wait for Dawn to recover to find out what had happened. It certainly required a follow up.

Chapter 4

Disappointment was etched all over his face, he had been so close; all that watching and waiting to no avail. His hands were scratched and sore from the brambles, he hoped the devious bitch's hands had been cut up too. How could she have jumped into that bloody river and escaped like that. It was deep, cold and flowing fast, he was sure she would avoid the river make for the mill on foot, then he would have caught her easily. He couldn't be sure but thought he'd caught a glimpse of her swimming down-stream maybe she was drowned; serve her bloody right. His search of the bank and the bushes nearby found nothing. He did not expect her to run so fast and her finding that dam tiny gap in the hedge was not expected either. Seeing her on her bike going down that quiet lane was an opportunity he did not want to miss. Next time he would be more meticulous, he would ensure there were no avenues of escape. If only Earnest had been with him like last time it would have been easy. Anyway no harm done he had learned a lot and would not make the same mistakes again.

He hurried back brushing the woodland debris from his jacket and trousers as he went, turned into the golf course entrance left the drive following the path through the trees to his van parked to the side of the clubhouse. He was a man unseen, no one took any notice of him, he could go wherever he wanted nobody questioned his right to be there, sometimes they spoke to him, not as someone they knew, but as a familiar figure seen, unnoticed, soon forgotten. This was a quiet time most golf club members had either finished their rounds and gone home or were in the bar. He saw no one and no one saw him as he started the van and drove off confident he would have another chance soon.

After his collection from Shenfield post office earlier he had tucked himself behind a large truck, being visible only as he left the post office roundabout. When viewed it would seem he had carried on north up the A33 but by hiding in its shadow he turned round out of sight and came back to the Wildmoore turn off in search of his target. His attempted abduction was unlike when he and Earnest had lifted the other girl, that was easy. George dropped Earn off to follow behind the girl as she walked away from her friends towards the bus stop, he followed in the van slowly passing Earnest, stopping alongside their target, he leant over opening the passenger door pretending to ask her directions, the road was clear both ways so Earn approaching from behind went unnoticed; as she leaned in to speak to George he pushed her into the front jumping in behind holding her still whilst George emptied the syringe into her neck, the nearest piece of bare flesh exposed to his drug filled needle. It took only moments they were gone. The girl had no time to react or scream, the vile fluid taking away any resistance she may have mustered in seconds.

His attempt to pluck this latest plum on his own was a complete failure, he thought she would be glad to come to him to retrieve her bike but something spooked her, chasing her was a big mistake, perhaps he should have waited till he and Earn were together. He was too eager; the need to rekindle the excitement of new skin to touch and to relish the fear in her eyes as they tightened the noose to the point of death, only to see it well up again each time they loosened the cord and consciousness returned. The thoughts of what might have been, made his inner need grow uncontrolled; he shouted at himself for being so impatient pummelling his hands on the wheel till his fingers splashed blood onto the windscreen and the self-inflicted pain took over releasing the tension that was about to explode his mind.

Having escaped she was bound to raise the alarm, that is if she managed to scramble out of the river in one piece. If not a missing girl would attract police attention; he would have to be extra cautious now, so waited at the junction of Wildmoore and the A33, knowing if he kept very close to any large vehicle in front on the outside lane he would be unseen by the camera, he could then return via an alternative route far from the main road through the villages of Lydd Green and Old Basing; no cameras there.

He returned the van to the sorting office yard, having wiped away his scattered blood drops from the windscreen and wheel, deposited his postal collections and went immediately to the staff locker room to change, not wanting any of his colleagues to see his torn, dishevelled clothes. The navy work trouser legs were snagged and muddied as were his boots; the jacket was embedded with woodland debris. He normally used a cleaning service who came regularly to the collection office but this time he bundled the lot into a plastic bag to take home for cleaning, he thought maybe he should dispose of them completely; he had a spare set in his locker and toyed with the idea of changing into these and finishing his shift but saw there was only ten minutes left. He was late getting back, normally when he'd completed his round he would be expected to go to help in the sorting floor. He put on his civilian clothes went to his supervisor saying he was sorry for being late back but he'd stopped on route as he was feeling unwell and thought he was going to be sick.

"No problem George, you go on home, call me tomorrow if you are still not right, I'll find someone to cover your round. By the way if it's more than a couple of days go and see the quack, you'll need a certificate. Do you need a lift home"?

"No thanks Joe, I'll walk it's not far and it might help clear this damned headache, don't worry about covering my round I'm sure I'll be okay by tomorrow, I'll call if not".

"Okay, take care, look after yourself".

George thanked him and left feigning a shambled walk head bowed. He never took time off except for official holidays so his lie of being ill was accepted by Joe his supervisor without question.

Joe was not one who left anything to chance so changed the collection rota anyway leaving George Grant in the depot tomorrow to help with the sorting should he recover and return to work. It would not be a problem if George didn't come in, it wouldn't matter as most of the guys liked a different routine now and then; if George wanted he would soon change it back a day or two later; in the meantime Joe was covered with no worries for tomorrows deliveries and collections.

Chapter 5

Constable Compton Busion enjoyed the role she had been given; she had developed searching the electronic world to a level where almost anything anyone asked of her and her young helpers, they could find. Breaking the rules to achieve her goals was not her way, however bending them a little was always a possibility. Scanning CCTV was never the boring task that other detectives found a chore, to her it was a joy looking for the smallest unexpected differences that led to catching those who thought they were untouchable.

Today her task; following Dawn's progress yesterday from school to home and home to the turn off at Wildmoore. It was not seamless, there were gaps as she left the coverage of one camera before being picked up by the next. The gaps were brief but did not detract from the picture Compton built of her journey. She was picked up on the town cameras jogging from the restaurant towards her home but was out of shot for twelve minutes after the Popley roundabout. She reappeared on the same camera this time riding her bicycle. She had been home, changed from her college clothes into riding gear with a very obvious yellow reflective over jacket. She was riding fast, being seen pedalling rapidly as she passed Chineham and again later at the new estate roundabout but after that nothing, no cameras until Shenfield; she did not appear there. The assumption she had left the A33 at Wildmoore proved to be true as she had just heard from Peter Andrews of Dawn's discovery in the adjacent woods. She went over the videos again not looking for Dawn this time but at all the other activity. Several run throughs built a picture of every vehicle that had been present on the journey, each had been timed and recorded. Nothing stood out. None of the vehicles followed her; those that would have been close at the time she left the A33 were seen to pass the Shenfield roundabout with no noticeable delay. The only vehicle that followed her in any way at all was a red post office van; it stopped at regular intervals on the way, the postman driver seen on occasions, where there was CCTV coverage, emptying mail from the various collection boxes on route arriving at Shenfield post office well before Dawn turned off. The van left Shenfield and was not seen again till it arrived at the Popley roundabout two hours later, this time coming from the direction of Old Basing. All this was reasonable and expected; after Shenfield the postman's route must have followed the country lanes back towards Basingstoke where no CCTV existed. She would check the postman's collection round with the post office later but was of a mind whoever had taken Dawn's bike and chased her through the wood must have been there already and had not followed her on the road. She phoned Peter, who had come in early and was sitting quietly scanning his report on the computer screen for errors before he submitted it officially; he went down to see the results of her search.

"Thanks Compton, it was just an idea that maybe someone was waiting for her at the college or her house and followed her to Wildmoore".

"I'll go through it again if you like in case I missed something".

"No I don't think that will achieve anything you've already been more than thorough. Our best bet is to interview Dawn and take a description of the man. SOCO may come up with something, though it was pretty messed up out there, some boot castings and maybe fingerprints from the bike and helmet are possible".

"Okay let me know if there is anything else I can do".

"Sure, thanks anyway, I'll call".

Peter left 'Compton's den' walking up stairs to the main squad room to see that Davis had returned and was sitting at his desk. The open design of this room, on the first floor, had small areas where desks faced each other in groups of four giving intimacy to the officers of the same squad but a small level of privacy from outside if needed. The centre of the room had a large long table where group discussions could be carried out. It was their boss Toni Webb who normally convened such meetings so it was used only on special occasions rather than daily. This table tended to become cluttered with overspill paperwork from the adjacent desks; a scramble to retrieve their files ensued when a meeting was called. Uniform officers who assisted the detectives were also housed at one end of this room separated from their colleagues only by the layout of desks. The exception being IT in their own suite and the traffic police who were housed on the ground floor close to their vehicles. Open plan was the order of the current police head office management; Detectives in separate offices was discouraged as was separation of uniform officers from plain clothes, if privacy was needed one of the interview rooms could be used. The older officers still did not like the arrangement but all had come to accept it and it did mean you did not have to go far to find someone.

Every desk had a computer linked by a closed local area network. Connection to the outside, such as police central databases, DVLA and the internet was available on two selected computers that were linked through the IT department's control on the floor below. Each computer was allocated to a unique officer with a personal password; central files were available to all but each officer could secure his own data, releasing it only through a central secure control. Two printers were shared by all. If officers were not on site their computers were automatically locked to any non-authorised activity. Compton's and her officers had their own independent system, they had access to everything. The IT engineer next door was responsible for maintenance and overall security and worked closely with Compton. Having once suffered a serious breach of security passwords were now allocated by IT and changed at random. Officers complained at first with the what seemed to be overkill on security but Webb soon let them know it is what it is, 'get used to it'.

Peter sat opposite Harrold not interrupting his boss who was on the phone. He opened his notebook looked at his file to make sure everything he had done yesterday was noted and up to date. He then opened a new file to make ready for the coming day's events. DI Harrold Davis closed his mobile and turned to Peter.

"Sergeant Andrews, good work yesterday it looks like you saved this young girl from the worst effects of the cold. That was June Owens on the phone she went straight to the hospital this morning; she says Dawn has come round now with no lasting ill effects. Her first answers to June's questions provide only of a vague description of the man. June says she was obviously very afraid at the time; all her energies were concentrated on escaping and not scrutinising her pursuer. It seems her bike was stolen from outside her boyfriend's house when she was round the back. She thought it was Charlie mucking about so she went looking for him; suddenly this man jumped out from a hedge holding her bike and threatened her. She just ran from him through the woods and when faced with the river barring her escape, apparently she can't swim, she threw her yellow jacket in the water by the bank then found a place to hide, she hoped he would give up the chase. Such quick thinking I'd say, probably saved her. We never saw or recovered the jacket it was probably washed away. She was too afraid to move from her hiding place so just lay there; much too long it seems. Unaware how much the cold was affecting her and her ability to rationalise, eventually her body succumbed and she drifted into unconsciousness".

"Well at least now she'd found out why Charlie hadn't called her. By the way Compton has searched the CCTV for anyone who may have followed her, nothing obvious. It may have been random; however I suggest we have a word with Charlie,

Dawn and her family to keep an eye open for strangers. Tell her not to go out alone and keep closer to home for a few days".

"You really think she is a target of some kind"?

"I hope not, but just for a while, it can't hurt to keep an eye open, at least whilst we see what we find out from forensics; they may come up with something which may help identify this man".

"Okay Peter have a patrol car follow the route she takes from college and back at the appropriate times, ask them to liaise with the family through Constable Owen, I don't want them becoming alarmed so tell her to say it is a normal precaution in cases like this, you know play it down a little".

"Good. How long Sir"?

"A few days at least till after next weekend, we should have discovered something, or nothing by then".

It was the 'nothing' part of that statement that concerned Peter; if this guy was a stalker or worse, he may spot the police presence and hold back, only to resume when the surveillance was withdrawn; he hoped they would make some progress before then.

"What shall I do now sir"?

"Come with me we need to look more closely at Wildmoore; this guy must have hidden out of sight if he was waiting for Dawn, which seems odd as her visit was a spur of the moment decision. More likely he followed her and arrived soon after so must've come by a vehicle of some kind; where did he park? There are'nt many places on that lane to hide a car out of sight. Let's go and see".

With that the pair stood and moved towards the door. Peter stopped and turned back letting his Harrold move towards the stairway.

"I'll see you at the car Sir, I want to organise the patrol car and let June Owens know what's going on, five minutes or so eh"?

"Okay Peter, I'll call in on Compton on the way out, see if she has anything new".

Compton Busion was always thorough and had been reviewing the CCTV again just in case she had missed something; it was fortuitous that Harrold Davis arrived when he did.

"Hello Sir, you seem to know when I have found something, a bit spooky if you ask me, are you a mind reader or a psychic"?

"I don't think so, does that mean you've found him"?

"Not exactly, it's just there is one piece of footage that seems out of place".

She loaded the relevant CCTV file and moved forward to the time slot she was interested in.

"If you look carefully you can just see a piece of a vehicle on the inside of the truck....there; only a brief glimpse eh"?

"So what"?

She stopped and replayed the image up to the moment in question.

"It's the colour sir; red with a yellow flash of some kind. There were no red cars on the route at that time, so where did it come from, I went back and there it was hiding in plain sight a post office van".

"Come on Compy don't keep me in suspense what is the significance"?

"I followed a postal van all the way from Popley to Shenfield with the normal expected stops. I dismissed it as not suspicious and assumed he went further along the A33 eventually finishing back at Old Basing part of his route. If this is the same van it's the second time he came to that roundabout, a forty minute gap between the two sightings. It may be nothing but I was wondering where he had been all that time, and why the dangerous manoeuvre wedging yourself on the inside of a truck like that unless you were trying to hide".

"A bit odd I agree; maybe he'd forgotten something so had to go back. Good work though, spotting the colours, I wouldn't have noticed until you pointed it out, I'm not sure of it's significance but I'll call the post office and check. I'm going back

43

to Wildmoore someone at the golf club may have seen something. Call me later, okay".

The almost hidden entrance and twisting drive's approach to the clubhouse displaying a tiny sign *'Wildmoore Golf Course'* eventually led to impressive stone pillars supporting a pair of open and equally opulent ornate wrought Iron gates. The car park at the end of the drive was large with allocated spaces clearly marked with the names of the officers and selected members on posts supporting engraved slate labels. Davis slotted into an unmarked space, dearly wanting to occupy the space reserved for the Club Captain, but he needed these people to cooperate and his anti-privilege thoughts would not work here. The Clubhouse was as grand as the excessive driveway entry had hinted; a tall single story building in a modern style, concrete, steel and glass everywhere; he liked it; he always was a sucker for good design. The covered entrance's single glass door slid silently into a hidden recess as he approached leaving him standing inside what he thought was akin to an upturned goldfish bowl; the glass dome, which was invisible from the outside, drowned the whole area with light. In front was a semi-circular reception counter at which stood a young woman immaculately dressed in black and white. He moved forward not intimidated but feeling he should be; this place was made to make you appear small.

"Good day sir, how can I help you"?

A clear crisp voice with a trace of Hampshire in the delivery put him immediately at ease. Much as he disliked the trappings that money and privilege bought the 'lucky ones' he could understand the excitement of being in a position to be a member of a place like this. He did not play golf, even though it was now available and affordable to almost everyone, this club was not one you just turned up for a quick game after work.

"Yes miss, I am Detective Inspector Harrold Davis and this is Detective Sergeant Andrews of Hampshire police, we would like to speak to the club secretary if he is available".

He knew the secretary was probably employed, whereas the owner, chairman or other directors were not likely to respond too easily.

"Brian's not here at the moment but the chairman is around somewhere, I'll give him a call".

She picked up a phone from the counter pressed a single button, the response was immediate.

"Martin, there's a Detective Davis here to see Brian but he's not in today will you deal with it? .... Okay I'll tell him".

She placed the phone back and turned to the two detectives.

"Martin will be with you in a few minutes, he's on the driving range at the moment, one of the ball collecting machines has broken down, he can't resist being involved, always wants to fix everything himself. Can I get you something a coffee, tea"?

No thank you miss well wait here if that's okay"?

She nodded and smiled returning her attention to the desk computer screen.

They stood looking around the room when in less than five minutes a tall very fit looking man in his late fifties, dressed in a grey track suit marched through the glass door, straight up to Harrold Davis and Peter Andrews.

"Good morning officers I'm Martin Matheson, Chairman of this establishment how can I help you"?

Davis came straight to the point surprised that this man was more than pleasant and obviously willing to assist.

"The day before yesterday a young girl was chased into the woods near here by an unknown man; she was forced to hide and remained hidden in the bushes all night, we found her the following day, unconscious suffering hypothermia. He may have used your driveway to hide himself and his vehicle. I would like any CCTV recordings you may have, to see if there are any vehicles or people who should not be here".

"My goodness, I hope she's okay. We know all our members well enough and don't normally have people that should not be here, they would stand out if they were; I will copy the recordings for you, We have a camera on the drive and one covering the carpark; two on this building at the front and the rear. They are activated by motion sensors, turning on floodlights after dark; they record for about three minutes after movement ceases. The video is stored on the main frame for a up to a month before it automatically deletes. Jenny can download the files for you onto a flash drive is that okay"?

"That would be great sir, the whole months recordings would be useful, not just the last few days".

"Did you hear that Sweetie, give the man what he wants".

"Yes fine Dad, it will take me about twenty minutes".

"I would be surprised if there is any unauthorised vehicles or people come to that, our members are well known to us and each other, I'm sure I would have heard from somebody if there was a stranger on the premises. Anyway I'll leave you in Jenny's capable hands I've a cantankerous old machine to fix, come back if you need anything else. I hope the young lady recovers".

"She is on the mend thanks; we'll be in touch if needed".

With that Martin Matheson left the way he came in.

"Follow me there are seats in the lounge next to the back office where you can wait in comfort; are you sure about the coffee"?

"Thank you miss Matheson we are fine; I thought your father would be at the factory".

The name was well known in the area and Nationally on most supermarket shelves; with factories in Basingstoke and several sites throughout the south Matheson Meats was a popular brand and a very successful family business.

"Good Lord no; my brothers run the business now, have done since he retired; this is Dad's baby now".

She said, indicating the golf complex with a sweep of her arm.

"Wait here I'll be as quick as I can".

With that she left them in the small lounge and disappeared through an adjacent door, closing it behind her.

"Wow I didn't realise he's 'Matheson's Meats'. Fancy owning a whole golf club as a hobby".

"More than a hobby Peter have you any idea of the fees to join, let alone play a round of golf".

"I'll start saving then, shall I"?

Harrold smiled at the thought, shook his head and settled back in the leather armchair to await the return of Jenny. True to her word she returned just before the twenty minutes with the memory stick in her hand.

"For speed I've copied the files in a compressed MP4 format I hope that is alright, if not let me know and I will download them in full but that will take much longer and need more memory than I have here".

"I'm sure that will be fine; we have an IT wizard on our team who can extract nearly everything from almost nothing".

"Call or come back if you need, I'm always here".

"I will, thank you for your time and cooperation; goodbye Miss Matheson".

"Surprisingly helpful people sir let's hope we find some useful stuff on the videos; I don't like the idea of some creep running around threatening youngsters".

"Nor do I, let's get back soon Peter, foot on the gas eh".

Chapter 6

Toni had been following the progress of the incident by the river and was concerned the man who had chased young Dawn would have done serious harm had he caught up with her. If he was of a mind he would almost certainly try again, not necessarily with Dawn, although that was a real possibility if he was fixated on just her, but it was now more likely he would target any vulnerable young girl. The sixth form college was a prime source where female students could be observed easily and by following any one of these possible victims he could learn their habits and routines, waiting for the right moment to come along when he could isolate them and exercise whatever his twisted mind had conceived. Dawn had been lucky, her presence of mind had laid a false trail and she had kept herself well hidden, another youngster may not be so fortunate or be able to react in good time. A general meeting was needed, there were no urgent cases in the pipeline and what was outstanding could be dealt with alongside any new investigation. She left her desk and went downstairs not knowing exactly what she intended but would see the reaction of her officers to the situation.

Almost everyone who mattered was in the squad room except for Compton and Jonny Musgrove.

"June would you mind calling Constable Busion to come here and find DI Musgrove if he is on site".

"Yes Ma'am, I think he is upstairs with the CPS and the Super shall I interrupt them".

"No just send him a text to come down as soon as he is finished".

Toni called the officers to order round the central table which miraculously had gone from a paper and file cluttered mess when she first walked in to completely clear before she had time to turn round.

"Good afternoon everyone I am here to pose a question or two concerning the incident of yesterday when a young girl Dawn Westcott almost died from exposure. The man who threatened her missed his target this time but I am fearful he will try again. It would be remiss of us to ignore this; we have a duty of care here and must prevent a recurrence or any new effort by this man to attack the young people that are our responsibility. DI Davis and his team have been investigating up till now but I want to expand our efforts to include all officers here today. Harrold will you put everyone in the picture".

"Yes Ma'am; we have been lucky so far in that Dawn was found in good time.....".

Compton Busion entered the room followed by Jonny Musgrove who quickly moved to stand by the table.

" .....as I was saying Dawn was saved from exposure and is now recovering. I spoke to her at the Hospital she told me it all started when she went to meet her boyfriend at the restaurant where he works, unbeknown to her had been taken to hospital with a burst appendix. She then went home to collect her bike and cycled to his house in Wildmoore to look for him, no one answered and whilst round the back of the house looking to see if there was anyone home her bike was taken. She thought it was her boyfriend playing a joke so walked along the lane to look for him. A man then jumped out in front of her holding the bike. She felt threatened so ran back diving through a gap in the hedge and across the woodland fields towards the river. She said the man followed as she could hear his footsteps, at the waters edge she stopped and took off her yellow safety vest and threw it in the river, went back across the field and hid in the bushes. She remember nothing more.

We found her the following day suffering from hypothermia and had her transferred to hospital. SOCO has found footprints of Dawn overlaid by those of a heavy treaded shoe size ten on the riverbank. The same footprints were discovered at various places including where we found the bike. There were fingerprints on the bike other than Dawn's or her family's so far unknown, not on record. CCTV has shown her progress to just before the turn off, the only vehicle to have followed her in anyway was a post office van. Although his stops were normal we have some CCTV anomalies and have yet to check this out. We have just come back with some CCTV from the local golf course as yet unexamined".

"Thank you Harrold, questions anyone".

There was a buzz of chatter for a minute or so before Jonny spoke up.

"It seems to me Ma'am, this man will try again so I suggest we track him down a soon as possible; why didn't she jump in the river to get away"?

"That was my first question of Harrold too. Apparently she is afraid of the water and can't swim. She felt too conspicuous in the bright jacket so threw it in the river, then hid hoping he would stop looking. Before you arrived I had already stated I believed he would not stop, it's nice to know you think the same. Right we have some but not too much evidence so I want the senior detectives to split the load using their teams to start door to door near the college, the restaurant and Wildmoore. People are nosey so someone will have been looking for sure; see if there was anything unusual in the past week or so, not just around the time of the incident, you know what's needed. This will be a bit of a slog I know but good old fashioned footwork will find who he is. Jonny, Harrold work together, allocate who does what; I'll go and visit Dawn, I want details about this man from her, she may remember more now she has recovered".

Dawn had left hospital and returned home the previous morning; Toni's phone call to her mother had paved the way for a visit in the afternoon.

The house was a typical Popley council estate house maintained in good order, the rendered front wall and wrought iron gate had been recently painted and the path with its short front garden was tidy the shrubs either side neatly trimmed. This home was well cared for as were many of these houses which had been sold off in the late eighties. Much of the estate was now privately owned with just a few left run by the local housing association. Dawn's was probably owned by her parents judging by it's appearance although many of the association tenants would also have displayed pride in their dwellings; Toni would soon find out. Her press of the bell push brought a rapid response, due she thought to her previous call.

"Mrs. Westcott, good afternoon I am Detective Chief Inspector Webb, I phoned earlier".

Toni's assumption that this was Dawn's mother, as she offered sight her warrant card, was confirmed by her being invited in straight away.

"Yes Inspector, I'm Margaret, please come through to the back room; would you like a tea or coffee"?

Toni accepted the offer of coffee as she sat in one of the armchairs. The home was more generous than appeared from the outside; it was as deep as it was wide. The back room spread across over half the rear elevation overlooking the quite large garden. This extended forty or more feet to a high wooden fence with its rear gate leading to a pedestrian path which linked all the houses in this row. The garden was neat and well looked after as was the rest of the house.

"Please have a seat I'll get your coffee; Dawn is in her room".

"Where is Mr. Westcott"?

"He's at work, should be home about seven or so".

Margaret Westcott left; Toni did not press her to fetch Dawn as it was obvious she wanted to speak to Toni beforehand. Toni scanned the room, which was obviously the one most used by the family. The two armchairs and settee were arranged in front of the open fireplace, a little worn but comfortable, several landscape pictures on the wall with family photographs among various ornaments on the modern sideboard all blending to emit a homely feel. The noise of kettle and cups could be heard through the open door followed by Margaret's reappearance a few minutes later. She placed a tray with two cups and a plate of biscuits on the small coffee table adjacent to where Toni was seated.

"How do you like it"?

"Black no sugar thanks".

With the formalities over and the offer of a digestive biscuit accepted, Toni opened the proceedings.

"How is Dawn faring"?

"She's recovered from the exposure, the doctor said she was lucky the temperature that night was not so cold to have any lasting effects. She's not been able to go out since you know; that man scared her so much she thinks he will be waiting for her somewhere".

"I'm sorry to hear that, her trauma, I expect, will stay with her for a while yet, we will help there and can provide counselling and some protection of course until we resolve the situation".

"I don't know if we want the police involved we can take care of ourselves".

"Of course we will respect your wishes but our offer remains if you need it. Would it be possible to meet Dawn, her actions at the time shows her to be very astute; if she's getting better like you said, she may have remembered some details that were not clear when my officer first spoke to her"?

Toni wanted to speak to Dawn on her own without the protective mother controlling events, she stood and continued.

"I just want to see this brave girl before I continue to track down and arrest the man who put her at risk. To save her coming down here perhaps I could speak to Dawn in her room".

Margaret Westcott was reluctant but couldn't resist Toni's request; although it was her original intention to keep this policewoman from speaking to her daughter, she now saw her as someone who could possibly help Dawn shake off her depression. She nodded and rose, walked into the hall and started up the stairs indicating for Toni to follow. Dawn's room was at the head of the stairs the door was closed. Margaret knocked with no answer, she called out.

"Dawn love, I have a police officer here who would like to speak to you. We are coming in".

With still no reply she opened the door and walked in, Toni followed. Dawn was sitting at a small desk looking at a computer screen. She turned as they entered looked at her mother and then at Toni eye to eye.

"What do you want"?

Toni forced a smile to counter the deep frown on the brow of this young girl.

"My name is Toni I'm the Detective in charge of finding the person who threatened you. I have more than twenty officers working to that end this very minute and I wanted to meet the young lady who had the good sense to lead him away and save herself".

"Well now you've met me, you can come back when you've caught him".

"That I will but if you want us to catch him I'll need your help".

At that point Margaret interrupted.

"She has already told your officer what happened so I expect her to be left to recover, she doesn't want to answer any more questions".

"I have read my officer's notes, they are very sparse".

Toni looked at Margaret and started coughing, she needed a few moments with Dawn alone.

"Would you be so kind to fetch me a glass of water".

53

Margaret, unaware of the subterfuge turned and left the room. Toni turned immediately to Dawn.

"You know of course, you are the only witness and your initial statement was given when you were very stressed, I am sure you may now have more to tell me; without your information we may never be able to catch him and I'm sure you don't want him roaming free".

It was just enough time to voice her demand, for Margaret returned in a few seconds having obtained the water from the bathroom next door. Toni thanked her, took the glass drinking slowly looking at Dawn for some indication of a response to her appeal.

"It's alright Mum, I don't mind a few questions and I do want to help catch the man don't I"?

"Well okay, but no too long mind".

Dawn looked round at Toni and smiled.

"You can sit on my bed if you like".

She spun her chair full circle so she could face Toni, in the movement she shooed her mother away with the back of her hand giving her a stare and a lift of her jaw silently indicating she wanted to talk to her alone.

"I'll wait downstairs then, remember not too long".

Toni then realised the fear of going out was Margaret's and not Dawn's and that she had been indulging her mother's protective attitude to keep the peace.

"How are you feeling"?

"Oh I'm okay, better than yesterday anyway; the cold was pretty awful, I'm glad that copper found me when he did I'd like to thank him in person, tell him to come round when you see him".

"Are you afraid to go out"?

"I suppose, a bit, but not really, it's Mum who's scared. I want to go back to college, I said I'd always walk with someone but she's a bit reluctant".

"Give it a day or two and your Mum will probably come round and let you go back to classes, maybe Monday next after the weekend. What are you studying"?

"Maths, Physics and Spanish".

"What would you like to do from there"?

"I'm not sure yet, University first, if my grades are good enough, maths is my favourite".

"That's what I did at Uni, if you need any help let me know".

"You have a degree in Math"?

"For my sins, yes, a long time ago though".

"Wow, isn't that unusual for a policewoman"?

"Not so much nowadays, the police have a wide range of degree qualified officers, do you know what you want to do"?

"No idea, certainly not the police, oh sorry I didn't mean to be rude I'm sure the police is a good job; I'm not sure I know what I want yet".

Toni laughed at Dawn's slip of good manners, it lightened the mood considerably, she was now ready to proceed with the interview.

"Don't worry, when I was younger I never dreamt I would end up a detective but here I am; you have plenty of time to find your niche, you'll be fine. Now what I need from you is a run through step by step; tell me your memories of that day from the time you left home to arrive at Bright Cottage, take your time any detail may be important; do you mind if I record this , I don't want to forget anything and taking written notes is slow and a bit disruptive, alright"?

"Okay, I'm fine with that".

Toni placed her small digital recorder on the bed between them, spoke to set the level and check it was working.

"That's good, you can begin when you're ready".

"Well after I left home, I was worried about Charlie so was riding quite quickly and arrived a bit out of breath so I stopped by the gate for a minute or two to recover before I went in. Charlies Mum's car wasn't there, which I thought strange for if he was sick she should be with him. I leant my bike against the fence and put my helmet over the saddle, I knocked on the door a couple of times with no answer, I looked through the front window it was dark inside I couldn't see anything. Then I went round the back to see if he or anyone was in, I thought he might be in bed and couldn't get to the door and maybe his mum had gone for medicine or something, I was thinking up all sorts of reasons why he hadn't called me. Anyway I peered through the kitchen window, nobody was there the whole place was in darkness. When I came back round the front my bike was missing; I didn't believe it at first I was only gone a sec".

"Did you hear anything or see anyone at all at this time even when you were riding down the road towards Charlie's house"?

"No nothing, no one. When I saw my bike had gone my first thought was that Charlie was playing a joke on me and had sneaked out the front when I was out back and ridden round the bend out of sight".

"What made you think that"?

"Oh he's always playing jokes and stuff, it's his way, he's good fun you know".

"Fine, go on".

"I walked along the road, no that's not quite right, I ran round the bend expecting him to jump out trying to surprise me, I was going to be ready for him and.....I don't know scare him back maybe; but nothing. I stopped when I came to the straight bit of road and had a clear view all the way to the end. I realised then it was not Charlie who had taken my bike. I turned to go back to the cottage as whoever had taken the bike could have gone either way and was long gone".

"Did you look up the road the way you came in when you saw the bike had gone"?

56

"I think so, yes I looked both ways but saw nothing. Anyway I changed my mind about going back to the cottage and decided to walk towards Shenfield where I could get help and a lift home".

"Why didn't you use your phone"?

"It had shut down; run out of battery I think".

Toni knew Dawn had relaxed and was in a good frame of mind to recall the events that followed. She would not interrupt again until she had finished, she'd leave any questions till the end.

"You are doing great Dawn. Now the next bit is important so think carefully and give me all the details that come to mind right up to the point when you fell asleep".

"Okay. I was annoyed I know that much; I love my bike and was really pissed off at whoever had pinched it. I started to march quite quickly as my heart was racing you know, I could feel it in my chest, probably from being angry I suppose. I went by the entrance to the golf course, I looked up the drive just in case someone had ridden up there, you can't see far though as there is a bend a little way along. I slowed down then and was walking normally when all of a sudden he jumped out from the bushes on the left holding my bike by the crossbar. He held it up and shouted that if I wanted the bike I had better come and get it. I stopped dead, I could see his eyes were looking straight at me, I was scared, it was his eyes you see. I could tell he was odd, he never blinked just stared with those scary eyes holding the bike in the air waiting for me to come to him. I turned and ran I can't remember how far but I heard his footsteps behind me so as soon as I saw that gap in the hedge I jumped through it I just wanted to get away. The brambles grabbed at my clothes and cut my hands but I couldn't stop running. I ran through the trees across the grass field hoping to come to the village before he caught up with me. I'd forgotten the river ran through that part of the woods, the only way across was to run to the old mill. It was much too far I'd never get there in time, he would catch me for sure. All of a sudden the river was there I'd nowhere to go. I stood on the bank staring at the rushing water unable to move. I heard him swearing as he tried to push through the small gap in the hedge, he was much further behind than I thought so he couldn't see me yet. I was scared cause I can't swim, or I would have jumped in or I think I would, anyway I took off my yellow jacket and threw it in hoping he would see it. I don't know if he did as the river was running quite fast and my jacket started to float away, at least I was less obvious without it. I looked around and still couldn't see him so I ran back towards the wooded area and hid in the tall grass. I was afraid to look but I think he'd reached the riverbank; he swore out loud, the 'F' word several times then he turned and went back; I wasn't sure if he'd gone because I could hear him walking off and then returning a couple of times, I suppose he was still looking for me. I waited and waited too scared to move. I don't remember anything after that".

"Quite an ordeal and very clever of you to ditch the jacket. Just a couple of questions if you don't mind".

Dawn smiled and nodded, glad to have told her story to a sympathetic ear.

"Are you sure he had not just found your bike and wanted to return it"?

"No way; if you had seen his eyes you would have known, besides why did he chase after me"?

"Okay; when he spoke did you notice his accent; can you describe his voice"?

"He was local I'm sure there was a definite Hampshire lilt and it was deep and a bit gruff, like he had a cold. It broke when he shouted".

"Good now do you remember what he was wearing"?

"He was in a suit, no not a suit exactly, but trousers and a jacket black or maybe navy blue".

"His face and figure"?

"Not really, it was so quick, he was old like, grey hair I think or could be fair; not very, very old you know over thirty though and well built".

"How tall"?

"He seemed big but then he was holding the bike above his head which made him seem taller. About one metre eighty anyway. Oh I've just remembered he had a badge on his jacket, red or yellow; both, I wasn't close enough to see exactly what it was".

"You know what Dawn we will leave it there for today; you have been great; all this will help us enormously. If a police artist comes over do you think you could help them sketch a likeness".

"I can try. Do you think you'll catch him"?

"Early days; I'll let you know when we do, by the way have you seen Charlie"?

"Yes my Dad took me to the hospital yesterday night; he's getting better he 'll be home in a couple of days, we phone each other as well so it's alright now".

"That's good, take care Dawn".

With that Toni rose from the bed smiled at Dawn and left with her smiling back. Mrs. Westcott was sitting on the stairs, obviously listening to what had been said, she rose as Toni approached the top of the stairs and went down in front. At the front door she paused and said.

"Thank you detective, you have certainly made an impression on our Dawn; you've got more out of her in a half hour than I have since she came home".

"Just give her time and space, she has suffered a traumatic event, getting back to a normal routine as soon as possible would be best".

"Am I being over-protective"?

"Just a tad, but you're a Mum so it's okay, for a while anyway. Your daughter is very smart let her be your guide".

"I'll try. Goodbye Inspector".

"Goodbye Margaret, we'll be close by".

Toni moved to her car happy with the information gathered today. She had shed light on some important facts; Dawn had almost certainly been followed, the circumstances of her stolen bike and the man waiting for her were not a random occurrence, the suspect was a local man from Hampshire, Toni believed Dawn's take on his accent was probably right; he wore a uniform of some kind, blue or black with a red and yellow insignia. His age was uncertain, as teenagers thought anyone over twenty five was really old. For now Toni would place him around forty give or take ten years; the sketch may help narrow it down later. Even though it was late she would go back to the station and feed this information into the case file; at this time of the evening most officers would have left, budget cuts did not allow for overtime without special authorisation from the Superintendent, however she knew Constable Busion would still be on site. She hoped other information her teams had found may enhance Dawn's description and guide them towards a suspect.

"Hello Compton, I've something for you; an interview with Dawn Westcott, sorry no notes just a recording, I'll write them up later and leave them on your desk before I go, you can add them tomorrow".

A recording was good for the detail but the impressions of the officer observing the subject were only possible through their notes and were an essential addition to the information in a recording. Toni left for her office to find a small pile of paperwork not related to this case. She knew it would be a late evening before she finished; it looked likely a Chinese takeaway would be tonight's supper not that she minded, the Chineham Noodle house was excellent. Her first task was an email for her two Inspectors to have everyone at an update meeting at ten tomorrow morning. Her intended meal with Nathan would have to wait; she sent him a text for if she spoke to him he was likely to persuade her to leave the paperwork, which she would regret the following day when the pile would have grown.

Chapter 7

Toni walked into the squad room several minutes before ten to find the table already cleared of its usual clutter and surprisingly an unusually quiet group of officers ready and waiting.

"Well, well, what's all this? I suppose there's a first time for everything anyway thank you everyone for being so prompt. It seems the incident with Dawn Westcott has touched a nerve; we've been lucky it was not more serious and that's largely down to our victim. I spoke to her yesterday when she gave a good account of what happened. The man is described as about six foot tall large build, grey or fair hair around forty years of age, dressed in a dark blue or black uniform with red or yellow motif. He may be local as he had a gruff voice with a recognisable Hampshire accent. A police artist is with her as we speak so we should have a likeness soon. I believe Constable Busion has coordinated all the reports and some interesting CCTV footage that I will leave her to explain".

"Err yes, thank you Ma'am. The description of the suspects clothing and CCTV has thrown up a possible vehicle of interest. A Post Office van number VG17RUJ has made some deliveries and collections that place it in the vicinity of the incident at the time in question. It also seems to have made deviations from its expected route on that day. The CCTV at the golf course shows the van arrived and left almost an hour later. It was out of sight when parked so the driver was not identifiable. Traffic are waiting on the route it is taking now and will apprehend the driver when he next stops. This morning we have asked for details of the driver from the sorting office, the manager is looking into it and will send us the details by email any minute. Fingerprints from the bicycle frame are ready for comparison along with casts of the shoe prints found by the river. If this is our man we should have him in custody within the hour".

"Thanks Compton; right we think he has been watching Dawn and maybe other girls from the College for some time waiting for the opportunity to accost them when alone and vulnerable. We have had no other reports or related incidents so think this was his first attempt to confront his intended victim".

A beep from Compton's phone sounded almost at the same time as Inspector Davis's mobile.

"That's the artist impression I expect, I'll go and see. If it is I'll print off some copies for everyone".

Compton said as she started to leave.

"The email should have come from the Post Office by now I hope".

Said Harrold, again rising to move just a few steps over to his computer, he sat at the screen and read aloud the resulting email sent by the post office manager.

"'*Mr Owen Jones (senior postman) is currently the driver. He is on the round from our Basingstoke office to Heckfield Place on the A33 returning along the A30 via Old Basing with fifty seven stops for delivery and six for collection'*. There is a route map too, Ma'am showing the collection points. Significantly the golf course has no official collection box, but he told me they do collect from there if they're making a delivery. It looks like we might have him even before he's had time to do any real damage".

At that moment Compton returned with a dozen A4 copies of the artist impression. A round face with large eyes and dark brows, grey hair, long and untidy with dark sideburns. Not brilliant for identification but certainly good enough for elimination.

Two hours later the red van was in a police parking bay and Mr. Owen Jones was in interview room three, courtesy of the uniform traffic police. Toni and Harrold Davis came down together as soon as he had been processed. They looked through the one-way glass and then at each other surprised. There sat a short thin man of around sixty who was almost bald. Nothing like the description or artist image.

"Did they check the bloody van number"?

"Yes, of course I saw the van in the yard Ma'am".

"Let's get in there and sort this out".

"Mr Jones, I'm Detective Chief Inspector Webb and this is Detective Inspector Davis, I need to ask you a few questions".

"And I need to ask you a few too. What do you mean interrupting me on my round I have post to deliver and collect you know? Royal Mail it is and shouldn't be interfered with isn't it".

Toni was taken aback; his broad Welsh accent and outburst was not expected.

"I'm sorry you have been delayed but an incident occurred which requires us to ask these questions".

At this point there was a knock on the door and Sergeant Andrews entered.

"You should see this Ma'am".

Toni moved to the door and took the paper offered by Peter.

"The prints don't match Ma'am and the shoe cast is completely different and much too small".

Toni realised they had the wrong man, but why, she was thinking. They couldn't have it all wrong could they?

"What do you want to do Ma'am"?

Toni rose and called Harrold to come too.

"Please wait here Mr. Jones, I'll be back".

"I don't mind helping but I have to finish my round, if I don't leave soon all the sub-posties will be calling my boss and I'll be in real trouble".

"I'm sorry I won't keep you any longer than necessary".

She stopped suddenly realised they had the right van but the wrong man.

"Mr Jones is this the van you always drive"?

"Lord no; I only started yesterday the man who usually does this round had gone sick".

"Whose round is it then"?

"That'll be Horse; we call him that, George Grant's his name though, he'll be doing sorting instead for a while, we swap around sometimes, boss says it keeps us from getting bored".

"Why 'Horse'"?

"On account of his hoarse voice and his initials".

"GG of course. You can go Mr. Jones, contact your office to have a replacement vehicle sent so you can take your post and finish the round; we will need to keep this van for tests; Peter take him to a phone. If there is a problem Detective Sergeant Andrews will speak to your boss and explain".

Harrold was looking dejected but had to speak up.

"Sorry Ma'am, my fault I never asked the postal Manager who was driving on the day, it never occurred to me".

"Don't fret, you were not to know, we must go to the sorting office right now. You go with a couple of uniforms, I'll go in my car, let's hope he's still there".

"Shall I phone the manager"?

"No I don't want him warned. Bugger".

"What's up"?

"Owen Jones is bound to have told his boss about us looking for George, my mistake, he'll either run or be ready for us. Let's go".

George felt so uncomfortable there was no way he could stay at work waiting for the inevitable. As soon as he heard that Taffy, the relief driver, had been stopped by the police, he was gone. Too late now, the realisation that leaving his station after pleading he was sick again would make the coppers think he was guilty of stalking the girl. No matter what he said he knew they wouldn't believe him but what could they prove, he hadn't actually done anything? He'd keep it together and stick to his story whatever they threw at him. He'd been foolish not thinking

65

it through. The coppers had been quick to trace him, God knows how? The girl, other witnesses maybe or cameras he didn't know about, what an idiot. It didn't bear thinking about, but what if he'd actually caught and taken her, they would probably have found him anyway by now and he be in a big load of shit. Earnest would never have made these mistakes he wouldn't try this on his own again. At least he had disposed of his dirty clothes, dumped in a rubbish bin the other side of town. He was using his new set now and had put an old set he had saved from the garden shed in his locker. He had changed into his pyjamas to back up his story of being unwell; sat in his favourite chair in front of a daytime television gameshow pretending normality to anyone who came knocking; for sure they would and soon.

Toni and Harrold were a minute behind the uniformed officers in arriving at the postal sorting office. Two of them had already entered the door with the third standing by the car.

"They've just gone in Ma'am".

"Good, let's hope he's still there; officer you wait here, Harrold go round the back in case he does a runner".

Toni followed through the open door to find a reception desk and a corridor to one side. The exceptionally wide corridor had one door either side, now closed; at the end a pair of double push-through doors were still swinging slightly pendulum like from her officers entering a moment before. She entered a large room divided into six bays with tall pigeonholed racks over wide tables. At the end of the bays a post code sorting machine was processing letters delivering them to the appropriate individual bay slots. Rejected letters were distributed to the tables where each postman was rapidly and skilfully manually sorting letters from the pile on the table and thrusting each into it's appropriate slot. She scanned each by trying to identify Grant to no avail. She saw her two officers were talking to a man in a glass walled office at the rear of the room; they came out together as she approached.

"This is Joe the supervisor Ma'am, apparently Mr. Grant has gone home sick".

"He was ill yesterday you know and went home; I told him I would cover his round but he insisted on coming in today so I put him on sorting. I had a call from Taffy saying you had the van and was looking for Horse; sorry I mean Mr. Grant; when I told him Taffy had been stopped and you were looking for him he said he felt unwell again. He said if the police wanted to speak to him they would find him at his house. I sent him home; what is going on"?

"We need to speak to Mr Grant concerning an incident not related to the Post Office, we were told by your manager that Owen Jones was the employee driving the van on the day in question, we now know it wasn't him, so sorry if that has caused you a problem, but I do need Mr. Grant's address, now".

"The manager must have just looked at the duty roster, he couldn't have known about the change, well no harm done I've sent Taffy a new van and another driver they can finish the round together. When will I get the van back"?

"Soon as we have finished, you'll receive a call to collect it. The address please".

"I'll find that for you now".

Toni turned to the two uniforms.

"Thanks guys you can go now; please ask DI Davis to come in, he's at the back of the building".

The officers left and Toni moved to the office to see Joe coming out with a piece of paper in hand.

"This is his address; I've put his phone number too, in case you wanted it".

"Yes that's good. Does he have a locker"?

"Err, yes I'll show you, they're not usually locked".

"Okay thanks".

Harrold arrived coming in through the corridor as Toni and the supervisor were at the door of the locker room. She shook her head to show that Grant wasn't on site and indicated for him to follow.

"This is his locker; do you want to look inside"?

"Yes but would you open it please".

If it was empty Toni wouldn't bother however if it contained anything interesting she would obtain a warrant before she removed it. There were some magazines in the bottom with some boots on top and a postman's uniform hanging on two hooks. The clothes looked dirty, a little worn too.

"Please seal this locker Harrold, call Sergeant Andrews to organise a warrant before we search it properly. The uniform looks interesting it might be the one he wore the other day".

Harrold moved to the car to search for some tape from the boot, he hoped the kit was up to date, he hadn't kept his in order but knew Toni would not be so lax. Sure enough the tape was where it should be why did he doubt her for even a second.

Having assured the supervisor he would have his van back soon and that another officer would be along with the warrant to remove the locker contents, Toni left with Harrold for the home of George Grant. She was not expecting to find him there, sure he had already made his escape.

George lived in a small house number twenty two Manor Gardens part of a large estate south of the Basingstoke ring road; the homes, built in the nineties, were rented out by a housing association and appeared in good order. They both approached the door where Harrold knocked loudly. To his and Toni's surprise they heard a shuffling behind the door and a gruff voice shout.

"Hold on a minute I'm coming".

The door swung back and a man in pyjamas unshaven with unkempt hair stood looking from one to the other. Dawn's photofit image of him was pretty good.

"What can I do for you, don't come too close I've caught a bug of some kind"?

"I'm Detective Inspector Davis and this is Chief Inspector Webb, are you George Grant"?

"Yes why what do you want? I'm not well you know so be quick I want to go back to bed"?

"I'm sorry you are feeling unwell but we need to ask you a few questions".

"Can't you come back in a few days when I'm better"?

"I'm sorry but we need some answers now".

"Does that mean you want to come in"?

"That would be good".

"Well its up to you; if you catch this bug it will be your own fault".

Toni nodded at Harrold indicating she wanted to take the lead; he stepped in through the door directly into the lounge then moved to the back wall where he could be out of sight, observe and take notes. Toni moved in behind the man who sat on the couch; she sat opposite him without being invited.

"Mr. Grant I need to know what you were doing in Wildmoore Tuesday afternoon"?

"Tuesday, yes that was an odd day all said and done. I'd missed Wildmoore to start with you know, I don't always have mail for there. There is no collection box except at the golf course. Although it's on the list it's not really official, we collect as a favour at the same time if we have deliveries, anyway when I arrived at Shenfield I found some mail that was for a couple of the houses and one for the golf club in the bottom of my bag so went back. I delivered the letters and was just leaving the club when I heard these kids shouting, I went down the path to see two lads with a bike, they were throwing a helmet back and forward to each other. I yelled at them something like 'what the hell are you doing' They threw the helmet at me and ran away leaving the bike. I picked it up when another kid came running

69

towards me, it was a girl I'm sure. Anyway I held up the bike and asked if it was hers. She turned and ran, I assumed she was with the others but was dressed different, I think maybe it was her bike. I followed to where she dived through a hedge I went to follow but couldn't it was all brambles; I cut my hands, see".

George held up his scratched fingers.

"What did you do then"?

"Well nothing really I went back up the path picked up my van and carried on with my round".

"When you went to the hedge how far in did you go"?

"I didn't go in. I couldn't it was too narrow".

"What happened to the boys".

"I don't know they were gone".

"What about the bike"?

"Nothing much, I put it in the hedge, someone might have run it over if I'd left it in the road; I thought whoever owned it would find it".

"Why didn't you report it"?

"Never occurred to me I just carried on with my job. I forgot all about it till you called just now".

"Can you describe the boys"?

"Just lads, about sixteen or so, dark clothes short hair".

"The girl"?

"Hmm; different she had a yellow jacket, as I said I thought it was her bike at first but when she ran, I wasn't sure".

"Why did you follow her"?

"I don't know, curious I suppose".

"Why use the path and not the road to go back and forth to the golf club"?

"The road has too many turns, the path is only half the distance. Look, a Chief Inspector asking all these questions is a bit unusual, seems to me a lot of fuss over young teenagers stealing a bike; what the hell is going on"?

"Thank you Mr. Grant when you are feeling better I would like you to come to the station and make a formal statement; by the way I would like to take your work clothes for examination".

"I suppose, of course, I don't know why you would need them, unless this has to be more than a bike theft, has something happened to one of those teenagers; won't you tell me what is happening"?

"Just routine Mr. Grant, we need to illiminate you from these enquiries so please come in as soon as you can".

With that Toni rose and waited whilst Harrold went with Grant to his bedroom to fetch the clothes; she then moved towards the door; Harrold followed, the bundle in his arms.

"Goodbye Mr. Grant, please come in as soon as you can".

He nodded closing the door behind them.

Harrold Davis wondered why Toni had not arrested and taken him in.

"Why not take the bastard in Ma'am the lying toad, his delivery was much too pat. He must have rehearsed that many times. We knew he was probably expecting us; but that story is a load of rubbish"?

"Not quite all, he has kept close to what happened in some respects and inventing the teenagers as bike thieves would be accepted by some as a credible explanation. I would have loved to give the bugger a good grilling but what we have so far will not stand up in court; as it is at the moment the prosecutors will not touch it with a bargepole. Even if Dawn identifies him he is not contradicting the situation that he confronted her, and we don't have any evidence of anything else. The only exception where we may be able to break his story is in his denying he followed her into the woods and by the river. We require proof he was there, maybe his clothes from the locker will give us what we need. Harrold call Peter, see if he has the warrant yet; if he does you can go with him back to the sorting office".

"We'll take his statement Ma'am and compare it with my notes; this man will slip up if we apply enough pressure".

"Let's go back Harrold. I will organise surveillance and have him watched openly; he will know we are there twenty four seven. The following week covertly, he will think he is in the clear then we'll be back in his face again, and again, we won't let this guy blow his nose without our knowing about it".

Detective Sergeant Peter Andrews was bagging the clothes and items from George Grant's locker with Joe Silvester observing.

"I can't see what you want his old uniform for, what's he supposed to have done. George is such a steady worker you know, never takes a day off and now sick twice in one week"?

"I'm sorry Mr Silvester this is part of an ongoing enquiry and as such is confidential. We don't know if Mr. Grant has done anything we just need to eliminate him; when he has recovered I'm sure he will be back at work and will tell you if he wishes".

"Hmm, I just worry that's all, I'll need to cover his round somehow".

"I'm sure you'll manage without him for a day or two".

Peter moved back to the car to wait for Harrold who had gone to see the Manager.

"Anything sir"?

"No not really; he apologised for giving us the wrong information as he only had the weekly roster that did not show the change made by Joe Silvester on that day. Joe deals with the sorting office, all local deliveries and collections. The manager lets him get on with it; says he has enough to do transferring the incoming countrywide mail to central office, organising parcels for collection, registered mail and all personnel matters like wages; he is sorry but keeping up to date with who's on which round is not his priority. I did make a printout of Grant's employment record, nothing unusual though, been working here for nine years. I see you've his clothes and stuff let's send them to forensics now, we could do with a break on this one".

"Listen up everyone".

The squad room had an unusual hush that Toni had never seen here before. The detectives and their teams were gathered round the big table all unhappy with the result of the interview with George Grant was inconclusive, even more so as no charges were possible with what they had so far.

"This man Grant is all wrong, God knows what he intended to do to Dawn Westcott if he had caught up with her. The very fact that he didn't is good, very good but has also left him with a story that covers his bloody arse and without evidence to show he deliberately took her bike or tried to follow her; we can't charge him. The forensics on his clothes matched diddley squat, those he was wearing that day must have been dumped somewhere, let's see if we can find them, search for where he has been since, try CCTV again. We know he followed her into the woods and up to the river but have no sodding proof. I want full time surveillance; Jonny that'll be you, organise a twenty four hour watch on him, at his house at the sorting office and follow him on his rounds. Let him see us, with no let-up. I want this bastard worried".

Jonny could hear an anger in Toni's voice and a decision out of character. This was not right; he asked.

"How long is this to go on for Ma'am"?

"I want him really rattled so one week to start with where he sees us every dam minute, then we keep an eye on him for another week but very quiet like, give him a chance to relax. Then back again in full view".

"What happens then"?

"We bring the bugger in again and run the question by him this time in an interview room, we'll ask Dawn to come in for an identification parade. We have to stop this man or he will do some real damage. I know we'll have other things to do so let's hope we are lucky with some quick results. Harrold do a full background check; finances, friends, go back to his youth too you know school as well and Compton look into his use of the internet".

There was a murmur as the group broke up and moved to their desks. Jonny was concerned so moved over next to Toni.

"Can I have a word Ma'am. In your office".

She turned and left with Jonny Musgrove one step behind.

"What's up Jonny"?

"With me, nothing; I'm worried about you, why are you being so aggressive about this man, using resources we can ill afford; a twenty four seven watch, what's that all about? The overtime alone will break the bank, have you even run this by the Super"?

"What do you mean coming in here telling me what I should and shouldn't do? This chap is dangerous and we must put him away".

"I agree with that whole heartedly but there are more acceptable ways and means. We don't want him complaining of harassment do we; you mustn't give him anything to help his case when we go to trial. Even if we prove he was lying we will only have minor offences to charge him with at the moment. The CPS will want more, you know what they are like, so why this over the top reaction, can't we go the more conventional route eh"?

"Oh Jonny I don't know; I've had this terrible feeling ever since we knew Dawn was missing. She nearly died and it was his fault and we can't touch him for it. It's all wrong. I just want to punish him; I want him to be afraid like she was, am I bad to want that"?

"Just a bit Toni, just a bit; it's not like you to go full on like this full of emotion, you usually think things through and discuss the alternatives with us first; perhaps we can modify this surveillance a little. No point in having a car outside his front door all night whilst he's asleep you'll only be punishing the poor guys on watch, not forgetting the three week overtime bill; in any case I doubt if the Super will sanction the cost for more than a couple of days".

"I know, I know, but let me tell you something. I've seen this before when I first started, a girl died; the DI knew, we all knew who did it but had no evidence. It was awful the case was eventually abandoned I vowed never to be part of anything like that in the future".

"This isn't the same; well not really, Dawn isn't dead".

"Only by luck this time I'll wager, her actions alone saved her, nothing to do with us and his cover up story has left us with a similar dilemma to back then; one we probably will not be able to solve. He thought he was going to take her with no one finding out, but now he knows we are on to him he will be more careful. He will wait till we have given up altogether then he'll try again. He will not stop, he may even have done this before, we just haven't found out about it".

"You're wrong about us not saving her you know, Andrews arrived there in time to do just that remember. Okay Ma'am we'll give it a go, just not so 'gung ho' alright".

"Fine Jonny maybe you are right, daytime surveillance for now and make sure he sees us".

Toni felt dreadful, Jonny was right of course, what was making her so irritable and aggressive when she was normally very calm and deliberate in her approach to problems. What she needed was some R and R and good night's sleep.

Chapter 8

George Grant was shaking and the sweat that ran down his sleeves during the questioning had started to dry, he could sense his body odour; he would shower later. He felt happy with the outcome but still nervous about them tracking him down so easily. The story was so close to the truth except his real intentions and the fact that he had stolen her bike and followed her to the river; they had no proof of either. He wondered what had happened to her, with this amount of attention he thought she must be dead. Thank goodness he had dumped his clothes. The ones they took and the others they would find in his locker, would tell them nothing. He had gone over the story in his head several times he would not forget when he had to go in and write it down. He'd wait a couple of days; giving him time to find out what had happened to the girl. Whether she had died or not made no difference, whatever they said he had not touched her. He did not want to tell Earnest what had happened, George was ashamed to have been so foolish; Earnest would give him a hard time if he knew. He was still in his pyjamas so decided to keep it to himself and go to bed, the shower could wait till the morning. He slept soundly confident he was safe. The day was spent watching television and drinking lager, he didn't even bother to dress. He peeped through the curtains every now and again seeing the officers in their car knowing they would leave when five o'clock came. He was determined not to let it worry him. The news at six had just begun when there was a knock on the door, he wondered who it might be; he opened the door carefully with the chain on.

"Oh it's you, what the hell are you doing here"?

George removed the chain and let his visitor in.

The two uniformed officers sat in the car outside the home of George Grant. Monday morning was the fourth day of their stint with no sign of their suspect leaving his home all weekend.

"Seems odd Sarge, we've been here all this time and no sign of him".

"The boss said he was pretending to be ill so would not expect him to come out for a day or two".

"Look there's been no sign of movement in any of the rooms, no lights or nothing, even if he was really sick you'd think he would watch the tele or something. Normally you can see the screen through the window during the day; he hasn't even drawn back the curtains like on Friday and Saturday".

"You know we are parked in full view; the idea is it would rattle him by us watching all the time; I bet he is just hiding in his bedroom scared shitless".

"You are probably right. Do you want a sandwich Sarge, I've either ham or cheese"?

"Your misses spoils you Danny; cheese is great. We'll eat our breakfast first, then after you'd better call the boss let him know it seems too quiet".

Jonny listened to the surveillance report from Constable Danny Joiner concerning doubts about the lack of movement.

"What makes you think he is not home constable"?

"I would have thought he would turn on a light or watch the TV but nothing for two days. The front curtains were drawn closed when we left at night and normally open when we come back in the morning. We saw some activity on Friday and Saturday, the odd light on and off and the TV reflecting on the window but now nothing. The curtains haven't been moved, closed Sunday when we arrived and still the same now. Even if he knew we were there and I'm sure he does, he would draw them like normal don't you think sir"?

"Seems likely, anything else"?

"Well we were told to expect him to come to the station to make a statement sir, I don't think he has yet, maybe he has done a runner, in the night".

"Thank you Danny anything else".

"No sir, that's it".

"Okay keep your eyes open I'll be there soon"

Jonny was concerned, he had expected George to come in by now but thought the surveillance had put him off. If he had done a runner that would be great, they would track him down and have a good reason to bring him in again. He decided to go to the house and see for himself.

When Jonny and Mel arrived at the home of George Grant; it was eleven am. The police car with its two watching uniform officers were parked directly outside. They pulled up behind and approached the officers.

"Anything happening"?

"Nothing sir all quiet".

"Mel let's go see if he's in".

They knocked once; a second time more loudly. Jonny shouted through the letter box for him to open the door; nothing. The front door swung back with two hefty shoves; not too hard as the jamb was a soft wood and the lock a simple Yale. He went straight upstairs to check the two bedrooms whilst Mel first looked in the kitchen and then opened the door to the front room she stopped dead when she saw the scene.

George Grant was in alright, but was going nowhere, still in his pyjamas sitting in front of the blank and silent TV, smelling worse than ever before, a few drops of blood down his front and some spots on the armchair between his legs had dried to a dark brown; the gash at his throat deep and wide the obvious source but why so little blood. The flies told her he'd been dead a while. Mel looked at the body, her first thought was 'bloody hell how did we miss this' and then 'how did anyone get in without him being aware'.

Jonny found nothing and on coming down he caught the odour of death well before he entered the living room;

"Shit, Mel; how the hell did this happen"?

"A bit of a sod eh! Either they had a key or picked the lock, we may never know as we buggered it on the way in; SOCO may be able to salvage something from that. I'll call them in and the doc too, by the way did you touch anything upstairs"?

"No the internal doors were open I just did a quick look; did you check he was dead Mel".

"No, I didn't see any need. I'll go check the kitchen again see if there is a way in".

He looked again at Grant's throat.

"I see your point".

Mel walked to the rear where the small galley kitchen led to a concrete yard surrounded by a high fence, she couldn't see over; there was no gate. The door was shut but not locked.

"It may be possible to break in through the back as the door was not locked, the fence is a bit high so I can't see where it would lead. I'll go and look".

"Okay Mel; let's get out of here we've disturbed the crime scene enough already".

They both left the house Mel heading off down the road to look for a back way in, whilst Jonny moved to the officers still in the car unaware what had happened. The Sergeant wound down the window.

"Done a runner then"?

"Not exactly, he's dead".

"Fuck me! oh sorry sir I... didn't mean to... bit of a shock. Err...shall I close off the area, do you want me to call anyone, indicating the radio".

"It was not what we expected to find I can tell you; but yes please seal off the house, but no radio, I'll call it in on my phone".

Jonny knew the press, especially freelancers, illegally monitored the police radio channels and would be all over this even before the doctor or forensics had arrived. Phone was more secure. He would call Toni with the news. A thought flashed into his mind and went as quick as it came. He shook his head no not possible. The chat with Toni a few days ago, her recent odd behaviour and her obvious frustration made him wonder for that split second if she somehow had solved her problem. He told himself to shut up and put it to the back of his mind.

"Hello Ma'am, I'm sorry to tell you George Grant is dead. Sergeant Frazer found him just a short while ago, his throat has been cut, been dead a while I'd say from the dried blood and the smell. The doc will be able to tell us though. I'll stay here and wait for SOCO and the doctor. In the mean-time Mel and the two uniforms who were on watch will do a door to door".

"Must have happened at night; I knew we should have had a twenty four hour watch".

"My fault Ma'am I talked you out of it".

"No, no, Jonny, it was my decision I was doing it for all the wrong reasons and you put me straight. We couldn't have foreseen the possibility of him being killed though".

"That's true; no one outside us few knew he was on our radar, and why a revenge for something that never happened, you couldn't possibly have known, in any case it looks like whoever did it entered through the back, we don't know when it happened so even if we had a car outside all night we may not have seen anything".

"Just a feeling Jonny, I have them now and then. A police car outside may have deterred the killer. Keep me informed. By the way any chance it was self-inflicted"?

"I don't think so, the size of the cut would suggest not, besides there was no weapon, that I could see; I would say a definite no to that".

"Well we now have a murder on our hands, come back when you have finished we will have a general meet. You know

Jonny whatever he has done or intended to do; he didn't deserve to die like that; due diligence for all eh"?

"I know Toni, I know. I'll call when the doc has been. Bye".

Mel came back to the car and spoke to Jonny.

"There is a narrow alley that goes behind the houses, not all the way to the end though; some have gates, some don't; Grant's is one that doesn't but it would be possible to climb over the fence, It's nearly two meters high so not very easy, I'll tell Soco, they can have a look see".

"Good. I'll wait here for them and the doc, do a door to door please Mel, ask the uniforms to help they'll be glad to stretch their legs".

Chapter 9

This was not what she wanted, she felt cheated wanting to break him down, make him suffer the consequences of his evil mind, needing him to be ridiculed and vilified. Whoever had done this had given him a quick way out. In a way she was glad he was dead, at least he would not be able to continue with his twisted ambitions. She could not understand why her anger continued.

She thought back to when she had tried to explain to Jonny how she felt; remembering her time as a trainee at Southampton; she had only been working a couple of weeks when there was a case of a missing teenager, she had been found in the woods, just like Dawn but she was dead, strangled. Toni wasn't involved being very new to the station, the pictures of the dead girl were posted in the murder file for all to view, she had been told to study the file as part of her training; awful images forever etched in her mind, she could see them now as if it was yesterday. There was a prime suspect, she'd never forget hearing them talking about how they knew who had done it, her neighbour they said, but there was no decent evidence. They brought him in more than once but couldn't break him. In the end he lawyered up and complained of police harassment. The upstairs lily livered lot conceded and the investigation was eventually dropped. The lead detective took the can and was put on leave during an investigation, he never came back. She shuddered remembering being told in no uncertain terms, to keep her nose out when she asked a question about where he was. It had stuck with her, that case, the poor girl and her family never receiving any help from the police or the justice they deserved. She knew all too well the power wielded by senior police officers and had come up against a few who abused it. She was sure those in power all those years ago had not been honourable but she was too junior and naive to do anything about it. Too late now as those involved had left or passed on; water under the bridge best forgotten, but it never would be. Her mind moved back to the current problem.

Was the killing of George Grant a vengeance killing or was there some other reason as yet to be discovered? It was now her job to find out, her and her team's. Toni called Dr. Debbie Taylor, at the pathologist facility in Richmond, used by most of the southern police, and a friend of some years. The message service was active indicating that Debbie was busy, maybe she was the doctor attending the scene; she left a message to call and waited.

"Toni love, sorry to have been so long getting back, been busy, third one for me today; I assume it's about your dead postman".

"Yes Debbie, thanks for getting back to me anything I should know"?

"Doctor Fletcher attended this one, he's a non-committal kind of guy so would not have said much at the time, I've sent the initial report to Jonny Musgrove, dead approximately forty eight hours. A bit of a messy wound; a knife cut through the carotid artery and the windpipe, quite a deep cut, not much blood, so his heart must have stopped almost at once, quite unusual. Odd how someone could get so close with no signs of a struggle, the autopsy should reveal more. Will it be Jonny"?

"More likely Mel Frazer"?

"Okay, I'll let her know when, it would be nice to see you though it's been some time since we had a chat; oh and I'm sorry I couldn't make your bash the other day, I was at a conference in Sheffield".

"That's alright you missed a good do though. You know what maybe I'll come with Mel, I have not seen you at work for ages".

"I could delegate the job to one of my guys and we could have a long chat".

"Whatever you like, a chat would be good, this ones giving me some gyp a friendly ear may help".

"Right you are on; I'll call as soon as I have him allocated a slot, a day or two at the outside".

"Thanks Debs; look forward to it, bye".

She sat back, perhaps Jonny had more, he would be back soon now the body was on its way to the Richmond Pathology lab. Her inquisitive mind was still reacting from the news of George Grant's murder, she needed to talk to someone not involved which immediately brought Colin to mind. 'I'll call him tonight' she thought 'when I've a clearer picture of what has happened'. In the mean-time she would let Jonny and Harrold carry on.

The room was less than half full but Jonny and Peter Andrews were there as well as Compton Busion along with the uniform back up officers who had been on surveillance duty and doing the routine door to door stuff. Toni decided to go ahead and start a breakdown of tasks with only half the information she needed. Delay and lack of coordination would not help here.

"Well we have enough of you to start at least; I presume the others are out".

"Davis won't be long Ma'am, he's with SOCO, we found out Grant had a car, the keys were in his jacket, it was parked further along the street; he's with them now checking it over. Mel Frazer is still at the house, it seem likely the killer entered the house by climbing over the back fence and through the back door, SOCO have some unidentified prints from the door frame and some blood-like material on the fence, also a single footprint in the alley, maybe from when they jumped down on the way out".

"That's good anything else Jonny"?

"They said whoever did this would have certainly had some blood transfer from the victim which may be what they found on the fence. Doctor Fletcher was in attendance, death confirmed as between thirty and fifty hours ago, so some time over the weekend; autopsy may narrow it down a bit, he wouldn't say any more. June Owens has gone to the Westcott's house; I asked her to find out where they were especially Mr. Westcott".

"Thanks Jonny. Yes Compton what is it"?

She could see Compton was fidgeting wanting to say something.

"It's the car Ma'am; didn't know he had one, as soon as I had a description and the reg. I started a CCTV search. Found him a couple of times from home to the supermarket but the morning after Dawn went missing he went to the under-cover area where the town centre shops take their deliveries. He left his car with a bundle in his arms and was off camera for a few minutes; he didn't have it when he came back. I told DI Davis; I believe he dispatched a couple of officers to do a search, they have big waste bins down there. It's been a few days so they could have been emptied, worth a shot don't you think"?

"Good work, you never know your luck; if it has been picked up already they may have to go to the dump; we'll cross that bridge if necessary".

"If it has been picked up we may lose it altogether as it goes to the incinerator from there, not a landfill site. The officers are aware and will follow it to the incinerator and may be able to catch it before it goes up in smoke".

"Let's hope so Compton. Right please start a murder file for George Grant. Jonny you will be lead on this as I will need to keep Harrold free, I want him to work on something else. If you need more bodies Peter or June can be used just ask Harrold to release someone. Use uniform for any ground-work. We now need to look at the life of George Grant in great detail, someone wanted him dead. Jonny, I presume Mel will be attending the autopsy"?

"Yes Ma'am, Dr. Taylor has called already, tomorrow morning at nine".

"Good; that's it; anything new, keep me in touch".

Before she arrived back at her office Toni heard her phone ringing down the corridor, she hurried along and picked up before it stopped to find Harrold on the line. Her head was so full of things she wanted to say and do that she spoke at speed a little disjointedly spilling out her thoughts even before Harrold had a chance to say more than a 'Hello';

"I couldn't wait for you to come back Harrold, I wanted to start straight away. I've made Jonny SO for the murder. I have a different task for you; unrelated; I'll tell you about it when you come back in".

She paused realising she had spoken out of turn.

"Sorry, I jumped in there Harrold, you have something for me"?

"Yes Ma'am, the lads at the town centre have found a bundle of clothes in one of the bins. Dead lucky they were there just in time as the bins are due to be emptied in a couple of hours. They've bagged them and are on their way back now".

"How do they know if they are the ones Grant dumped"?

"A good chance they're right, they could see the red and yellow insignia of the Post Office on the jacket, there's boots too so I've been told".

"Sounds like good news, at least if they are his it will confirm Grant was lying. Too late really, if we had this earlier he would have been in custody. No good crying though, come and see me when you've finished".

Toni sat back reflecting on her recent actions. Her normal calm controlled management of any situation had been seriously lacking this day. Much to her surprise self-control was proving difficult to restore, she couldn't understand what was going on. The fact that she should have saved George Grant caused her an overwhelming emotion of guilt. It was made worse by the underlying feeling she was glad he was dead. The conflict of duty

86

and her opposing inner thoughts were dragging her towards the abyss of despair; she had been there before when her premature baby died. The symptoms of depression were invasive and growing; she needed help and soon. The lifeline of Colin beckoned, before then she had the down to earth insight of Debbie Taylor to call on. She picked up the phone and called Walter Munroe.

"Sir I'd like to take a couple of days leave, some personal things that need my attention in London. DI Musgrove is handling the murder of George Grant and DI Davis is following some leads I have given him concerning Jake Snell, you remember from the transplant cases of two years ago".

"Ah yes, he's the one that disappeared, I remember. What about him"?

"Well you may remember Sergeant Bonington of Anti-corruption, you know the unit they now call the IOPC, (Independent Office of Police Conduct) he's been promoted to an Inspector in the same department; anyway he called last week and told me Snell was back in Country, he says under a new name Jeremy Shore, he found out from a friendly colleague in the serious crime squad through one of his immigration contacts apparently; he thought as it was our case to start with we might like to follow it up. I've checked with immigration and a man with that name came in via the Channel Islands and Weymouth in Dorset; it may be nothing but worth a shot don't you think"?

"Yes of course why not, I don't like villains thinking after time has gone by that we have forgotten them any more than you do and coming back here after what he did is something he should regret; go after him with my blessing. Oh, and the leave is fine, take as long as you need, just call in daily, in case anything develops whilst you are away".

"Thank you Sir, I'm sure Jonny and Harrold will cope without me for a couple of days. I'll be going to Grant's autopsy tomorrow on my way to town, DS Frazer will be the officer in attendance I just want to receive confirmation on the cause of death".

Her next call was to DI Harrold Davis.

"Hello, Harrold are you back in"?

"Not yet Ma'am, won't be more than ten minutes I think".

"Okay come directly to see me as soon as you are".

Toni sat back to wait, glad for the ten respite minutes promised; she close her eyes and tried to blank her mind, her rhythmic breathing calming her a little. Unaware the ten minutes had drifted to twenty, treasured tranquil moments finally disturbed by a knocking on her door. She opened her eyes to see her detective through the glass; beckoning him to enter she stood, shaking off a concern that she had dozed off, covering her disquiet by moving over to her favoured appliance.

"Coffee Harrold"?

"Yes please Ma'am".

She spoke as she prepared two cups and pressed the button on the coffee machine for a double shot.

"You remember the case of the transplant kids"?

"How could I forget, why what's happened"?

She carried the hot black espressos to the desk they both sat at the same time.

"Well it looks like we have a chance to finally arrest the one who got away".

"You mean Jake Snell, why has he been caught somewhere"?

"Not exactly, our old friend Bonington has given me a heads up that he thinks he is back in the UK. Calls himself Jeremy Shore now. Here's the file he sent me it shows how he eluded us last time, he used a false ID then, which he changed a couple of times since. Seems he spent most of his time in France, went to Jersey and then back here a week ago on the ferry to Weymouth.

Immigration later spotted an error in the passport so informed the police but they have not been able to put the finger on him".

"Why'd they give it to us, now he's so close to home I'd 've thought they would jump at the chance to bring him in"?

"Politics I think, plus he feels they owe us from before".

"Politics"?

"When the two corrupt officers Vale and Branch were sent down we weren't sure if they were at the top of the pile. A certain ACC and a Commander brought a lot of pressure on Chief Superintendent Smith to downgrade the corruption charges. Trying to save the force from scandal they said but he wasn't too sure that was their real motive. The French press put a stop to any cover-up; anyway these guys are still around and the Independent Office for Police Conduct have gone as far as they can with this without exposing themselves to those who may have ulterior motives. An out of the way DI like yourself investigating quietly may not be noticed".

"I understand, a single team job, nothing traceable I suppose, I report just to you"?

"Got it in one, use your team where you need to but keep the details from them, absolute need to know only. Work on your own Harrold; a one man job as much as possible. His old bosses may not know he's back but that may not be the case for long; they have tremendous power and resources; if they find Snell before we do I am afraid he will be eliminated. He may know nothing but they won't take that chance. Now drink your coffee, I have to leave".

Harrold shuddered at the bitter unsweetened mouthful, picked up the file and left. 'How does she drink that stuff every day'? He must remember to refuse next time; maybe not just the coffee either' as he looked at the bombshell of a file in his hand. He would be careful with this one, very careful. He didn't need reminding of their terrible crimes, the images of the defiled dead children would remain with him always.

Chief Superintendent Vale and Detective Chief Inspector Branch had been controlling organised crime in South London with Grimes and Snell the leading villains for many years. Together they ran protection, prostitution and loan sharking but their main source of income was abducting kids and sending them abroad to use their organs for transplant operations. Although Grimes and Snell were not into the drug scene, it was thought the two police officers protected those that were but it was never proven. Vale had secretly banked over a million euros overseas and Branch the same. Grimes, Vale and Branch were eventually caught and sentenced to life imprisonment but Jake Snell managed to escape overseas leaving no trace.

Chapter 10

The ride to Richmond was uneventful, the motorway being clear with Toni leaving very early to avoid the rush hour congestion; she expected Mel to arrive much later, only a little before the autopsy which was scheduled for nine. She knew Debbie would be in her office at eight so was aiming to arrive at the same time or earlier. She drove into the car park at the pathologist's facility, built a few years before to centralise the service; one that was previously inefficient, it being spread all over the south. She selected a parking space where she could observe the arrival of her friend Doctor Debbie Taylor and waited. Debbie headed up the laboratory with a team of pathologists and scientists to assist with the business of dealing with justice for the dead. Most died from natural causes or obvious accidents, the few exceptions being from suspicious circumstances. Even so the majority of these were from suicide or an accidental cause such as an overdose; only the very few like that of George Grant were from murder.

As expected Debbie pulled up at ten minutes to eight, looked up from locking her car door and unsurprised saw Toni a few yards away walking towards her. They met and hugged briefly as a was their familiar greeting.

"Thought you'd be here waiting, let's go in and have a coffee".

Toni nodded but did not speak or smile, just fell in behind her friend as she walked up the steps to the facility's entrance. After Toni signed in and clipped on her visitor badge they went up in the lift to the second floor.

Debbie ushered Toni into the chair opposite her desk and sat in front of a pile of papers left in the tray overnight. She spun round in her swivel chair and turned on the coffee machine behind her.

"Give me a minute while the coffee warms up".

Said Debbie as she leafed through the papers to see if anything was urgent.

"Nothing here I can't deal with later".

Coffee poured, papers pushed to one side, Debbie waited for her friend to speak looking at her intently. Toni looked down breaking eye contact and spoke in a sharp voice, unlike her normal tone.

"What"?

"What do you mean 'What'? You're the one who wanted to see me. You are clearly troubled so speak up girl".

"I don't know what's up with me Debs, I'm making all the wrong decisions. I give an order then change my mind. I put a half-hearted watch on a suspect when I know it should have been full surveillance and because of that he is killed. I feel so guilty, even though he was a dangerous bastard he did not deserve to have his throat cut. You know what, when I first heard I was disappointed because I wanted to be the one who punished him. Then I had this wave of joy, I was glad he was dead. I'm still glad and I can't shake off the conflict of guilt and euphoria, it's blowing my mind. If only I knew what it is…..".

Debbie held up her hand a flat palm towards her friend's face.

"Hey there, stop a second, enough of the rambling. You have a dilemma indeed, but not unexpected considering what happened".

"Unexpected for me, I never had feelings like this before, I can't believe that I am happy for someone to die, it goes against what I've believed in all my life".

"How are you feeling physically"?

"Okay I suppose just tired most of the time".

"Does that mean you're not sleeping"?

"I sleep alright, in fact I find myself dozing off in the chair sometimes and that's not like me".

"Do you wake up in the night"?

"Yes sometimes but wake up all of a sweat; what's all this about my sleep patterns? What does it have to do with my mental conflict"?

"Your job is one of constant pressure, you hardly ever take a day off let alone go on holiday. The mind needs a rest as well as the body, if not it will not function as you expect".

"I've done this for years I've always been okay, why now there is nothing going on any worse than usual"?

"There is another possible explanation".

"Do tell. I'm all over the place at the moment, it takes a real effort to deal with even the day to day stuff at work".

"Toni love don't be offended; I think maybe you are going through the 'change'. Have you missed a period lately"?

"What! No... err, maybe. Not exactly missed but a bit late and then early a couple of times. I put it down to....I don't know what I thought.....It can't be can it....I'm not old enough....am I"?

"It can come at any age; it could be stress related but what you have told me is symptomatic of the start of menopause. Your mental state particularly indicates a change in hormone stability. Look go and see your GP he will explain more, he will do a blood test and probably recommend replacement therapy. You'll be back to your old self in no time".

Is that what it is a hormone imbalance. The menopause; she'd not thought that was a possibility it hadn't even crossed her mind; I'm not that old; then maybe I am; any age Debs just said. Toni's eyes welled up with tears. The fear she was going mad or senile or something had been lifted; the relief made her let go with emotion like never before. She felt embarrassed and couldn't speak.

"Hey, hey Toni this is quite normal, take a deep breath it will pass".

"I can't work like this can I; what do I do? I can't tell the Super or anyone at work either".

"You won't have to, take some leave see your GP, HRT works; there are possible side effects, mostly minor, he will explain these, so you'll have to weigh them against getting your life back. Do it now, you will notice a difference very quickly".

"You are an angel Debs, I thought I was going mad; I'll call him today; I still have a few things to clear before I can take time out".

"Get the treatment started as soon as you can, things will start to improve in a few days. At least now you will recognise the symptoms for what they are and stop fretting. Work when you feel up to it and take time out when you don't. You are the boss down there, no one will question your actions, you'll be fine soon enough. Another coffee before we go down to see Grant's autopsy"?

"Good idea, thanks, can I have just a tiny bit of sugar though"?

Debbie laughed.

Toni and Debbie arrived at the glass fronted mezzanine observation floor to see Melanie Frazer and a young constable sitting opposite the window adjacent to where the covered body was lying ready. They both stood as the two approached.

"Morning Ma'am".

"Good morning Sergeant, Constable".

"This is Constable Sheevert Ma'am, he's one of the new recruits fresh out of Hendon. I've brought him along for the experience, it is his first time".

"Welcome young man, look and learn".

"Yes Ma'am I will; thank you for the opportunity".

The three looked at each other all wondering if he'd be thankful in an hour. Toni saw the pathologist enter the room.

"Today its Doctor Hart, good here she comes".

Penny Hart looked up at her audience as she pulled on gloves and slipped her mask and glasses into position. She waved an acknowledgement of their presence and spoke to her assistant to turn on the recorder and comms. The speaker above the heads of the observers burst into life, loud and clear. Penny began.

"The subject is a white male, one point eight metres tall, forty to forty five years of age, a fit physique with only little excess fat. There is a large obvious wound to the neck, looks like two separate cuts from left to right angled upwards suggesting cut from behind by a right handed person. The lack of arterial blood indicates the cuts were post-mortem. No obvious defensive wounds or other visible marks".

Penny and her assistant turned the body on its side where she examined the back and under the arm. Rolled him to the other side and repeated the examination.

"No obvious damage to the back minor bruising to the torso".

She next examined the arms and hands, taking samples from under the fingernails followed by the legs looking closely at the feet and ankles.

"Arms and legs show signs of being bound recently. Thin bruising lines around the wrists and the same at the ankles. The nails were dirty; I have collected samples but it looks like every-day grime rather than anything left by his assailant. His feet are in poor condition, corns and partially healed blisters suggesting bad shoes or maybe just a complaint common to postman".

She returned to the wounds of the neck cleaning the area adjacent to the cuts.

There are signs of strangulation marks almost hidden by the cuts, fine lines like on the legs and wrists suggest wire or a thin rope was used. I'll know more when I look at the skin under magnification. The lines appear in at least five different places. I think this man was subject to being throttled several times before death occurred.

She next took a scalpel to open the area to reveal the nature of the wounds.

"A strong smooth blade was used ten or more centimetres long, a domestic carving knife perhaps, the first cut partially severed the windpipe, the second the carotid artery. So little blood the cuts were inflicted at least half an hour after death and possibly even later.

She lifted his eyelids and used a magnifying glass to examine the nose and face closely.

There is only small signs of Petechial Haemorrhage so not full suffocation; probable cause would be repeated partial strangulation, this would lead to a lack of blood to the brain that would have meant drifting in and out of consciousness each time; death would have followed within a few minutes unless the restricting wire was released. I will need to examine the brain to see if that is the case but I think not as facial colouring has not changed. I suspect the restriction of the vagal nerve is most likely what happened here, affecting the parasympathetic nervous system which results in stopping the heart. This can happen with only minor pressure to a particular area of the neck; I will need to examine the heart to confirm.

I don't believe the assailant intended to kill here, pressure on the vagal nerve was a mistake, it requires a sudden strong impact or prolonged low pressure to a very specific point to cause this type of reaction. The cuts I believe were made to try and hide evidence of torture; the assailant may have had only a little or even no blood transferred to his hands, arms and clothing. The blood pressure left in the system after death would fade very quickly once the heart had stopped beating; if the cut was made very soon after death, it would allow for perhaps a minor squirt of blood, if much longer than five minutes almost no blood at all especially as he was in a sitting position, as gravity takes over".

Penny moved to the head looking in the ears and eyes finally to the top of the head.

96

"Well, well, some significant trauma here, looks like the assailant grabbed his hair violently tilting the head back whilst performing his task. Some considerable amount of hair pulled out by the roots. I should find some DNA here, the skin from his hands will almost certainly have transferred, providing he was not wearing gloves of course. Some of the hair will have transferred to the assailant's clothing no matter how careful he was".

She took samples. Next came the Y incision and the extraction of the organs, Toni did not expect to learn anything new from this process so decided to leave. Mel would let Jonny know if there was anything different. Blood and tissue analysis would take a day or two, she would see the report all in good time. Whatever happened; Jonny and the others would do their job she need not worry. She said her goodbyes and left noting that Constable Sheevert looked a little green but could not take his eyes off what was going on. 'He'll do', she thought.

"Seems our inquisitor was angry, perhaps he was annoyed that his victim had died too soon. I expect he wore gloves but you never know we may be lucky; do you want to come back to the office"?

"No thanks Debbie I'll be off, lots to do. I'm so pleased I came here you've been a great help even if needing HRT reminds me I'm getting old, and yes I will deal with it as soon as I can".

"You are not getting old; you are younger than me so you can't possibly be old, so there. Don't wait too long".

"Have you err…."?

"No, not yet but my turn will come. Off you go, let me know what your GP says. Okay"?

"Okay. Can I leave my car in the car park for a day or two, I want to go into London so will catch a train, I hate the traffic"?

"No problem; I'll tell security, do you want a lift to the station"?

"No I'll walk it's not far".

97

Toni took the overnight bag from her boot and set off for the half hour stroll to Richmond station. The Independent Office for Police Conduct her next port of call, followed by a visit to see Colin but before then she would find a hotel in town and think things through.

Chief Superintendent Vernon Smith was surprised to be told that DCI Webb was waiting in the lobby requesting to see him. It had been a long time since he'd had contact with her. The Vale Branch corruption case the one and only time they had been closely involved. His plans for the day were pretty full but decided to spare her some time as he was sure she had a very good reason in coming to see him in person without an appointment. He told the reception security officer to send her up.

"Well, well; Toni Webb it is nice to see you again it's been a while hasn't it. Come along have a seat".

She accepted with a "Thank you sir. Yes it has".

"Enough of the sir. Its Vernon okay. Now what brings you all the way to us like this, why not use the phone"?

"I think you can guess; phone calls are not always safe".

She looked round the room wondering if it was safe to say what she wanted here either.

"Don't worry this is a shielded area and is swept daily, what goes on here stays here unless I say otherwise".

"Right good. You know of course Jake Snell has reappeared under a new name"?

Vernon was surprised but nodded, curious about how she had found out.

"Well I have started a quiet investigation; I presume that is what you wanted"?

The penny dropped. So that's how Bonington had interpreted his orders to carry out a clandestine search and apprehension of Snell by the best means possible. Clever bugger, giving it to Webb was a streak of guile that may well pay off; he'd never thought to go outside his department. He would not let her know he was unaware of Bonington getting her involved.

"For sure I want to find him before other parties have wind of his presence; it seems you are sufficiently out of the limelight and are probably our best resource towards achieving that".

"How much does Assistant Chief Constable Brown and Commander Blakewood know"?

"Nothing up to now, but that does not mean they won't find out; if they do and find Snell before we do, he will be gone and our best chance of catching them will be gone".

"I thought we had cooked our goose with those two anyway; they're too well covered and much more powerful than the likes of me. Maybe Snell knows nothing, Grimes never gave anything away so why should Snell"?

"I never given up with routing out corruption in the force, they will make a mistake eventually. I hate the thought they will remain free on my watch, however if nothing else they will retire and be gone, but it is possible Snell knows something and will be willing to trade. It appeared Grimes was the one in charge but Snell was cunning and played his submissive part well; clever enough to be the only suspect in the whole group to escape. I'm certain he would have hidden some insurance to protect himself from his hidden bosses. Enough time has passed so most everyone will have forgotten him; we'll hide him here and be free to question him without the pressure of the brass baying for blood".

"Not exactly legal, we'd be harbouring a criminal".

"You have to catch him first Toni, that won't be easy but when you do I want him here where you and I can finally put this baby to bed ".

"I have to go now Vernon, keep your eyes and ears open for activity from the brass, I don't want to be caught out nosing where I shouldn't".

"They still think I'm on their side, they won't find anything to the contrary until I take them down. If there is any untoward interest I'll hear about it and let you know".

"Thanks Vernon I'll use Bonington as a point of contact. I won't come here again, well not until it's close to a resolution, eh".

"Goodbye Toni, good luck".

They shook hands and parted each with a smile.

Toni didn't doubt he would warn her if there was any danger but she thought he may have a hidden agenda. She needed another insider to look out for her interests.

The mobile clamped to her ear, as she walked to the cab rank, rang without answer, not even transferring to a message leaving response. She hung up wondering if it was worth a trip to the Yard if only to find Colin elsewhere. She stopped at the rank and tried the call again to no avail. She took a cab back to her hotel resolving to call him later. Perhaps it was for the best, her visiting Scotland Yard may cause someone to notice, gossip abounded there so better to meet Colin privately.

Her next call to her GP surgery in Basingstoke was answered almost at once, she made the appointment for two days later, should give her enough time to see Colin and go back without rushing. She lay back on the bed fully clothed intending to rest for just a minute, her eyes closed; she slept.

Waking slowly she realised, just as slowly, where she was but unaware of the two hours that had passed. She checked the time accepted the loss and called Colin again, this time there was an answer.

"Hello Toni, how are you"?

"Could be better Colin, any chance we can meet"?

"Today, where are you"?

She thought for a second, wanting to go back to sleep.

"I'm in London. Not now, tomorrow will do if you're busy".

"It'd be better for me, I'm on a job right now and won't be finished till late. Tomorrow; call me early and we can have breakfast together".

Colin was tucking into the 'big' breakfast whereas Toni had settled for a simple omelette. They ate in silence for a while, Colin spoke first.

"You didn't come all the way here for a breakfast with me so what's up Toni"?

"The Vale corruption case has reared its ugly head again. This time Police Conduct and possibly Serious Crime too I think, have dropped it in my lap".

"They wouldn't do that if there was any chance of an easy outcome; you're going to have to watch your step; tell me what made them drag it up again".

"Vernon Smith gave our friend Bonington a file which he very discreetly passed on to us; apparently Jake Snell escaped via Denmark using a genuine issued passport, under the name Leonard Bartram, he left in a car registered in the same name. He has since dumped that name and the car; he is currently using a passport in the name of Jeremy Shore; he arrived in Weymouth via Jersey last week. I have no idea where he is now and how he acquired these documents; they are not full on forgeries but were issued by the passport office from apparently valid proofs of identity. The common point being the photograph which showed up from facial recognition, during the monthly immigration audit, as being the same on two passports. Immigration informed Serious Crime who used a similar face identification application to discover it was Snell. The file is very sketchy it does not contain all the facts it doesn't say how Conduct came to get hold of it; I suspect someone from serious crime passed it on; probably Inspector Paul Fortune, as he was the officer who took over the original case from us. When I saw

Smith earlier he told me nothing except he's hoping we catch Snell for him to interrogate covertly; he's after the bigger fish".

"I guess what you need from me is a watching brief to see if top brass show an interest"?

"Anything you can find without being obvious will help, we have nothing much at the moment. He obviously came back for a good reason".

"He may have run out of money and has a nest egg hidden here somewhere".

"If he is skint, he may be here to squeeze his old bosses for a handout".

"I hope not for his sake and yours too if he has any sense; they will then know he's here and your little investigation will be impossible to hide; besides which I am sure they will either pay him off or arrange a disposal. More likely the latter which will leave you with nothing. Look I'll do what I can to help but I cannot afford to stir things up even a little. Small ripples on my patch tend to turn into waves".

"Thanks Colin be careful though. Sorry I didn't ask earlier, with my being so wrapped up in my own problems; but how's the family".

"They are all fine growing fast. The promotion and the move back to London was a godsend really; a much bigger house and with Sonia's and my parents being close by, it kind of completes things for us. The kids have a whale of a time with their grans and grandads, yes it is good".

"I envy you that, and I dam well miss you being around but am so glad you went back".

"What about you, seeing anyone"?

"What do you think? No time much lately, I'm so tired when I get home I just want to sleep. I go to the pub now and then with Josie and her brother my neighbours, especially when I can't be bothered to cook; that's about it for my social life".

"What about the brother, what's he like"?

"Nathan, he's okay we get on fine".

"Hmm. All work and not much play eh! not good Toni do something about it whilst you can".

"I will, just let these cases conclude first, then I'll take a holiday; I may go and visit my brother, he's back in Nigeria you know".

"Yes you told me last time we spoke, sounds like a plan; maybe take Nathan with you".

"We're not that close".

She smiled inwardly 'there's a thought'.

"You said cases what else is going on down in Hampshire"?

"Oh just the murder of a 'low life', Jonny Musgrove is handling that one and I've given Harrold the Snell job, I just need to be on top of both, you know how I am".

"Indeed I do, now finish your coffee I have to go back to the Yard, I'll drop you off at Victoria station if you like it's on my way".

"Good I have to go to Richmond to collect my car".

The ride to the station was conducted in silence each deep in their own thoughts.

"Well goodbye Toni I'll be in touch soon as I know anything".

She leant across and kissed him on the cheek then said closing the door behind her as she climbed out.

"Thanks Colin you're a good friend".

By the time she arrived back at Richmond she saw Mel's car had gone, the autopsy being over long before. Debbie's car was still in its allotted space but Toni did not want to disturb her again, so left without stopping.

There was plenty of daylight left when Toni arrived home, however she couldn't face going to her office and the inevitable pressure to become involved with her officers' problems. Her priority was to sort herself out first, with that uppermost on her mind she called her GP to see if he could fit her in later this evening rather than wait till her appointment the following day. She had only been to the doctor a few times since coming to Basingstoke once for a couple of stitches and tetanus shot, when she cut her arm in the garden; the other times for her police required health checks. She was in luck; he would add her to the end of surgery at seven o'clock. In the mean-time she decided to relax with a book she had been meaning to read for ages but had never quite found the time.

A pork pie and oven chips with a glass of chardonnay followed the first of the HRT tablets she'd collected from Boot's late night pharmacy after her consultation. Although the results of the blood test would take some time the doctor was sure she had all the symptoms, so decided to start her immediately on HR medication. The adverse side effects were explained but Toni was not interested she just wanted to feel normal again and the sooner the better. She would have to call him the following week for the blood results and again after three more weeks to check if she needed to increase or reduce her dose; she wondered how soon the tablets would have an effect.

Her supper finished Toni went to bed more relaxed than she had been for some weeks. She lay there thinking about Larry and Nathan too. Larry's calls always upset her, reminded her of what might have been; held her back; Nathan's presence was exciting, urging her to move on. She resolved to stop Larry's half-hearted efforts at pretending he cared; she didn't need him checking on her like he still had a stake in her life; he deserted her when she needed help the most, so the hanging on had to stop. She reached for her phone selected Larry's number and put a block on his incoming calls. She's write to him later when she'd had time to think about what to say; she knew very well what she would like to tell him but was also aware she probably wouldn't commit those thoughts to paper. Another time. Sleep soon followed.

Chapter 11

Two days leave produced a mound of paper, Toni wondered if it was all necessary, but these are the days of accurate record keeping, mostly generated to protect the force from outside criticism, in other words to protect the bosses arses rather than to help solve crime. Still it had to be done so she settled into reading and signing, she never signed off anything she had not read; some officers just signed the lot without reading a word, relying on whoever generated the paperwork knew what they were doing. That wasn't going to happen in her station. Two hours later with the pile reduced and mostly transferred to the out tray she briefly wondered if they weren't right as she had found nothing amiss; not this time anyway. She picked up her phone.

"Jonny it's Toni, come and see me if you are free".

"I'm in the middle of something right this minute boss, half an hour should do it, okay"?

"Fine, bring the Grant murder file when you come".

Although Toni had digital access to the information, it contained photo-copies of officers original notes not the often watered down versions that were entered via their computers. Photographs were original too as were the comments added in the margins of reports by officers when they were actively investigating the case. All involved were encouraged to read the file regularly, to help refresh their memory or spot something new another officer had noted. Subtle things seen in the file often led to a breakthrough, it was key and the most important document concerning each and every case.

Jonny Musgrove carefully placed the file the right way round in front of his boss.

"Well Jonny give me a run through; what have you been up to whilst I was away"?

"Compton has started a search through his finances, shows nothing untoward so far, no big debts just a credit card with two hundred owing. He manages on his wages well enough. There are regular payments to his former wife for child maintenance, he has a son fourteen years old, he used to see him one weekend every month. He's been divorced three years. His official work record is limited but good, reliable and regular, rarely mixes socially with his work colleagues but no conflict recorded or mentioned. We could find no one who may have had a reason to be even mildly upset by him. We interviewed a couple of his workmates, both saying he was a bit of a loner but pleasant enough. Here's where it becomes interesting, his laptop had some password protected files, Compton found her way in to expose sixty seven images of nine different girls taken from a camera with a long range lens, there were five of Dawn Westcott amongst them; the images are time stamped and cover a ten month period; we haven't recovered a camera, if we had that the internal memory might show more; I think the killer may have taken it. No other images or files that were questionable and there has been little internet activity just a few emails. There is one possible lead; he belongs to a photography club, the emails are about club meetings and technical tips from other members; seemed harmless at first but in view of the pictures we found I'll check it out . Compton is currently trying to identify the girls. I questioned his former wife at her home yesterday, she is single with no current partner; an agency shorthand typist, not working at the moment, claiming Job seekers; her son was at school at the time I visited. She was very cagey about why they separated; it was cited as unreasonable behaviour. When I asked if he was ever physically violent towards her she became regressive and refused to speak. Again unresponsive to questions of possible infidelity. Some deep wounds there I suspect; I did not press it. One odd thing, she did not seem even remotely upset by the news of his death and offered no reason she could think of why

106

anyone would want to kill him. I did not mention why we were looking at him with regard to Dawn, I've saved that for a second interview when the son is home; I want to give her time to recover from the shock, I'm sure there is more to come about George".

"Have you identified any suspects"?

"Not any that stand out Ma'am. Up to now we have made little progress in identifying anyone other than Dawn's father Adrian Westcott. Could be a revenge killing, a weak motive I know still he has no alibi for the time when George could have been killed. The wide time frame too makes me doubtful. I've spoken to the family liaison officer, she owned up to telling Mrs. Westcott that we had a person of interest in custody".

"She should never have done that".

"I've already questioned why she told her; said she thought it would give the family peace of mind, she never said a name or anything more. Mrs. Westcott did not ask questions about who it might be, in fact expressed little interest. It is probable that she mentioned it to her husband who could then have checked and somehow found out about George Grant. We have his prints which we took as elimination samples, they don't match the ones found on the door frame of George's back door. I'm not sure we have a case to apply for a warrant to search the house or obtain a DNA sample from him".

"Well Jonny you are right to consider him; when no other suspects exist, the one you have is the most likely. We have Dawn's DNA don't we"?

"Yes we do, ah! Why didn't I think of that; of course we can compare Dawn's against those found in the hair samples from autopsy. It won't be a match but if it was her father there will be enough pointers to justify a warrant".

"Quite right it could also exclude him too. By the way have you asked him to provide a sample voluntarily"?

"I didn't. I thought if he refused he would know we were interested giving him time to rid himself of any evidence".

"Maybe. If it isn't him you will have saved a lot of time. Not to worry do the test with Dawn's DNA. Anything else"?

"Only one other thing that seems coincidental. Mr. Westcott works at the Wildmoore golf course, he is their head groundsman; he was working there the day Dawn went missing, mind you that's not unusual, he is there almost every day; also he could have had access to the video before we did and seen the postal van".

"Hm. I'm not too sure he's the one; you know I don't like coincidences; go back to the course see if you can trace his movements on the day George died; use their CCTV; also find out if he has access to the recordings. I find it hard to believe he would go as far as cutting the guys throat especially if he knew we were close to arresting Grant; still he's the only one in the frame at the moment so press on".

Toni did not want to interfere too much but, those images found on George Grant's computer worried her. Were these past victims or just voyeurism on his part. She would go to Compton and see for herself.

"Good day Ma'am, how can I help, is it the murder, or maybe the return of the wandering Snell. Could it be some other villain you are chasing"?

"Hello Compy, I was wanting to see the photos from George Grant's computer".

"Oh yes the girls, hang on I'll pull them up for you. They are grouped in files with two letter names, I think it may be their initials but that's a good guess as the five pictures of Dawn are in a file named 'DW/r' there are nine different files sixty seven images altogether; the images are time stamped and cover a ten month period Dawn's being the most recent. I have no idea what the '/r' means it occurs in two other files; there are three other suffixes to the initials '/m', '/n,' and one with '/d'. I've looked through his files and can find no reference to these anywhere else so have no clue at the moment as to their significance if any".

Whilst she was speaking Compton the uploaded files appeared on her screen for Toni to look at.

"As you can see they are mostly facial images; close ups with the background out of focus, typical of a telephoto lens. Some shots are full body images; their clothes varied but all appeared to be young teenagers in an open air environment. The full body shots had some background detail but nothing obvious as to location".

"Have you managed to identify anyone other than Dawn"?

"Maybe; I've used missing persons, locally and in adjacent counties with the initials on the files as the main search parameter, the only result being a Karen Small who went missing two months ago from Reading and has not been found as yet. I'm waiting for the report and photo from Berkshire police, 'KS/d' being our file with those initials".

"A real puzzle those file names, let me know about Karen Small, if it is her Jonny Musgrove will need to know immediately".

"I've already kept him up to date Ma'am as soon as the picture comes in he will have it. I did have an idea with regard to the initials and suffixes but it didn't work out; also it worries me that there was no camera or anything at his house that would be able to take this type of shot, his mobile was certainly not up to it. He may have some other place where he does his photography, leave it with me a while I'll let you know".

"Now, what has Inspector Davis asked you to do"?

"Nothing yet; he did warn me we were going to carry out a deep financial search concerning our old friend Jake Snell, I'm still waiting to hear from him".

"Okay, good that's all for now, call me".

"Ma'am".

Toni left and went up one floor to the squad room looking for Harrold Davis. She'd asked him to keep it to himself and already he had involved Compton Busion, she wanted an explanation. She found him at his desk head down in a rather thick file. She approached and cleared her throat to attract his attention. He looked up not quite aware who was there, being so engrossed in his reading.

"Ah. Harrold there you are".

"Oh sorry Ma'am have you been looking for me"?

"I was but only just this minute; I can see you are well into something".

"I'm going into the old files covering all the incidents leading up to the arrest of Grimes and the two bent coppers. There is a lot to go through and I want to have it all in my mind before I tackle looking for Jake Snell. It's never been proved but I think he was the one who killed Reynolds and his Mother".

"As good a place to start as any. I hear you've roped in Constable Busion; she tells me she's awaiting your instructions".

"Ah yes I have an idea, following the money is the way I want to go. I'm sure he has come back to recover some of his ill-gotten gains. Wherever he hid it he will have made sure no one else knew. I doubt if it is in a bank, our boys at serious crime will have found that for sure, a safety deposit box is an alternative, but still risky for him although there may be some of his cash hidden like that. I think the bulk may be with a trusted friend; hidden in such a way that even the friend does not realise what he has been sitting on all this time".

"How on earth are you going to find that out"?

"I'll wait for the results first before I tell you Ma'am, you know me I have my fraud squad ways and with Compton's IT skills we will prevail, I hope so anyway. I have other irons in the fire, with DS Owens".

Toni looked sideways at him with a glare to freeze blood. He understood that look and continued quickly so as to calm her obvious disquiet.

"I know you said covert as possible Ma'am 'a one man show' and all that; it still is one man really, just me, I'm the only man here; however the two ladies are essential if I am to progress anywhere with this, they know the rules and will be as quiet as mice".

Her frown dissipated at Harrold's excuse and terrible attempt at humour, she realised he would need their help if he was to succeed.

"I wasn't kidding when I told you to keep it very quiet Harrold these men are dangerous, if they find out we will all be in trouble".

"Don't worry Ma'am if Compton Busion and I comes up trumps Mr. Jacob Snell will come to us like a cat to the cream".

"Well Harrold I'll leave you to it but don't be so secretive that you forget I'm here".

They parted with Harrold giving a polite chuckle to what he thought was his bosses joke. Toni smiled too, happy that she had chosen well with both her detectives. She formed an email to Superintendent Munroe outlining the state of play with George Grant's murder only mentioning that Davis was dealing with a missing villain without mentioning who.

Toni sat back in her office closed her eyes to wait for events to unfold in their own good time. She did not have to wait too long.

Chapter 12

Gregory Small had no idea where his daughter had gone. One minute she was walking from sixth form college to the bus stop the next she was lost. The ride from Basingstoke to south Reading usually took less than an hour. She boarded the bus, he was told, people remembered her including the driver, however no one remembered where she'd left the bus; he doubted that she ever was on it. Her usual stop is a short walk to her home only a few minutes away. The Reading police had not responded very quickly, at eighteen she was an adult so he was forced to wait till the day after she disappeared before they initiated a missing person report. They said many youngsters go off for a day or two and return unharmed so not to worry. It wasn't their baby who was lost so they had no idea how he felt, he had slept rarely since she went missing awake most nights. Karen had only recently turned eighteen and was due to sit her 'A' levels soon and was ready to go to university the following year. She had already secured her place at London, subject to satisfactory exam results. She and her father were in no doubt concerning her grades, her place was secure; or it was before she disappeared. Karen had no regular boyfriend although she had dated a few times, the only activities she was involved with were swimming three days a week in the college pool and preparing for her exams. She normally used her free periods during the day for these activities, seldom staying late and always home by six pm, whatever else she had planned for later. There were no clothes missing, her purse with a few pounds and her bank card were still in her room, she only took her bus pass and some change with her when she went to class.

Detective Sergeant Linkman had kept him informed of progress, what little there was. No sightings since the day she went missing. CCTV saw her walking towards the bus stop chatting to some friends; they had all been interviewed confirming they had parted their ways a hundred yards from the stop. The cameras did not cover the stop itself but the bus was picked up at the Chine roundabout, the quality of the image was poor so, although people were seen on the bus, identification of individuals was not possible. Linkman traced most of the users of that route at that time who seemed to confirm her being there, but he thought familiarity with her regular presence was clouding their memory, by assuming she was there when she wasn't. It took a couple of days before he secured the digital printout from the bus company, her bus pass had been used in the morning but not in the afternoon. She had not boarded the bus so should have been seen somewhere on camera, but no. Even though her card had not been used he checked the next bus which left fifty minutes later; no one there remembered seeing her. The people who travelled these routes were nearly all regulars who knew their fellow passengers well enough to know if a stranger was amongst them; his conclusion, there was not.

A wider search of the towns CCTV produced nothing. The investigation moved towards Reading as Linkman was certain she had been given a lift by someone and possibly someone she knew.

Detective Sergeant Melanie Frazer rang the bell and waited, a few minutes later she faced Gregory Small. He was stooped with dark ringed half closed vacant eyes, unkempt hair dressed in a grey T shirt and black trousers, his feet were bare.

"Yes"?

Melanie held out her ID saying.

"Mr. Small, I'm Detective Sergeant Frazer could I please come in"?

The eyes opened wide, seeming to grow as if a great fearful image had presented itself.

"Have you found her"?

He could already see by Mel's sombre face the answer before she spoke; the light in his eyes faded, tears replacing the fear.

"No Mr. Small I am sorry; however we have a lead which may help us find her. I am from Basingstoke which I believe is where Karen went to college. We have found another girl who went missing under similar circumstances to your daughter and although we don't know where your daughter is we believe the two are linked. I can't go into details yet but I thought you should know she hasn't been forgotten"?

"Did Sergeant Linkman send you"?

Mel realised that reporting her missing in Reading had left the Basingstoke police in the dark, even though the two towns are fairly close they are in different counties. It wasn't that the two do not cooperate, just there is no structure for automatic liaison when cases overlap. She must find and talk to this Linkman asap. She did not want to lie to Mr. Small so made light of the lack of information interchange. Melanie was concerned with seeking the whereabouts of his child; so replied without answering his question directly.

"Reading and Basingstoke are cooperating in looking for Karen; Sergeant Linkman will continue to be part of this investigation. One or both of us will keep you informed of our progress. You look tired sir are you able to sleep, we can provide a family liaison officer if you wish they can help in many ways".

"I've had one here already so no thanks I don't need that anymore. Work keeps me busy takes my mind off it a bit but It's hard to sleep when you keep wondering, you know. I do doze off a little, it's just not knowing. You think she's dead don't you"?

"We never give up hope sir".

She gave him her card.

"Please call me anytime Mr. Small".

She left with many unanswered questions; all she really knew is, he's a single parent; she had no idea of the family circumstances. He seemed resigned to his daughter's death; he never pushed Mel for answers; never asked who the other girl was or if she was dead or alive. Her gut was twitching, this man was behaving very oddly but his position was so awful who knows how anyone will react in similar circumstances. She needed to find out a lot more about the Small family before she came back. He looked dreadful; was that a lack of sleep and fear for his daughter or is there more to him than appears?

Back at base Mel sat with Jonny going over the interview with Karen's father; Jonny Musgrove sat quietly listening not interrupting her flow as he wanted to feel what she was feeling, to consider the misgivings she hinted at concerning Small's odd attitude.

"One thing sir I did not press him as I had little knowledge of the case. I did not want to put him on his guard with a silly mistake on my part. We need to contact Linkman before we go any further".

"I agree Mel, I think I have the answers to some of your missing info. Apparently Linkman did visit the sixth form College here in Basingstoke where Karen went to school; he informed us through the desk sergeant of his pending visit, it was entered in our daily log as a missing person investigation by the Reading officer, but we of course did not become involved at the time. It is only now that the fact the two girls were at the same school has become significant. One more very unexpected item of interest, Small works as a groundsman at Wildmoore golf course".

"He does, does he? well that's a coincidence we can't ignore. Look shall I go and speak to this Linkman or will you"?

"You go ahead Mel; you've a good idea what you want to ask him, I'm going to the golf course, the coincidences where both girls go to the same college and both fathers work at the same golf club bothers me too much; maybe Small has more to tell than he has given up. Keep in touch after you've finished with

Linkman; when I've done at the course we'll go and see Small together".

"What about Constable Crane sir".

"Keith's still clearing up paperwork with the prosecution service lawyer on the car theft. I'll call him in if our visits prove fruitful and we need more help. We'll brief him before we go to see Small, he can go see Westcott when he's finished with the CPS".

They left the office together and went their different ways from the car park.

Jonny drove at a crawl through the golf course entrance along the twisted driveway, surprised how well the whole place was hidden from the road. Wildmoore Golf course was busy the car park almost full. He parked in one of the few remaining places and walked slowly, looking about him taking in the landscape as he had during the drive in. The fifty yards walk to the impressive club house entrance took just long enough to give him an overview of the nearby course design and the buildings layout.

Jenny Matheson was at her usual place behind reception, Jonny was impressed by the glass open structure even with just a brief glance but concentrated his mind on what he was intending to ask the young lady smiling at him as he approached. He held out his warrant card.

"Good morning I'm Detective Inspector Musgrove I need to ask a few questions as a follow up to my colleague's visit the other day".

"Yes sir, I remember I hope the recordings were useful".

"They were indeed thank you, however I need to find out a little about a couple of your employees, are you able to do that for me or do you need to call someone"?

"You've caught us at a busy time so most of the staff are out on the course; it depends on what you want to know I may be able to help. You will have to forgive me if a member comes in I will have to deal with them so cannot leave the desk".

"That is fine. I'm sure you are aware Mr. Westcott's daughter encountered a problem nearby the other day. I need to know his attendance over the past week. It's just routine to fill in the timeline of everyone involved".

"Yes we know Adrian has told us about it and was so relieved when she was found. I can print off his work schedule from here if you like"?

"That will be great, also you have a Gregory Small working here too, could I have his printout also"?

"Oh yes of course, his daughter too....I see; she has been missing for some time have you found anything"?

"Not yet. Have Adrian and Gregory talked about this do you know"?

"Of course, we have discussed it on several occasions, Adrian is Greg's boss by the way, a bit of a coincidence both girls, don't you think"?

"Possibly, did they know about the recordings you provided"?

"Oh yes we all had a good look but couldn't see anything unusual, did you find anything"?

"Not much, but you never know sometimes little things become significant later when we have more information".

"Hmm.. are they connected do you think"?

"We have to investigate every possibility. By the way what did you mean by we all had a good look"?

"Well there was Gregory, Adrian, Brian the club secretary and my Dad oh and me of course".

"Was there a discussion"?

"Not really, we just looked and when it was finished kind of shrugged our shoulders as if to say looks alright to me. Dad said there was nothing to be gained here, best leave it to the police, we then went back to work".

"Did Mr Westcott or Small say anything"?

"No they watched in silence".

"That's it then no more questions".

"Well good luck detective, if you need anything else or need to talk to my Dad just call first so I can make sure he will be here".

Jenny ducked under the counter to retrieve the schedule printouts.

"Thank you Miss Matheson you have been very helpful".

So the two fathers were privy to the video of George Grant being nearby, Jonny wondered did they know more? He sat in his car and left a text for Mel to let her know he was finished and was ready to meet her at Small's house later.

Chapter13

Melanie Frazer sat next to her opposite number from Reading in her car. They had met in a layby on the A33 midway between the two police stations. Detective Sergeant Linkman had been looking for Karen Small for ages without a trace, he was hoping this young officer from Basingstoke had some answers.

"Thanks for meeting me sergeant Frazer this case has frustrated me like never before; I've had so little to go on; all my efforts to find Karen anywhere after she left Queen Mary's College failed, nothing on CCTV and no reliable witnesses. I hoped she had run away but that was a forlorn wish as every indication was that she had been abducted. She had only the clothes she was wearing and almost no money in her possession. Her phone was either switched off or had run out of battery. I questioned her friends in case she had confided in one of them, but nothing unusual was apparent. The girls she walked with from College parted company at their usual place. No message to them or anyone since no note or call to her father to give him hope. I was at a loss till you contacted me".

"Hamish isn't it, enough of the sergeant just call me Mel if you want".

"Sure thing Mel, please what can you tell me"?

"We now have a good idea that a George Grant may have abducted Karen, her initials appeared on a file with photographs we found in his laptop; there were several others too including our girl Dawn. George Grant was questioned earlier as a person of interest before we gained access to his computer; unfortunately we had to release him as we had no concrete evidence at the time and he had a good explanation for his presence at the scene. We kept an eye on him though during the day, but someone entered the house one night and killed him. It's when we discovered his body we found his computer and the photos. Forensics and the discovery of hidden clothing confirmed our suspicions, too late for us, he was already dead before we could bring him in".

"Too little too late for Karen I fear, do you have any idea who may have killed him"?

"Not sure yet, one of the fathers maybe or both, we have forensics being analysed as we speak, I just wanted to let you know where we are and to offer you a chance to become involved if you want. What can you tell me about Gregory Small"?

"What! You think Small killed this Grant out of revenge, how did he know about him anyway"?

"I'm not sure yet there are a couple of coincidences that make it possible, however when I met him briefly he was so distraught he hardly functions, so sad. The autopsy indicates the death was not intended but came about during a violent interrogation maybe Small tortured him trying to find his daughter and went too far".

"Well I am a bit shocked I don't rate Gregory Small as violent in fact quite the opposite, he lives up to his name slight build and quietly spoken, obviously grief stricken but he kind of accepted the situation that we were doing all we could. He wasn't at all pushy and asked few questions. Still you never can tell, if he thought this Grant had taken his daughter it may have triggered a reaction no one could guess he was capable of. Still how the hell did he find him"?

"That is something we are looking into, look when I leave you here I am meeting my boss, we will be going to see Small directly, follow me if you want, Inspector Musgrove may like to have you nearby as you are familiar with him and he does live on your patch. He'll probably ask you to wait in your car but at least you'll be aware of what goes down".

"Thanks Mel I will, better than sitting on my arse back at the station waiting for you to call me".

Mel saw that Jonny had finished from his text and would be at Small's Reading house in fifteen minutes; her message back said she was on her way along with Linkman. He acknowledged with no objection to Linkman's presence.

Three cars parked behind each other outside Gregory and Karen Small's home. The officers had gathered outside with each explaining what new information had come to light. The consensus was that Gregory Small was now a serious person of interest but they would question him informally here and only make an arrest if circumstances proved he was truly a prime suspect. The results of DNA testing and other forensics had not yet come through, even though Mel's earlier contact with Small was inconclusive Jonny was not prepared to wait before he questioned him. He surprised Mel by asking her to wait in the car as three officers were too many at this stage, he tasked her to check on forensic progress. He said her idea that Hamish Linkman being here may prove useful as Small knew and trusted him. She agreed to wait outside, glad she had invited Hamish along.

"Sergeant I will leave you to introduce me but beyond that I will conduct the interview, even if a question arises in your mind please wait until I have indicated you may speak".

Linkman nodded his acceptance; they approached and knocked. Small peeped briefly through the front room curtain a few moments later he opened the door. He stood in clothes that looked like he had slept in them, unshaven, hair awry with tired dark ringed eyes.

"Hello Gregory, remember me Sergeant Hamish this is Detective Inspector Musgrove may we come in".

Small stood back his hand still on the door lock, they passed by and he closed the door behind them. His face and voice were expressionless, even their visit offered no hope.

"Have a seat, can I get you something"?

"Thank you no, we are fine".

Jonny waited to see how Small responded to the silence. He just stood saying nothing for almost a minute. Eventually Jonny continued knowing his silence was odd; he offered no question as to why they were there or had they found his daughter. Jonny decided to go straight in hard, see if he could shock Small into an emotional response.

"Just a few questions Gregory if you don't mind".

"Your girl was here already; still if you must, okay".

"When you went to George Grant's house what did he say".

Lance Small turned from grey to white and almost fell into the armchair opposite the two officers. He did not answer.

"Did you not hear me, what did Grant say".

"Who said I went there? I didn't see him he wasn't in. I don't know who he is either do I".

"So you've never met him"?

"No I don't know who he is".

"You said when you went there he wasn't in, is that right"?

"Yes, no, I don't know".

"You don't know if he was in or not"?

"He wasn't in, I never went there".

"How could you know he wasn't in if you never went there. Its Manor Gardens I believe what number"?

"Twenty two, I meant I never went in, the door was shut"?

"Did you try round the back"?

Small had regained a little composure so thought before he responded again.

"No I went home".

"Good; how did you find out where he lived".

"It was Adrian who found it, we viewed the pictures at work when we saw the postal van we both thought the same; the postman. The family officer girl who came to his house told his misses they had someone who they thought had chased his girl and that they were keeping an eye on him so she shouldn't worry as Dawn would be safe. Adrian went to the sorting office pretending a parcel was missing and asked if the postman who delivered to the golf course could have accidently left it in his van. The manager said the man was off sick but went to ask one of the other drivers to look in the van. Whilst he waited for the manager to come back he chatted to some of the workers who told him it was George Grant who was off sick. I think he found his address from the electoral register or something".

"Did Adrian go round to the house".

"I don't know, though he told me a police car was outside most of the day, not at night though so I suppose he must have gone there if he knew all that".

"What did you go there for"?

"I'm sorry, I just needed to do something, I know I shouldn't have, I just wanted to ask him if he had seen my Karen. He wasn't there or he wouldn't answer the door. I was foolish; if he was the one who had taken her he wouldn't tell me anyway and if he wasn't he wouldn't know. Adrian said the police would sort it and I should forget him".

"And did you"?

"I tried but I am still wondering; you will question him won't you, see if he knows where my baby girl has gone"?

His eyes full of tears and his plea to Jonny left him almost certain that Gregory Small was not the killer, but not quite. He would have to eliminate him without doubt, before he could remove him from his suspect list. He looked at Linkman a silent request for him to question Small if he wanted.

"Would you mind if we took a DNA swab Gregory, just to rule you out from all the stuff we've collected".

"Okay, if it helps you find my Karen".

"I'll go and fetch the kit from my car, won't be a moment".

They all stood at the same time; Linkman left Jonny with Small who turned to him moving in close so they were face to face.

"I know she is probably dead but please ask the postman if he knows anything; you are good a questions and will see if he is lying or not. I just need to know, so I can say goodbye you see; I might be able to sleep then".

At this point Linkman returned and quickly took his sample, put his hand on Gregory's shoulder and said.

"Not at work today"?

"No I had a rough night; Adrian said I could be flexible, he would cover my work as long as I let him know, I'll go in tomorrow".

"Do you need family liaison again; they can help you know"?

"The family lady is nice but I'm better on my own thanks, just keep looking eh"?

"Of course. You take care I'll be in touch soon".

Mel was standing by or rather leaning against her car when they came out. She quickly stood straight and walked towards them.

"Well"?

"It's not him".

They said almost in unison. She looked from one to the other.

"How do you know"?

Jonny spoke first.

"I faced him with it, his visit to George's house, he genuinely seemed unaware Grant was dead, I think he is either telling the truth or he's the best actor in the world".

"I told Mel he was not capable".

"I know Hamish but it is not a proven fact yet just a gut feeling we both have; I still need to check his story and find who really did kill Grant. I know the missing girl is still your responsibility but the murder is ours; the cases are so intertwined I suggest you give the DNA sample to Mel before you leave she can have it checked against what we found at Grant's house; she will keep you posted. I presume you are still on her case so why not stay with us we can work on it together".

"I'd like that but will have to clear it with my boss first".

"If you want I will ask DCI Webb to formally request your assistance".

"Good, I'll stay with you then if that's okay"?

"Fine. Our next call is to see Dawn's dad, but I want to go back to the station first, make sure we have all the facts before we tackle him. Bugger..... I've just remembered; Keith may have already gone there give him a ring Mel call him off, I hope it's not too late".

"You know what sir, someone rid us all of a nasty piece of work but killed the only chance I have of finding Karen".

"Don't lose heart Hamish there are a ways to go yet".

Keith Crane was speaking to Margaret Westcott on her doorstep. She told him her husband Adrian had returned to work as soon as he knew his daughter was safe.

"I see madam how did he know that Dawn was safe"?

"The family liaison officer told us, she said the man who took her bike was now safely out of the way, so we assumed it was okay to go out again; I hope that is right you do have him locked up don't you"?

Keith was surprised that the FLO had told them so much, he did not want to let on that George Grant had been set loose or that he had later been killed he needed to speak to Jonny before he went any further. He was in two minds if he should go to the golf course to speak to Adrian Westcott, his decision was to call Jonny before his next move.

"You no need to worry Mrs. Westcott this man won't be bothering you or your family".

"You had me worried for a minute you see Dawn has also gone back to college. What was it you wanted I'll tell Adrian when he comes home"?

"Just a courtesy call to make sure you are all okay, but you are fine I can see, I won't keep you any longer, goodbye".

His mobile shook him from wondering what to do next.

"Oh hello Mel, what's up"?

"Have you spoken to Adrian Westcott yet?"

"No, he wasn't in I saw the wife though, it seems the FLO was a little loose tongued, he could have known about Grant. I left saying I was there on a courtesy visit, and not to worry".

"Good, cancel the interview and come back to the nick".

Chapter 14

Harrold Davis was sitting at his desk alone glancing at the hive of activity and chatter coming from Jonny Musgrove and his team. He wondered how their investigation was going. He made a point to collar Jonny or Mel later for an update. He forced his mind to ignore the events taking place across the room and came back to his unenvied task. Not convinced the motives of the Serious Crime or Conduct were what they were said to be, he would proceed with caution; if things went sour he wasn't going to be the scapegoat to cover up their skulduggery. After a detailed briefing with Chief Webb he now knew that she suspected other senior officers in the force had eluded detection during the investigation two years ago. Having removed two corrupt detectives and several villains after murder and a series of crimes involving the trafficking of children, Toni told him of her doubts concerning two police officers, namely Commander Newton Blakewood head of the Met and Montague Brown, the Assistant Chief Constable of Hampshire. He did not want to believe that corruption at that level existed so close to home but nothing surprised him about how low people would stoop in their greed and lust for power. Her argument was sound and with suspicion backed by some friends in Police Conduct and Serious Crime he had to concede the possibility had some serious weight. His quarry, Jake Snell, much lower down the pecking order, was in fact the only villain to have escaped before the net closed. The fact that he was now back in the UK, this dangerous, clever murderer would leave the corrupt policemen vulnerable. He had to find Jake before they did.

He had been going through the rather complex case file where a network both in England and France had been abducting children to harvest their organs. He closed the last page having made notes in his pocketbook concerning various names and places which would give him a starting point in his search for

Jake Snell. When he finally looked up the squad room had almost emptied, a few uniform officers were still at their desks but all the detectives had gone. He placed a call to June Owens; the line was busy so sent her a text message to meet him downstairs as soon as she could. He locked the file in his desk, stood slowly, for his back had become stiff and unyielding after sitting so long, he stretched to full height moving gingerly towards the exit on his way down to seek out his friend and colleague Compy B.

Anticipating Harrold's need for her full attention she had delegated the enquiries for Musgrove and his lot to Constable Masie Archer, one of her team of ferrets who would serve them every bit as well as anyone here.

Compton Busion had a special liking for Harrold Davis; this Inspector from London had a unique talent when it came to identifying anomalies in financial documents. He could glance at a page and see even a minor oddity in the pattern of figures. His skill had tracked down many a suspicious entry when he worked as a detective sergeant for the fraud squad in London. When he came here he soon combined his ideas with her computer skills and were able to uncover more than a villain or two.

Today she had been asked to help him trace a former suspect who had disappeared abroad just in time to escape capture. The knowledge that he was back in England surprised her but was a fact she would use to advantage. She and Harrold surmised lack of money was the reason for his return; this is where they would trap him. Exposing himself now was foolish so he must be desperate; he probably left a considerable sum here when he ran in haste almost two years ago, enough it seems to force him back. The larger the sum the harder to hide; she was thinking 'Harrold you can spot a missing penny in a pot of gold so Jake take heed he is coming'. She of course knew it would not be so easy and would require a good slice of luck as well as skill, she would enjoy the chase regardless of the outcome.

"Hello there young lady are you ready"?

"Yes sir, where do you want to start"?

Chapter 15

Mel, Keith and Hamish gathered around Jonny's desk, all waiting for the result of forensic material found at Grant's house hoping it would reveal who had been there, the three junior officers were convinced it was to be Adrian or at a pinch Gregory who had climbed the fence. No other suspects fit the situation as they knew it and were keen to be gone. Jonny urged caution saying he would not approach Adrian Westcott until he had more information, they should wait for Compton's assistant Masie Archer to contact them. Eventually the call came, Jonny listened slowly shaking his head. He hung up with the three looking intently at him for the result.

"Not good I'm afraid, none of the prints or DNA found at Grant's house match our two dads, however we still need to speak to Adrian to be sure. A new lead has come to light however; George Grant was a keen photographer and belonged to a club based in Hartley Wintney. They meet in the village hall once every two weeks, I have the name of the club secretary here somewhere, he may lead us to finding where Grant kept his cameras".

"Hartley Wintney"? Hamish Linkman asked.

"It's a village five miles outside Basingstoke on the old A30". Volunteered Keith.

"Lots to do today so we need to split up. Mel you and Hamish go there and seek out the secretary".

Jonny was shuffling through the file as he spoke.

"Ah, here it is, his name's Paul Lewis, works at Fullers Estate Agents in the high street. We must find Grant's equipment, there may be more photos in his camera's memory; ask for a membership list you know what to do. Keith and I will interview Adrian Westcott, he will be at work now so we will be at the golf course. Masie is still doing her thing with his computer and finances you never know what she may find that one. We still

130

need to interview his ex a second time, I want to do that here; Mel will you run that one, tell uniform to bring her in and the son if he is there, keep them separated, she is hiding her feelings about Grant, you may encourage her to open up; I was stone walled by her last time. If you have no joy with her the son may be more forthcoming, have a care though, remember he is under-age; by the book, okay".

"Don't worry, kid gloves me; we'll call if anything crops up".

On her way out Mel spoke to the desk sergeant explained what was needed with regard to the former Mrs. Grant. She felt buoyant today for some reason, maybe it was because she was more than happy to have the opportunity to work with this sergeant from Reading. His soft Scots accent pleased her, it reminded her of her Dad; she had never acquired his accent herself, having an English born Mum and going to school in the south were too strong an influence. She had a warm feeling about him; not often she had the time to socialise outside of the station, although her colleagues and the others who worked there were friendly and pleasant enough, Hamish Linkman triggered something in her a little more basic; sensuous even. The sudden thought that he was probably married took the smile from her face. 'Sod it'! she almost said out loud, she would have to be careful, hide her feelings until she knew more about him.

All four left the squad room at the same time moving down the stairs to the rear car park in silence. Jonny and Keith climbed into Keith's car and were gone, Melanie Frazer almost ambled, with Hamish ahead of her, enjoying what she was seeing.

"We'll take my car Hamish; I'll drop you back here when we've finished" she said. "do you have to be home at a certain time"?

"Fine, nay my times my own; I had a text from my guvnor to say there's no need to come back, just to call him once a day till I've finished here".

They settled in the car and Mel set off for the short ride to Hartley Wintney.

"You live in Reading I presume"?

"Aye, a small flat rented for now, I did intend to buy a place but it's so expensive down here I'm not so sure. I was in the Borders police last year based in Kelso; I lived with my Dad till he passed on, three years ago now. I've put his house up for sale but what it's worth will hardly buy a garden shed down here. Still it will be a good deposit if ever I decide to buy. Anyway I had no chance of promotion in our small community and with Dad gone I had no reason to stay; I stuck with it till I'd passed the sergeants exam but it took the move south for the promotion to happen so when this job in Reading came up I jumped at the chance".

"Regrets"?

"Nay I love it, always busy, a lot more crooks down here you ken". He said with a big grin.

Mel laughed at his quip.

"Yes all the best villains live in the Thames valley".

The sat nav's impersonal voice interrupted their joke telling them they had arrived at their destination, Fullers Estate Agents, to which satellite technology had guided them within a few yards. Typical of similar establishments with a central recessed glass door splitting display windows either side with pictures of local residential offerings. A one room office with two desks and various filing cabinets lining the walls. They walked in to be greeted by a man in his late forties, well dressed in a grey suit white shirt and green tie emblazoned with the company logo; the usual uniform of a salesman out to impress. His smile and offer of help quickly faded when they showed their warrant cards and introduced themselves. Mel asked to speak to Paul Lewis.

"I'm sorry miss, Mr. Lewis is out with a client at the moment, he should be back quite soon. Err... I could call him on the mobile if you like"?

"Thank you Mr....?"

"Oh sorry Earnest Palmer Miss".

"Mr. Palmer, do that, tell him we are waiting and please address me as either Detective or Sergeant".

"Sorry.... Sergeant, I'll call him now".

Earnest Palmer moved to behind his desk and picked up the phone pressed a single button and waited. It was answered almost at once.

"Hello, Earnest here, there are a policeman and woman here who want to speak to you.......I don't know they didn't say....... I can't help that...... well leave them and come back they are waiting.... I said I don't know.... Just get here and you'll find out".

Earnest hung up.

"He wasn't best pleased, wanted to know what it was about; none of my business; anyway Paul said he'll be back in fifteen minutes maybe a bit longer. I can make you a coffee if you like".

"No thank you Mr. Palmer, we'll wait in our car, we can see him arrive from there".

They walked to the car which was parked right outside where they could see into the office to wait for Paul Lewis to return.

"Why no coffee Mel, and coming out here to wait"?

"I want to see the reaction between Palmer when Lewis returns, before we go in".

"Why is that, do you suspect something"?

"No not really just a feeling I have sometimes, I always take notice of it, it has stood me well in the past".

"A bit of a psychic eh"?

"Just careful Hamish; someone murdered George Grant in a very violent way, we don't know who yet; it could be anyone we come across during our investigation; you may be face to face with a killer without realising it. Seeing peoples reaction to

133

different situations when they think they are alone can be very revealing".

"I bow to your experience; an old head on young shoulders".

"I've had a good mentor".

"DI Musgrove"?

"Oh no,....well yes, him too I suppose; mostly the Chief really, Toni Webb, you have yet to come across her, she is formidable when it comes to pursuing villains. We've all become very respectful of her example".

"Can't wait ; I think".

"Don't worry she's a sweetie, you'll be fine".

An Audi pulled up sharply some yards in front of the waiting pair, a man identifiable as their quarry by being dressed in the standard suit and tie slammed the door and strode purposely into the estate agents office. The two officers watched as he moved towards Palmer's desk arms waving and pointing. Palmer stood hands raised in submission. It was obvious Lewis was complaining about being called back and was giving Palmer a hard time. They followed close behind Lewis only to mute the heated conversation which ended abruptly as they entered.

"Mr. Paul Lewis I am Detective Sergeant Frazer and this is Detective sergeant Linkman we have a few questions we need to ask you in connection with a serious incident".

Lewis turned sharply the anger still spread across his brow.

"What's this all about, you've probably cost me a sale making me come back right in the middle of a viewing"?

Mel could see Palmer was pretending to look at his computer but was straining not to miss any of their conversation. She threw a look from Lewis to Palmer and continued.

"I'm sorry about that but we do need to speak to you preferably in private".

Paul Lewis saw the pointed look and understood, his face taking on a more relaxed and controlled countenance.

"We can go through to the back, it's a small restroom and kitchen but private enough".

There were only two seats by a small table, Mel indicated that Lewis take one, she sat opposite. Hamish stood by the door which he had shut behind them. Earnest left his desk and crept towards the closed door he wanted to hear what was being said.

"Mr. Lewis you are secretary of the local photography club, is that correct"?

"Yes I am and have been for several years, why what is all this about"?

"Do you know a Mr. George Grant"?

"Yes of course, we have a small membership about thirty regulars and a few who come and go. George is one of the regulars, been a member so long I can't recall when he joined even, why what's the problem that you had to see me so urgently"?

"We will come to that in a moment, how well do you know George"?

"We speak at the meetings obviously but I have never socialised with him outside the club; he's a good photographer, very skilled; he's a great help to our newcomers teaching them the tricks of the trade if you like".

"What about his equipment, his camera; what do you know about that"?

"Well he has several cameras, two old Nikon SLRs for use with film and his latest digital is a state of the art Fuji. He has an early Leica very rare, he brought it to the club once; I don't think he uses it though. He produces some fine prints, in his studio workshop I presume, I've not seen his printing equipment but must be able to develop and print from film and also an A3 digital colour printer from the quality of the stuff he brings to the meetings. We don't have shared facilities, we all have our own to

135

varying degrees, we only use the village hall you see, for our meetings".

"Where is George's workshop"?

"I've no idea at his house I would think".

"What type of subjects do you photograph".

"Almost anything really, I like flowers and trees, George was good at long range shots of wildlife, his work with things such as squirrels, woodland mammals and small birds is second to none".

"What about people"?

"Portraits and the like you mean. I do family and friends, some of the others too but no, not George as far as I know, I've never seen any".

Paul stopped and looked closely at Melanie's stern expression wondering why this serious face, asking questions about his favourite hobby. Something was not right what sort of shots had George been taking to bring the police to his door?

"Are you hinting that he has taken some unsavoury pictures, is that why you're here; will you please tell me what this is all about what has George supposed to have done"?

"I'm sorry to inform you Mr. Lewis that George Grant has been found dead and we are trying to trace everyone who may have known him".

"Bloody hells fire, that is a shock, what can I say. A heart attack was it"?

Paul Lewis sat in silence a bemused expression on his face. Mel decided to face him with the truth.

"He was murdered in his home. We know he was a keen photographer but could find nothing at his house, no cameras or equipment of any kind we need to locate his studio or whatever you call it".

"Wow murdered you say; I can't think why, he was such a nice man; you think someone killed him for his equipment; a burglar; I know it is worth quite a lot of money but to murder someone for a camera seems far-fetched to me".

"We don't yet know why he was killed, but probably not to steal his equipment, a forensic search indicated his studio was never located at his home, we hope one of your members knows where his workshop or studio is located. Please provide a list of members past and present with their address and contact telephone number. Was he friends with anyone in particular"?

"Not really he mixed with everyone. I still can't believe it. The membership records are at home I can run you off a copy and bring it to the police station if you like".

"Is the list not on your computer here"?

Paul looked askance at Mel indignity in his voice.

"Oh no, no, I would never bring the club material to work".

"Okay. Here's a police email address please forward the details as soon as you arrive home".

"Oh yes I can do that, I see, saves a lot of time indeed, good".

Linkman stepped forward and spoke for the first time in a deep and penetrating voice.

"Now listen, this is important, do not mention this conversation to anyone hear me, one of these people in your club could be the killer and you don't want to inadvertently alarm them or attract their attention. Take this warning seriously Mr. Lewis very seriously".

They stood, thanked him for his cooperation and left with him still sitting in the chair. Earnest Palmer was back at his desk head down, he had been tempted to listen in at the door but once he heard that George was dead he went back to his seat, afraid they might catch him at it; he remained silent and didn't even acknowledge their departure. Back in the car Mel turned to Hamish.

"A bit strong that last remark; did you see his face, scared or what; do you really expect him not to say anything"?

"I don't know but did you notice he seemed shifty when you mentioned pictures of people, immediately jumped to the conclusion that George might be taking dirty photos and protested far too much at the suggestion he did club business on the work computer; if anything is amiss he will not keep quiet, we should be able to pick up on that when we interview the members".

"You are right he was uncomfortable, perhaps he is running through the files this very minute deleting anything dodgy".

It wasn't Paul Lewis deleting files but Earnest Palmer who had been busy as soon as the officers took Paul into the back room. The need to go home was intense, clearing his house and computers of pictures and anything connected to G.G. a priority. He thought he'd already covered his tracks at the office and was surprised they had traced George here so quickly.

"You all right Paul what was that all about"?

"Nothing much just some club business concerning one of the members".

He had the officer's warning fresh in his mind so would say nothing more.

"I have something urgent to do so need to go home early will you hold the fort Earnest, please".

"No problem off you go".

He sat at his desk not sure what had just happened, he couldn't believe it as soon as he heard George was dead he moved away from the door afraid to be caught eves dropping, so missed the fact George had been murdered. Earnest wondered how he had died, he seemed healthy enough; a heart attack maybe or perhaps an accident in his van. As soon as enough time had passed for Paul to be well gone Earnest Palmer made a short phone call, put up the closed sign switched the office phone to divert to his mobile and was on his way home.

Mel and Hamish arrived back at Basingstoke station earlier than expected. She found out from the desk sergeant the uniform officers had not yet returned with the Grant family, he said they were waiting for her son to return from school. She re-read Jonny's notes on his interview to prepare for when they came in. She would question the mother first and then the son. He was fifteen so would need to have the mum or some other representation present during the interview so arranged for family liaison to be available. Jonny felt neither of them were anything more than persons of interest but thought Mel would find out more than his first efforts revealed. Mel was not going to caution them but keep it very informal; more likely to achieve some rapport.

The gist of Jonny's report showed Julie Grant was a non-working agency shorthand typist on Job seekers; nothing known about her son. The couple divorced due to unreasonable behaviour. No response to Jonny's personal questions and did not care that her ex was dead and showed no surprise that he was murdered. She was not told of George's link to Dawn Westcott and the other girls in the photos; that did not mean she was unaware of his activities in that direction. Mel was ready to push hard. Being unsure if the presence of Linkman would seem threatening she decided to keep him in the observation room at least for the first part. He might be more help with the son; she would decide as the interviews progressed.

Chapter 16

Jonny pulled up outside the Popley house ready to tackle Adrian Westcott. He asked Keith Crane to wait in the car as he did not want to put Adrian on guard with an overpowering police presence. He was not sure about Adrian but thought it less likely for him to want revenge as his daughter had been found and was safe, unlike his colleague Gregory Small whose daughter Karen was still missing. Adrian was not at home.

From the Westcott's home in Popley it was a ten minute drive to the golf course at Wildmoore. Margaret Westcott had told Jonny that her husband had been called in to cover for Gregory who had phoned in sick, no doubt brought on by Mel Frazer's earlier visit. The golf course was not where he planned to confront Adrian so decided to let Keith conduct the questioning, more forthright than he intended but needed to observe Adrian's reactions which often told more about what was true than any answers given. As always Jenny Matheson was at the desk.

"Well, well, we are becoming popular, you'll be taking out membership soon".

"Not on my salary Miss Matheson".

"What can we do for you today? My father is not on site if that's whom you want to see, I did ask you to call if you remember".

"No it's Adrian we've come to find, we did expect to meet him at home, he is here I hope"?

"Oh yes, Gregory phoned in sick, poor guy he is all over the place at the moment, we give him some slack with time off; he'll need his work if he is to survive the loss of Karen. Adrian kindly covered for him today, he's a good man".

"Can we see him please"?

"Out on green five at the moment, quite a way over there though. I'll call him, he has a buggy with him so he won't be too long; if you go to the lounge I'll send him along as soon as he is back"?

"Don't tell him we are here though".

"Why; do you expect him to run"?

"No of course not; I don't want to worry him he's probably still on edge".

The two policemen walked across the foyer to the lounge on the far side, as Jenny spoke through a walkie talkie requesting Adrian to come to the reception. They did not hear his response or any further words from her; they entered sat on the comfortable chairs to wait. Keith picked up a golf magazine from the coffee table, he was not a golfer and after a quick flick through its pages saw him discard it with a shrug of disinterest.

"Do you play golf sir"?

"No Keith, you need a lot of spare time for this game as well as a lot of spare cash. I'm saving it for when I retire, I'll have the spare time then; not sure if I'll have the cash though".

Ten minutes passed in silence; Jonny was about to go out to find what was going on when Jenny Masterson entered the room.

"Look I'm sorry Adrian will be a little while yet the buggy has broken down, he's been trying to fix it but no joy. He started walking back another ten minutes I would think, as I said It's quite a way on the far side of the course. Can I make you a coffee or something"?

"No we are fine, thanks for letting us know".

"Do you think he has scarpered sir"?

"No, where would he go; I'm sure it's genuine, however if he's not here in a quarter of an hour, we'll go find him".

Well under ten minutes had passed when Adrian burst in the room hot and breathless.

"Is Dawn alright and Margaret why are you here"?

"Calm down Adrian there is no problem, I told Jenny not to tell you we were here I did not want to upset you".

"She didn't tell me; I saw your car from the eighth and started to run I thought something had happened".

"I'm sorry you are upset I did try to avoid you anticipating a problem, we just need to ask a couple of questions that's all".

"Thank God for that; it's difficult to put it out of your mind I see bad things round every corner. I want to stay home all the time to protect them but can't of course, I have to work. I know it's irrational but I can't help it".

"I understand Adrian" said Keith "It will become easier. Sit down and get your breath back, we need to clear up a couple of points concerning how you found George Grant".

"Oh, is that all. Margaret was on about how you had someone in custody and it was alright for Dawn to go back to college. She said the lady family liaison girl told her. I wanted to make sure it was safe that's all".

"That still doesn't tell me how you found who he was and where he lived".

"We were running the CCTV pictures here, the same ones you had from Jenny, when I saw the postal van. It made me curious so when I came home I pressed Margaret about her conversation with the lady family officer. She'd told her they had someone who had chased Dawn and that they were keeping an eye on him so we shouldn't worry as Dawn would be safe. I put two and two together, the same as you obviously did after seeing the postal van at the golf course and went to the sorting office; I found out the driver was George Grant but he was off sick. I found his address from the electoral register. When I went there I saw your two guys in their car keeping watch. It confirmed I was right".

"Did you go back later"?

"No why should I, you lot were watching him he wasn't going anywhere was he".

"Did you tell anyone"?

"I told Greg; he had an idea about the postman anyway when we watched the video. Oh and the Misses she was happy you were watching him, it made her feel safe".

"Did Gregory go to Grant's house".

"He might have done I don't know he never said".

"I shouldn't tell you but you'll find out soon enough, George Grant is dead, he was murdered in his house".

"Bloody Hell. Murdered wow; I can't say I'm sorry but how.....Hey, wait a minute you think I did it. You can't, I know it's not me....so....no hold on you can't be thinking of Gregory can you, that's why all these questions no, no, that's not possible Greg's a gentle soul".

"We don't know who did it yet, we have to consider everyone".

"You think we did it together don't you, I know I went there but I never went in, I couldn't do a thing like that. Not me or Gregory you must look elsewhere".

Jonny interrupted before Adrian became too agitated.

"Don't worry Adrian we are following other leads; Grant was a very nasty man who had enemies elsewhere you two are very low on our list of suspects but we still have to ask these questions. A simple DNA test will eliminate you and Small".

"Oh you had me worried for a minute, do you want a sample now".

"No Adrian its fine, we will take it later if we need to. You go back to work and don't worry any more, I'm sure we are done with you. We are still trying to find out what happened to Karen, so tell your friend we are on his side and encourage him to come back, working will make it easier for him to deal with not knowing what has happened to his daughter; staying alone at home is not good".

Chapter 17

Julie Grant had been placed in room two, a standard almost bare interview room with two chairs facing either side of a small table, her son Gabriel was in room one, a more pleasant room with a sofa, two armchairs and coffee table, along with the FLO Constable Liz Dawson.

"I'm Detective Sergeant Melanie Frazer, Mrs. Grant I am one of the team investigating George's death. Your name is Julie isn't it"?

Julie nodded but did not speak.

"You and your son are here because I am required during our investigation to ask you some questions relating to your former husband George. You are not under arrest or caution so whatever you tell me here is merely to help us find out what George was like. Do you know if he had any enemies who may have wished to harm him"?

"He may have done I don't know though; we've been apart for ages now".

"Why did you keep the name Grant after your divorce"?

"Where is my Gabe"?

"He's next door with one of our female family liaison officers, probably having tea and biscuits by now I should think".

"Oh, he doesn't understand what's happened, he loved his Dad, they kept in touch regularly you know".

"I'm sure it must be a terrible loss for him, and you too I imagine. Why keep the name Grant"?

"For Gabriel's sake, he couldn't have understood why I would have a new name. Me and George were good in the beginning and he always provided, still does; did. Where will the money come from now he has gone"?

Mel felt sorry for this woman and wanted to provide her with information where she might find some support.

"Social services will help you now, I'll arrange someone if you like, we'll talk about it later. You are doing fine so let's continue okay. Why did you divorce George, Julie"?

"It's too embarrassing, I can't".

"Hey, it's only you and me here and now, I won't tell anyone, did he hit you"?

"No nothing like that".

"Was he unfaithful"?

"Sort of but not as you might think".

"I don't think anything Julie tell me".

Julie cried. Mel passed her a tissue and waited.

"He wanted to do things I did not like. He brought his photography friend to his studio. He made me pose for him, you know".

"Go on Julie get it off your chest it will help".

"I had to take my clothes off and things".

"What things, what did he make you do"?

"I can't, I can't it's too painful".

"That's okay don't worry I understand. How did you manage to leave him and proceed with a divorce"?

"I left one day when he was at work, I took Gabe he was much younger then; I found a refuge, a lady from the home came and helped us".

"Did he follow you, try to force you back"?

"No he said if I didn't have any spirit he didn't want me anyway, He said he would give me a divorce and pay maintenance if I kept quiet about the stuff; you know".

"Where did you go then"?

"I went with my sister for a while then I had an agency job and rented this flat, we were fine until now. I've been promised some more work from the agency but now George won't be sending us money I don't know if we can manage".

"Family liaison will help you find the help you need; give it time you will be fine. Do you know the names of his photography friends"?

"Not really there was a man I heard George call him Earl or Earn, something like that I think, he was the worst; he was there most times one other came I don't know who he was".

"If I show you some pictures do you think you will recognise them"?

"Oh yes I think I could but it was a long time ago and I don't really want to. No, no I won't; I want to forget".

"That's okay Julie don't worry you won't have to do anything you don't want. Where is his studio, did he keep his equipment there, you know cameras and stuff"?

"He used to keep it at home but after I found pictures of young girls we had a blazing row so he moved it all out to a rented lock up in Market Street, one of the industrial units I don't know which one, when he took us there it was always dark. It was after this he started to make me pose; just for him at first, then he brought in the others".

"I'll leave it for now you have been very brave. I need to speak to Gabriel next; you can be with him if you like".

"No you mustn't speak to him; that was all years ago he won't remember anything; you can't tell him what I have just said".

"Don't fret I will be discreet and I will keep it brief. Look come next door and see Gabe; it is much more comfortable than here".

Mel led Julie along the corridor to room one. Gabriel was sitting next to Liz on the sofa, he jumped up immediately upon the sight of his mum. They hugged and Julie smiled obviously holding back the tears.

"Liz make Julie a cup of tea I'll be back in a minute".

Mel returned to the viewing room adjacent to room two.

"Well Hamish what do you make of that"?

146

"What a bastard eh. That poor woman; I'm almost glad he's dead. Good lead with the location of his workshop, we should be able to find that easy enough. This photography club looks like a source of some nasty characters. The probable abduction of young girls by this lot is a real worry. We need to copy pictures of the members and show them to her".

"I won't do that, not yet anyway; I need her to do it willingly I'm not going to spring it on her, you saw and heard my promise; she's been through enough with my dragging it all up again. Come through you can interview Gabriel, I will observe from inside".

Liz had already returned with Julie's tea and a coke for Gabe. Mel and Hamish entered and waited some minutes for them to become used to their presence. Hamish smiled and directed his attention to the boy.

"Hello Gabriel, my name is Detective Sergeant Hamish Linkman. Mrs. Grant I would like to speak with Gabriel if you don't mind, just a few questions".

Julie turned to Mel who had positioned herself in the corner and asked.

"Why not you"?

"It's alright Julie, Hamish is my partner, Gabe will be fine with him".

"Okay then". Julie turned to her son smiled and nodded. "You answer them true Gabe there is no one to protect now; we are safe".

"You are fifteen is that right"?

"Yes sir last month".

"I am very sorry about your Dad; you were close I believe"?

"Sort of; I loved him you know he was alright with me we got on, no rows or anything but he was not always good to Mum".

"You saw him regularly, where did you go"?

"Nearly every month but not always. Nowhere special, mostly MacDonald's or Kentucky, once when it was raining we

147

went to his house to watch videos. I liked going to the river fishing, we didn't catch anything big though. He took me in his van on a post round once, it was boring we didn't do it again".

"How often did you go to his house"?

"Just one time, soon after we left".

"You were very young then did you never go back later"?

"I said didn't I".

"Did he give you any money"?

"No, not normally, only Birthdays and Christmas, he said Mum should give me pocket money he pays her enough. He did pay for everything when we were out though he bought lunch, sweets and ice creams and stuff like that, you know".

"When was the last time you saw him"?

"I'm not sure about three weeks ago I think, he came to ours, mum sent me to the shops to buy some milk, we didn't need it she just wanted me out of the way. I know we were short of money so there was bound to be a row".

Julie butted in then.

"No, no, that's not what happened. He'd missed a bank payment and came to give me the cash, he only stayed a minute there was no argument. I did send Gabe off because George can be a bit aggressive especially about money but it was alright".

"That clears that up then, when you went out did he pick you up from your house"?

"Not always, he would phone and I'd meet him somewhere in town, usually in the shopping centre".

"You are at the Everest school aren't you what subjects are you doing, GCSEs this year isn't it. I expect you will go to Queen Mary's after"?

"Yes I'm doing six subjects History and English Lit. are my best. I'd like Queen Marys if I can get in".

"I'm sure you will".

"I thought you might have taken up photography like your Dad"?

"He wouldn't let me touch his stuff. They don't do that at school either, anyway Dad never did photography when I was around, I don't like it, it's horrible".

"Why's that"?

"Waste of money and its boring".

"Did he ever take your picture maybe when you were out".

"No he didn't, he doesn't take good pictures, why are you asking me that"?

"No reason just thought with it being his hobby he'd want pictures of the family. I'm trying to have an idea of what your Dad was like when he was alive; if we are to find who hurt him we need to know him better".

"He didn't take pictures of me or Mum she wouldn't allow it so there, don't ask any more do you hear. He only did that stuff with his weird mates at their club; if you want to know about his pictures go and ask them. I don't want to answer any more questions. Mum can we go home"?

"Hey Gabe, it's alright don't be upset, I've no more questions you can go anytime you like; I'll arrange a car. Both of you have been most helpful".

Melanie stepped forward and placed a hand on Julie's shoulder, she could see she was close to breaking down, and hoped to avoid this in front of her son.

"Julie we have finished you can both go home and put it all behind you. None of what has been said here will be made public through me or Detective Linkman, your privacy is important to us. We shouldn't need to trouble you again except maybe later to let you know when we have found out who killed George. If you have any problems or misgivings you can call me anytime. Would you like Liz to accompany you home"?

"No just a lift will do; please let us be, we have had enough".

Mel pressed one of her cards in Julies hand.

"I know Julie, you and Gabe have been more than brave; don't forget I'm here if you need me and do let Liz Dawson help with your finances at least".

Liz accompanied the mother and son out of the station to find the police car that would take them home. Mel and Hamish sat in the two armchairs of room one unable to speak for a full minute. Hamish spoke first.

"That was awful, not only the wife but his son too from his reaction. If he wasn't subject to that abuse he was certainly aware of his mothers suffering, you could feel the dread emanating from the lad when talking about his father's so called hobby".

"Julie is in denial; she believes Gabe doesn't know what she went through but I'm certain he knows very well what has been going on for a very long time".

"Now for those bloody club members eh"?

Said Hamish expecting to go straight out and start arresting these awful men.

"All in good time, I need to run this by the Jonny first, I am sure he will involve Toni Webb before we do anything. First we must find the Grant workshop or studio, I know Jonny will insist we research all the club members before we rush in making arrests. Remember our aim is not only to find who killed George but primarily to trace what happened to your Karen Small".

"Sorry, Mel, I hadn't forgotten her, but for a moment I was so incensed with these guys, all I wanted was to go and drag them in by their necks and give them hell. Karen and anyone else they may have corrupted must be our priority. Let's go and find Inspector Musgrove I'm too wound up to sit still".

They went back to the squad room; Mel was looking for Keith or Jonny, nowhere to be seen. She thought 'not back yet'.

"Lots to do Hamish you can help if you like, I'll log you on as a guest to Keith's computer are you familiar with this set up"?

"Yes, looks like ours, what do you want me to do"?

"See if Lewis has sent the email with the membership list, it should have come in on the group mail address, find out as much as you can about each of them and make a file for each. I can't give you access to our current files as a guest, you will need clearance first, you should be able to work with what's available".

"I'll be okay, what are you going to do"?

"I'm going to the Market Street industrial estate to find Grant's workshop".

"Couldn't you do that online"?

"I doubt if Grant used his own name, a photo and asking around will be quicker".

"You are right again of course then you've been at this a lot longer than I have".

"Still wearing your L Plates then".

"I'll never stop learning even from one so young as you".

Hamish blew her a kiss as she swaggered out the door a big smile on her face.

Chapter 18

Armed with a picture of George Grant Mel set off for Market Street which lies between the motorway and the town's southern residential area. No longer a market, the name harped back to the early days when Basingstoke was a town serving the surrounding agricultural community. All traces of the original cattle market had long since gone the area eventually being taken over by a series of small industrial sites. The one she was looking for specifically would have self-contained lock ups, there were two fitting that description in the area and she hoped it was one of these. The first was the smaller of the two with some thirty units of two different sizes. She drove into the shared driveway where several vehicles were parked, the units were arranged in two rows, small units to the left and larger units to her right. In the far right hand corner were three men unloading a large van carrying their packages inside through an up and over door. Moving to an adjacent parking space she climbed out and approached the group.

"Excuse me guys can you help me"?

They all turned to see who had spoken, one stopped what he was doing and moved towards her, the other two continued their work.

"What ya want love"?

Mel produced her warrant card and un-pocketed the photo of Grant holding it out for him to see.

"I am Detective Frazer I'm looking for this man have you seen him"?

"Oh police is it, what's e done"?

"He's not done anything but I believe he has a unit here and I need to find it".

"Why don't you ask him where then"?

"I can't he unfortunately died recently and I thought someone around here might have seen him coming and going".

"Give us a gander at the photo".

He studied it for a moment, then suddenly moved off into the building taking the picture with him. Mel was surprised but waited a couple of minutes before deciding what to do, just as she was about to go in the man returned with the picture and handed it back to her.

"Sorry love no one here's seen him, we've been in this place a long time, the girls in the office know everyone on this site, he's not from round here. You know there's another lock up complex a ways up the road, he may be from there".

"Thanks I'll go check it out".

Before she'd finished speaking he turned back and continued to help his colleagues. Although she couldn't rule out this site completely on the say so of one local, she thought it best to try the other place first. It was just a short drive to the next site. This was much larger and had about eighty units. Single units were on the right but were all joined together in a long block, all the same size only a little larger than a double garage. Other units on the left were at least twice, sometimes three and one four times bigger. Four other units at the far end were big two story affairs with large frontages. She thought a bit of luck when she saw the entrance was gated with a small security office. If it was manned they would surely know who rents each unit. The gates were wide open so she drove through without challenge and parked at the first space just inside. She moved to the security hut and looked through the glass door to find an older man sitting on a well upholstered chair a newspaper over his face fast asleep. She tapped on the door frame, with no response. Her second knock this time was much louder which woke the slumbering guard with a start.

"Hey, you, what goes on there; what do you want"?

"Mel held up her warrant card to the window".

His response was unexpected and slow. He stood or rather stumbled to attention and almost saluted. Ex police or an old soldier she thought. He then beckoned her to come in.

"Sorry Sergeant; caught me there, double shift does it every time".

"The names Melanie and you are"?

"Dave Dingh sergeant"

"Right Dave I need your help".

"Sure thing; let me sit down a minute first. Right, that's better what can I do for you"?

He looked very shaken, the shock of being woken suddenly she thought.

"Are you okay"?

"Fine just give me a mo. will you".

"Take your time and when you're ready I'd like you to have look at this picture, I believe he rents one of the units here".

Dingh reached under the counter retrieved some ancient looking reading glasses, the kind you buy on a market stall for a couple of pounds, before studying George Grant's features.

"An odd picture you've given me here, he looks dead".

"He is, do you know him".

"I'm not sure, it could be the guy from one of our units number fifteen I think".

He took off his glasses and gave them a wipe with the tail of his shirt, put them back on and stared again more closely this time.

"Yes I've seen him around for sure, it could be any one of those units around that number; let me look it up".

He dived under his counter again and brought out a grubby folder from which he extracted an A5 notebook. He flicked through the pages stopping several times.

"Ah here he is Palmer, that's his name or anyway that's the one who pays the rent. Haven't seen him around for a while now I don't know why".

"Number fifteen you said"?

"No I got that wrong luv, it's seventeen, look".

Dave held up the book for Mel to see but took it back again before she could focus on the page.

"I remember now looking at this, fifteen is an overflow store for the shoe company; they have one of the big units at the end. Number sixteen is empty your man is definitely number seventeen".

The name rang a bell for a second then she realised Palmer was one of the two estate agents, too much of a coincidence, this was definitely the right unit. Palmer paid the rent but George used it or maybe both.

"Tell me Dave are you supposed to keep a record of who comes and goes"?

"I used to but not now, we had CCTV and everything when I first came; it was a proper job then we had uniforms and the gate was electric. Mind you that was when all the insurance was paid for by the company that owns the site. They slowly sold off the units so it was down to each individual to do his own insurance. Only twenty units left owned by the original company. All we do now is sit here, close the gate when the last one goes home and open up again when they come in the next morning, we don't bother to lock it anymore. The cameras are still there but they don't work, we've lost the recorders and screens, when they broke down they stopped fixing them".

"How many of you are there"?

"Should be four but at the moment only three so we do double shifts; I don't mind, the extra money comes in handy. We do six till six and rotate so that we all get a fair share of the nights; time and a half you see and you don't have to do much. Two walk rounds each shift, twelve and four, there's a time clock here when we start and finish with one at the far end of the site to show we've not been dossing. I'm sure they only keep us on to comply with some safety regulation or other".

155

"Have you noticed anyone else using that unit"?

"Maybe I'm not sure, let me think about it, lots of people come and go you know, if they are not regulars it's difficult to see which unit they are going to".

"If I show you some pictures do you think that would help"?

"Probably let me see".

"I don't have them with me now but I will bring some later, by the way do you have a spare key to number seventeen"?

"I do but it is a simple mortice lock; many of the single units put on their own padlocks, we can go see if you like".

She stepped down from the small hut, Dave followed with obvious difficulty and a noticeable limp. Mel could clearly see he had an artificial leg and struggled a bit when walking. He noticed her looking and that she had politely averted her eyes.

"I see you noticed the leg, lost it at Goose Green, you are too young perhaps to know about that".

"I'm sorry; I do know about the Falklands though".

"I was lucky some of me mates never came back except in a plastic bag. I tried one of those articulated modern ones but still prefer my old faithful they gave me years ago, it's not so pretty but more comfortable".

"Sorry I didn't mean to stare".

"It's okay love don't worry about it, I don't. Come on lets go and see this dam lockup".

Sure enough even when they were several yards from unit seventeen they could see two large padlocks, one on the central up and over door and another on the smaller inset door.

"What do you want to do miss Melanie"?

"Wait here Dave I won't be a moment".

Mel went back to her car and returned with a roll of tape. She affixed the 'police do not enter tape' across the door in the form of a cross.

"I will be back soon with a warrant and some big cutters, don't let anyone near this unit".

"That'll be my pleasure see you later then, do you know what time you'll be back I have a change over with Alan at six, but I'll wait if you like".

"If you don't mind that would be great. Give me your number I'll call you if we are going to be any later than six. By the way I owe you a drink".

"Nah no need for that, glad to help; I'm curious though when you come back perhaps you'll tell me how the poor bugger copped it".

"I might just do that, over a pint perhaps"?

Mel returned to her car, called Hamish with the news and more importantly asked him to contact any deyective he could find to set in motion acquiring a warrant and a couple of uniforms with bolt cutters to come to the Market Street industrial complex.

"I was just about to call you, are you coming back, I think you'd better I found something you should see"?

"I was going to wait for the uniforms to arrive but I will if you need me; what is it, what have you found, is Jonny there"?

"I can't not on the phone you really need to see. Just come back now I don't know who to tell, there's no one here".

"Find Davis he will be with Constable Busion downstairs ask anyone they will show you, ask him to start processing the warrant for the unit. I'm on my way".

Mel pressed the speed dial for Jonny Musgrove.

"Yes Mel what is it"?

"Where are you"?

"On my way back what's wrong"?

"I have found Grant's workshop Hamish is trying to obtain a warrant to break in".

"You don't need a warrant if it is Grant's, this is a murder have you forgotten"?

"I know but It's not rented in his name; I'll explain when I see you. Another thing Hamish is having kittens about something he has found. I presume your interview with Adrian went okay".

"Yes, he did trace Grant's whereabouts but only passed it on to Small. He swears he did not go there after our guys left but has no real alibi for the whole time frame, he remains of interest but that's all. We'll be back in ten minutes".

"So will I".

Chapter 19

Toni was standing in her small conservatory looking out over her recently neglected garden, she had no intention of going into work till much later, debating whether to deal with the encroaching weeds herself or call on her gardener. The knock on her front door soon made that decision for her.

"Saw your car there; not going in today"?

"Morning Nathan, maybe this afternoon".

"Sounds good, I'm not working today maybe we could bring our date forward a few hours, lunch instead of dinner"?

"Very tempting, I was going to tackle my overgrown patch this morning, come in, let me see".

Toni picked up her mobile, selected a speed dial number and waited, hoping he would answer.

"Hi there Jorden, it's Toni Webb are you free today......just a couple of hours weeding mostly, you know what to do........Good.....key in the usual place.....no not till late....I'll leave your money in the tin...okay thanks".

"You sorted that out quick, he's a good lad coming at short notice like that".

"Well he knows I won't nick him for doing his own 'weeding' if he is good to me".

"Does that mean what I think it does"?

"I caught him once when I came back unexpected; he was working, earphones on full volume puffing his heart out, I smelt it even before I reached the garden. He nearly shit himself I can tell you. Anyway we came to an understanding".

"I bet you did you crafty minx".

"Well where are we going, what delights do you have in mind"?

"You spend your days in dark places with dark people and even when you go out you go to dark dingy pubs and drink dark beer. Today you are going to see some light. Your carriage awaits madam, put on your coat and hat and don't forget you handbag, your treat I believe".

"Cheeky sod, if I'm paying I want somewhere I chose".

"Not today lady; this you will enjoy".

"Toni did put on her coat but no hat, she opened her bag and put thirty pounds in a tin on top of the cooker and shut the door behind her".

"What about the key"?

"It's always in the same place, Jorden knows where".

"A bit insecure don't you think"?

"I'm a Chief Inspector remember, no one robs a copper if they know what's good for them, anyway they'd never find them".

Nathan had his doubts about that.

"I suppose you know what you're doing; ready? Let's go".

Nathan's Mercedes was a lot more comfortable than her old Vauxhall and they were soon moving away from Basingstoke along the A30 north. She wondered where they were going but was happy to let it happen. She sat back taking in the scenery as it presented itself; when she was working she was either driving, had her head in a file or on the phone, so never saw anything of the surroundings she passed time after time. They turned off the A30 onto a minor road; a sign indicated they were heading towards Odium. Odium was by-passed in a flash soon leaving Hampshire heading into Surrey; they began to follow a steep rising road fringed by bushes and trees; there were no houses. Now she was really curious.

"Are you going to tell me where we are going"?

"Be patient, wait and see, enjoy the ride".

Nearing the brow of the hill was an impressive group of buildings that stood on their own. The trees had diminished to a few saplings leaving a clear view that spread for miles in three directions. They pulled up outside.

"Welcome to the Hogs Back Hotel".

"You know what I have never been up here, I've heard of it of course but what a stunning view".

"Yes, this ridge rises even higher and runs for quite a few miles, trees block the views along the way but there are places to stop where you can take in the scenery from both sides of the road".

"Well what we can see from here is pretty special".

"Wait till you see inside the hotel, It has been refurbished recently; they moved the restaurant from the ground to the second floor, you can see south for miles over the Surrey countryside".

"You know what this is great, now I don't mind paying".

"We are a bit early for lunch let's walk a bit along the Hogs Back, it'll give us an appetite".

"Whatever you say".

She hadn't felt this happy in years, whether it was the hormone therapy or the company, probably both, she didn't care, this was going to be the start of a good day. She reached into her bag switched her phone to silent without looking; held on to Nat's arm as they strolled aimlessly along the grass verge. The walk, mostly silent except for the occasional pointing at some interesting feature of the landscape was an appetiser to a superb lunch. Toni tended to eat fast food rarely cooking and only using the Four Horseshoes when in need of a change. A glass of Sancerre with the best ever whole sea bass in a sauce to die for was the highlight a bowl of fruits to finish with coffee left her sated and happy. The view from the new panoramic glass window was even more inviting than what they had seen on their walk, she sat quietly, occasionally glancing across at Nathan wondering if she could find some time in each day to be with this man.

Inside the Hotel Nathan had gone to use the toilet; Toni waited outside the entrance taking the opportunity to look at her phone. She knew it; the mobile's silence had given her only a short respite; when she glanced at the screen and saw that during their walk and wonderful lunch, seven messages and two emails had arrived, all urgent, or so it seemed, each demanding attention. She closed off the screen they could wait, her officers were competent enough to deal with anything, well anything that wasn't political that is. She was tempted to look but resisted, they were not going to spoil these last hours of a perfect afternoon.

"Where to now"?

She said looking at Nat framed like a full sized portrait in the Hotel doorway; this man had awakened something in her she had forgotten; she was unsure if this was the right moment to expose her feelings; caution won out for now 'let's see how it goes maybe next time'.

"I don't know, let me think. We could go for a slow country lane drive take potluck where we end up. If you like, Guildford is just down the hill at the other end of the Hogs Back, we could wander round its old streets; a bit touristy but there are some unusual little shops. It has a fine modern Cathedral if you've never been there. You choose".

"A slow ride would be nice, but in the direction of home please. I would love for this to go on all day but needs must".

Nathan's bottom lip dropped in a pretend sulk which broke out into a smile a moment later.

"I know work calls; you can't escape for too long can you"?

"Nature of the beast I'm afraid. Look I don't have to go back immediately, I haven't looked at my messages yet they can wait a little longer. Take a slow ride back, drop me at the station I can find a lift home later or walk if it comes to the push".

"Tell you what, I'll drive back very slowly, when you have finished call me and I'll pick you up, we'll go for a nightcap nice end to a nice day eh"?

"I'd like that a lot, 'Lay on Macduff'".

"What"?

"A favourite quote; take no notice just go".

They sat in the car park at the station reluctant to part. Toni leaned across and gave Nat a kiss on the cheek. He reached out and held her arm returning the kiss briefly to her lips. The embrace lasted longer than he intended as Toni responded in kind.

"Thanks Nathan the best day I have had in a very long time, sorry it has to end".

"Maybe it doesn't, remember what I said, give me a call when you've finished, I'll pick you up".

"We'll see; once I'm in here it is difficult to get away, I won't promise".

"If you can't that's fine, another day then".

"For sure, bye, Nathan".

"Bye, Toni".

As Toni entered the station proper the duty sergeant, who was at the front door collard her.

"Excuse me Ma'am, everyone and his dog has be looking for you, there's a bit of a flap on. I don't know what but DI Musgrove cleared the squad room for a private meet with all the detectives, I'm normally first to hear what's going on, but this time nothing".

"Thanks for the warning sergeant, strange you haven't heard, I'd better go upstairs before they all come looking".

"Hope it's nothing serious good luck Ma'am".

The feeling of apprehension rose in her breast, a lock out of the uniforms meant some shit was flying about, she knew it was about to land on her desk. She wished she had stayed out with Nathan and left it till tomorrow before coming in.

Approaching her office the frosted glass obscured the two shadowy figures sat inside; as she came closer she saw Harrold and Jonny. They were resting silently, not moving but certainly not talking either.

The shit had already landed.

Chapter 20

The three officers arrived in the car park at the same time. Mel was first to the squad room Keith and Jonny, seconds later. Jonny spoke before he reached his desk.

"Right listen you two, Keith call Busion; Mel find Linkman I want everyone here in five minutes".

"What about Harrold Davis and his lot".

"Just Davis but not the others. Well Mel you said you found the lock up but couldn't break in, something about it's not in his name so you need a warrant".

"The man renting it is an Earnest Palmer he was one of the estate agents I met earlier. He works with the photo club secretary name of Lewis. Hamish Linkman has been checking the membership for me and has come across something odd. I don't know what yet he wouldn't say over the phone. As far as the warrant is concerned I did not want to compromise any evidence we may find in the workshop by breaking in knowing it was not Grant who officially rented it. What if Palmer is part of this, any dumb lawyer would have anything we found ruled as inadmissible if we broke in without due cause"?

"Your right of course it has happened before I know; the CPS would be a mite pissed if we screwed up. Good job".

"Sir DS Linkman and DI Davis are with Constable Busion they will be here directly". Said Keith Crane

Thanks Keith I need to put all this in order, a lot has happened and I want everyone to be up to date with where we stand, I feel we are moving in the right direction with the camera club especially now we have found the workshop. Let's hope there is some concrete evidence there. Ah, here come the others".

Jonny waved them over to the central table which was a little cluttered as always. Keith and Mel slid the offending overspill files along the table; leaving room for the officers to sit together at the opposite end.

"Everyone who matters is here I think. Inspector Davis I believe you are working on your own case at the moment but as you were involved at the start of this one I thought you might like to know where we are heading".

Harrold nodded a thankyou as they all sat at one end of the long table.

"First things first, we have almost ruled out Adrian Westfield and Gregory Small, I say almost because any case against either of them is weak there being no prints, DNA or any other evidence linking them to Grant's house. Neither men have alibis however and both have a motive of sorts. I think we should move away from them and be looking for new suspects. Our interview with Mrs. Grant and her son revealed they are still traumatised, not by Grant's death but from his unbelievable ill treatment of them over several years. Although they left him some time ago and she obtained a divorce, the wounds are still there even though, years have passed. They are obviously in denial and may always be so. However I 'm not sure if either of them capable of revenge they were much too afraid of him. One thing is certain Grant and maybe others have taken pictures of girls pertinent to our abduction enquiry and at least one of these youngsters continues to be missing. The pictures and we hope the workshop are our best leads so this is where we will concentrate our efforts. Now how are we doing with the warrant"?

Harrold had taken the information from Hamish filled out the appropriate forms and went upstairs to explain its urgency.

"It is with Superintendent Munroe, Jonny, he will send it to us as soon as he can, maybe this evening if he can find the right people that is. You say you have ruled out George's former wife, I've never met her so bow to your experience with her, but don't you think her motive is strong enough to make her a person of interest; family first eh"?

"Thanks Harrold he has some clout does the Super so we should have the warrant soon. Mrs. Grant you say, hmm....I'm fairly sure about her but you're right to suspect her involvement, I'll definitely keep her in mind. Now Sergeant Linkman you have something you found in the list what is it"?

"A few things stand out sir, first Earnest Palmer is a member of the photographic club and as he pays the rent for the studio unit we must assume he knew Grant very well; he has no record. The membership list is all male now and fairly complete, with addresses, phone numbers and emails. There were two ladies once but have let their membership lapse three years ago. Most of the current members seem genuine that is they have no police record however I found two with form; Liam Kerridge; bound over and a hundred pound fine for being drunk and disorderly two years ago, this when he lived in Bristol; next is Barry Finn, from Belfast, six months for aggravated assault, time served in Northern Ireland, released eighteen months ago. I've sent for both files. One other member worries me though, I think we should talk in private".

"We don't keep secrets here Sergeant let us know what you have".

"At least clear the room sir, keep it to this group only otherwise I must decline".

Jonny was not in the mood to muck about but saw Hamish was adamant so took his demand seriously, if it turns out to be bullshit he would ball him out later. He stood, rapped loudly on the table, with a paperweight he grabbed from a nearby desk, to gain everyone's attention and announced in a raised voice for all to hear.

"Listen up you lot I want everyone not involved here to leave the room until you are called to return, go and have a cup of tea we won't be long; last one out close the door please".

The background noise ceased for a moment to resume more loudly as officers closed down their computers and prepared to leave, there were a few moans on the way out concerning the CID division, none of it complimentary.

"Keith please check that no one has hung back to eves drop".

Keith crossed to the door and watched as the last of the uniforms had left the corridor and disappeared out of sight.

"All clear sir".

"One of the disadvantages of an open plan system. Right now Hamish what is it that requires all this secrecy".

"It's one of the names on the list sir it could be a problem".

"Come on man spit it out who is it"?

Hamish leaned forward followed by each officer doing the same in a semi-circular huddled together with heads almost touching; he spoke in a whisper.

"This particular club member is one of your own; Assistant Chief Constable Montague Brown".

"Oh Fuck! Not him".

The huddled group shrunk back as far and fast as they could without tipping over their chairs, trying to move way from what they had just heard. The silence was tangible following Harrold Davis expletive. It was a long moment before their involuntary held breaths released. Jonny put his hands up to calm the shocked faces, he didn't want this to generate into a free for all discussion. He looked directly at Hamish Linkman

"I'm glad you insisted we clear the room; this would have been all over the station in five minutes and on the internet five minutes after that. I know there will be speculation right now but please keep your thoughts unspoken; no one will say anything to anyone or even discuss it amongst yourselves do you hear, security is paramount. Police stations leak like a sieve when it comes to gossip so keep shtum, you never know who is listening. Leave this with me. Mel use this search warrant as soon as it arrives, do the search tonight no matter how late, take Hamish with you. Keith take over from Linkman, you have access to more secure computer levels than he does, identify the rest of the members, gather as much information as possible without there being even the remotest possibility any of them will detect what you are doing. Ensure the list is secure, remove any reference to 'you know who' that Hamish may have inadvertently left on the general system, work with Compton on this. Harrold you and I better meet together with the boss this has turned political".

"You don't know the half of it Jonny, this has thrown a spanner in the works for both of us".

Jonny and Harrold were in Toni's unoccupied office having phoned and texted her with no response. Jonny was pacing frustrated.

"Where the hell is she and why doesn't she answer"?

"She took some leave, personal things I heard".

"How come you know and I don't"?

"Grapevine news and you've been out".

"Bloody gossiping lot. Another thing Harrold what the hell did you mean when you said, it has buggered both of us and why yell out 'not him' on hearing the name"?

"I can't tell you that Jonny; shock I suppose it just came out. Let's wait till Toni is here".

"What are you investigating, has it anything to do with the case you're working on, whatever it is"?

"As I said, let's wait for Toni and you'll find out. Just leave it okay. Sit down and take it easy".

"Bloody secret service you; we could be here all night do you know how long she planned to be away"?

"I've no idea, could we not go to Munroe if you're that concerned"?

"Not yet Harrold; he's busy getting our warrant, I don't want that to stop just because the Acting Chief Constable has found himself involved with a dodgy lot of perverts. They'll close ranks, that lot always do. I'll bombard her with texts and messages first".

"For what it's worth I don't think Superintendent Munroe will do what you said".

"Maybe, but I have my doubts. We'll give it an hour; I'd prefer to run it by Webb first. Let's go and get a cuppa".

"Best idea you've had today".

"Shut up".

Chapter 21

Melanie and Hamish were on their way to Market Street with warrant in hand, the uniformed sergeant Mick Anvers was driving with Mel and Hamish in the back, a huge pair of bolt cutters lay across the front passenger seat, it's business end extending into the foot well. Mel had phoned Dave the watchman who was waiting even though it was well after six.

"Your Superintendent certainly knows how to pull strings, that warrant would have taken a whole week to process in Reading".

"Well connected, is our Munroe, Hamish, he knows when things are important and works with you not against".

"You are lucky working here, there was too much back biting where I came from, Reading's a lot better, but it still goes on there especially among the DIs ".

A chuckle came from Mick.

"You should see our lads when they get going, Traffic verses Patrol".

"I thought you all got on well"?

"Handbags at dawn, sometimes Mel, daft lot we are, nothing serious though".

Mick stopped at the gate where Dave and another man stepped out of their hut to greet them.

"Hello Sergeant, this is my oppo Alan Fellows".

"Hi, thanks for waiting Dave; the Sergeant here will open the unit. Here's the Warrant I want you to witness what we do please".

"Alan's the one officially on duty after six, shouldn't he be the one"?

"You're quite right; hello, Mr. Fellows I'm Detective Sergeant Melanie Frazer would you mind witnessing us open unit number seventeen".

"Sure thing, this is quite exciting, I've never had anything like this before, follow me".

Alan took the warrant, stood tall and marched towards the bank of units containing number seventeen. Dave hobbled behind, he didn't want to miss anything.

"Go on, tell her about the other night".

Said Dave to Alan whilst they watched Sergeant Mick go to work with his cutters.

"Why"?

"Why not it might be important, go on do it now".

"Alright; stop pushing.......excuse me Miss".

"Yes Alan what is it"?

"Dave thinks I should tell you about the other night".

"What about it"?

"Not last night but the night before last, a guy came to the site about ten o'clock, he walked in pushed the gate open a bit, he didn't see me, well I don't think he did cause he never said anything. Not many people come in this late so I kept an eye out like. Anyway he went to unit seventeen opened the small door and went in; he had both keys so I didn't think anything of it. He came out ten minutes later with a bag, one of those soft holdalls, pushed through the gap and shut the gate behind him and was gone".

"No car"?

"Come to think of it I don't think so; odd how he got here then. He could have parked up the road I suppose I didn't hear anything though".

"Did you recognise him".

"It wasn't the usual chap from seventeen, you showed Dave a picture of him; dead; he said, is that right? Anyway this one was alive for sure and yes I think I've seen him before".

"Thanks for that Alan, any information is helpful no matter how trivial it may seem at the time".

A loud crack told them Mick had finally cut the padlock free from the clasp placed the bits in a bag and returned to the car to wait. These detective could be a long time and he didn't fancy standing around outside. Alan stepped forward with the mortice key and opened the small door".

"Please step back now".

Demanded Hamish having donned gloves and shoe covers as he stepped through the door.

"Light switch should be on your right sir".

Volunteered Dave. Hamish ran his hand along the wall to find a cluster of switches. He carefully flicked them all. The fluorescent fittings spluttered into life one at a time till all six had flooded the area with white light. Melanie now suitably gloved and booted step over the threshold into the lighted area. Two long tables dominated the central area, one had a large projection unit for producing enlargements, the other heavy duty rectangular dishes of varying sizes, she presumed for development processes. Over each table were two red lights also glowing in their dish-like shades but their glow was overpowered by the intensity of the long white tubes. Several wires were strung between the tables with rows of bulldog clips hanging from each. At one end was a large plastic container half filled with what appeared to be water. The walls on either side had metal rack shelving with an assortment of cardboard boxes; some items were sticking out, thermometers tongs and tools used in developing and printing. A small and large guillotine, sheets of plain white plastic and many sizes of photographic paper in protective envelopes filled one rack. Bottles of chemicals lined the rack on the other side.

"This will take forever to go through we'd better have a forensic team over here".

Hamish ignored the photographic equipment and moved to the back of the unit where a multi-tiered desk had the space for a computer, a rectangular dust fringed shape showed where it had

172

recently stood. The power lead, and remote keyboard left behind told him it was a stand-alone Apple. There was no sign of a blue tooth mouse, perhaps it was hard wired. An A3 photo printer rested on the upper shelf, which was his target.

"No sign of any cameras in the open, plenty of cupboards though so could be in one of them. The PCs gone I'm afraid but whoever took it left the keyboard and printer".

"Not much good then" Said Mel.

"I don't know, whoever took it was maybe unaware the memory in the printer will have held a copy of at least the last file printed. This looks to be a sophisticated machine with a processor and firmware of its own; not relying on drivers from the main computer. With luck it'll hold a history of many more than just one image; I bet Compton will be able to extract whatever it may contain".

"Nothing else seems to be staring us in the face as being of immediate use, we will leave it to SOCO to do a thorough search. Leave everything else just bring the printer, I don't think we have a bag big enough, I'll cut up some smaller ones to wrap it before we transfer it to the car. Is it heavy by the way"?

"Probably but I'm sure I can manage, bring the car down here though I don't want to lug it all the way to the gate, when you arrive ask Mick to cut the other padlock, Soco will want it open sometime or other and it will save him having to come back ".

Hamish wrapped the printer in the opened out bags using tape to secure them. It was lighter than he expected so easily transferred it carefully to the back of the car, whilst Mick cut through the second padlock.

"Hamish, you go back with Mick; take the printer to Compton I'll wait here till SOCO arrives. Have you remembered the power lead"?

"Yes it's in the wrappings, I'll dust it for prints before Compton's IT boys have a go at it. How will you find your way back"?

"You can come and collect me if you like".

"Hm, you want a personal taxi service do you"?

"Beats walking".

"Okay call me when you're ready".

Chapter 22

Hamish and Compton sat the printer on a desk next to one of her computer terminals, they had called Scientific Services to come and take prints and any other samples they may find. The two detectives stood back eager to delve into the machines memory whilst the young science officer took photographs, thoroughly examined the unit finding several prints and some possible skin samples from the print cartridge securing clips.

"Finished now Constable Busion all done, I'll put the prints through a search and place the results to the general file, the DNA if there is any, will take a few days. You'll hear a 'ping' when those results are ready".

Constable Compton Busion knew the results were likely to be sensitive so decided to prevent the information being available on the general police data banks.

"Thanks, Dennis, I want you to send the processed prints direct to my email, I will do the search myself also when the DNA results come back I'll send someone over to collect them. Nothing is to go on general release".

"Okay, what's so secret, you can tell me"?

Hamish Linkman saw a problem, nosey SOCO's always wanting to second guess the detectives.

"You don't know me Dennis, however if I find out you have discussed this with anyone, you will see a side of me you will not like. The lives of children may depend on the results found here being kept strictly to those who need to know, you are not in that group, so mouth shut and mind on something else, you understand"?

"Oh dear me. Sergeant, sorry I didn't mean anything".

"Good lad now go and do your job".

Dennis was gone far quicker than he arrived.

"You are a scary son of a bitch, Hamish Linkman, Dennis is alright really; still all the scientific guys are naturally curious so I suppose you are right to ensure he keeps this under wraps".

Hamish had not seen Compton at work before and was as surprised as everyone when they first see her in action. She turned away from Hamish and focussed her attention to the printer; attaching the power lead and inserted a connecting cable to one of three USB sockets. She began to talk to the machine as if it was alive.

"Let's get down to it my friend what are you hiding in that little old silicon brain of yours"?

Her screen came alive with streams of letters and numbers that meant nothing to Hamish but seemed to please Compton. A few moments later she attacked her keyboard with a gusto and speed he had never thought possible.

"Now we have you come to mummy. Wheeee".

A few seconds later the screen filled with something Hamish recognised. A page of file names with their type and size in organised columns with the date last opened.

"Let's see what you have here".

"I can see some JPEG and .docx files Compton are we able to view them"?

"Oh you're still here. Sorry Hamish of course you are, I get carried away sometimes. What shall we look at first; the latest picture file, I suggest"?

Hamish leaned forward as Compton called up the file named DW9. There it was one of the images of Dawn similar if not the same as those recovered from Grant's home. Compton scanned down the list DW8, DW7 and so on to DW1 all images of Dawn Westcott.

"Let's try KS if you can find one" said Hamish.

Compton scanned down the page to the last JPEG file. There were no files with the name KS.

"The limit of data here is about one month Hamish, Karen was abducted before then wasn't she"?

"Yes well before, lets look at one from as far back as you can".

"Here we have files HJ17 going down to HJ4 which is the earliest".

HJ17 was a full body shot of the back of a female standing naked apart from a pair of trainers on her feet, the hair was short and dark, her thin muscular frame made her appear youngish, difficult to tell with no facial features. HJ16 was of the same girl, for girl it was, as the full frontal image revealed her face. They jumped to HJ4 to show pictures taken in a similar fashion to Dawn's found on George Grant's laptop, long range telephoto head shot. Hamish scanned through the page one at a time.

"Let's try one in the middle, look that one there KD18".

The file opened both looked, not shocked as they had both seen worse but Hamish recognised the picture.

"Bloody hell turn it off its Karen Small".

Karen was naked sitting on a carver dining chair, her wrists bound to its arms; her ankles were tied back tightly to the rear legs of the chair exposing her front for all to see. Her eyes were heavily made up with dark lipstick almost black emphasising the white of her cheeks. Her eyes seemed blank as if she were blind, the whole face expressionless. Compton had not turned it off as Hamish demanded instead she zoomed in on her face and focussed on the eyes.

"Hamish look at the size of her pupils, she is heavily drugged I would say, and the date this was processed only just about two weeks ago".

A thought ran across Compton's mind 'If they kept her this long she could still be alive, not likely, the date's when it was printed not when the picture was taken, that will have been earlier'.

177

"Can we see if there is a text file with the same name or date".

"No, I can't do a file name search as they are unnamed just consecutive numbers. If we had the original computer the names would be there, the text files were randomly sent unattached to the image files. The printer doesn't need them to print images; the fact they are there at all is due to a crap bit of software design. There is no way of knowing to which images they were attached. There are two with the same date though".

She pulled one file into her pages ap. It streamed in as pure text in lower case with no spaces or punctuation making it almost impossible to read but certain words did stick out. It seemed to be a list of names all mixed together. She tried another file at random with a similar result,

"This is meaningless Hamish I will need to do a lot of work on these and probably all of them, if they are to make sense. I also have an idea where we may be able to go back further in time and retrieve more files; leave it with me I'll call you".

Chapter 23

Toni opened her office door, her two Inspectors turned in surprise and both stood at the same time.

"Thank God you're back".

"Do you need me that much Jonny"?

"No. Sorry Ma'am, I mean yes I do….err".

"Is that a declaration of love I'm hearing"?

Harrold was laughing at Jonny's embarrassment.

"This is serious Ma'am".

"I know it must be Detective Musgrove, just trying to lighten the atmosphere. A lock out in the squad room and two DIs taking up residence in my office tells me some crap is about to descended on the head of Toni Webb. Come on out with it".

"A lot has happened whilst you were out Ma'am, I'll go through it in detail after, but the gist is this; in looking for George Grant's murderer we have found what appears to be one or more men abducting girls and using them for dubious photoshoots. Dawn was an intended target, Karen another still missing and we suspect others as yet unidentified. Our big problem is this, the Assistant Chief Constable is a member of the photo club, therefor could be part of this group. He may be innocent and have nothing to do with what is going on, but I am obliged to include him in our investigation as much as any of the others".

"Hold it there Jonny. Harrold have you told him what you are working on"?

"No Ma'am, I haven't but I think we should don't you"?

"It seem impossible not to in light of where this might lead. Jonny what I am about to tell you goes no further not even to your team, well not yet anyway".

"ACC Montague Brown is a person of interest in connection with the illegal abduction and organ transplant case of two years ago, I'm sure you remember that Jonny. We have been asked by Smith of Police Conduct to quietly look into a particular individual namely Jake Snell who may try and contact our ACC. We strongly suspect he was a leading figure within the organisation controlling the two corrupt officers Vale and Branch who were part of this elaborate scheme".

"Bloody hell Jake Snell, I remember he was Grimes lackey wasn't he, I thought he was long gone overseas somewhere".

Toni continued.

"He's back in the UK now and looking for money he has hidden here. We are trying to stop him getting at his stash. We think he may contact Brown to try and extort some money from him. This is Harrold's job. He will give you the details later. I was hoping to keep this very discreet but too many people know about it now, we will be lucky if it doesn't leak".

"None of my team will say anything".

"I know Jonny not deliberately anyway, but during any investigating we do leave a trail, you know that from the past. We have plugged the holes and removed the bad officers, but only the ones we know about. It's the ones we don't, who will trip us up. That is only part of the problem. Brown is great friends with the Met Commander Newton Blakewood".

"Are you saying he's involved"?

"It is believed so by some at Serious Crime and our old friend Vernon Smith is certain he is bent. There is no hard evidence and anyone who would provide even the smallest negative information about either of them is either too scared or has been eliminated. If they find Snell before we do he will disappear. We have tried both Vance and Branch with offers of better conditions and even open prison but they won't budge, I don't blame them either if they say anything nowhere will be safe and they know it".

"A Commander and an Assistant Chief Constable, two powerful men what chance do we have"?

Toni had no confidence in the outcome because she knew Jonny was right in his reaction, however she endeavoured to instil some enthusiasm in her two detectives.

"If they are bent, and I am sure they are, the evidence will be out there somewhere and when we find it their power will count for nothing. There is always someone more powerful who will be glad to see them gone, we have allies in that camp, so go and find it. Harrold fill in Jonny with the details concerning Snell, set a plan of action, keep the investigations separate for now at least until a concrete link is established".

Harrold had an idea, he thought significant in establishing the link between Brown and Grant.

"This is how I see it Ma'am; abduction of children and murder was what Jake Snell was involved in, on the orders of the two corrupt officers Vine and Branch now in prison. We believe they were in their turn controlled by Brown and Blakewood. We have Grant and likely other persons abducting children, albeit older and for a different purpose; with Brown possibly amongst them; is that not link enough"?

"You may well be right but until Brown is definitely found to be involved with Snell and has more than an innocent reason to be a member of this photographic club, we will not rock the boat okay. Jonny, you will continue the murder enquiry openly but ignore Brown's possible involvement, proceed as if he is innocent. Harrold you will discreetly continue with your task as instructed, find Jake Snell; let me deal with Montague Brown. Jonny if you find Brown has something to hide keep it to just you and me, we may be able to use it to our advantage in tracking down Jake and a possible lever into Blakewood, however your main task is to find George Grant's killer. As the cat is now out of the bag, only partway at the moment let's hope it stays that way. Neither of you take your eye off the ball, find Jake and find the killer anything else is a bonus. Remember no phone calls or texts and certainly no computer data, with the name of Brown or

Blakewood anywhere near; tread very carefully. Off you go, let me have a few hours to deal with the politics".

Now was the time she had to rely on her instincts about Walter Munroe, she trusted him but there was this niggling doubt that politics would force him into a corner. She would not tell him everything but enough to achieve the desired outcome.

"Ah Toni come in, I hope this is just a friendly visit to tell me all is solved or soon will be".

"Not quite sir, I do have a problem where I think you would be the best one to handle it".

"Hm.. sounds ominous".

"It's not that bad but it could get out of hand if not dealt with quietly".

"Go on. What's up"?

"This murder of George Grant has taken a turn in a new direction and I think we are close to identifying his killer".

"One of the girls father's is it"?

"That's what I thought, but no they have been cleared, or at least reduced to persons of interest rather than suspects, no real strong motive and no match to our forensic evidence".

"So who is next in line"?

"You know we found pictures of our victims at his house, well it turns out he is a member of a photo club, not unusual in itself but no sign of any cameras or equipment at his house. To cut a long story short we found his studio workshop, full of equipment and although his digital camera is missing and his computer also, we have obtained photographic evidence from his printer. Pictures of girls forced to pose in dubious positions slightly pornographic, more sadistic I would say. We think one of his club colleagues is the murderer, knowing Grant had been caught trying to abduct young Dawn whoever killed him was trying to cover up their own involvement; finger-prints and DNA will almost certainly identify the suspect".

"So what's the problem, you seem to be almost there".

"You are not going to like this sir but the ACC is a member of the club".

"Monty is in the photograph club"?

"I'm afraid so".

"Blow me this is a problem what do you want me to do"?

"I can't appear to be anything but straight, I have to treat every member of the club the same, finger-prints DNA computer and camera equipment has to be checked. I have to include the ACC in this or if it comes out later that he was dealt with differently it will cause an almighty furore".

"You are right Toni, we must be seen to act fairly, his prints and DNA are on file we can check those discreetly and record the fact on the file do you want to interview him"?

"No of course not, I just need to eliminate him as quickly as possible. I need his personal computer or laptop or both if he has them, oh and any cameras he may have. He will have them back the same day they just need to have been in our possession and logged as having been checked you know for proprieties sake. Do you think you could do that sir, a phone call maybe, I could send someone to collect them"?

"No Toni leave it with me I will go see him myself to explain. Who else knows about this"?

"Just my team Ma'am and one or two others. I have sworn them all to secrecy, they will be okay. The problem will come when we know who did it and make an arrest, the lawyers will find out soon enough, then we and the ACC will need to be prepared".

"Not how I expected to spend my day but I will try and nip this in the bud, I'll call you later".

Toni left the office feeling guilty at having kept him in the dark regarding the expected outcome. Munroe couldn't fail to have wondered if Monty Brown was involved, the case of two years ago must also have given him pause but he said nothing.

Toni didn't know how much he had been told by Smith either. She wondered what will transpire.

Back in her office all was quiet, the pile of paper in her in-tray ignored she opened her phone.

"Hello Nathan, is it too late for a lift home and what about that drink"?

"I can't let you walk can I? I'll be there in fifteen minutes".

"Great, meet me by the back steps, the Shoes will still be open, bye".

Chapter 24

'Good God, Monty Brown, what have you been up to'? A silent question in the mind of Superintendent Walter Munroe on hearing from Toni Webb what had been found in the membership list of the photographic club and at the workshop of George Grant. He had little choice but to face his senior officer with the request for him to hand over his computers and cameras. He would use the standard cliché of all police, 'just routine the need to eliminate him etcetera'. It would sound lame but he hoped Monty would react sensibly and understand the significance of what would happen if he refused to cooperate. He was a belligerent self-important bastard most times but Walter could not believe he was really involved with child abduction and cruelty but you could never really know. He remembered Toni hinted he may have been involved with that corruption business of two years ago. He reluctantly picked up the phone.

"Hello sir, I need to see you it's a very urgent matter.....I understand but it really can't wait that long........no sir I cannot discuss it over the phone..........its personal.....no not personal for me but for you.......that's what I said......I'll explain when I see you.......yes only you can deal with this and my sincere advice is it must be done now.........I will come to your house......more discreet......yes this evening......good in one hour then, thankyou sir".

Within minutes of the call Montague Brown rapidly climbed the stairs to his study on the first floor. The death of George Grant had been a shock when he saw the monthly report on cases pending; he should have anticipated this visit. He unlocked the door and made a beeline for his laptop. He sat wondering if what he feared was really what Walter Munroe wanted or was it nothing to do with Grant. His insistence on seeing him about a personal matter worried him; the guilty feeling about his involvement with Palmer and the club made him cautious, he decided to be on the safe side and clear his laptop of anything incriminating. He selected the files related to the HW Photo Club deleted them en masse. He went to his photoshop application and deleted all files associated with that too. Next his photo albums were deleted if they contained anything he felt remotely connected him to the club. He kept a few scenic pictures and lots of family photos a few letters to the club and some advertising material: It would seem odd as a club member if there was nothing. He scanned everywhere on his laptop for anything that might raise a doubt. When he had finished he selected the trash symbol and emptied it. He again scanned through a third time sure that every doubtful file had gone. He felt safe now, he was glad he never did his own developing or printing, keeping it all on this one machine. He suddenly remembered his camera, and took if from the desk drawer, he looked at the current batch of pictures but was sure there was nothing on there to worry him, he had not used it for quite a long time; it was clean just family stuff. The last visit to the club had been a show by one of the genuine members, architecture he seemed to remember. He had kept that block of pictures which would back up his innocent association. His only visit to Market Street was way back three months ago. He'd not taken pictures there only watched, leaving early. Palmer later gave him a memory stick with the pictures; he had destroyed the device as soon as he had uploaded the pictures, but these were all gone now.

Monty returned to his lounge mixed a large scotch and soda, not much soda, a little ice. He did not flap easily but the thought of what would have happened if they had just arrived and taken his laptop made him break out in a sweat. He drank his whiskey and poured another, feeling better by the minute. The doorbell rang.

"Get that will you".

He called to his wife who was in the kitchen; obediently she stopped what she was doing and went to answer the front door. She shouted from the threshold.

"It's Walter Munroe" .

She opened the door wide.

"Come in Superintendent Munroe, he's in the lounge".

Walter followed Mrs. Brown in silence along the hall, he turned into the lounge, she continued to the kitchen. Montague Brown stood as Walter moved into the room, his hand outstretched. Walter took it and felt cold fingers with a clammy palm. He resisted the urge to wipe dry his now dampened hand.

"Well, well, Walter, what is all this secretive stuff about. A scotch or something else eh"?

"No thanks Monty I'm driving".

"Of course. Well what do you need from me, what is this personal stuff"?

"I'll come straight to it then. I understand you are a member of the Hartley Wintney Photo Club"?

"Yes, have been for a number of years why"?

"I am sorry to say one of the members has been murdered".

"Good lord who"?

"A George Grant sir".

"Oh dear the postman, I saw the report but it didn't register who it might be, I know him...knew him...I should say...he was a good man taught us quite a lot at our meetings. Murdered you say. Now I can see why you are here".

"We believe one of the members is the killer, requiring us to interview all those in the club".

"And that means me too of course".

"Not really sir, unless you can shed some light; we must however be seen not to show favouritism by excluding you from the usual processes".

"I understand. I can't help much I haven't been there for several weeks".

We need your prints and DNA; I'd like your permission to use those we have on file".

"No problem, anything else"?

"Do you have a computer sir"?

There it was, the expected request; thank goodness he managed to ditch everything. Do they know about the clandestine under current outside the normal membership? If they don't now they soon will.

"One at Central of course but that is only for work. My personal laptop is in the office upstairs, that's all, I don't use it much. Do you need to take it"?

"Yes sir I'm afraid I do, just a quick look to say we have done so. You know what will happen if we miss anything and it gets out especially the press. When it goes to trial it will be impossible and counter productive to hide your membership. If we can show we have treated you the same as all the witnesses there will be no comeback. We must do everything by the book and out in the open to protect you".

"Quite right too, I'll go and fetch the laptop".

"I'll come with you sir if you don't mind".

"Oh of course, by the book; yes indeed".

They came down to the lounge having collected the laptop and his camera. Munroe felt uncomfortable not knowing whether to call him by his name or with just a sir, he ended up doing both.

"Sure you won't have a small one Walter"?

"No not this time thanks Monty, I'll be getting along. Someone will bring these back to you tomorrow; one more thing sir would you make a statement, you know about your membership and any interaction between you and Grant, mail it to me I will add my notes, list it as our interview so as to comply. Sorry you have to deal with this just because of a hobby eh; goodbye Monty".

"Farewell Walter thanks for your discretion".

Superintendent Walter Munroe drove to Basingstoke incredulous for Monty to have acted so out of character; cooperative was not how he expected to find him. Alarm bells were ringing, this was going to grow nasty.

How did he find himself in this situation; Monty really didn't need to ask that question he already knew. Ambition to start with, then greed and finally indulgence, if only he could put the clock back. As a young copper he was tolerant and fair, he had a good wife whom he loved and he knew loved him. It all started to change when he met Vale and Branch, they were senior detectives and he just a constable; under their influence he rose to sergeant and Inspector rather quicker than normal. They were old school bending the rules to achieve results; at first he just closed his eyes to their faults, unaware he was becoming more like them, eventually doing their bidding without question. When he moved from London to Hampshire he took their influence with him, adopted a hard line whereas before he would be understanding, he became demanding of his junior officers at the same time sucking up to his superiors. His wife saw the changes in him creep insidiously into their home. He treated her more like a servant than a wife. Love died; fear replaced harmony. He secretly maintained contact with Vale where money changed hands when certain factions of the underworld were given leave to continue their activities undisturbed. His wealth grew in line with his ambition; chief superintendent and Assistant Chief Constable; Chief Constable his target. His ties to Vale continued secretly, until Vale and Branch were put away. He was lucky to avoid being swept up in the aftermath of their activities, Newton Blakewood being his salvation there. His innocent hobby photography was a relaxing one he enjoyed for many years, the meetings at club he belonged to in the next village, were a pleasure to which he looked forward. He came to know most members and after some time saw him being invited

189

to a special session by one of them, Earnest Palmer. It started innocently enough when the model just posed seductively but watching them take pictures of the girl in more extreme poses excited him even though he knew it was not quite right. His marriage had disintegrated to where the only physical contact with his wife was when he slapped her for some minor domestic failure. These pictures seemed to fill a gap somehow. The pictures Palmer gave him were violent in their nature, and the girl's obvious distress excited and appalled him at the same time. He resolved to no longer involve himself with Palmer and the others and had not been there since. He even decided to leave the club altogether. All the evidence was gone now; Munroe would ensure his involvement would be minimised sending his laptop and camera back tomorrow. Four whiskeys later Monty was sad he had missed out on a normal life, but bolstered by the power and wealth his corrupt actions had generated; he fell asleep in his chair feeling smug and safe.

Chapter 25

Harrold Davis was not going to let Jonny's investigation distract him from what he intended, he'd wasted enough time already. He picked up the phone and selected his favourite number.

"Compton, it's Harrold, are you free to start?....Okay in an hour....I will. See you then".

Jake had acquired a passport in a new name; Leonard Bartram genuine to all who saw it because it was not a straight forgery but issued by the passport office. The fact that it was fake, was only in the image; the photograph on the document was of Jake but the name wasn't. The application had genuine documents to support its issue along with Jake's attested photo. Somewhere there was a real Mr. Leonard Bartram whose identity had been stolen or more likely bought. Harrold would find the real Bartram. The new name of Jeremy Shore could be significant; the same initials as his given name; were the J and S necessary for some reason, why chose that name? He knew criminal methods for hiding their funds inside out; four years in the Fraud Squad had taught him that. Find his money find the man. J S and L Bartram would unlock the money he just had to beat Jake to it. He gathered his files and took the stairs to the floor below.

"Not quite ready Harrold; take a seat I won't be long".

"At last, I'm finished".

Said Compton, having transferred the updated password changes of each of the officers to her central security program. This weekly routine to safeguard files had come about since a serious breach where information had been accessed by an outsider a few years earlier.

They sat side by side, each at a terminal which could connect to almost anywhere they wanted; the search was about to begin.

"You now have my undivided attention Harrold, phones off, door closed. It all started in Camberwell so I'll go back there, electoral register to start with. Leonard Bartram first see if he is on the role and Jeremy Shore too while I'm about it. What about the passports"?

"I've already covered that, the addresses given were for different numbers in the same apartment block in Camberwell Road. Both conveniently unoccupied at the time the passports were issued. Jake had gone to a lot of trouble to cover his escape even to registering his false names onto the electoral register at the Camberwell road addresses; the passports were sent there by post so he obviously had access. Facial recognition was not operating at the passport office back then so it wasn't picked up that the two applications were for the same person. The people living there now have no connection to Snell or any of the others. The block used to be owned by a company called West London Estates; sold off over a year ago to a Camberwell housing association, which was partly funded by the local Council. I suspect West London Estates was being 'protected' by Grimes and Snell in some way. I might follow the Estates company further if we achieve nothing with today's search".

"Seems it'll not be so easy Harrold too long ago; I suggest for now you look for safety deposit companies and secure storage facilities in the same area; I can't see his money being in a bank account".

The two investigators began with high hopes of a quick result. Twenty minutes passed without speaking when Harrold looked across to Compton with an enquiring frown.

"I'm getting nowhere, there's only one safety deposit facility in Camberwell with Metron Bank, I can't extract any information from them about their depositors. They have only been open for a year so I think they are out of the picture. The only other storage is a short term furniture facility owned by Pickford's Removals; they have no record of a Bartram or Shore. I'll expand into the surrounding districts, what about you"?

"Nothing in Camberwell, but I've a hit in Peckham and another in New Cross. Both surnames Bartram, first name Leonard and the other Larry, I'm in the process of following them up".

"Where is this Leonard living"?

"38, Culver Street New Cross".

"I'll switch to that area, see what safety deposits are available near there".

"How about you go visit Culver Street"?

"I will, but I want more ammunition before I do".

"Don't you mean information"?

"In our game information is ammunition".

Compton knew the truth of that statement so smiled inclining her head in agreement.

"Another half an hour then we break for a cuppa, okay Harrold"?

There was no need to answer; the two turned back to their respective screens.

The time for tea had not arrived when Compton exclaimed.

"Bingo! We have him".

Harrold's glum face lit up in anticipation.

"What"?

"They lived next door in Camberwell and were at school together as kids. Jake and Lenny went to Old Kent Road Primary, way back. Jake moved up to Holt Street Comprehensive but Lenny went to a specialist school for disabled children. He had a genetic heart condition which only showed up when he reached ten years old; it grew progressively worse before secondary school. He had several operations which saved his life but he ended up a paraplegic. Spends his life in a wheelchair. This has to be how Jake obtained the passport. I wonder if Lenny knew"?

"Go back to his bank records about the time Jake escaped see if any money changed hands".

The searched continued.

"Harrold look, it's all here, Bartram's credit card was used to book a ferry; it doesn't say where from. A day later a thousand pounds cash was paid into the same account".

"He must have gone by car or van if he left on a ferry, how much was the fare"?

"Just shy of nine hundred pounds a booking website so no details of the ferry company. I could probably go deeper and find out".

"Not necessary we can guess; it doesn't matter anyway. Unlikely Dover then; a longer trip, Portsmouth to Spain perhaps".

"No it doesn't cost that much one way, more likely from a northern port to Scandinavia, much less obvious for us to have looked there too. I think Jake Snell is a clever fellow".

"Whatever, we have the right Leonard Bartram for sure, how long has he lived in New Cross".

"Ten years at Culver Street, it's a Council House".

"Does he own a car"?

"Hold on I'll see. No...wait yes he did two years ago a van was registered but has been marked as scrapped, soon after Jake dissapeared. He doesn't have a drivers licence".

"What about insurance on the van".

Compton did a quick search.

"Nothing here, Jake could have taken out a policy at another address and in another name, there are too many insurance companies, it will take ages to cover them all. The van was taxed and tested at the time".

"I'll search around New Cross for a safety box company whilst you go for your tea. If I have nothing by the time you come back I'll hand over to you. I'm going to see our Mr Bartram at Culver Street, see what he has to say for himself".

"Bit of a drive into London".

"I know but we are closing in, we can't delay or Snell will have come and gone; it wouldn't surprise me if he hasn't already done so".

"I hope not, shall I bring you back a cup of something"?

No thanks Compy, I'm fine, soon as you're back I'll be off".

Harrold picked up the phone, he didn't want to use his own car it would be too slow and he wanted June to drive.

"June I need a patrol car we're going to London meet me outside in about ten minutes".

Chapter 26

June Owens was driving whilst Harrold assembled his notes and thoughts ready for a face to face with Lenny Bartram. His search for deposit companies had produced two results. Marshalls Depository Ltd. had a record of Jake Snell having rented a box, last used three days before he left for pastures new. The rental had been cancelled at the same time so the lady on the phone was happy to release the details. She refused to release information about current depositors without a court order. He thought maybe another box in the name of Shore was possible but she would not confirm he was a customer. He would follow that up when he had finished with Culver Street.

The second deposit company was Safe Store First a small storage unit who were more willing to talk but did not trust answering questions over the phone. This self-store site was located on an industrial estate on the borders of Peckham and New Cross, it seemed promising as it was possible to rent a small lock-up about quarter the size of a single garage. He had not delved further as Marshalls were the most likely and Compton had returned by then and he did not want to delay. He would visit that site too when he had finished with Bartram.

The M3 section was fairly quick, and as they were in a fully emblazoned police car they were able to take advantage of the traffic moving out of their way on the slower M25; once onto the south circular heading to their final destination they settled to the inevitable slow pace, London traffic dictates. Culver Street was typical of specialised council property. Single story identical semi-detached units, with plain rendered frontages, a shallow tiled roof and plastic double glazed windows; the space between the pavement and the door of about three yards was hardly enough to be called a garden; reminiscent of the prefabs constructed after the war but not quite as large. The front door of number 38 was wider than standard, obviously made to accommodate a wheelchair. They parked right outside; there were no other cars as the double yellow lines were all along one side of this narrow street, Harrold remembered of old, how it was near impossible to keep a parking space close to home in the suburbs; he was glad he had moved out to Hampshire.

Harrold and June were at the front door together, June rang the bell Harrold stood back. A few minutes passed with no answer, June was about to knock when the lock rattled, the door opening wide to reveal a middle aged man in a wheelchair.

"Yes, are you from the clinic I've not seen you before"?

"No sir we are the police I am Detective Constable Owens and this is Detective Inspector Davis, are you Leonard Bartram"?

"Ah I should have guessed now I can see the car. Yes that's me I'm Lenny Bartram. I thought you had come for my physio session, my usual bloke is sick, he phoned to say he was sending someone else. Anyway what do you want"?

"May we come in sir we have some questions concerning an old friend of yours Jacob Snell"?

"Yes okay, I'll have to back up, give us a sec. Jake eh? What's he been up to I thought he's in France"?

Lenny backed his wheelchair down the hall and turned into the living room on the right. He looked round at June as she entered.

"Close the front door for me love will you please".

June obliged and they followed him into the room.

"Sit down anywhere you like; I get cheesed off looking up at people all the time; what can I do for you. By the way if you want a cup of tea or anything you'll have to make it yourself my helper doesn't come in for a couple of hours"?

"We'll miss the tea for now; when did you last see Jacob"?

"I'm buggered if I can remember near a couple of years ago I think maybe a bit less".

"Hasn't he phoned you recently either"?

"No he couldn't have; I've got a different phone since he went; a new number he wouldn't know it".

"When he left he used a passport in your name with his photo, were you aware of that"?

"The cheeky bugger, no I didn't but I'm not surprised; we look alike you know people thought we were brothers. I've never had a passport, no need really I'm not going anywhere".

"So you didn't give him your birth certificate and ask your doctor to sign the photo he used"?

"Put it like this we were close, he was a good mate; I was very sick for a while; before he left he helped me here a lot; lived in a bit did everything for me to so he had access to all my stuff. Whatever he did, I didn't know about, I wouldn't have cared at the time neither; what was mine was his too".

"Did you give him your bank card"?

"Of course; he bought all my food and anything we needed, he could spend what he liked, he put in more money than he took out anyway. He gave it back when he left; I still have it".

"Does he pay anything into your account now"?

"Not since before like; he gave me a couple of hundred in cash the day he went that's all. I get by alright you know I receive benefits and a disability allowance".

"I see you bought a van number XRT825T, was that so you could go out with your wheelchair"?

"That wasn't mine I can't drive; don't want to either. The van was Jakes, he kept it here a while; took it when he left".

"Why did he leave the Country in secret"?

"I thought you of all people would know that; Jakes boss, a copper named Branch, had been rumbled and Branch's boss was after Jake, he owed him money I think or knew too much; would've nicked him or done him in more like if he'd caught up with him".

"Who was Branches boss, was it another policeman name of Vale"?

"Nah, Vale was just a front, he was caught too I heard; it was someone bigger a real high up, I don't know who, Jake never told me, said I'd be safer if I didn't know".

Harrold liked the loyalty this man was showing to his friend, even thought the friend was a thorough villain. He also was pleased with the apparent honest answers he had been given. He decided to take a chance with his next few questions.

"If I tell you Jake is back in England would that surprise you"?

"If those other guys are still around yes it would, he was dead scared of them, and the likes of you coming here tells me they probably are".

"Why did you say 'they' when you only just told us Branch had one boss"?

"I assumed there was more than one because Jake said 'they' were after him and he had to go".

"Indeed 'they' still are and I'm the one trying to stop them, I need to find Jake before they do or he will be killed for sure".

"Says you; how do I know you aren't working for these big wig bent coppers"?

"You don't, but if I were, why would I tell you about Jake being back here. It's obvious you didn't know what's going on and have been answering my questions straight enough. I was hoping we could trust each other".

"I've never trusted a copper before and I'm sure not going to start now".

"Alright then how's about a little bit of you helping me with some other things: still to do with Jake and his old boss but nothing related to his whereabouts; not that I think you know where he is, I don't".

"Okay lets see where you go, but before we start would the lady constable make a cup of tea I'm gasping, I expect you are too"?

June stood and moved towards where she thought the kitchen might be. She liked Lenny and his apparent open if not too honest way, you didn't notice his disability from his manner, refreshing somehow. The tea served and the first mouthful downed, Lenny looked at Harrold.

"That's better now fire away".

"Did Jake leave anything with you"?

"Like what"?

"A letter, a packet, a contact address, a telephone number, anything really".

"Apart from the cash, no I don't think so; he didn't give me anything in particular. There was a box he kept in the spare room from when he stayed, he never took it with him when he left. You know what, I bet it's still there. Young lady if you go to the back bedroom you'll find it bottom drawer bedside cabinet an old oxo tin".

June up and left to retrieve the box wondering what an oxo tin was.

"No one's slept there in years apart from Jake, I just use it to store my medical stuff".

The tin arrived and was placed on the coffee table.

"Do you mind if we look inside Lenny"?

"Help yourself".

June opened the lid and tipped the contents on the table. A small signet ring looked like gold. Some receipts for petrol with one from a Jeweller in New Cross for watch repairs, no watch though. A well used comb, a small fruit knife and an empty key ring with a logo from a Casino in London.

"Not much here, I do remember the ring though it belonged to his mum".

"What about the watch receipt and the key ring"?

"No idea about the watch, the key ring is from a club up west, Jake went there a few times, he wasn't very lucky though he never won anything. He said it was a rip off; he stopped going".

"Do you mind if I keep this. If it turns out to mean nothing I will return it"?

"I suppose but not the ring eh, I think I would like to keep that, just in case, yes just in case".

"That will be fine. I don't think there is anything more except tell me if he does turn up or calls you; I don't expect you will but please tell him who I am and that I am after the bigger fish. You can give him this number and tell him we may be able to come to some arrangement".

Harrold gave Lenny his card with his personal mobile written on the back. Lenny pocketed the card without looking at it. June took the empty cups back to the kitchen. Lenny called after her.

"There's no need to wash them up love, Mandy will be here soon to cook my dinner, she'll do that".

"We'll be going now but I may be back later. Look after yourself Lenny you have been a great help".

Lenny saluted from the doorway as the two police officers walked towards their car. He looked both ways for signs of his physiotherapist, no joy. 'Never mind he'll be here soon' he thought.

"Right June, Marshalls on Duke Street first".

Sat Nav showed it was only a mile up the road, June was on it straight away. Marshalls appeared to be a simple shop front on the outside; a dark wire-glass window with the name in gold paint discreetly written behind the glass hinted at the somewhat different interior. Harrold could see a wind-down metal shield built in above the frontage. The entry door had no handle or any visible means of entry. A single bell push with a camera and speaker grill built into the wall were the obvious way to gain attention. Harrold having left June in the car, stood in front of the door and pressed.

"Good afternoon sir, Marshalls; how can I help you"?

Harrold held his warrant to the camera.

"I'm Detective Inspector Harrold Davis could I please come in and speak with you"?

"Ah the phone call of earlier, I'm not sure if I'm allowed to tell you more than I already have".

"I have a photo I would like you to look at".

There was a buzz and a click the door swung back. Harrold stepped through into a small vestibule with another door in front. The door he came through closed behind him. The second door now opened where Harrold heard the voice of the woman on the speaker.

"Please come through".

He stepped into a corridor with a door set in wired glass wall to his right a window halfway along and a second door facing at the end. She appeared at the window now open.

"I'm Emily King what is this photo you want me to look at"?

Harrold had already removed the pictures of Jake, Vale and Branch from the file; he passed all three through the window together.

"Do you recognise any of these men".

Emily looked carefully at the three pictures in turn.

"Just this one".

She said holding up the shot of Jake.

"You told me earlier that a Jake Snell once had a box with you, account now closed. I know you said you would not release information about other clients without some official documentation, but I am investigating a murder and the abduction of a young girl. Just tell me did this man rent a second box under another name. You don't have to tell me the name just say yes if he did".

"I did say I needed a court order to comply with data protection, however I don't think I will be breaking that code if I answer your question".

Harrold waited; King studied the photo again.

"Is this man your murderer"?

"We believe he is".

"Well, then the answer is yes".

"Was it under the name Jeremy Shore"?

She nodded her head but said.

"I can't answer that".

"I quite understand, tell me how do your clients gain access to their box"?

"Simple enough, when they rent a box we give them a key, it has a code letter on it related to their particular box number, they come with the key we check it is genuine, let them into the safe room, we activate an electronic lock to their particular box, they open it do their business and ring the bell when they have finished, we let them out".

"Can anyone use the key"?

"Oh yes, customers often send a friend or relative, it doesn't matter who it is as long as they have a key. They will have to know which box number though, if they try to open a different box an alarm will alert us".

"What would you do if that happened"?

"I leave the door locked and call our security, someone will come and find out why".

"You don't call the police then".

"Good Lord no, it has only happened twice in all the time I've been here. Security checks them out; both times a genuine customer who has just forgotten their number".

"Can your company open boxes without a key"?

"No, there is only one key if is lost we would have to bring in a specialist locksmith to gain access".

"Has that ever happened"?

"Unfortunately yes but rarely; the box is classed as abandoned six months after failure to pay the rent or someone dies and the relatives can't find the key. A legal process to go through too".

"Mrs. King you have been most helpful. I will return with a warrant. In the meantime If a certain gentlemen phones or comes here please call me at once. You have excellent security here".

"I like to think so; unless you are known to us or have a key you won't get past the second door".

"Or back out of the first door, if I am not mistaken".

"Possibly".

"Well thankyou again Mrs. King here is my card please call me".

"It's Miss King detective, I'll let you out, goodbye detective Davis".

Back at the car June was sitting half asleep when Harrold almost jumped into the passenger seat.

"Blooming hell boss, you gave me a start".

"We're in luck June he's going to come here".

"How do you know".

"He has a box here".

"We know Jake had a box but he emptied it ages ago".

"No not that, before he left he rented another one in the name of Jeremy Shore. She wouldn't confirm the name without a warrant but hinted positively when I showed her Jakes picture. We need to put a watch on this place and another on Bartram's house. We can't afford any delay he could turn up any minute. I must call the boss; local police would be the easiest but we can't keep it quiet using them, Toni will know what to do. Remind me we need a warrant to open Jeremy Shore's box just in case he doesn't turn up".

Harrold's call to Toni lasted a good twenty minutes, he ran over the interview with Bartram and Emily King explaining the need for a twenty four seven watch on both places. She agreed, told him to wait, she would call him back. As soon as he hung up Toni placed a call to Bonington. Ten minutes later she called Davis.

"Two plain clothes officers will deploy one at each site Harrold they should be there within the hour, they have your number and will call when they are in position. You can come back here now; I want you to track down that warrant asap. By the way you did well I did not expect to find him so soon".

"I'm not counting my chickens yet Ma'am, not till we have him under lock and key, Do I have to come back I want to make this arrest".

"Yes you do, this is Bonington's case and you are right, Jake is such a wily bastard he may yet slip away so I don't want you anywhere near to carry the can if he does; still we do have a shot at him thanks to you, if it works out and he is captured you will go back, I don't want Smith to shut us out till we have brought down Brown ".

"Okay Ma'am, I'll stay till the surveillance boys are here".

"What now boss"?

"We wait June".

Only twelve minutes later two calls one after the other, very much to the point. That was quick, he thought; Toni Webb knows how to pull some strings that's for sure.

"Culver Street, on station sir".

"Duke Street, on station sir".

Harrold looked around but couldn't see anyone. 'Good enough' He thought.

"We can go now June".

"Thank goodness I'm getting hungry".

"You'd better hurry up then; no sirens you hear me, I want to sleep on the way back".

Chapter 27

"I've made a quick scan of all the files; the documents are mostly personal letters, some downloads of articles from magazines, newspapers, and correspondence. One or two letters to the various committees he sits on. Nothing much concerning the photographic club just minutes of a meeting two years ago, a letter complaining about the failure to give notice of a cancelled gathering, it seems he turned up and no one was there. The image files are family pictures, holidays mostly very old these nothing recent with the family. Under his club photo files were a few scenic shots, buildings, some flowers and the odd wild-life picture. All that would seem normal".

Constable Compton Busion and DCI Toni Webb were sitting side by side with ACC Montague Brown's laptop under scrutiny. It had been Superintendent Munroe who gave it to Toni, much to her surprise. Compton was explaining what she was doing and was about to do. Although Toni could use her computer for the more common applications she only had a layman's idea how these machines worked, the technical jargon, often expounded by Compton, threw her completely leaving her to accept the end result without question. This time it was more sensitive and she wanted to know the how and why and when. She would have to concentrate and curb Compton's enthusiasm if she were to understand.

"On delving into the hard drive I found a mass of deleted stuff, it's a bit all over the place most are only bits of files but a few image files are over forty percent complete with pictures he would not want anyone to see, like this".

A picture appeared on the screen with sections missing.

"That looks like one of the girls. Why are they not complete, can we find the rest of the image"?

"The answer to your second question is yes we can recover them within limits, the fact they are incomplete is more complex, I'll try and put it simply".

Toni thought here we go, here's where I go into tilt. She let her continue ready to interrupt if she lost her way. Compton continued without a pause.

"When a hard drive is new it is like an empty book-shelf, some of the space is taken up with program data and that stays where it is placed with a bit of spare room for modifications. The next part contains an index, in other words a list of all the files by type, name and where they are stored, this will grow as files are added and shrink as they are dumped. Most of the space is taken up with files. Because not all files are the same size, the space is allocated so that there is no wastage. Unlike books which sit side by side, you can break the files into smaller sections so one file may occupy several different spaces on the shelf, that is different locations in the memory. The index knows where all the bits are so when you ask for a file it goes to each location in turn and reassembles the information as if it came from one place. Now comes the tricky part, are you okay so far"?

Toni replied.

"Yes I think so, go on".

"If you delete a file it is not actually deleted, all that happens is the index is set to indicate the space, or spaces, are free and available for new data, at this stage however if you wanted you could retrieve the information, effectively undeleting the file".

"Why can't you do that with these files then"?

Because they have gone one step further having been emptied by the user as no longer needed, in other words the index has been wiped and the space is now free to be used again".

"Ah so it's like when I select the empty dustbin symbol on my computer all is lost and cannot be undeleted".

"That is almost right Ma'am, you haven't actually emptied the bin just that the index no longer exists for that file; the data is still there but fragmented with no way to reassemble them into a complete file, each fragment now being available for new data. Under normal use it has effectively gone for good. If any time later I were to create a new file it will use the freed up space, however if the space is not big enough it will look for another free space in a different location".

"Come again I'm not sure if I understand that".

"The computer will always try and use the largest spaces first but as that is not always enough eventually all the files in the system will be stored all over the place in small fragments. Genuine files and deleted files all together in a congealed mass, however all is not lost. In older computers the fragments for just one file could run into dozens of locations so retrieval would take ages. A program of maintenance allows you to defragment your files, something you would do once a month say. Modern computers do a similar exercise automatically, that is it brings the locations of files closer together and reduces the number of fragments. Deleted file data is never lost unless a new file has over-written it. Well are you any the wiser now"?

"I must be but I'm still a little confused, are you saying that the files Monty deleted could still be there if he has not written new ones to take their place but he would think they are gone anyway".

"Yes and no, you are right in that he would think they are gone, but defragmenting software will automatically have overwritten some of them and those are likely to be incomplete. The bigger the memory the less fragmentation there is".

You said you can recover these deleted files even though they have been binned is that right"?

"Sometimes yes. Here's what I can do. I'll separate the files he kept from the ones he deleted; what remains are unlikely to be complete files, even if I find all the fragments I will have to look manually at each one to see if they belong together, a bit like a giant jigsaw puzzle with an unknown number of pieces almost impossible with image files, however I have software that will reassemble text files. It choses wrong sometimes but about eighty percent are good enough. Image files need to be fairly big fragments to make sense".

"Hence the partial pictures you showed me".

"That's right, we are lucky in one respect it seems he deleted and binned all these files quite recently and has not used the computer much since if at all, so many of the files will not have been overwritten".

"Will you please try and extract as many part pictures as you can, and the same for the text files"?

"Of course. I tell you what I will do; strictly not the correct procedure, unless he is under arrest or a warrant has been obtained; I will copy everything onto a new hard drive, swap drives so you can give him back his computer and he will not know the difference. I will keep the original drive and assemble as many files as I can from the fragments. I can inhibit defragmentation in this hard drive so nothing will change it can be kept and offered as evidence; the serial number of the original drive will be etched on the frame of the of the processor so if it comes to a prosecution he cannot deny its authenticity".

"That is great Compton, what would we do without you. Even the one half picture I have seen so far tells me he is not squeaky clean. I don't know about a warrant though that may be more difficult".

"Don't worry just arrest the bugger and we can legitimately do it anyway".

"I don't think that will happen either, bigger fish to fry before then I fear".

"Bloody politics".

"You can say that again".

"One more thing before you go, shall I cross check the pictures I find with those in the printer recovered from Market Street"?

"Good idea it will tie Brown to having been there".

"Remember you will need a warrant before you can reveal we have his hard drive or use it as evidence. Bending the rules gives us the knowledge but does not satisfy protocol".

"I know but what powerful leverage".

"let's hope so, I'll call you Ma'am when it's done".

Toni left thinking she had understood all the Compton had told her; still unsure how deleted files weren't really gone however she was more than glad they could be recovered. If she had even a couple of dodgy pictures to hand, Munroe and Smith would be able to apply considerable pressure on Brown, she hoped enough to make him vulnerable.

Chapter 28

Jonny had the membership list. He'd divided it into four sheets scanned all the names to see if any of them rang a bell; nothing leapt out except the names of Paul Lewis and Earnest Palmer. Palmer struck him in two ways one he was one of the estate agents along with Lewis and the name Earnest was something he had seen somewhere but couldn't put his finger on. He kept the sheet with names of Montague Brown for himself along with Liam Kerridge and Barry Finn; the two already found to have form and passed the remaining sections to Mel Frazer, Keith Crane and Peter Andrews. Peter was not normally part of his team but Harrold Davis was happy for him to lend a hand.

"Listen up everyone we have some twenty nine people to go through from this list of club members, there are seven for each of you, I have the rest. Full background checks; see if they have a record, bank accounts, phones, internet, families and friends the lot, you've done this often enough, you know what to do, try and find photos if you can, drivers licences or passports should do that. Finally does the name Earnest mean anything to any of you"?

Melanie's ears pricked up at the name.

"Yes it does, there was something Mrs. Grant said, let me see".

Mel flipped through her notebook.

"Here it is, word for word. 'I heard George call him Earl or Earn, something like that I think, he was the worst'. I remember now; it was when she was being forced to pose by her husband, another man was there too she said, not always the same one maybe, not sure; she recalled hearing the name of one man who was always there".

"Could this 'Earn' be Earnest Palmer, whoever has him check him out first".

They all looked at their sheets, it was Keith who responded.

"He's mine boss".

"Okay let's get started; Keith let me know what you have on Palmer straight away. Melanie where is Linkman"?

"He had a call from his boss so's gone back to Reading, he didn't say why, only that he hopes to be back tomorrow".

"Good an extra pair of hands is welcome".

All four moved almost in unison to their workstations to begin the task of finding all they could about the individuals on their lists. Keith Crane was the first to break the silence.

"I've only just started sir but I thought you would like to know what I have so far. Earnest John Palmer, forty eight. Married to Katherine two children, John 20 and Michael 17. 72 Gardeners Road Hook. Works at Fullers estate agents Hartley Wintney, been there eleven years. No record of any kind, not even a parking fine. I've requested his bank accounts, be with me later, and are about to look at his online activity".

"Thanks Keith, do you have his car number"?

"He doesn't have one in his own name his wife does though, it's a red 2016 Ford Escort".

"Do a CCTV search along all the roads that lead to the Market street estates, evenings most likely, also around George's place about the time of his death".

"I was coming to that sir, give us a chance, only been on it five minutes".

"Sorry Keith, I'm an impatient bastard at times".

Keith just nodded his agreement with a grunt; the other two couldn't help but smile. Jonny shrugged his shoulders at his own impatience; he knew he needn't instruct his officers in their every action so went back to his own search saying nothing more. Paul Lewis was his first subject but in spite of Melanie's reported misgivings his first search could find nothing to show him as anything but straight. As with Keith's search of Palmer the basic data concerning all his six other members appeared to be as expected. The next step was to dig deeper.

Three hours later Peter stood and stretched his arms above his head, took a deep breath and let out a big sigh.

"I need a break, coffee anyone"?

A universal 'yes please' sent him across the room to the machine on the far wall returning five minutes later with four cups, two in each hand.

"Sorry there's no milk".

He said, taking a spoon out of his pocket along with a handful of sugar packets which he tipped onto the central table next to the cups. No one said anything but moved from their workstations to the table to retrieve the much needed refreshment. They sat quietly sipping the hot liquid when Jonny broke the silence.

"I know you would have said already if you had anything significant. I've almost done with my lot with nothing to note. I'm still waiting on some bank records, as you are no doubt, unlikely we'll have them today".

Keith spoke next.

"I've almost done too it seems Palmer is a definite fellow to look into but he's the only one in my lot. From the CCTV I've spotted the wife's Fiesta all over the town, and she's dropped him off at work a couple of times; there's a camera outside the post office in the same parade as the estate agents and another outside the village hall; he has a drivers licence but she seems to be the one who does all the driving, maybe he drinks a bit and won't risk a DUI. I'm still waiting on the camera shots from the Market Street approaches; they are not on a through route so not linked to traffic central but download to remote boxes. I sent one of the uniforms to pick them up ages ago, shouldn't be long. None of the other members have anything out of the ordinary".

Peter was waiting for Melanie to speak and she for him, the pair sat in silence.

"Nothing from you two then"?

Queried Jonny looking from one to the other. Peter glanced at Mel who indicated to him to go first.

"No sir, I am waiting on some bank stuff and the same CCTV from Market street as DC Crane sir. Apart from that they all seem fine so far".

Melanie had been biding her time, she had found information that triggered her sense of unease.

"I have two possibles; newish members, Samuel Rivers and Thomas Carter. Both in their forties and living on the same road in Rotherwick; they joined on the same day six months ago, they first went to a meeting where GG gave a lecture on long range photography and the use of the telephoto lens. They only went to meetings when George was present. Lucky for us Paul Lewis was like a school master in keeping attendance and other records. One thing I found is all members were given a membership card with their photo, copies of which are in his files. Apparently showing the card allows them discount's at Dixons and other photo suppliers. They came to the meetings in different cars which was strange seeing as how they are neighbours and live within walking distance; again like Keith and Peter I need to see the Market Street videos and bank statements too".

"Good some progress, at least we'll have something to work on, when this stuff arrives. I didn't pick up on the photo membership cards Mel; Good work. Can we print them off and perhaps a visit to Market Street to see if the watchmen recognises anyone; the same for Mrs. Grant, she may recognise them.

"I'll go visit the watchmen Dave and the others when we've finished here but not Mrs. Grant sir; well not until we've exhausted all other avenues".

"Getting soft are we Mel"?

"A promise that's all, sir. Shouldn't uniform be back with the footage by now"?

Keith had a phone to his ear.

"They're on their way; ten minutes".

"Great, time for another coffee; anyone?"

Positive replies saw Peter gather the empties and cross the room again. Mel's phone vibrated in her pocket; she had put it on silent so as not to disturb the others whilst they were working.

"Yes ….good…..okay….thankyou…..I'll tell her…..Bye".

She hung up and redialled.

"Hello Compton, Dr. Taylor has sent the Post-Mortem test results I believe…..good……..No. I'll come for them myself".

"Is that what I think it is"? said Jonny.

"Yes sir PM and forensic results too, shall I bring them now, Compton was going to post them on the general file, I said not to, you know why"?

"Good, yes go now".

On her way down Mel passed the awaited uniform officer coming up the stairs.

"Constable Joiner are those the videos from Market Street"?

"Yes Sergeant, sorry I've been a long time I had to wait for someone with a key to open the boxes. I've just three discs covering the last month, do you want them"?

"No Dan, take them to DI Musgrove he's in the squad room. Dan this case is a very sensitive, please keep what you are doing for us to yourself, chat amongst the lads is the last thing we want".

"I understand Sergeant. Mums the word".

She continued down to Compton's office and came back with four copies of the report. Jonny called everyone to stop what they were doing.

"Listen up, we have some important additional info. I know you are still tracking data from your lists but Grant's Post-Mortem tests have found unknown DNA in his hair, strongly pointing to being that of his killer. Extensive search of NDNAD

(National DNA Database) produced no match. The marks on his neck were made with a length of twine or wire however those on his wrists and ankles were made by dark grey plastic cable ties, these were removed after death and taken away presumably by the killer. From analysis of SOCO's finds; the blood on the fence at the back of his house is a match for Grant and details from footprints at the same location are included here. Prints on the rear door frame produced negative results from AFIS (Automated Fingerprint Identification System). We've reached a point where we now need to interview these guys. It will take too long to apply for warrants so we'll go on without. We'll start with those who seem to be most likely but must not ignore the others even though they seem to be straight. Finish up on anything you are currently looking at, you can come back to this later".

He waited for his officers to close their terminals and clear their desks.

"If you are all done gather round".

He handed each of them a copy of the PM and SOCO reports.

"Melanie you will go and bring in Palmer, Keith you will fetch Samuel Rivers and Peter your man is Thomas Carter. All of you go with uniformed officers in police cars; remember one of these men could be our killer so be careful. If they won't come willingly arrest them; I'd prefer not to at this stage, I don't want them under caution yet either; 'help with our enquiries: the need to eliminate them' is the best approach, be polite, nice and gentle even. They should all be home from work by the time you turn up, if they are not home find out where they are and bring them in, I want to have them all here at the same time. In the meantime I will apply for search warrants and deal with Liam Kerridge and Barry Finn. Both seem to have been clean since their brush with the law; full time working and families now. Their DNA and prints don't match anything so maybe their past form means nothing. Yes Mel what is it"?

"What if we can't locate them immediately"?

"Leave one of the uniformed officers to wait at their home in case they come back whilst you search; I want their phones and computers before they can muck about with them. If they are not the killer they could still be involved with the abduction of Karen Small so may not be too willing to come quietly. Anything else?....Call if you have a problem. Good hunting".

Jonny filled out the twenty eight warrant application forms and passed them through the internal mail to the Super to expedite; he didn't speak to him for whichever judge Walter applied would be none too pleased so he didn't want to be around. His visit to the homes of Kerridge and Finn to find them both at work, he'd have to come back later. On arriving back one hour later Palmer and Rivers were seated in interview rooms two and three.

"Peter why are you here; where is Carter"?

Peter Andrews responded explaining why he'd returned empty handed.

"Not much I could do sir. Thomas Carter's on holiday in Spain with his family and will not be back for another four days. It puts him out of the frame for the murder as he was out of the Country when Grant was killed".

"I've had the same problem my two were working away and won't be back till tomorrow night. We still need to interview them and Carter as they could still be involved with the abductions and dodgy photos. Arrange to pick him up as soon as he comes back".

Jonny was annoyed as he wanted all suspects in the station together, collusion being a real possibility.

"Right let's begin with the ones we have".

217

Chapter 29

"Why have you brought me here, your Sergeant said that as I am a member of the same club as George Grant she had to exclude me as a suspect. Surely you don't think I had anything to do with his death".

"Quite right Mr Palmer; thank you for coming in this evening, we shouldn't keep you too long just need to eliminate you, easily done. You are not under arrest and can leave anytime you like; we just need your cooperation, answer one or two questions if you would".

"Oh is that all. I don't know anything I can tell you that might help".

"Mr Grant was a postman so came into contact with so many people it will take us ages to go through them all. Do you mind if we take a DNA sample it only takes a moment"?

"Is it compulsory".

"No of course not but it will seem very strange if you refuse when you offered to cooperate. We could obtain a warrant but I'm sure you don't want that".

"I was only asking; I don't mind go ahead".

Jonny nodded to Peter Andrews who stepped forward.

"Just open your mouth for a moment sir".

Peter inserted the swab and wiped it around the inside of Palmer's cheeks, placed it into its container and bagged it with a label which he filled out with the name time and date.

"That was easy wasn't it, we'll take your prints next if you don't mind".

"What you never said; all that ink and mess".

"No that's old stuff we have simple scanners now, look".

Peter stepped forward again, this time with the FP scanner. He gently took Palmer's right hand placing each finger one at a time on the sensitive screen. Palmer passively offered his left hand; the process was repeated with the right.

218

"Is that all can I go now"?

"Not quite just one more thing. I understand you rent a unit on the Market Street industrial estate, what do you use it for"?

What little colour was in Earnest Palmer's face drained in a moment; his vision blurred and beads of sweat blossomed on his ghostly white brow.

"I err don't know what you mean, I gave that up a long time ago".

"Then why do you still pay the rent"?

"It is a five year contract with a penalty clause if I terminate early, so I sublet it out".

"Who"?

"What, I'm not sure what you mean"?

"Who is your sub-tenant, surely you know who pays you rent"?

"Yes, yes it was George the postman".

"So you must have known him quite well, what did he use it for"?

"I think he did his photography there".

"You seem unsure how come, you must have been there from time to time".

"Only once or twice in the beginning when he first took it on".

"So not recently then"?

"Oh no not for ages, months and months ago".

"Hm. Strange, the security men identified you as being one of several people who came there on occasions in the past weeks. How do you explain that"?

"I can't they must be mistaken. Anyway what has this to do with anything, it was just George's studio"?

"We think it has everything to do with why he died. How do you explain if security were so wrong, you appear in CCTV footage recovered from the road leading to the site"?

This was a real stretch; what little they had in the way of video, left them unable to identify any complete car numbers or individuals but Jonny thought Palmer wouldn't know that.

"I forgot I might have gone there but I didn't go in".

"You expect me to believe that"?

"I don't care what you believe I want to leave now, you said I could didn't you".

"Okay you can go but just one more question before you do".

Jonny produced the picture of Karen Small, tied to a chair, extracted from Grant's printer found at the lock up.

"Can you tell me who this young girl is"?

"Oh my God where did you get that. I don't know who she is I've never seen it before".

"Are you sure Earnest, it's not a nice picture, she looks willing enough or do you know different. Help us here, could it be you have been used by whoever took this picture and had no control over what has happened"?

"I can't say anything I don't know anything you have to let me go home".

"Fine you may leave now but we will be bringing you in again very soon; next time you may be under arrest. We will come for you when we have assembled all the evidence; you could be charged with very serious crimes. We have several members of your club here right now under questioning; no doubt they will blame you for everything; if you cooperate now you may be able to avoid the murder charge and some other major offences. I'll leave you here to think it over for a while. When I come back you can either cooperate or go home and tomorrow face the fate others have laid out for you".

Jonny and Peter left the number two interview room and moved to the observation space behind room three.

"Peter send the DNA off to the lab now and check his prints against those from the door frame".

Samuel Rivers was sitting at the table with Keith Crane. Mel moved from room two viewing into the viewing area of room three where Jonny was ready to observe her interview of Rivers.

"That went well sir, I think he will break".

"I hope so, I've given him the chance to think up more lies that we can bury him with. I'm not sure though, I have a feeling he is pretending to be weaker than he is. He is certainly guilty of something I'm not sure what. Anyway your turn next".

Melanie Frazer stepped into the sparsely furnished room to be faced by a Samuel Rivers eyes. They stared at her without blinking for several moments in such a way she was almost forced to break the eye contact. He was under six feet but appeared to dominate the space. Very broad shoulders and dressed in a grey T shirt and Navy chinos that emphasised his physic. He obviously worked out; a lot.

Good evening Mr. Rivers I'm Detective Sergeant Frazer and this is Detective Constable Crane; I would like to thank you for coming in at such short notice. You probably know George Grant was found dead the other day and as a member of the photo club to which he belonged we are asking everyone a few questions to help us find out a little more of George's life. You only recently joined I believe"?

"Yes, about three months I would say; what happened to Mr. Grant that I need to be here at this time"?

"I'm afraid he was murdered; what can you tell me about your relationship with Mr. Grant"?

"Murdered wow that is a surprise! Relationship you say. No not me, I hardly knew the man".

"Tell me what you do know"?

"Not much; he was just one of the people at the club, he did a demonstration at one of the meetings I remember it was when I first went there, he seemed to know his stuff. On one occasion we went to his studio come workshop, just a few of us after the meeting had closed, he gave a lesson on colour development and

221

printing, he was quite knowledgeable and a good instructor. I saw him at the meetings once or twice more I think, that's about the sum of it. He seemed to be an ordinary bloke to me. I'm curious why do you think he was he murdered"?

"We don't know yet, he knew a lot of people and we have to go through them all to eliminate them one by one".

"And that includes me I suppose; fire away do your elimination".

"First would you give us a DNA sample and your fingerprints please".

"No problem; but hey remember I went to his studio that time so my prints may be there. I don't think I touched anything though".

"Don't worry the prints we are interested in were found at his home; unless you went there at some time"?

"No, never been there don't even know where he lived, so that's fine, take your samples".

Keith took a DNA sample followed by the scanned prints.

"That's a neat bit of kit, I was expecting the old inkpad and paper. Are we done then"?

This man was easy going and relaxed; it didn't feel right; people are normally nervous when it comes to being questioned by the police and even more so when murder is involved. Melanie shifted from the formal Mr. to calling him by his first name to see his response.

"We move with the times Samuel, just a couple of questions then you can go, the officer will drop you back home".

"Thanks; what else"?

"Your friend Mr. Thomas Carter also joined at the same time I believe; did he go with you that time to the studio"?

"He's not a friend you know it was just a coincidence we joined at the same time. The village delivers a newsletter once a month, there was an article about the club, by the secretary guy Lewis, with an invitation for anyone interested to come to the hall at Hartley; that's right, it was when the Grant fellow gave his lecture. Mr. Carter must have seen the same article. I found out he lived in the same road later, never knew him before then have hardly spoken to him since. As for the studio visit I'm not sure, he could have been there I didn't take any notice sorry".

"That's fine, thank you for your help, Detective Crane will show you where to pick up your ride. One more thing before you go, we need to look at your PC or laptop would you give it to the driver we will return it tomorrow".

"I don't know about that I need it for work".

"I understand Samuel, I'll ask our technicians to check it this evening and we will return it first thing before you go to work, I promise".

"In that case I suppose it's okay".

"Well goodbye Mr. Rivers you have been most cooperative I don't suppose I will see you again, take care".

He smiled and rose slowly from the chair, the eyes again fixed on hers until he reached the door.

"I hope you catch him, detective, goodbye".

He was gone with Keith one step behind; she immediately called the desk sergeant.

"Sergeant please tell Constable Danny Joiner to take Mr. Rivers home and to collect his computer also to make a note of how long he is kept waiting before it is handed over; better send another officer with him I don't trust this guy".

Mel moved to the viewing area behind the interview room where Jonny and Andrew were talking.

"That was strange I think he is too calm sir and those eyes staring at me, cold as ice, I didn't like it".

"We both noticed his reaction to learning of the death, I'm sure he knew already; his manner was too relaxed he is acting out a role".

"Either that or he is taking something".

"You are right Peter a distinct possibility; whatever, I rate him higher than Palmer. By the way Mel, Peter couldn't match Palmer's prints to the door frame at Grant's so unlikely to be him, the DNA will confirm. What do you think Mel"?

"I don't like him much but that doesn't make him a killer, we need evidence. His willingness to give us DNA, fingerprints and computer makes me think we won't find it that easy".

"Back to the drawing board we need to dig deeper. The CCTV footage hasn't given us much hope we fare better with the bank statements, they may be here tomorrow. It's getting late let's call it a day. Early start eh".

Peter had already cleared his desk so said his goodnight and was gone. Mel locked her files away and switched off her computer.

"Good night Jonny, I'll tell Keith to finish up as soon as Dan Joiner arrives back with Rivers laptop".

"Oh yes, tell him to take it down to Compton, I'll have a word with her. Your promise to have it back first thing means one of her guys is in for some overtime".

"Sorry about that Jonny, I wanted to keep him sweet; I'll come in early and take it back to him. What about Palmer"?

"I'll probably let him go home tonight and bring him in tomorrow, he is certainly mixed up with the dodgy pictures but as to abduction, maybe I don't know; I bet he won't sleep much tonight. Go home Melanie; you sleep well".

"Don't worry boss I'm bushed, like a log me. Nite".

Palmer sat in the room with a uniformed officer standing by the door statue like, silent. He had waited long enough.

"Can I go now; I want to leave"?

The officer did not respond.

"The detective said I could leave when I wanted".

Still no response. Palmer was afraid to get up and go, although he was desperate. The thought of his wife questioning him if he did not return soon gave him the courage to stand. A slight hesitation but seeing no movement to stop him he walked towards the door. He felt the perspiration form on his brow running down the side of his face, he reached the door and pushed gently, it didn't move.

"Please let me out now".

His voice raised and shaking. The officer reached across and gave the door a good shove with the palm of his right hand; it swung back with a bang as it hit the stop on the wall outside, Earnest jumped.

"The way out is to your right sir, good evening".

Earnest took one look and trotted out and along the corridor towards the exit and daylight as fast as he could.

Sergeant Banks chuckled to himself as he closed the door and returned to the squad room.

"Palmer's gone sir".

"Thanks sergeant".

Chapter 30

Compton was sitting in Toni's office waiting for her to come in, clutching the DNA results to her breast as if protecting them from whoever. She and Donna Grover, one of her assistants had been up half the night checking and cross checking the results, there were still some to come from yesterday's suspects but that didn't matter what she had was going to be a shock. Mel Frazer had already collected the laptop belonging to Rivers, which had checked out okay, even the deleted stuff had nothing in it to worry about.

"My, my, Compy you are a surprise what brings you up here out of your comfort zone to the big bad bosses office".

"Good morning to you too Ma'am, I wanted to phone last night but it was early hours really and I knew you need to sleep. This is going to upset your, or should I say DI Musgrove's, investigation".

"Well what is it that has you all of a tizz"?

"It's the DNA results".

"You have a match; it's not the ACC is it"?

"Oh no nothing like that, it's not a match exactly we don't have a sample to compare it with".

"Come on out with it stop dithering".

"The skin sample from George Grant's hair is a partial match to himself".

"That's crazy it must have been contaminated somehow".

"No Ma'am it's a complete chain for an individual not George but a close relative".

"What do you mean how close"?

"Very close; a parent, a brother, a sister or a child".

"Oh my God; you mean his son Gabriel don't you"?

"It seem most likely, or a sibling if he has one. If we had his mother's DNA it would help as a partial match to both would mean it would more likely be the son rather than George's brother or sister; we need a sample from Gabriel to be certain".

"This certainly changes things with regard to the murder but this dodgy photo club lot has thrown up the possibility of finding out what has happened to Karen Small. Keep this to yourself for the moment I will tell Detective Musgrove. Young Gabriel Grant is still a minor, we need to be careful this news stays confined to need to know only. Thanks Compton leave those results with me".

Compton placed the DNA results on Toni's desk and left. Toni followed a few minutes later after switching on her coffee machine, to see if anyone had arrived in the squad room. Finding it almost empty she went down to the desk sergeant who was currently handing over to the day shift officer.

"Good morning sergeants may I interrupt for a moment. Please ask Musgrove and Davis to come straight to my office as soon as they arrive".

The two men returned the greeting, with the day officer acknowledging her request. She turned and climbed the two flights back to her office, pressed for a double espresso and sipped the hot shot of caffeine, wondering what would be the best plan of action.

Compton returned to her domain to see how her team were getting on with the computer downloads. Brown's data was already dealt with and logged with the report encrypted available to Toni and Munroe only. They had Palmer's scrutiny almost done; full of interesting stuff she'd been told. River's hard drive was clean but had been copied ready for deeper examination next. She was not impatient knowing how long some of these things could take, her girls were no slouches they'd let her know as soon as they were done.

Chapter 31

Jonny Musgrove and Harrold Davis sat in silence unable to absorb what they had just heard. Toni waited for a very long minute to let it sink in before continuing.

"It is hard to believe that a young boy did that to his father but the DNA evidence is pretty strong. I know the case is not yours Harrold but you need to be aware of the way things have changed. The link between Monty Brown's sadistic images found on his computer and the abduction of Karen Small may yet prove to be the way we use him to draw in Snell and in turn Blakewood so you will keep an eye on his investigation as well as pursuing your own lines of enquiry. Jonny you must proceed with the arrest of young Gabriel under caution, ensure you follow procedure to the letter; a duty solicitor may not be good enough, speak to the mother Julie and make sure he is adequately represented. The half DNA evidence is not enough alone, take a sample from him, you need his prints too and his shoes and clothes. Tell SOCO to search his house. Don't do any of this without the necessary warrants even if he or the mother give permission to search. I don't want anyone to find us lacking in support of the rights of Gabriel and his mother. These two have been abused so will have a very sympathetic audience, if it turns out Gabriel is guilty he shouldn't go free at trial because we failed to follow the rules okay".

Harrold finally found his voice.

"You know what Ma'am nothing should surprise us in this job but it bloody well still does. People like Grant don't deserve to live, yet when someone does something about it we have to track them down and lock them up and all because we have really been the ones to fail".

"Justice for all Harrold or we will have anarchy".

Jonny voiced the standard cliché without any conviction. Toni did not want her officers to go about their tasks feeling despondent although she understood their reticence.

"Come on you two, it's not for us to Judge, you know that, we are here to start the process of putting things right. We find the evidence arrest those we believe are guilty and leave it to others to follow through. Even if George Grant deserved to be punished it should not have been like this and if you don't agree you should never have become a detective".

"I know you are right and I'm sure Harrold feels the same, it is difficult to be dispassionate but we will be professional when it comes down to it".

"Yes I'm sure you will".

She looked at Harrold, quiet as always, who presented both palms up and shrugged his shoulders in submission and nodded his agreement.

"Until we have this fully wrapped up we have to keep this out of the press if and when it comes to trial it will be out of our hands but at the moment we have control, don't let it leak tell your teams".

"Yes Ma'am".

Agreement from both detectives was the cue to leave, Jonny to the squad room and Harrold to Busion's den one floor below.

Jonny sat at his desk not sure how to break the news. He moved to the centre table pushed the pile of papers to one side.

"Gather round you lot, this is going to hurt".

Melanie, Keith and Peter huddled together looking at each other wondering what the bombshell might be. They sat in a tight bunch and looked for Jonny to explain himself.

"First I want to thank Peter for his help but we will be discontinuing our investigation of the club members for a while. You are needed elsewhere; DI Davis wants your return. We will come back to the club later, I think your task with Harrold has a bearing on that too so we may all be working together again later".

It was obvious to Peter he was expected to leave before DI Musgrove would to continue; he said his goodbye and left to seek out his boss, his curiosity unsatisfied.

Once out of the room Jonny vented his feelings of frustration, more at himself than his two trusted aids. His voice was quiet, almost whispering through clenched teeth.

"What have we not done that all murder investigations should prioritise. Who are always prime suspects from the outset"?

They all knew of course but did not answer the obvious rhetorical question.

"Family; sodding family. What did we do? We sympathised emphasised and everything but check them out properly. We did not take DNA samples, we did not take prints, we did not verify alibis if they indeed had any".

" You are taking about Julie and Gabriel aren't you"?

"You are dam right I am Detective Sergeant Frazer. My fault as much as yours I went along with it, side-tracked by this bloody tacky photo club, wasting our time on people who had nothing to do with the death of George Grant, well not directly anyway".

"Come on what has happened sir, where did we go wrong"?

"Our best evidence from the outset was the DNA found on the skin left in Grant's hair when the killer pulled his head back as he cut his throat. When there was no match with Dawn's or Karen's family and nothing from NDNAD, we let it pass, stupidly waiting till we perhaps had some luck with the club members. Thanks to some quick thinking lab technician we now have a great dollop of egg on our face. He found a match to a near relative of George. He had no siblings so that leaves his son Gabriel. We could have had that news days ago if we had done our jobs properly".

"We couldn't have known that at first sir; the lead to the club seemed so strong and the pressure from above with the ACC being involved left us little choice; is it any wonder we went down that route".

"Keith, we still should have checked them early on and everyone will know it; still all is not lost. The partial match is not enough we need Gabriel's DNA to confirm. Securing corroborating evidence is also vital if we are to close this out quickly and carry on with the club case. I think the abuse sustained by Gabriel and his mother from those scumbags may be the reason George was killed".

"What do we do now"?

"We'll divide the workload Melanie; you will secure a search warrant for their house and an arrest warrant for Gabriel too; I know that is probably not necessary but I want to be certain we are protected from criticism; the DNA report should be enough due cause for both. Call Linkman back here, he has a rapport with Gabriel I want him to conduct the interview. Ask Toni to request his help".

"Who shall I use for the warrant"?

"Ask the Super he will know which Judge is available".

"What about representation for Gabriel"?

"Mel, you've enough to do. Keith, that will be your job, you know the duty solicitors quite well pick the best and have him here this evening. Also organise someone from child services, explain we are about to charge a minor but no details okay. I don't intend to arrest Gabriel until he is here at the station, I want to keep this as covert as possible, no nosey neighbours seeing anything unusual. Organise a search team, two officers in plain clothes should be enough they must arrive in an unmarked car after the boy has left. I want you to serve the search warrant then bring Julie Grant here in your car. Find Gabriel's phone, leave everything else to the search team. Meet back here by four o'clock; we'll go to his house soon after, I want him to be home from school. That's it, if you think of anything I have forgotten just do it and let me know later".

"Where will you be if we need anything"?

"Where do you think Keith; I've been called to see the Superintendent; he wants an explanation I expect".

"Bloody politics"?

"As always".

Chapter 32

At four thirty five Jonny, Melanie and Emma, the child support officer arrived at Julie's and Gabriel's house. A car with the two search officers was parked out of sight in the next street. Melanie left the car alone and approached the house, her press of the bell brought Julie to open the door, she looked shocked for a second.

"Sergeant Melanie, do you have some news?".

"May I come in Julie".

"Of course".

Julie stepped back as Mel entered ensuring the door behind her was left ajar. She walked into the living room. Mel asked.

"Where is Gabe"?

"Upstairs in his room, he has only just come in".

"Will you call him down please; I need to talk to him"?

Julie went to the bottom of the stairs and shouted for Gabe to come down. A few moments later the rumble of heavy feet as he came down heralded Gabe's arrival.

"Mum there's a car outside; oh it's you again".

"Hello Gabriel, please come outside for a minute".

Melanie almost herded Gabriel towards the front door, still open, allowing Gabe no alternative but to pass through. Jonny and Emma quickly left their car to face Gabriel on the doorstep. Julie followed behind unaware of what was happening.

"What's going on, are you taking him somewhere"?

Melanie turned and ushered Julie back into the sitting room leaving Gabriel on the doorstep with Jonny and Emma.

"Hello, Gabriel remember me"?

"You're the other detective what do you want now"?

"That's right I'm Inspector Musgrove. I'd like you to come with me to the police station again, is that alright".

"I expect so, as long as mum comes too I don't mind, is it about dad"?

"Of course your mum will be there, this is Mrs. Emma Francis, she is from child support she will accompany us in the car and be with you whilst we ask you some questions".

"Why do we need her"?

"She's here to make sure we do things right because you are under sixteen".

"Humph. I'm not a kid you know. Can I bring my phone"?

"I'm afraid not. Do you have it with you"?

"No it's in my room".

"An officer will find it and bring it to the station; you can have it later. Let's go".

"What about mum"?

"She will come in the other car, she needs to check the house and lock up, she won't be far behind".

"Julie take it easy sit down, he'll be with Detective Musgrove going to the station, we will follow them shortly, I'll let you know what is going on in a minute".

"Is it about George and those men like I told you, Gabe has nothing to do with it. It was just me".

"We have to search your house Julie, this paper is a warrant, in a few minutes two officers will come to make the search, and we will go to the station".

"Why, what are they looking for there is nothing here to find. Why are you taking Gabe without me, he hasn't done anything"?

The ring of the bell told Melanie the search team had arrived, she rose and let them in leaving Julie on the couch clutching the warrant bemused. Mel spoke to the two men in the hallway as the put on their neoprene gloves.

"Okay let's start, I'll take Mrs. Grant to the station and send your car back, take any mobiles and computer directly to Constable Busion".

"Julie come with me now, we are going to the station, don't forget your handbag and a coat it's a bit chilly out".

"What's going on why have you taken my Gabe, I should be with him"?

"You'll be with him soon Julie, shall we go"?

"Okay, okay; give me a minute. I don't understand, are we leaving these men here alone; what about locking up"?

"Don't worry the officers will be very careful and will secure the house when they leave".

Mel helped Julie on with her coat and guided her to the car; they sat together in the back; nothing was said during the short drive to the station. The driver dropped them at the front steps, returning to the house to wait for the officers to finish their search.

Keith had contacted Brian Marchant, the best of the available duty solicitors, who was waiting at the door when Jonny, Gabe and Emma arrived. He had been warned by Keith of the situation and that an arrest warrant was available but was to be held in hand subject to how the interview went.

"Hello Gabriel, my name is Brian Marchant I am a solicitor who will look after your legal interests and ensure you are treated fairly".

"I thought she was here for that".

Said Gabe, pointing to Emma Francis.

"Emma is here for your physical welfare I am here to make sure the police follow the rules of law. This officer is going to take a DNA sample and your fingerprints do you have any objection"?

"Can I refuse"?

"You can, but if you do the police can obtain a warrant and oblige you to give them what they want. My advice is to agree as they will be able to take it anyway, it just delays things a little and won't look good for you".

"Okay I don't mind".

Chapter 33

Julie was taken to the comfortable room one, with a WPC in attendance, whereas Gabriel was now seated in interview room two. Jonny took up position in the far corner, Detective Sergeant Hamish Linkman sat opposite Gabriel; Brian Marchant was to the right of Gabriel, to his left Emma Francis. The stenographer Constable Faye Tenison was at the far end alongside the recorder. Melanie was in the viewing room.

"Gabriel Grant I am about to conduct an interview with you; it will be recorded; don't be nervous you are just here to help us".

"I remember you, your that Scots detective from before; where's my mum"?

"She is next door you'll see her soon enough. Constable Tenison please switch on the recorder".

Hamish tested the recoding was running then opened with the formalities by introducing those present in the room along with the time day and date.

"Gabriel Grant you are being interviewed under caution in connection with the death of your father George Grant. You do not have to say anything, but it may harm your defence if you do not mention when questioned something you later rely on in court. Anything you do say may be given in evidence. Do you understand"?

Gabriel stood there silent.

"Gabriel do you understand what I have just told you"?

"I suppose so, you said I didn't have to say anything so I didn't".

"Gabriel, for the recording, please answer yes if you understood or no if not"

"It's yes but I didn't ....."

Marchant leant across and quickly placed his hand across Gabriel's mouth.

"Gabriel please say nothing until you speak with me first, I am here to protect you; what you tell me stays with me, what you tell the police officers the court will hear. The caution is to be taken seriously you only have to answer the officer's questions if you want to, you say no more than you need to, okay"?

"Yes sir".

"Look at me after each question, if I nod you may answer if you do not wish to answer just say no comment, you may then tell me privately why you don't want to answer I will then advise you".

"This is weird but okay".

Hamish Linkman had no knowledge of Brian Marchant but was impressed and a little wary he would have to be careful how he worded his questions. At the moment he only had the partial DNA as his lead he'd have to wait for the fingerprints and anything they find at the house to bear fruit. The reaction to questioning before showed a damaged side to Gabriel he wanted to reveal again; Brian Marchant, not to mention Emma Francis might make that more difficult. He would begin slowly and try to bring out Gabriel's hidden self.

"You remember when we spoke last you were talking about your father's last visit. You said you had been sent out to the shop so your mum could talk in private. Were you gone very long"?

"About ten minutes or so the shop is on the corner of our road".

"When you came back was your father still there"?

"I can't remember, what did I say last time"?

"What you said then doesn't matter it's what you remember now that counts was he there".

"I think he was about to leave, yes he went soon after I got there".

"Was your mum there too"?

"Yes she was on the doorstep".

"Was she alright"?

"How do you mean"?

"Did she seem happy"?

"I don't think so, she had been crying"?

"How do you know"?

"She had marks on her cheeks, you know from her black eye shadow, it had run down".

"Did your dad say anything"?

"No, not to mum; he did wave at me though when he got in his car. I think he was saying goodbye but I couldn't hear him".

"I believe your dad missed a payment and your mum was short of money".

"That's right he came to pay her in cash, mum said".

"Did you see the money"?

"No".

"Is that no, you didn't see it or no, there was no money"?

Gabe was tapping his lips then looked at Brian for guidance. The two whispered together for a minute. He told Gabriel to continue.

"I didn't know when I saw you before I thought he had paid mum. I found out later he'd only gave her half and that's why she was crying".

"How did that make you feel"?

"I was angry, mum said we couldn't manage unless she could find some more work"?

"I can understand that, how did you feel when you found out that was the last and he wasn't going to pay any more at all"?

"I never said that, how did you know"?

Brian stopped Hamish before he could ask the next question.

"Please be careful Sergeant, my client never said anything like that, are you are trying to put words in his mouth"?

"Indeed, I have no intention of that, however we know Mr. Grant had cancelled the standing order made payable to Gabriel's mother two weeks before. There was a telephone conversation between George and Julie on the day the missed payment had left her with nothing; that same afternoon he came round and paid her half and I believe told her that was the last".

"Gabriel did you know your dad was not going to pay your mum ever again".

"Not then I didn't, I only found out when I found her crying a few days later".

"I presume you were upset so went round to see your dad to ask him to change his mind, what day was that"?

"I didn't see him, there was a police car outside so I left".

"When did you go back"?

Gabriel paused and looked at Brian, who shook his head.

"No comment".

"Was it the Saturday night after the police car had left"?

Brian stood and called a halt.

"Enough sergeant, I wish to speak with my client".

Hamish terminated the interview with everyone leaving the room barring Gabriel and Brian Marchant.

Jonny went to the viewing room it was empty.

"Where's Keith and Mel"?

He asked the uniform officer guarding the door.

"They said they were going down to Constable Busion to check on something".

"I'll go find them Hamish; you carry on when Marchant has finished, you are doing well".

Hamish Linkman waited outside with the others for a further five minutes when Brian opened the door and called them in.

They all sat in silence whilst Constance started the recording. Hamish stating the time of the restart, naming those present.

"Gabriel after your first visit when you saw the police car, did you go back again that night"?

"No".

"Did you go round to the back of the house to have a look; sometime later maybe"?

"You can't see anything from there the fence is too high".

"You could have climbed over".

"I might have lifted myself up for a peek, but I didn't go in that way".

"Was that the way you came out then"?

"I don't remember, anyway I never said I went in did I"?

"No you didn't, but I do believe your dad let you in later the following night when you were sure the police car had gone".

"No comment".

Again Brian called a halt and whispered to Gabriel.

"I think my client has answered that question he said he did not go into his father's house. Can we move on".

"That was not a question Mr. Marchant but a statement of fact. It's based on forensic evidence showing Gabriel's presence inside the house".

"What evidence"?

"We will come to that soon enough; I was hoping Gabriel would offer the information telling us what happened voluntarily and not be forced to concede when faced with irrefutable evidence. This time I want a straight answer. Did your father let you in to his house on Saturday evening"?

Again Brian spoke to Gabriel in a whisper, but before he could answer Jonny Musgrove entered the room, he gave Hamish a note and moved to his previous position in the corner. Hamish spoke for the recording.

"Detective Inspector Musgrove has entered the room".

Hamish looked at the note.

"I repeat did your father let you in"?

"Yes".

"I am glad you are being honest Gabriel as we know you were there, your fingerprints and DNA show you were with your

240

father the night he died, and that you left by the back door, climbing the fence, more detailed processing of the forensic evidence found in your house will confirm this and more. We will take a break there. Gabriel if you require refreshment please ask Emma or the uniformed officer he will find you something".

They all left the room leaving Gabriel with the PC who was earlier waiting outside and Emma Francis.

Brian Marchant tackled Jonny as soon as they had cleared the room.

"What is this evidence, Sergeant Linkman is almost going too far, remember his age"?

"Look Brian, the evidence is damming; I have enough to charge him with murder right now but I was hoping he would tell us what happened, if he does it will make it much easier for him in court. This is a pretty sordid tale I don't wish to have it presented in court for the press and public to gloat over. A confession and a sympathetic CPS could see a much better outcome. His dad was a bastard who deserved to be punished but not by Gabriel, not like this".

"Tell me what you have I'll see if I can persuade him".

"You know I can't do that Brian, but if he answers Hamish's questions honestly we will put all our cards on the table as the interview progresses. To remind you, we still have to interview the mother she has more to do with this than she is telling".

"I would normally tell him to say nothing at this stage, but we have known each other long enough, I trust you to be fair by this boy".

"I will Brian I promise. I'm going to interview Julie Grant now. I suggest you have a break spend some time with Gabriel; do advise what's best for him; then we will start again".

Chapter 34

Jonny Musgrove opened the door of room one. Julie was sitting in one of the armchairs with a uniform WPC standing by the window.

"Where's Gabe, I've been here for ages; what have you done with him"?

"He is fine up to now Mrs. Grant, we have started his interview; at the moment he is having a break and some refreshment. A lady from social services is with him to ensure his physical well-being and we have provided a solicitor as his legal representative".

"Why would he need a solicitor, I can't afford anything like that".

"Don't worry there will be no charge for his services".

"What do you think he has done that you are interviewing him in such an official way"?

"I'll be honest with you Julie; we believe Gabriel was involved in the death of his father George".

"No, no, that can't be; he wouldn't, why would he"?

"We have forensic evidence placing him there at the time, he has admitted under caution that he went to see his father on the day he died. What do you know about that visit"?

Julie looked down at the floor, shook her head several times but did not respond.

"You asked why he would do such a thing when I think you know already. Was he angry when he discovered George was not going to pay you anymore"?

"We both were, he was supposed to help with money until Gabe left school".

"What did you decide to do about it"?

"I know stuff about him he didn't want made public; I told him he'd better think again. He threatened me.......well I mean he swore at me, a lot. Told me to F off, he'd done with paying".

"This stuff you know about him, is it what you told officer Melanie Frazer".

"That was confidential she promised not to say. Where is she anyway"?

"She didn't say anything or give details, Mel just told me you'd had a difficult time. She would never betray a confidence".

"Well good. I thought….it doesn't matter what I thought; anyway it's true he was not nice that's why we divorced".

Jonny thought Mel might be able to befriend Julie as she appeared to fear anyone knowing about what had been done to her and Gabriel.

"Look I just came in to explain what we were doing with Gabriel. Would you prefer it if Sergeant Frazer was here to explain rather than me"?

"If you want, I don't mind; you can stay if you like".

"I'll go fetch her; I won't be a moment".

Jonny left room one and went to room two viewing area to find Melanie sitting making notes. He could see through the one way mirror, a part consumed mug of tea or coffee on the table and a can of coke. Marchant and Gabriel were talking, sitting opposite was Emma holding her mug close to her lips, not drinking, listening; the sound to the viewing area having been muted.

"What do you think"?

"He'll come through although there's this niggle I have; he's holding back, don't know what"

"Come with me I need you to interview Julie, I feel her about to block me; go on your own I'll stay here".

"I've not prepared".

"You'll be fine, try and open her up into admitting she knew he was at the house".

"Hello Julie".

"Hm, did you tell him about me"?

243

"You know I didn't, I had to report our meeting but limited what I told him to just that you were unhappy in your marriage for very personal reasons".

"That's what he said but he seems to know".

"I'm sure he has a good idea but he didn't find out from me. Photos and digital images have been found of young girls in compromising positions so he suspects you may have been used in a similar way. It's going to be difficult to avoid the truth".

"He seemed to think Gabe was involved in George's death, why"?

"I think Gabe knows about what happened to you and possibly more. Did George ever take him to his studio in Market Street"?

"He used to take him out every so often I don't know where every time; it's possible he went there he never said".

"Do you think Gabe would retaliate against his dad for stopping your money".

He did say dad should pay, especially after what he has done".

"What do you think he meant by that"?

"I don't know".

"Come on Julie you must have some thoughts".

"Well if he knew what George had made me do, he never said, but it could be that I suppose".

"When he went to see his dad on the evening he died, did you go with him"?

"What makes you say that"?

"Something Gabe said".

"He shouldn't have, I told him to keep his mouth shut".

"It's perfectly understandable that you would both go to ask him to reconsider".

"Gabe said he was going, I told him not to, but he insisted. I couldn't let him go on his own could I"?

"Of course not, knowing George's violent side I would have done the same. Did you both go in"?

"Not at first it was just me but when I didn't come out straight away Gabe banged on the door so George let him in".

"What happened inside"?

"Nothing at first, we both pleaded with him to start paying again. George was quite drunk, all he did was swear at us he wasn't listening. He went to hit me but Gabe stuck his foot out and he fell".

"What happened then".

"I can't. I mustn't. We agreed to say nothing if we were questioned, Gabe didn't want to but I said to keep quiet".

Come on Julie what happened when George was on the floor"?

Julie was red in the face her eyes wide; her voice raised an octave almost shouting. Mel could see she was reliving the moment.

"George cursed a lot and was calling him a cissy and worse; the drunken bastard couldn't get up and lost his temper. He rolled over onto his knees grabbing at Gabe's legs trying to stand, said he was going to give Gabe a good hiding. Gabe pushed him down again and said how would he like a taste of his own medicine".

"Please go on Julie what did he do next"?

"I can't I promised, you will have to ask him, I won't say another word".

Mel realised she had reached Julie's limit. She would come back to her later when she'd calmed down and her resistance to further questions had abated.

"Okay Julie we will leave it there for now".

Mel left the room to find Hamish and Jonny; she needed to tell them what had transpired before they continued with Gabriel's interview.

Chapter 35

Interview room two was again ready with the recorder running and everyone present noted. Hamish, armed with the information Mel had obtained from Julie, knew he could relieve this mentally tortured young boy of his pent up guilt and emotion.

"Gabriel remember you are still under caution. I'd like to go back to where you said your father let you in. I want you to think back was it perhaps your mother who opened the door"?

"No it was dad, mum was inside".

"So your mum went in first"?

"She only went to ask him to carry on paying, she didn't do anything, it was just me".

"We know he went to hit your mum, what happened then"?

"I stuck my foot out he fell on his face, I sat on his back he couldn't get up, he'd been drinking see".

"Did he say or do anything"?

"He did swear and shout at me to let him get up; said he'd hit me when he did".

"I told him he shouldn't hit mum and should pay what he owed. He started to push himself up then, so I was afraid he would break free and hit us. I lifted up and sat hard on his back again. He collapsed and lay still for a bit so I tied his feet together then his hands".

"What did you use to tie him up".

"Oh, just some cable ties".

"You had them with you"?

"Yes. Not usually though, they were what he'd used on me and mum before; I'd brought them with me, I wanted to wave them in his face when I told him I was going to tell everyone what he was like. I never had the chance though. When he fell, they were just handy".

"Please go on Gabriel".

"Mum and me lifted him into the chair; he was shouting at us to let him go; said I was a faggot and mum a whore, said he would fucking kill us both when he got free. I stuck my hanky in his mouth it stopped him shouting a bit. Mum wanted to go and leave him but I knew he would get free and come after us I wanted him to know what it was like; being tied up and choked; I wanted to get my own back. I went to the kitchen and found a ball of string I cut a piece off with a knife. It's what he did to mum and me and some others; I'd seen the pictures so I knew we weren't the only ones. He would make us take our clothes off; I didn't want to do that with him; then he would tie us to the chair. He'd pretend to strangle us and take pictures, he would touch our bits and when we had almost passed out he would release the noose, time and time again he would tighten and loosen. He'd play with himself and keep doing it do it until he'd finished. You thought you were going to die when you couldn't breathe. I decided to do it to him so he'd know how it felt. I'd tighten the string and he'd go all dizzy then I'd loosen it, he yelled at me each time to stop but I couldn't. After a few times he shut up, so then I did stop but he just never said anything. I shook him but he didn't move. I didn't mean him to die it was an accident; I just wanted him to know what it was like".

"What did your mum do while this was going on"?

"Nothing she just watched. When he didn't come round she said we had to leave but had to cover our tracks first. I used the scissors to cut the cable ties and removed the string. Mum took them when she left; she said she would go first and I was to follow in five minutes and meet her at the end of the street".

"You left by climbing the fence why not go out the front"?

"I stayed looking at him he seemed so peaceful it wasn't fair I wanted him to suffer. I did what I'd been wanting to do for years; I cut his throat; I know he was dead already but it felt right. As I went to go there was a group of kids outside; they were right by the gate. I waited but they were sitting on the wall

247

next door talking, it didn't look like they were going to move. I didn't want to be seen so I went out the back and climbed the fence".

"Why did you cut him twice".

"I thought I hadn't done it properly first time cause he didn't bleed you see, so I did it again; I suppose it was because he was dead already".

"What happened to the knife, cable ties and string"?

"I met mum up the road and we walked home; she dropped the stuff in a dustbin on the way".

Hamish stood, his mind numbed by the story of retribution brought about by years of evil abuse, he didn't know how this would end but thanked God he wasn't the one to make that kind of decision.

"Gabriel please stand. Gabriel Grant. You are under arrest for the murder of George Grant. You are still under caution. Do you understand"?

"Yes sir, can I go now"?

"I'm afraid not Gabriel; you will remain here for the time being, your solicitor will explain what happens next".

Jonny left Gabriel and the others to deal with the formalities and went to room one.

"Oh it's you again, where's Melanie and what's happened to Gabe"?

"Your son Gabriel has been charged with the murder of his father. Julie will you please stand. Julie Grant, you are under arrest for the murder of George Grant. You do not have to say anything, but it may harm your defence if you do not mention when questioned something you later rely on in court. Anything you do say may be given in evidence. Do you understand"?

"It was all me it wasn't Gabe. He just happened to be there, I did it, I killed him, you have to let Gabe go".

"Julie do you understand the charges and the caution".

"Of course I do; you bastards pretend to be nice and then you do this to me and my boy, you come after us quick enough when all the time that fucker gets away with terrorising us for years and years. You didn't do anything about that did you"?

Jonny thought she was right in a way but her display of temper reminded him of Mel's earlier niggle. Maybe Julie was the one who incited Gabriel to do what he did or even did it herself. It's up to the lawyers now, he would of course plant that notion in Marchant's mind. Julie still had to be interviewed formally not a job he wanted; she certainly wouldn't respond positively to him, and he suspected Melanie would not be flavour of the month either. He went upstairs to let Toni know of the charges; she would decide the next course of action.

Toni listened to Jonny's report and news of the arrests.

"A good result Jonny but it does leave a nasty taste in the mouth doesn't it".

"Yes Ma'am, I have to follow up with the formal interview of Julie but she shows such aggression towards me and Melanie I don't think we will achieve much".

"The forensics you have already and Gabriel's confession are enough, do your best with her, it won't matter what she says, the two of them were there together when he was killed; I know there are plenty of loose ends to tie up, forensics and statements to be completed, put your guys on that; for you its case closed. When the paperwork is finished give everything to the CPS; they will evaluate the charges, work with them, it's a good outcome. Now you can go back to work on Palmer".

"Thanks a bundle".

"You're welcome. By the way keep in mind you still need to keep the ACC for Harrold to work on; he is closing in on Jake Snell; between the two of them we may be able to eradicate the other rotten egg".

"Don't worry he can have that one any day of the week".

Chapter 36

All the time in the world, Jake thought he'd go see his old mate Lenny Bartram. He'd used his name for a long time but was back now with his new disguise just in case the boys in blue had found out about his little passport ruse. He'd been using trains and cabs since he'd been back, buying a car would have been nice but expensive and risky, in any case his funds were limited at the moment. He told the cabby to drive slowly by the house to the end of the road. The black car parked on the double yellow lines fifty yards along gave him pause, the man sitting in the driver's seat appeared to be sleeping. He knew the wardens used to be hot and unsympathetic around these streets; he did not think that had changed so who could sit there without being disturbed; only one answer to that question. He told the driver to go to the next street and drop him approximately level with Lenny's house. The houses here were almost a mirror of those on Lenny's street with the gardens back to back. He walked to where he thought Lenny's house backed onto and used the side gate to enter it's garden. He kept close to the fence at the side moving towards the back. He climbed the fence to the rear of the garden which turned out to be one to the left of Lenny's. The fence was low enough and no barrier to Jake when in a few minutes he found himself at the ever open back door to Lenny's kitchen.

"Well ,well, I wondered when you would turn up".

Jake bent forward and the two old friends hugged.

"Good to see you Lenny how are you"?

"Not bad, all the better for seeing you. I presume you noticed the ever present visitor out front seeing as how you used the back door"?

"I did but I'm wondering why".

"Something to do with a visit I had yesterday, seems you've been a naughty boy and nicked my name; I've a card here from an Inspector Davis, he was here with a bit of skirt copper asking after you. I'm supposed to ring him when you turn up. Said you should call him if I decided not to, you can come to some arrangement; it's about him wanting a bigger fish than you".

"Davis hm! I don't know him; seems they're aware I'm in the UK, I was hoping to come in and leave without anyone noticing. Shall I make us some tea and you can tell me all about what you've been up to"?

"Biscuits in the yellow tin; by the way he took your oxo tin from the bedroom, I managed to keep your Mum's ring though".

"Nothing in the tin except the ring and my watch, did Davis take that"?

"No watch Jake, just a receipt for a repair".

"That's right, I forgot, it had stopped and I took it in to have it fixed. I wonder if it's still there; never mind I don't need it. Thanks for saving the ring though, I'd like that".

Jake passed a pleasant hour with his pal before leaving with his mum's ring in his backpack and Harrold's card in his pocket; he went out almost the same way he came in. Phone in hand, the uber, three minutes away, picked him up as he dusted himself off. He made a mental note of the house number in case he needed to return. Bigger fish indeed; he knew who they were but was hoping to land one of them for himself but considering the cop Davis's message perhaps there was another way. He asked the taxi man to find a hotel near New Cross. He chose a local B and B, over the chain hotels, as it would take cash with no questions, he thought if the police were looking for him around New Cross they may have put the main hotels on their guard. The walk to Duke Street from his digs was less than a mile, Marshalls Depository holding his nest egg was very close, he would check it out later today and go there tomorrow. After checking in at the B and B and asking after the local restaurants, he set off for an evening stroll. Halfway to Duke Street he stopped off for a pint and a look at the menu, in the 'Canal Bargeman'; one thing he missed in France was a decent ale, the beers were okay and the wine usually good but there was nothing like a pint. As he approached Duke Street it was closing in on six o'clock, plenty of traffic; but there it was the stationary black waggon with its sleeping man, fifty yards from the Depository parked on a yellow. He eased into a doorway well out of sight and waited. Sure enough almost on the hour of six, Marshalls door opened and Emily King stepped out, Jake noticed she'd hardly changed in two years, the door closed behind her, she paused listening for the electronic click as the security locks engaged and the shutters came down; satisfied all was secure she set off for home; at the same time the black car left it's spot. No imagination these guys, six hour shifts on the dot only watching when the shop was open; still he'd bet they were mounting a twenty four seven watch on Lenny. He'd have to go in at night to recover his box without them catching him. He watched Emily walk along Duke street cross the bridge and turn left, he waited a few minutes and followed. A quiet street only a stroll from her office Emily King was glad to be home; Jake Snell a few yards behind was glad too. He hoped they hadn't obtained a warrant and opened his box already but as detective Davis was here only yesterday he didn't think he could have obtained one in so short a time; if he had, that would be sticky for a certain big fish and would make it harder for Jake to apply the squeeze. He'd find out from Emily tomorrow not in her office but in the comfort of her bedroom. He was about to change her opening hours. Now he was ready for the Boatman's mixed grill and another pint.

Chapter 37

On his bed still dressed, Jake couldn't sleep, he was agitated, the police had sussed out Lenny and had a watch on Marshalls too, what were they waiting for. Did they think he would just walk in; no they were not that stupid; why keep a watch and leave it so obvious. Was there someone watching he had not seen; were they leaving a clear time out of hours to tempt him? If he was going to do it, it must be now before they had time to set the trap. He put on his jacket and back-pack quietly descended the stairs leaving the guest house, gently closed the front door so as not to disturb the landlord, it was just after midnight.

He walked on the far side of Duke Street carefully scrutinising the parked cars, no sign of surveillance, he felt safer but because he saw no sign it did not mean there was none. He pressed on. Emily's house was in darkness, her semi had a side entrance with a wrought iron gate; it did not appear to be locked. Jake stayed on the oppose side of the road walking fifty yards each way checking for surveillance. None to see. The adrenalin was pumping now the excitement building it was now or never, he crossed the road and entered the garden of the house next door, moving silently to a break between the houses where the hedge stopped short, he found the gate fastened, as he'd thought a latch no lock; he lifted the latch, winced at the squeak emanating from the hinges, as he pushed it open, sounding like an out of tune violin; he slipped through closing it slowly to reduce the expected screech. It was silent, 'funny that' he thought 'makes a racket when you open it but not when closing. "Concentrate" he whispered to himself, he crept round the back to find a small conservatory all its double glazed windows closed tight, he peered inside to see a sliding glass door to the main house also closed. Beyond the conservatory what looked like a bathroom window with its frosted glass; the top vent slightly open. Here was the way in. He reached into his rucksack and found what he had put on the top earlier, a simple tool made from a plastic ruler and a small wire hook taped to one end. He inserted the business end into the crack between the frame and the small vent fishing carefully inch by inch, his practiced hand felt the resistance of a handle, he pulled gently teasing the handle up slowly so the makeshift hook did not to slip off; click the window was open. Not a large opening but certainly big enough for Jake to climb through, he took what he needed from the back-pack stuffed them in his pocket, leaving the pack on the ground for now; he'd recover it later. No bath, just a small cloakroom. His eyes soon became accustomed to the dark seeing no light from under the door he eased it open to reveal he was in the corner of a large square hallway, the stairs to his right and the front door to the left; immediately opposite were two closed doors. He moved to the stairs listening, all was quiet. He climbed the stairs keeping his feet away from the tread centres in case of loose risers whose sound would be familiar to its owner subconsciously warning them of an unexpected approach. He needn't have worried Emily was well asleep, which he found to be the case when he opened her bedroom door and stood over her. He removed the bindings from his pocket hovered over her head struck at his target like a snake, immediately winding the knotted scarf around Emily's face and over her mouth. Still half asleep and not sure if what was happening was real or just a nightmare, Emily's legs and arms were bound tight in seconds she couldn't move. It wasn't a dream it was real; a real nightmare. Jake unwound the scarf from her eyes keeping her mouth and nose covered. His face was inches away, his hot breath buffeting her eyes. A silent scream from Emily lay smothered unheard within her chest as he spoke.

"Miss Emily King, I'm sure you remember me and if not I think the police will have reminded you recently. I want one thing only then you will be set free. If you try to scream or fail to do as I say I will cut your throat and watch you bleed to death, if you understand nod your head".

Emily nodded furiously, she was wide awake now and terrified; she wasn't going to disobey this maniac, the police said he had killed before and she knew he wasn't bluffing.

"I am going to remove the covering from your face keep very, very quiet".

Jake unwound the cloth from her mouth and watched her take a deep breath but no words or noise of any kind came from the horrified face. This would be easy.

"You must tell me how I can enter the depository and get to my box. I have the key and the box number and will not touch anything else, when I have my box I want to know how I leave without triggering an alarm. If you do all of that I will phone the police and tell them where you are and they will set you free. If I see any sign of the police or do not get what I want I will come back and kill you. One more thing I will bind your face so tight your breathing will be very restricted, if I am caught you will probably suffocate in a few hours so you'd better be right or no one will know you are here until it's too late. Right now speak to me".

Emily tried to respond but couldn't, the tunnel of her throat seemed to have dried and her tongue stuck to the roof of her mouth all she emitted was a croak. She swallowed, a little moisture from her saliva glands broke the involuntary seal allowing her to utter a few words in a squeaky croak.

"If you have the entry code....my key....you can get in".

She coughed almost choking. Jake looked around and saw a glass of water on her bedside table. He took the glass to her lips.

"Here drink this... Hey, hey, take your time".

She managed to sup some of the water spilling it down her chin and onto her body. Her throat cleared, she continued fearful of what he might do.

"You can press the code button in the office, same as the one on your key it will open the vault and enable your box; the key will release your box".

"That sounds too simple tell me all the details".

"I'm sorry I forgot you must also stop the alarm".

"How do I do that"?

"Just put in the code".

Her voice so weak Jake could hardly hear what she said. Emily started to sob her breath coming in gasps, tears ran down her cheeks dripping onto her breasts; the drops on her exposed body triggered an awareness of herself; her nakedness was a shock; her vulnerability to this evil man disturbing. She became angry at his invasion; her ire engendered a determination not to break down. A deep breath followed her decision; she'd give him what he wanted and be safe.

"You can stop the bloody crying it just makes me irritable".

A vicious poke in the ribs emphasised his point and brought a yelp of pain from Emily.

"I'm not going to wait all night. Run me through the whole process step by step no mistakes hear".

A second jab ensured Emily was not going to resist. She knew the procedure routinely doing it every day.

"My key opens a panel in the wall to the left of the building. Put in the five digit code on the panel, this will free the electronic lock and open the shutters you can then open the entry door with the same key. Once inside there is a panel on the right it is behind the door, you will have to almost close the door to reach the panel and deactivate the alarm with another code, four digits this time. This will release the inner door to the office, you have forty seconds to do this".

"How do I get into the vault"?

"You can open it easy enough there is a panel on the desk it is covered by a plastic screen this is where you enter the code of your box, this allows access to your box all the other boxes

256

remain disabled. Next press the red button on the desk; this opens the door to the vault; you can then open your box with the key. To exit the vault press the green button by the door, I then press my red button again and let you out. If you touch any box other than yours the door will not open and the alarm sounds. I don't know how you will open the door to leave if you are on your own".

"What if I wedge the vault door open".

"It may work I don't know I've never tried it".

"How do I get out of the office and the front door"?

"The same it is the red button that releases the locks on all the doors you just push".

"If it goes wrong are the police called automatically"?

"No we have a security company that responds"'

"How long".

"Ten minutes maybe a little more".

"Give me the code numbers".

"What if it goes wrong how will I escape".

"You'd better hope it doesn't, numbers please".

Emily recited the two codes and told him the key was in her purse. She had no idea if wedging the door to the vault or the office in the open position would allow access to the box or trigger an alarm. She prayed all would be okay and he'd tell the police where she was. He came back with the key and held it up so she could see.

"Is this it"?

"Yes. Please don't cover my face I won't call out I promise".

He twisted the scarf three times covering her eyes nose and mouth. She tried to scream but all that happened was her hot breath made the cloth stick to her face. It was too late now; she forgot to tell him the building was time alarmed. If the front keypad was opened between when she closes and seven am the following day the security company will see an alarm. She was sure he would be caught and leave her to die.

Jake was nervous, it would only take a moment to find his box, even if wedging the doors triggered the alarm he had ten minutes to enter, open his box and leave; he figured that was plenty. His only doubt was if wedging the front door open interlocked with the vault door so he couldn't open it. The only way to find out was to try and see. He'd forgot to ask if the alarm was silent and time sensitive or both; would the security team be alerted at the moment he entered without him realising. If he couldn't enter and be out in under ten minutes there was no point in trying. He'd assume the worst and time himself, start the count as soon as he opened the panel in the wall and be gone in nine minutes, with or without the stuff in his box. Jake left her house the way he came in, collected his back-pack and walked slowly towards Duke Street. A black car had appeared fifty yards from Emily's house. They knew he was coming but this guy hadn't seen him; his exit through the garden of the house next door and staying inside the boundaries of several others along the road had kept him out of sight.

"Please Ma'am I need a warrant to open Jake's safety box, is there any way we can do this without all the fuss"?

"Sorry Harrold obtaining a warrant to allow you to open a safety deposit box when you have no proof that the named person actually owns such a box, is not going to happen. You said the woman who runs the Depository refused to confirm the name of Jeremy Shore as a customer, you thought she hinted that he was; that won't convince a magistrate. Jake's own box was long gone so without more evidence even the friendliest of judges will balk at the idea; any deposition will have to be watertight and it won't happen overnight that's for sure".

"I'm certain Jake will be there soon if not already, so what do you suggest"?

"Bonington has put a full watch on Lenny's house and another on the depository; no sign of him so far. The watch on

Lenny should deter him as it is quite visible. The one on Duke Street is the same but only covers opening hours so if Jake is going to try anything it will be at night".

"Seems reasonable but the security is pretty tight; how do you think he'll get in when it is all locked up"?

"He's a killer with no qualms about using violence so thinking like he does he will probably go after the King woman".

"Risky for him Ma'am but if he is desperate to find his box he may well resort to violence. We should put a watch on her as soon as possible".

"He will spot anything simple like a car outside, we need to put a man inside her house and someone to follow when she goes out. I'm not sure if we should tell her as she needs to act normally or he will see somethings up".

"She will have to know Ma'am if we put a man inside, she seemed quite strong I will be up front with her. Peter Andrews can be with her at home, June and I will shadow the walk to and from her work. I'm really worried about her".

"Okay Harrold I'll call Bonington to add someone to watch over King and let him know, his guys can stay in place in case there is a change we don't know about, radios channel four if you need back up from them".

"I suggest a night watch on the depository as well, tonight if possible, we'll go over first thing".

None of them realised their security arrangements could be too late. This meeting took place only just before Emily's interrogation by Jake.

Chapter 38

Duke street was quiet, the parked cars were the same as earlier, no suspicious additions. He approached the Depository stopped outside keeping his eyes open for any activity. He walked on twenty yards turned and stopped. If anyone was watching they were not showing themselves. 'Now or never' was his thought. Key in hand he opened the keypad in the wall, the rehearsed numbers entered he waited. At first he thought nothing was happening, that bitch of a woman had lied given him the wrong code, the rising tension abated at the whirring sound of a motor and seeing the shutters begin to rise. His clock was counting; the shutters seemed to take an age although it was only fifteen seconds for them to fully retract and the whirring ceased. The key opened the door at which point a regular beeping became the object of his attention, he stepped inside the sprung door pressing to close itself behind him, he let it go back so far but stopped it from shutting completely by the piece of cloth torn from one of his tee shirts placed in the jamb. The alarm panel, now accessible was lit with a red glow the insistent beep emanating from somewhere within. Jake punched in the numbers. Silence and white light replaced the red. He estimated eight minutes to go. The streetlights outside had lulled him into forgetting how dark it would be inside, the obvious bank of four switches next to the alarm panel would solve the problem, he hit them all at once. The place was bathed in light: the inner door to the office area pushed open easily, another piece of his T shirt held it ajar. From the corridor he reached through the window lifted the plastic cover ready to select his box code but stopped, he couldn't see a bloody red button anywhere. Thankfully the side door into the office itself was not locked pushing through he saw the offending device hidden from the view of customers on a shelf under the desk. He quickly selected box sdg, the code etched on his key, pressed the red button, almost ran round to the corridor up to the vault entrance. Jake held his breath and pushed; he was in; again the piece of cloth in the door jamb did its work. He went directly to number 187, its location etched in his memory; he'd waited two years for this day. The key he'd kept on a cord around his neck for the same long time poised over the lock; he prayed that blocking the doors from closing did not also stymie access to his box. The key turned the clicking sound of a lock released were music to his ears as the box slid free. He did not wait to check its contents he knew what was there. Two thousand pounds in cash but more importantly the two USB memory sticks. Cash into his pack the USBs to his inside pocket, he couldn't believe how easy it was, six minutes tops, he would be halfway to is digs before the security arrived. He tugged at the vault door, no problem the same for the office with only the street door to negotiate. He stopped turned off the lights not wishing to be framed in a halo of brightness as he stepped out. Pulling the door back enough to see outside he had a good view both ways all was quiet. Seven minutes all done. Jake marched along the street pleased with his night's work.

Constable Neil Portman was annoyed at being called out so late, he had been about to go to bed when he received the call from Inspector Bonington. Two long shifts watching the Depository saw it secure when he last left at six; he wondered why he was to return. The sergeant ordered him back at once, as the target was expected to show up any time soon, but instead of an open and obvious deterrent, he was to keep himself out of sight. A back up team was being assembled and would be close by within the hour. He was only to call in back up if there were any sightings; follow the subject at a distance but not to approach were his instructions. In order to remain covert he would have to park some distance away and walk in; there were not many places to hide near to Marshalls, all the shops either faced directly onto the street or at night had shutters over doorways where he might stay concealed. The street lighting didn't help much either but the few parked vehicles might afford him some cover; he'd have to play it by ear when he arrived. In the original briefing all the surveillance team had been given a photo and a profile of the man they were seeking. Jake Snell, currently using the name Jerry Shore, known to use violence and assumed to be armed. Neil had studied the face and was sure he would recognise him easily enough. Dressed in jeans and a warm sweatshirt with a fleece lined jacket, he was determined not to get cold standing outside half the night. The officer on nights posted outside Lenny Bartram's house was his mate Thomas Gwent. Tommy was not too far away he'd give him a call when he was on site. He was told that a DI Davis and his number two would be along later; Neil had been given Davis's mobile number if needed. The car was cold as was the night air when Neil set off; glad of his choice in clothes, for the journey to Duke Street was hardly far enough to stimulate the car heater into providing any kind of comfort. He parked in a side street five hundred yards from his quarry checked his radio and phone were secure, locked up and walked slowly towards the Depository. He stayed on the opposite side keeping low using the cars as shelter from anyone looking from the Depository. Soon he was close enough to see the building and was shocked to find the shutters were up and the lights were on.

"DP one, this is DP two over".

"What's up Neil are you in position. Over".

"Just arrived I need back up now. The depository is compromised the shutters are up, the lights on, subject may have left already or could still be on the premises. Over".

"Hold fast back up with you in ten minutes. Over".

"Shit the lights have just gone out, subject is leaving he's turned west along Duke street, I am following. Over".

"Wait for back up. Over".

"Can't sarge it will be too late; subject will be gone. Over".

"Stay well away Neil this guy is dangerous keep the radio open update your position as you go. Over".

Neil stayed on the opposite side to his target moving at the same steady pace a safe distance but close enough to keep his subject in sight. A vehicle approached from behind Neil it headlights on full beam, he ducked down behind a car waiting for it to pass. The vehicle stopped he looked back to see it pull up outside the Depository, a man climbed out walked up to the door and went inside. Neil was in two minds who the hell was this guy. He spoke into the open channel ignoring radio protocol,

"Another suspect has just pulled up in a van and gone inside the depository, I'll stay with original subject ask the back-up team to deal with the van guy".

"Okay, be careful Neil. Over".

In the brief time Neil had turned his subject was out of sight, Neil hurried along Duke street ever nearer to its end. The approaching crossroads gave him three alternative routes he hoped he would see his subject before then or he may be gone. Relieved to see Jake had crossed over to the same side as Neil some eighty yards ahead and was about to turn left. Neil pressed against the wall and froze, he hoped Jake would not glance back, for he was totally exposed with no cars or any cover to hide behind. It seems he was okay even though Jake did turn and appeared to look straight at Neil but not reacting to his presence; Jake was now out of sight having turned into the street on the left. Neil reported his position over the radio and halted at the corner. A brief glance around the side of the corner building was enough to spot Jake disappear into the shadows of a private house. Neil crossed over and moved to almost opposite the house. The bed and breakfast notice in the window was clear to be seen. The door was in darkness no sign of Jake; Neil presumed he had gone inside.

"Subject entered twenty seven Halliburton Road. It's a B and B, waiting and watching. You'd better hurry I can't cover the back he could be gone already".

"Stay where you are the back-up team will be with you soon; they are investigating the white van; I'll keep you posted. Over".

The six man team arrived in two vehicles one behind and one in front blocking the van in. Two armed officers approached the depository. A man came to the door dressed in green overalls with a Secure System Ltd. logo on his breast pocket.

"Am I glad to see you, someone's done a good job here alright".

The two officers were not taking any chances; the guard was immediately secured and cuffed much to his surprise. A quick check proved his credentials were genuine so he was released to be questioned in detail by one of the team. The team leader called Neil.

"Sorry we are a bit behind Neil, one vehicle is on its way now. The van guy's from the security company Marshalls use, he came out thinking there was a false alarm, he's worried about the lady that runs the place he says no one could open up without her key and all the codes. There is an officer on watch at her house already, I'll ask him to check. Be with you in five. Over".

"Good don't be too long suspect may have seen me I can't cover all the exits from here, I don't want to lose him now".

Harrold Davis received the call at one thirty am, it had all kicked off earlier than he thought, the upshot of the report from Bonington was; 'suspect has been isolated arrest imminent'. He dressed in record time and was on his way to New Cross stopping to pick up June on his way.

"What's up boss where are we going"?

"Jake's broken into Marshalls, he's been followed to a hotel in New Cross, Bonington's response team have secured the premises. That's all I know. You drive you're quicker than me".

The night drive reached a hundred mph on occasions but the journey still took a frustratingly long time. An hour and ten minutes later the Basingstoke duo found two cars blocking the road, three fully protected uniform officers and one in plain clothes attending. The chief of the team greeted them.

"Sergeant Meaker sir, site secure, us three plus three others at the rear, suspect believed inside, Detective Constable Neil Portman there followed him from Marshalls to this house and called us in; no sign of movement since. A message from Inspector Bonington sir, he says he will leave it to you to make the arrest".

"Good work, what about Miss King".

"She was found traumatised but physically had only minor injuries from being tied up. She's been taken to hospital by ambulance a female constable from the local station is in attendance".

"Thank goodness for that sergeant, this fellow has no qualms about killing anyone who finds themselves in his way. Do you know how many people are in the house here"?

"No idea, except the landlord Theo Jackman and his wife, four letting rooms are registered with the local authority but we don't know if they are occupied".

"I can't believe he hasn't spotted this lot; he's not going to just walk out if he has".

Harrold thought about Bonington leaving him to reap the rewards of his efforts or perhaps he's protecting his ass in case Jake escapes, either way he was stuck with it. He beckoned indicating for Neil to come over.

"Constable Portman, I'm Detective Inspector Davis I understand you followed the suspect from Marshalls, did you recognise him"?

"Not one hundred percent sir, but it looked like Jake Snell, the photo we have is not too good".

"You're right there but it's all we have. Did you see him go into this B and B"?

"I'm sure he did, he stopped outside and approached the door but it was too dark to see from where I was; when I came opposite the door it was closed and he was nowhere to be seen, if he hadn't gone in I would have seen him, there was nowhere else to go".

"Did he spot you"?

"I don't think so but there was a point when I was exposed so it's possible".

"How long after you arrived before the team secured the building"?

"Five minutes six tops".

"Time enough for him to have left out the back".

"I suppose sir, I bloody hope not, surely if he had seen me he wouldn't have gone in would he"?

"Perhaps he didn't".

"Didn't see me you mean"?

"No Constable. Didn't go in".

Harrold knew there was only one way to find out; before then he walked back with June to the car; he wanted her out of the way if Jake decided to become aggressive.

"June, find out which Hospital where they have taken Emily King; go and take her statement while it is fresh in her mind, use the phone not the radio to keep in touch".

Jake thought he'd caught a glimpse of someone following a moment before he turned into the street of the B and B. He deliberately hadn't tried very hard to avoid being caught once he'd secured his insurance; in any case he knew it was only a matter of time; at least this way he could keep out of the reach of Brown and Blakewood. After Grimes, Vale and Branch had been

266

caught, he became a prime target of those other two, he now had the safety net he wanted. The USB chips were inserted and glued securely into the carrying strap of his back-pack; two small compartments he'd prepared earlier were deep inside the straps' padding; they were undetectable. Although his room faced the rear overlooking a tiny garden, the bathroom at the front gave him a good view of the street below, the police presence was now significant both front and rear, he couldn't escape even if he wanted to. He lay on the bed and waited. His hopes of blackmailing Monty Brown or even Blakewood were a long shot anyway, with his money almost gone and little chance of securing enough to stay abroad in comfort, this was the best solution; he hated life on the run anyway. Giving evidence against the two corrupt senior officers would provide him with the chance of witness protection and a new start, or at the very least a shorter sentence in an open prison. It all depended on Detective Davis following up on his invitation. Jake heard the persistent ring of the doorbell. 'Here we go', he thought, standing ready to leave, his backpack left lying on the floor next to the bed.

"Sergeant we need to see if Snell is actually in there, a direct approach is our only choice, we could be here all night waiting for him to come out only to find he has gone already. I want your two men one each side of me, alert your guys at the back in case he makes a break for it, remind them he has used firearms before, so no risks if he decides to run. You and Constable Portman remain here in case it goes sour".

"Do you want a jacket sir".

Harrold opened his coat to reveal he was already suited.

"Been there before Sergeant, I don't fancy being shot but thanks for the concern, call your guys I'm going in now".

At three fifteen Constables Troy and Kettering stood next to Harrold Davis as he pushed the doorbell holding it down for a full thirty seconds. It was loud enough to be heard clearly from where he stood. He paused for another thirty then rang again followed by banging with the side of his fist on the wooden frame. A muffled voice emanated from within obviously moaning about the disturbance at such a late hour but too garbled for each individual word to be understood. The door opened a few inches to the full extent of a safety chain.

"What do you want; don't you realise what sodding time it is; we are full anyway"?

The two uniforms closed in on Harrold's shoulder clearly visible to the occupier. Harrold held up his warrant card followed by Jakes photo.

"Sorry to disturb you Mr Jackman sir I am Detective Inspector Davis we need to come in at once; I believe you have a dangerous man staying here this is his picture".

"Bloody hell, that's Mr. Short or something, dangerous you say, what's he done" ?

"Open the door please sir".

"I'll have to shut it first; the chain".

Harrold stepped back the door closed for a moment to open fully a few seconds later. Troy and Kettering went in first bypassing Jackman; Harrold stayed back.

"Mr. Jackman where is he"?

"Second floor top of the stairs number four".

The two officers moved together to the foot of the stairs stopped and waited for the instruction to go.

"How many guests do you have, you said you were full".

"I said that to get rid of you, only Miss Harvey, room one first floor, the others are empty".

"Where is your room"?

"That's down here out back".

"Go fetch your wife now and bring her here".

Harrold pointed at the smaller of the two officers, he didn't know which name belonged to which.

"Officer Troy"?

"Yes sir".

Pleased he'd guessed right, he wanted them to do the initial search as they were more experienced and trained for this type of situation than he ever was.

"You go to room one and bring out Miss Harvey, as soon as she and the Jackmans are clear we go. Kettering you check rooms two and three on the way up, if Jake is still somewhere in the house all this noise will have alerted him; he'll be ready and waiting so take extra care".

The Jackmans and Miss Harvey were herded outside to the waiting Sergeant Meaker. Again the two officers went ahead. Room two on the first floor was clear, the same for room three on the second. The two uniforms stood either side of room four. Harrold to the right, Kettering reached across and banged on the door.

"Jake Snell this is the police the house is secure there is nowhere to go please come out".

"Who is it"?

Came a voice from within. Harrold responded.

"I'm Detective Harrold Davis please come out with your hands visible above your head. Armed officers are in attendance so be warned they will not hesitate if you resist with violence".

"Ah Inspector Davis you took your time, I have your card and your message, I've been looking forward to meeting you for our little chat. I don't have a weapon I'm coming out".

The door opened, Jakes hands where they were requested to be. Kettering stepped forward, pulled his arms down one at a time, put the cuffs on Jakes wrists behind his back and patted him down.

"Nothing sir".

"Good. Jacob Snell you are under arrest for burglary at the premises known as Marshalls Depository. You do not have to say anything but it may harm your defence if you fail to mention something when questioned that you later rely on in court.

269

Anything you do say will be given in evidence. Do you understand".

Jake smiled and nodded. The took him downstairs securing him in the police van, Harrold approached Meaker.

"Sergeant please call Inspector Bonington he will tell you where to take him".

After they had taken Jake away Harrold went back up to room four, made a quick search to find it empty apart from an old backpack on the floor. He tipped its contents out onto the bed; some clean underwear, two shirts neatly folded a pair of socks. An old daily Mail newspaper well read by the look of it. A mobile phone and its charger, a plastic ruler with a small hook taped on the end, a ladies ring, one Harrold had seen before, two passports one in the name Lenny Bartram the other Jerry Shore. Finally an envelope with his name on the front; inside a note saying 'Please Inspector pass this on to my good friend Lenny B' with the signature 'Jake Snell'; it contained a wedge of fifty pound notes. Harrold piled it all back into the bag and walked downstairs; he'd deal with it later. The note puzzled him and the earlier comment about a 'meeting and a chat' were an indication he expected to be caught; no, not expected exactly; Jake wanted this to happen.

Chapter 39

Jonny Musgrove had Earnest Palmer in room two and Samuel Rivers in room three, he was thinking the Super was almost ready to tackle ACC Montague Brown but needed these two to be charged first with their statements implicating Brown in the bag. The recovery of his deleted computer files and some CCTV images were enough to question Brown under caution but third party confirmation would seal the deal; he would tread carefully at first. He knew Harrold was still tracking their old friend Jake Snell who may be able to add spice to the mix and confirm Brown was party to murder and kidnapping. He would love to be the one conducting the interview but if questioned under caution any officer of his rank could demand one of higher seniority be his questioner. Superintendent Walter Munroe was the most senior officer in Basingstoke so if they had to bring in someone to do that he would an outsider, which they dearly wanted to avoid. He wondered what Munroe and Toni had in mind.

The three were gathered in Walters office, putting forward his plan. Walter was leading the meeting; he'd been waiting two years for this moment.

"Here's what I think; let's keep it simple. I will call Monty Brown to come here he still thinks of me as a friend trying to help him out of a possible embarrassing situation, much as I'd done in acquiring his computer. When presented with the evidence his reaction will dictate my next step".

Toni couldn't wait for Walter to continue.

"That bastard would either try to bluster his way out by pulling rank or would capitulate looking for a way to save his worthless self by blaming everyone else. I'd bet my house on the latter".

"Remember Toni he is a slippery worm and will try to wriggle free, so no one's taking bets here. The sadistic images

271

will open the door, but his past dealings with Vale are what I'm really after; once he admits his involvement with Palmer it will only be considered a minor infringement, unless we can prove he knew about the abductions; that would be much more serious. Establishing a connection to Vale and Branch was going to be our aim, if we do that a long sentence will be staring him in the face".

Toni hit the nail on the head when she said.

"He's a bloody arse creeping coward who'd give up his own mother to get out of that one".

"One step at a time Toni, I'll have him in my office he'll be more relaxed and feel safer here than any interview room".

Jonny was concerned they do things right.

"Whatever he says in here with you sir, is not going to be any good in court, even if you record the whole thing it will be seen as entrapment, without a caution this won't work".

"I doubt if charges relating to Grant or Palmer will ever be taken to court, Jonny; however this will put him on the back foot, just the threat of revealing his involvement will be enough to make him talk. Once he admits even the slightest connection to Vale or any of his people, I will place him under caution, transfer him to the conference room and bring in all the paraphernalia, a police lawyer, his chosen representative the lot, he'll be shitting himself. Don't worry Jonny, Toni Webb has Chief Superintendent Vernon Smith's big guns ready. He has been waiting as long as we have to end this".

"What about Inspector Davis, is he any closer to arresting Snell"?

"Last report he was heading to New Cross expecting to make an arrest soon".

Ever cynical, with 'later' rather than sooner in mind Jonny couldn't hold back.

"We all know what that means Ma'am".

He wished he'd bitten his tongue before he spoke seeing Toni look at him with a scowl.

"We do indeed but Harrold Davis always means what he says, you of all people should know him by now".

"You're right, of course Harrold will come through. It's up to me now with Palmer and Rivers".

Once out of the office Jonny went immediately to the interrogation rooms where Mel Frazer and Constable Faye Tenison were waiting in viewing room two.

"Okay Melanie you can tackle Palmer this time, I'll observe from here; caution him first we have enough to charge him but I want to find out what happened to Karen. You have the stuff Compton extracted from his computer and his prints being all over the Market Street studio. Give him a way out if he gives us information about her. I'm not sure about Rivers you know we don't have much so need Palmer to give us a way into him. His laptop was not productive like the others, Compton thought he had deleted some files but no more than he would have in normal use. What she recovered was largely innocent or unidentifiable. He may not be involved at all but your gut says different I know. So go and find me something I can use".

Melanie entered the room with Faye ready to begin the interrogation, Constable Faraday remained standing in the corner where he had been keeping watch over Palmer.

"Mr. Palmer I'm detective Sergeant Melanie Frazer...".

"Where's the other one, Detective Musive something or other".

"I presume you mean Inspector Musgrove; he's busy elsewhere. I was about to say, I am here to interview you formally with regard to your activities at Market street studio and the death of George Grant. The interview will be recorded and Constable Faye Tenison will take notes".

Faye switched on the recorder then Melanie began the ritual process.

"Interview with Mr. Earnest Palmer; present in the room are me, Detective Sergeant Melanie Frazer, Constables Faye Tenison and Alan Faraday".

The officers spoke to indicate their presence as did Earnest when prompted.

"Earnest Palmer, you are not under arrest at this time but I must caution you that during this interview you do not have to say anything, but it may harm your defence if you do not mention when questioned something you later rely on in court. Anything you do say may be given in evidence. You may have a solicitor present if you wish, if you cannot afford it one will be provided for you. Do you understand"?

Palmer just bobbed his head.

Please speak up Mr Palmer for the recording.

"Yes, but do I need a solicitor"?

"If you wish, however it is not necessary, you may of course ask for one at any time during the interview. Do you require one now"?

"I haven't done anything I didn't kill George Grant so I don't need one. No".

"Regardless of what you told Inspector Musgrove I hope you will think about your answers this time as we have evidence of your having visited Market Street studio on several occasion. When you were there did you take photos of young people in various states of undress"?

"No never".

"How come we have images of these taken from your computer"?

"It was George who took the photos, he sent them to me in emails I didn't ask for them I thought I'd deleted them".

"Indeed you did but not until after we came calling at your work place the other day; these images have been viewed many times before you ditched them, why is that"?

This was a bit of a stretch by Mel as there was no way of telling how many times they had been looked at but Palmer didn't know that.

"Oh dear I don't know; they were just there I didn't see any harm they were only pictures".

"Did they remind you of the time when you watched George take them"?

"I didn't want to watch he asked me there I didn't know what was going to happen".

"Had you met Karen before that day"?

"What do you mean, that was the first time I'd seen that girl".

Melanie produced the photo of Karen taken from Georges printer memory by far the best of the images but similar to those from Palmer's hard drive. Mel knew he had seen it many times before and probably instigated the whole exercise. She was going to offer a scapegoat, see if he bit.

"This girl here; is she the one George tied up for everyone to take pictures".

"Yes, yes, it was George he did all that, some of the others took pictures but not me".

"Interesting do you think one of them killed George"?

The fact that Gabriel had killed George had not yet been made public so Melanie used the fear of being charged with murder to elicit the names of those on which Earnest might want to lay the blame

"What? I don't know, it could be I suppose".

"So it wasn't you then"?

"No, no it wasn't me; it must have been one of them".

"I only have you we don't know who the others are".

"I can't remember their names".

"Well you'd better start remembering or I will quickly run out of patience and conclude this interview and send you to the cells".

"Hey; don't do that give me a minute to think".

Mel said nothing just leant forward head cocked to one side looking Palmer in the eyes. Palmer looked down obviously debating who to give up first, not realising once he had mentioned even one name the flood gates would have been cracked.

"Err... there was um...a bloke called Simon".

"Simon who; your club doesn't have a member with the name Simon"?

"Maybe I got that wrong it's difficult to remember, George brought people who weren't members you know".

Again Mel knew he was making up lies; she said nothing just waited. The silence saw the sweat break out on the brow of Palmer; he was about to concede.

"There was this one chap I'd seen a couple of times his name was Brown I think, George called him Manny. He took photos of his own I saw him one time".

Is that it, just one name, was he a member"?

"Yes I think so, you'll have to check with Lewis he knows all the members".

"Did Lewis go to the studio".

"Good God no he's a right stick in the mud, I'd never invite him".

Mel couldn't believe her ears, Earnest Palmer had no idea what he had just said, he wasn't thinking straight; she'd change tack now press towards finding out where Karen might be. Constantly changing the subject ignoring, as unimportant, anything Palmer revealed in his confusion.

"We'll come back to which members were invited later. Now what can you tell me about the girl Karen; who brought her to the venue".

"I don't know she was just there".

"Did she come with George"?

276

"She must have done, although it was Rivers who took her when we left".

"How did you make her pose; I hope you didn't hurt her when you tied her up".

"No. I was always careful".

"I'm glad about that, she looked a bit drugged, did George do that too".

Palmer dropped his head into his palms realisation he had gone too far he didn't know how he was going to get out of this.

"Look I don't want to say any more I want a solicitor, you made me say things I didn't mean to".

"I only asked the questions you answered of your own free will. Do you have a solicitor and would like to telephone them"?

"No; you said you'd give me one".

"That's fine Earnest I'll call the duty solicitor".

Melanie thought she'd had a real good run up to that point much more information revealed than expected. She'd allow him his solicitor and speak to Jonny before continuing. Brown and Rivers being a bonus she knew were involved.

"Melanie Frazer, I can't believe you just did that, the guy's an idiot, did you hear what he said".

"Oh yes sir I did indeed. Who's duty brief"?

"Don't know the desk sergeant will call them in for you, whoever it is let me speak with them before he speaks to Palmer. I'm going to start on Rivers".

"Hang fire a while sir, now we know he's involved let's see if Compton can give us more details about him before you start".

"Okay Mel chase that up whilst you wait for the brief, I'm not sure if Palmer dropped the name Rivers just to confuse us, don't forget his computer was clean".

"Never thought of that, you know, giving up all that was a bit too easy wasn't it, maybe Palmer's not the fool he seems, then again maybe he is".

Chapter 40

Melanie was buzzing and wanted to calm down, a slow walk downstairs to the desk Sergeant to organise a solicitor for Palmer and then on to see Compton Busion, who would give her pause. The almost confessional session with Palmer should not be taken at face value until there was some verification. Her target must be to find out what happened to Karen Small, not seeking a prosecution for making some dodgy photos. The possibility of Montague Brown's involvement would assist Harrold in his task but for her it was still only a side issue.

"Hello Mel, what can I do for you"?

"Need a duty solicitor Joe for Earnest Palmer in room two who's on call"?

"Maitland or Jarvis"?

"Either will do can I leave you to organise it for me. DI Musgrove would like to see him before they contact Palmer"?

"No problem".

"Whoever it is warn the other one he may be needed later, the guy in room three, that's Sam Rivers, will probably demand a brief from the off".

"Busy day? Don't worry I'll sort them".

"You bet, thanks Joe".

Compton was at her desk as always, looked up at Mel's knock on the glass door beckoning her in with a broad smile.

"Hello Compy, I'm not disturbing you am I"?

"No its fine, what can I do for you today"?

"Samuel Rivers, have you anything new"?

"Nothing significant he seems straight enough, finances, work, home life all normal. Nothing in his past, served three years in the army, when much younger, discharged on medical grounds with an excellent conduct record. I've dug as deep as I can legally, he seems okay".

"What was the medical problem"?

"An eye condition, retina pig….thingummy, I can't remember what it's called exactly. Anyway it means he is almost blind except for the central vision, like looking at everything through a tube apparently: there's no cure".

"So what does he do for a living"?

"He works for a software house writing code".

"How on earth does he do that if he cant see properly. Does he drive"?

"I shouldn't think so, he doesn't have a licence".

"That explains a lot. Right now what have you found about Earnest Palmer, since"?

"He does drive although the family car is registered in his wife's name. I thought that was odd so dug around and found he has an insurance policy on a van registered to a John Smith".

"How did you find that".

"Although the DVLA has a different name and address he used an E. Palmer credit card to pay the insurance premium, I just back tracked from there".

"You amaze me; I'm glad I'm not a villain in your sights. I suppose you have the address and vehicle number too".

"Of course. Welland Park, Rotherwick and the van is an old blue Transit VYB 46R".

"I don't know Welland Park".

"Me neither, so I used Google Maps. Here we go; there it is; looks like an open space behind Tinkley Hall. Wait up, let's print off a satellite image".

As Compton zoomed in on the wooded area at first it seemed like nothing was there but on full size and closer examination a shed or caravan could be seen hidden amongst the trees.

"Best I can do, there are no ground level images though, there never are in such a remote site. Looks like a narrow lane off the one that serves the rear entrance to Tinkley; probably the only way in".

"Can you print a copy of that off for me"?

"No problem, anything else"?

"I think you've done more than enough; I'll leave you to go back to whatever you were doing before I barged in".

Rivers, oh Mr. Rivers, I think I have it all wrong with you, its Palmer all the time, playing me with his misdirections. Melanie was angry at herself for being so obstinate in her view concerning Rivers, keep an open mind was always Jonny's way she should have learnt the lesson by now. Her walk back to the interrogation rooms settled her ready for the next session; on her way she diverted to the squad room looking for Peter Andrews. Peter was at his desk writing in his notebook when she found him.

"Peter have you got a minute"?

"Yes Sarge just putting my stuff in order, how's it going with Palmer"?

"Okay I suppose, he's being tricky, pretending to be a bit of a dipstick, giving us names to lead us away from him. Anyway what I want from you is to go and see what you find at a place called Welland, it's next to Tinkly Hall or behind it, here's a satellite map think you can find it".

"I know Tinkly Sarge should be alright: what's there, what am I looking for"?

"On the photo there's a caravan or a shed in the trees, the site belongs to Palmer or he uses the address anyway. Take one of the uniforms with you go and check it out. I don't know what you may find it may be nothing play it by ear, log it in your notebook as a possible location of a missing girl".

"You think it might be Karen"?

"I don't know, just going with an idea, stay in touch Peter. Any sign of anything odd, treat it as a crime scene. We are looking for a blue transit too the numbers on the back of the photo. The Google sat. picture is not up to date so just see what's there now okay".

Back at the interrogation room, Mel found Jonny still in the observation area.

"Bit of info about Rivers sir, he doesn't drive so how did he arrive at Market street. His eyesight is shot so what's he doing at a photographic club. If he can answer those two satisfactorily he drops out of the frame, for me that is".

"What wrong with his eyes"?

"Can't remember the name but Compy says he can only see like looking through a tube".

"Ah tunnel vision, a serious disease. Now you know why he peered at you last time".

"Yes, I saw him stare and jumped to the wrong conclusion, typical me eh"?

"Don't worry Melanie I'll keep it informal for now, see what he has to say. Has Palmer's solicitor arrived yet"?

"No, I've told the desk sergeant to send him to you first".

"I was going to prime him with what we have but now we think Palmer is yanking our chain, let him go in cold. You go in there as soon as you can".

"I'm going to wait a while; I've left Peter Andrews chasing up a lead on a van that may belong to Palmer; be nice to know the result before I start".

"Okay but don't leave him too long with his brief ".

"Sorry to have kept you Mr. Rivers I'm Detective Inspector John Musgrove. I thought you should know we have made an arrest connected to the murder of George Grant".

"Oh is that all, you could have told me that on the phone, anyway I'm glad you've been successful".

"Before we proceed to trial we have to have a clear picture of all possible witnesses no matter how unlikely. The defence often use tactics criticising how we conduct the investigation to throw doubt on the evidence we put forward".

"Am I a witness"?

"I don't believe so but we must be able to justify our decisions with facts. I have a couple of questions for our records".

"Fire away".

"I believe you don't drive so how did you go to the meetings and more particularly the studio demonstration".

"My wife's the one who drives she drops me off and picks me up after. As for the demonstration at Market street I was invited at the last minute. We followed George Grant in our car and she waited for me outside, she's good like that".

"You write software programmes for a living, why take up photography"?

"An odd question; still I'll try and answer. I have a problem seeing things outside a very small area; it's called Retinal Pigmentosa. Using my computer I can expand and shrink text and figures to whatever size suits my vision without which I could not work. When I take a photo or look at an old one I can only see the centre I have to move my head to scan the whole picture a bit at a time. I wanted to learn how to compress images into the space where my vision is good enough to see it all at once. George Grant had some good ideas using fish-eye lenses to help me".

"How many times did you go to his studio"?

"Just the once".

"Who else was there"?

"Palmer for sure, he spoke to me, the others I can't say, two perhaps its difficult if people are not directly in front, even then I have to concentrate to recognise anyone. I'm better with voices".

"Fair enough Mr. Rivers I don't think we will be troubling you again do you need a lift home".

"Not necessary, my wife is waiting in your car park, she is very patient".

"Tell her thank you from me, for her waiting that is".

"I will, goodbye and good luck with the prosecution".

Melanie left the observation room and caught up with Rivers as he reached the exit door.

"Do you mind if I walk with you to your car, I'd like to ask your wife a question"?

"What; don't you believe what I said"?

"Oh no; don't think I'm questioning your statement not at all, it's just whilst she was waiting she may have seen something".

He did not speak but indicated that she follow; he walked to the passenger door and started to climb in as Melanie approached the driver's side. Mrs. Rivers wound down her window.

"Is everything okay".

"Yes of course, I'm detective Sergeant Frazer I have a simple question for you".

"Do you want me to come inside, is it to confirm Sam's whereabouts"?

"No nothing wrong there, just when he went to Market Street after one of the club meetings you waited for him outside".

"Yes I remember, Sam was chuffed when he came out said he'd learnt a lot, anything to help him cope you know; I don't mind waiting, I listen to the car radio mostly".

"I'd like you to cast your mind back, did you see any other vehicles arrive or leave, a van maybe"?

"Hm...I don't recall anything, only the car I followed it was parked in front of me. It was quite dark when we left, I don't remember any lights or other vehicles I'd say I was alone.

"That's fine, I'm sure we won't be troubling you again".

Melanie walked back in and along to the interview rooms, Jonny was talking to Richard Jarvis the duty solicitor brought in for Palmer. Melanie nodded a hello, Jarvis acknowledged, turned and entered Room three allowing the attending uniformed officer to leave before closing the door.

"Where have you been I thought you were observing"?

"I was but wanted to have a word with Mrs. Rivers before they left, just to see if she'd seen anything while she was waiting at the studio. No joy".

"Give Jarvis a while then if he's not out in fifteen minutes knock and move him along. I'm going upstairs so bell me just before you start I want to see this".

Chapter 41

With Jonny gone Mel leant against the wall going over in her mind her planned questions for Palmer. With her phone set in silent mode, the feint buzz and vibration against her breast broke her concentration.

"Peter that was quick speak to me".

"There is a small static caravan all shut up not sure if I should break in, I don't want to fuck up a crime scene or make anything I find inadmissible without a warrant. Tyre tracks indicate a vehicle coming and going lots of tracks all the same tread so several visits. What shall I do"?

"Protect the tracks; take prints if you find any, note the time and report over the radio to Central that you have no response from knocking and are breaking in as you suspect the possibility of a child in distress. Disturb nothing whatever you find, anything suspicious call in SOCO; note everything, no time for a warrant".

"Right Sarge, I'll call you".

"If I don't answer at once hang up; I'm in interview, I'll call back".

Mel was becoming excited she wanted to call Jonny but suspected he was with Walter or Toni so held back. The door to room three opened, Jarvis poked his head round looked at Mel.

"We are ready Sergeant".

"Be with you in ten minutes Mr. Jarvis".

Mel found Faye and Alan in the canteen.

"Okay you two here we go again".

The room was settled with everyone seated except Constable Alan Faraday who stood in his usual corner.

"Continuation of interview with Mr. Earnest Palmer. This interview is being recorded. Present in the room is me Detective Sergeant Melanie Frazer, Mr. Palmer, his solicitor Mr. Graham

Jarvis, Constables Faye Tenison and Alan Faraday. Mr. Palmer you are still under caution, do you understand".

Palmer looked at Jarvis who nodded.

"Yes".

Mel had the feeling this was going to be a 'no comment; interview she would have to work hard to open him up again, this time without the bullshit. Now Palmer had a solicitor present it was necessary to be careful, withholding information that a suspect had been charged with George's murder could raise an objection in court concerning anything admitted in this interview.

"Before we start I have to inform you a suspect in the murder of George Grant has been charged. I'll go back to my last question was Karen drugged".

Mel saw Palmer sneak a wry smile at the news.

"No comment. Who killed George then"?

"Mr. Palmer I ask the questions you provide the answers. If you didn't drug her was it George"?

"Probably there was no one else".

"Not true , I believe several people were at these sessions".

"No comment".

"Did you try to stop George giving her drugs"?

"I didn't know she was drugged".

"You were there, do you think she was allowing herself to be stripped, bound and strangled willingly"?

"I suppose so, George said it was a kind of morbid art".

"Why are you blaming George for everything, is it because he is dead and can't refute your accusations".

"No he was my friend; why won't you tell me who killed him"?

"You said earlier Mr. Rivers took her away after the session, is that correct.

"Yes he was the one".

"Would it surprise you to know Mr Rivers doesn't drive".

"Who says"?

"I do. Mr. Rivers is almost blind, he has never driven. I believe you are the one who took her in your van, by the way where do you keep it"?

Palmer looked at Jarvis who leaned forward to hear what Earnest was whispering; Jarvis shook his head.

"What van is that"?

"The blue Ford Transit, VYB 46R, insured in your name".

"Not mine you've made a mistake, there are lots of people with the name Palmer".

"Indeed there are but not using a payment from your bank account to insure this particular van I would think".

No smile on his face now, the brow being furrowed wondering what was coming next.

"No comment".

"Earnest, tell me when did you last go to Welland"?

Palmer placed his hands on the table leaning as far forward as he could towards Mel and shouted almost hysterical in her face.

"What the fuck! How the hell do you know about that. No bloody comment so there, here me bitch no bloody comment; I won't answer any more of your stupid questions; I didn't kill George, you said that yourself, so I want to leave".

He turned sharply and poked Jarvis in the chest.

"Your my so called solicitor, you tell her to shut up and let me go".

Mel saw the fear in his eyes and knew she had him. She felt three sharp vibrations from her phone and hoped Peter had come up with the goods, she decided to take the chance.

"I'm afraid it doesn't work like that Mr. Palmer you will not be leaving; please stand".

Jarvis knew what was coming so pulled Palmer to his feet and spoke in a loud whisper directly in his ear.

"You listen to me; don't you dare touch me again. Be quiet, keep your stupid mouth shut; I warned you to say as little as possible but you couldn't could you. Now do as you are dam well told".

Palmer stood his shoulders slumped eyes wide in disbelief, as Melanie and all in the room rose to their feet.

"Earnest Palmer I am arresting you on suspicion of the abduction and imprisonment of Karen Small. You do not have to say anything but it may harm your defence if you fail to mention something when questioned that you later rely on in court. Anything you do say will be given in evidence. Do you understand. For the tape Mr Palmer"?

"Fuck you, yes".

"Constable Faraday take him to the cells".

As soon as they were all gone Mel pressed speed dial for Peter Andrews; he spoke before she'd even said hello.

"Sarge SOCO are here I called them when I saw, there's so much here, girls clothes in the van and other stuff, we've even found cameras they could be George's; you have to come and see; there are pictures stuck on the wall too. I searched the area nearby; nothing but I found something hidden amongst trees some distance from the caravan. Some freshly dug ground been covered in leaves, I'm afraid of what's under there. Are you coming"?

"Of course Peter, on my way".

Mel didn't wait to call Jonny but bounded upstairs two at a time. Toni's office was empty so she continued apace to the Super's on the next floor. Gasping she knocked but didn't wait to be invited, just barged in.

"We might have found Karen sir…. you have to come now".

Jonny held up his hands to stop her impending tirade.

"Slow down a bit Sergeant, catch your breath; tell us what's made you so all fired up".

"Sorry sir, DC Andrews found a site where Palmer keeps a caravan there's signs of girls being kept there and a possible freshly dug grave nearby. I've arrested Palmer he's in the cells with his brief. SOCO are on site".

Toni had a wrenching in her stomach at the mention of a grave, she'd kept up to date with the interviews so far and wanted everyone to be aware of the overall situation, not knowing even minor details can lead to bad judgements.

"That is good, if she is there SOCO will find her. Some good news from Inspector Davis too Sergeant, Jake Snell has been arrested and is now with Smith. I believe Palmer stated that Brown had been to the studio of George Grant, Davis tells me Jake Snell is ready to give up some important evidence we may at last be able close an old case and bring the real villains to book. Jonny you and Mel go down to this caravan. I'm going to London to be with Chief Superintendent Smith during the interrogation of Snell".

"What about DS Linkman Ma'am, after all its his missing girl shall I let him know"?

"Yes of course Jonny, tell him how to find the place, he should be there even if they find nothing".

Superintendent Walter Munroe watched silently as the three officers interacted, pleased it was all coming together.

"It seems you have it well covered, even if we don't find Karen we may know what happened to her and bring closure to her father. Harrold and I will deal with Brown, good luck, we are all on the final lap".

When alone, Walter picked up his phone and made the call.

"Hello Walter, I didn't expect to hear from you so soon I must be popular".

Again a camaraderie so unlike Montague Brown; 'tread carefully' thought Walter Munroe.

"It would be nice if you could come and see me sometime soon Monty, the problem we have is not quite resolved".

"How do you mean, I've had my computer returned, I thought you had the killer under lock and key"?

"We do, we do, it's not that. Look too many ears on the phone I need to keep this is between us, if this leaks out some unfriendly soul will make two and two equal five. Come and see me so we can close this anomaly for good".

"Up to my ears today, will tomorrow be soon enough"?

"That will be fine sir; I suggest you come straight from home in your own car, your driver hanging around our station here will draw attention to you. Chat amongst the uniforms exchanging news won't be good, speculation and putting their own spin on why you are here is bound to happen, you know what gossips they are".

"All very clandestine but if you insist, about ten and Munroe you'd better not be wasting my time, hear".

The soft easy going voice returning to its normal brash tone; Walter was ready for a battle.

Chapter 42

Vernon Smith and Toni Webb were in an interview room unlike any Toni had ever seen before, no windows, one steel lined door a table with one chair both bolted to the floor. Jake Snell was sitting in the chair his handcuffs secured to the table by a shackle. There was no other furniture, no one way mirror, a single light in the ceiling illuminated the table leaving the fringes of the room in relative shadow. Toni stood in the corner almost invisible in the gloom. Vernon walked around the table once, twice, turned back the other way and circuited again eventually stopping behind Jake. He put his hands on Jakes shoulder pressing down, leaned forward to be close to his left ear.

"Well at long last Mr. Snell it has come to this. This time, this place; you had chances to escape, but you chose to come to me for some reason best known to yourself. Whatever you heard from officer Davis he is not the one you will be dealing with. My name is Smith, I am the only one here who has the slightest interest in what you have to say. No questions from me, no games from you, just say your piece and be done".

"I have something you want Smith; you have the means to make this all go away. My piece, as you put it, is to give you information about some people you have been interested in for..... I don't know how long, but quite some time. I have pictures, conversations, texts and much more, enough for you to do what you do best. I lived a simple, if not entirely honest life before they came along. I want to be gone with a new life, yes a new simple honest life; you give me that and I will give you everything you need to wreak havoc among the corrupt criminals running your precious army of boys in blue. Do we have a deal"?

"No we do not".

Vernon and Toni left the room, the door slammed shut behind them darkness prevailed, Jake Snell was left alone.

"Do you really think he has all that info"?

"Well Toni I hope so, he could have escaped easily enough with the two grand and the information; he allowed us to pick him up, he wouldn't have done that if he had nothing to bargain with".

"Why didn't he try and extract some money from Brown or Blakewood".

"Maybe he did but was blown out by one or both men, maybe he's running scared of them, so giving himself to us saves him from their wrath, at least for now. He must have stashed the information somewhere between leaving the depository and the arrest at his digs. Did your men search everywhere"?

"SOCO covered his room virtually the whole house and the route he took, they even searched the depository but nothing. The constable who followed him said he did not stop for even a moment until he went inside the B and B, we have his stuff in a tatty backpack nothing there either just the money with the note. Maybe he is bluffing".

"He can't be, he wouldn't have gone to all that trouble to recover his safety deposit box for a few lousy grand. He knows he won't achieve anything from us unless he gives something in return; he's hidden it somewhere; it has to be genuine information we can use to bring down Brown and maybe Blakewood".

"He obviously wants immunity and some sort of witness protection; can you do that"?

"I can, but not easily you see here is my problem if I try the official route the very people who can approve protection are people at Blakewood's rank; if I approach them he is bound to find out. I have one possible solution and that is to go someone outside London and the Thames Valley".

"Well if you do and have approval, are you going to offer him a deal or read him his rights and charge him".

"I don't know; not yet anyway let him sweat for an hour or two. By the way the man in there doesn't have any rights, you see Jake Snell is still abroad, whereabouts unknow. Coffee or tea"?

The suddenness of their departure left Jake in no doubt of their tactics; the instant darkness was impenetrable not even a glimmer from under the door. As time passed his pupils widened and he imagined he could see an outline of the doorframe but knew it was his imagination, for wherever he looked false images presented themselves. Smith was playing a waiting game; the dark was to wear him down, the shackle to leave him uncomfortable and the passage of time to generate fear; Jake was troubled by none of these. He crossed his palms as best he could with the restrictions of the cuffs and leaned forward resting his head on naked forearms. He would pass the time in sleep; the period of respite would prepare him for what was to come.

There was no viewing area to the interrogation room housing Jake, A hidden camera and recording system was in operation continuously, the formalities of reading Jake his rights would only be used if and when charges were to be brought. Smith and Toni entered the room as before.

"If I was to offer immunity what can I expect from you, what do you really have apart from vague promises"?
"Before I say anything more, I want recorded assurance from you in front of an accredited officer of the witness protection programme, that I will receive immunity from prosecution".
"Immunity in respect of what exactly"?
"Everything of course".
"You will have to be more specific; we can't give you freedom to do anything you want without fear of prosecution.

We have no idea what crimes you have carried out, we will need to know so they can be listed in the agreement".

"You tell me what you think I have done and I will see if that covers what I want protection from. If you are going to do this get someone from witness protection and a lawyer down here now then we can talk. As a sample of what to expect I have recordings; one is of a fellow called Blakewood ordering Vale to remove a particular person who was causing him a problem. If what I give you is not up to scratch lock me up and throw away the key okay"?

Jake was removed from interrogation to a cell. Toni and Vernon went to his office.

"Are you going to do what he asks"?

"Wait and see Toni, I have Brown here as well as Jake, Brown is backed into a corner over the pictures, I'm going to front him with Jakes information if there is any".

"This is tight Vernon; how long can you keep Brown here without charging him. It could take days to secure immunity for Snell and checking what he gives you against Brown"?

"I wont have to keep him here; he still thinks I am a friend looking to find a way out for him. I'll give him a fright and send him home. The man's an idiot he only rose to be an ACC by arse crawling, remember those in real power always want someone not too clever as their number two, it makes them look good. Surrounding yourself with obedient and loyal fools is expedient. Look I need to organise witness protection so go and have yourself a cuppa, the restroom is on the first floor, we are on the fifth the quickest way is to take the lift to the ground and walk up".

Toni took the hint, she had meant to ask why no lift to the first three floors she do it later, she decided to take the stairs. At each landing she glanced into the corridor to see the same set up on each floor except for the first where the door from the

294

stairwell led directly into a large area with armchairs, random desks, a wall full of books and a table with the makings of tea, coffee, even a tub of instant hot chocolate. The room only had one occupant, Detective Inspector Bonington.

"Coffee if I remember rightly Ma'am, no milk or sugar"?

"Thank you Simon, nice to see you".

"How's it going"?

"Don't know really, Snell thinks he has enough to secure immunity and get into a witness protection programme".

"I can't see the guvnor letting him get away with that, I bet he has something up his sleeve".

"I do too but I can't think what. By the way what's with the funny lift set up here"?

"Everyone wonders that but you're the first to ask in a long time. The lift goes from ground to four and five only as you've noticed. Floors four and five are offices, interview rooms and cells used by IOPC. The first floor was converted to a rest area and sort of self-help canteen when we took over. Two and three are data storage, paper files and evidence, there is also a secure computer room. In the event of a security breach, which we've never had by the way, the stair well doors lock automatically so the only way out for anyone trying to escape is via the lift which can only go to the ground floor where armed officers will be waiting. None of this is of our making we inherited it, a daft idea but now we're stuck with using the stairs".

"Must have been a paranoiac lot before you"?

"You could say that, bent coppers chasing even more bent coppers. Not true of everyone though, but if you share a barrel you get tarred just the same. Another coffee"?

"Why not. Ta".

Chapter 43

Never one to rush Jonny was not his normal self, urging Mel to drive faster. Welland lay hidden in a green wood, one narrow lane the only way in, far from any made up road. The thought of what may lay hidden was exciting him but tinged with feelings of dread. It wasn't dark but the light would be fading soon enough. They parked in the lane as the area near the static caravan was crowded, Peter Andrews closest, a uniform police car and two SOCO vehicles filled the available space in front of the caravan. The twenty yard walk towards the van found Peter and a uniform constable waiting for them by the taped off area.

"Sir, SOCO are still inside and the other team are over there in the woods. I can't begin to explain what's inside there are pictures you know; you will have to see for yourself".

"What about the disturbed ground Peter, is it a grave"?

"I asked, they won't tell me what they think, the guys are digging now, I watched for a while they are being slow and careful, I suppose not to destroy any evidence. I heard your car so came back here".

"Mel you go and see what they have found so far, don't let them put you off; I'll wait here I want to see inside that van".

"Sir".

Melanie moved towards the wooded area thinking Jonny was passing the buck, she wanted to have a look in the van too rather than the unknown discoveries at the dig site. The crime scene guys had taped off the perimeter and erected a tent over the suspect area along with some portable lighting. Even though there was plenty of natural light the floodlights glow was visible through the trees guiding her to the spot. Without the artificial source nothing would have seemed out of place, invisible to any casual glance. Whatever Peter saw in the van had obviously triggered him to make an unusually thorough search among the surrounding trees to have discovered the disturbed ground; a normal recky would have missed it. The uniform officer standing guard by the tape held up the palm of his hand at her approach.

"I'm DS Frazer, Constable don't worry I won't disturb them yet, they will come and tell us soon enough if they find anything".

"I have some gloves, mask and shoe covers if you want Sergeant"?

"Thanks, what's your name lad"?

"Constable Greg Levin Sergeant".

"Well Greg I may take up your offer later, are there any signs so far"?

"Oh yes, one of them came out with something, put it in an evidence bag, don't know what it was. Detective Crane wanted to go in the tent but the SOCO boss told him to clear off and wait till they'd finished".

"I can guess who that was; met him before; he'll be right with me, but I'll wait a bit anyway".

"A wise choice".

She waited ten minutes and when no one came out Melanie cupped her hands and called towards the tent.

"Sergeant Max Treddle is that you in there"?

A few seconds later a head poked out the tent flap.

"I thought it was you; young Melanie indeed, have you come to annoy me too"?

"Of course I have, move your arse over here and tell us what you have, I don't want to be standing out here all night".

Max lifted the flap clear and strode over to Mel.

"Excuse the garb, been busy, do you want to come and see"?

"Only if you've finished".

"I think we will be some time yet, there's a lot in there we have to be careful. So far one female, I think naked or nearly so, its difficult to tell as she's wrapped in several layers of plastic, not been there very long a week or so I'd guess. I've called pathology so we won't move her till they've been".

"What do you mean so far"?

"There is a second body under the first, been there much longer by the state of the decay".

"Anything else"?

"There could be more, the ground around has been dug very deep, we can't know until the first one is removed, then we can see to the one underneath".

"Can we see the girls face".

"Not yet, the plastic has several layers it's not very clear we can't cut into it yet, not till the doc says so".

"Constable Levin here said you'd removed something".

"Just a roll of tape, it was tucked down the side of the body, looks like what was used to bind the plastic wrapping. I'll carry on now if you don't mind a lot of earth and debris to sift through before we disturb the body positions. By the way there is another area fifty yards further in that looks doubtful, Its been taped off, we'll go to it after this".

"What another burial site"?

"Could be, don't know yet".

"Do we need a second team"?

"Not my call, it was only found an hour ago it may be nothing".

"Okay Max, thanks, I'll come back when the doc arrives. Jonny Musgrove will decide on the second team. He'll probably want you to check on it before you've finished here, just to make sure it's worthwhile".

With that Max turned back and ducked under the flap out of sight, Melanie was picking her way back to the van through the ever darkening woods.

"Two bodies sir, maybe more, one female now fully exposed, the other no idea of the sex yet its buried under the first, doctors on their way".

"Is it Karen"?

"Can't tell, she's all wrapped up, doc will have to open the plastic covering the face. They found a second site deeper in the wood, you should go and talk to Treddle, see if you need to call in a second forensic team to excavate".

"I've had a call from Doctor Taylor she missed the entrance but is on her way back now, go and meet her take her directly to the site, see if we can identify Karen. Whilst she is busy ask Max to look more closely at the second site, if he has an idea there may be something there I'll call in another team".

Melanie entered her car just as another car pulled up behind. She walked over expecting to see Doctor Taylor but it was Hamish who stepped out.

"Have you found her Mel is it Karen; I came here as quick as I could"?

"Hello Hamish, we don't know yet, there is more than one body but we....".

The sound of another car pulling up behind Hamish's interrupted Mel. She held her palm up to Hamish and pointed at the new car.

"This will be doctor Taylor, Hamish; I have to take her to the burial location well talk later okay".

Hamish nodded and stood to one side. Debbie donned her usual white suit, boots and gloves then hauled her kit out of the boot.

"This way Doctor I'll show you where to go".

"Hello Mel, a bit out of the way here, who's SOCO leader"?

"Max T, he's waiting. This is DS Linkman, from Reading we think it could be his missing girl".

Debbie gave Hamish a smile of acknowledgement; she followed Mel passing the caravan where Mel saw the techs had finished and were standing outside, Jonny and Keith were nowhere to be seen she presumed they had gone in. At the entry to the wooded area she turned to make sure the doctor and Hamish were close behind. The light from the tent guided them through the gloom. Constable Levin straightened up at their arrival. Debbie ducked under the tape calling Max's name at the tent flap.

"Wait up doctor there's no room for all of us in here".

A moment later Max and two others emerged from the tent; four bodies dressed in white from head to toe stood together, eerie figures in the half-light; Debbie slipped her mask over her mouth and nose, bent under the tent flap and entered where the target of her work lay partially uncovered.

"Max it looks like your lads have finished in the van, any chance you can have a look at the other site, DI Musgrove said he would call in another team if you couldn't manage".

He turned and spoke to one of his colleagues who moved out of the wood towards the van.

"Jeff will take the other two and have a start, I think we can manage, there is enough light at least to make an assessment. Who is this young man"?

"Sorry Max this is DS Hamish Linkman, it may be the girl Karen missing from his patch, he has been looking for her for some time".

"Welcome to hell DS Linkman, I hope this is not your Karen as it will give you hope you may yet find her alive but if it is it will give you closure; either way welcome to hell".

Max walked away head hung down.

"What's he like! Melanie"?

"Take no notice Hamish. Max is okay really. He's seen too many of these I think he grieves for everyone he finds, makes him grumpy".

They stood awkwardly for a while saying nothing, staring at Debbie's grey image moving across the fabric of the tent like a shadow puppet show. Mel had given up smoking over a year ago but this minute craved a cigarette like during her first week of abstinence; she sucked the scented woodland air in through her teeth imagining the bitter-sweet taste and the satisfying surge as the nicotine laden smoke hit her lungs instantly satisfied the addictive desire. Debbie emerged from the tent and called to Max.

"You can move her now Max, have her transported to Richmond, I've called a waggon, I'll examine the other one when you're ready".

She moved over to Melanie and Hamish removing her mask and gloves as she walked putting them in a plastic bag hanging from her suit.

"I've cut through a large section of the plastic so you can see her face, it has started to degrade a little but you should be able to identify her. She appears to have been strangled, ligature marks around the throat, as always autopsy before I say more. I can't give you an accurate time of death, the plastic wrapping changes the decaying process but at least a week. You can go in Mel and look, see if you know her".

Hamish stepped forward and held Melanie's arm as she was about to duck under the tape.

"Let me do this Mel...please"?

She stepped back gave him a mask shoe covers and gloves, held the tape up for Hamish to go through. She followed but stood back as he entered the tent. He knew almost at once that it was Karen who lay in the makeshift grave; he had studied the photographs provided by Gregory Small for weeks and knew every feature of her once laughing face. He backed out pulling his mask off using it to wipe away the tears forming before he turned to speak to Melanie.

"It's her Melanie, it's Karen; Max is right this job is hell".

"We have Palmer for this Hamish he will pay. Finally Gregory can at least lay his daughter to rest; you couldn't have done more".

"Thanks for letting me come, I needed to be here, look I'm going to go and see Mr. Small now, he should know from me, the poor bastard is going to find it hard, I want to be around".

"You go, I'll call you later, eh"?

When nearing the caravan he was approached by Peter Andrews.

"I've moved your car into the lane, along with the doc's, mine and the boss's; need room for the path-waggon it's due any minute. What's the news from the dig site"?

Hamish struggled to speak, throwing a gruff reply over his shoulder striding down the narrow lane to look for his car.

"Sorry Pete; ask Mel, I have to go".

Peter guessed why Hamish was so upset, he had found his Karen; he couldn't resist going to the graves to find out for certain. Mel was still by the tent as Peter approached, she looked at him when he reached the tape. He asked the question anyway.

"Is it her"?

Melanie nodded but remained where she was. Peter was not shocked just saddened. They hardly ever found missing people; those who had run away from home because of abuse never wanted to be found, those who were forced to leave by uncaring family ended up on the streets with nowhere to go and no future and those like Karen who were taken almost always ended up dead; rarely was there peace in the minds of those that survived and no quiet found for those left behind. Two forensic officers returned as Doctor Taylor left the Tent, she removed her mask and gloves, spoke to them then walked with Melanie to where Peter stood.

"Sergeant Andrews please go and direct the pathology technicians here the forensic guys are bringing her out very soon".

Doctor Taylor returned to her car to wait whilst the forensic and pathology techs removed Karen's body to their van.

Chapter 44

"Come on Munroe what is so serious that I have to come here almost incognito to answer your dumb questions. It had better be more than some stupid paperwork exercise"?

There it was, the usual belligerence 'I'm too important for the likes of you to be telling me what to do' attitude. Walter Munroe was of a different mind, thinking 'well Monty Brown you won't be calling the tune when I've finished with you'.

"I had no choice Monty the paperwork has to be done but more to the point, the truth has to be told don't you agree"?

"What are you talking about man, get on with it I have a busy day ahead and your flaffing is putting me all behind".

"It's like this we have a Mr. Earnest Palmer in custody for abduction he stated under caution that you attended meetings where the abducted girl was exposed to apparent torture. We found he has pictures of these scenes in his computer as did George Grant".

"The man's obviously lying, I went to the studio just once but saw no such thing".

"Well how do you suggest I deal with the situation, when the same images were found on your computer"?

"What are you saying. That can't be I de......No, no, he must have sent them, I didn't know they were there, you can't tell anyone, it will ruin me".

"I repeat how do I deal with it"?

"I don't bloody know, it's his word against mine, surely you believe me and not this dam criminal".

"It won't make any difference in court; his lawyers have his statement and will use every bit of leverage to have a go at the police during the trial. They will probably accuse you of collusion or even being the head of this group; the press will crucify you; I don't know what is best".

"You can't tell anyone about the pictures on my computer; you must interview Palmer again make him detract his statement about me, offer him some kind of deal, a reduced sentence or something".

"Are those your instructions sir"?

"Well yes, what else can you suggest, this can't be happening"?

"I don't think I can remove the pictures we found on your computer, too many people know about it, it would surely come back to bite you, besides it is highly illegal. I suggest you make a public statement about how you belonged to the club and say how the pictures came to be there. If you do this now you will pre-empt anything Palmer's solicitors might do".

"If I do I will be forced to resign, there must be another way".

"I can't think of one, at least this way you will avoid prosecution".

"What the hell do you mean prosecution"?

"Tampering with evidence for a start".

"I haven't done that".

"You did when you deleted files containing pictures of a criminal nature from your computer, when you should have reported them. I know it may seem to be a minor infringement but a man in your position and rank should have known better".

"You cheeky fucker, you can't talk to me like that, I'll have your job you'll see".

"I'm sorry but the IOPC also have this information and wish to interview you formally".

"What the hell are you talking about, what have you been saying to the Conduct lot. You shouldn't have done that; are they going to interrogate me, are they charging me with something"?

"I don't know sir, not for me to say, I am to call them when you leave, you know their office I'm sure; Chief Superintendent Vernon Smith will be expecting you soon; I suggest you explain everything to him, it will be your best and quite frankly your only course of action".

"Fuck you Walter, I thought you were on my side; I thought you were my friend".

"Fuck you too Monty, I don't take sides and you were never my friend".

Monty slammed Munroe's door so hard it was a stroke of luck the glass didn't shatter. Walter had a big smile on his face as he reached into his desk and turned off the recorder, picked up the phone and dialled.

"Is he coming"?

"He is Vernon, I have a car following just in case he decides to make a diversion, they will bring him to you if he tries. I'll email a copy of the recording you should have it long before he arrives".

Monty sat in his car in a daze he needed advice, he called Newton Blakewood, using his unregistered mobile number. When he spoke and Blakewood realised who it was, what was said frightened Monty so he couldn't move for a full minute. Monty drove fast, his temper was up; thank God it was Smith he was going to see and not some keen copper hunting nerd. When this all blows over he would sort out that shit Munroe. Those pictures were worrying though, how did Munroe find them when they'd been deleted, maybe he was bluffing. He kept his foot down, the sooner he arrived the better, Smith would sort it out.

This was a place where police officers were very wary. In the past the Anti-corruption unit went under different names but now it was known as the Independent Office for Police Conduct (IOPC) or Conduct for short. Before then it was not so independent; it had a chequered history, being a police department monitoring itself it was open to criticism. Still manned by serving officers but no longer a police department; its powers were more far ranging; able to deal with complaints from all sources and particularly not answering to anyone outside. If you were called there your life would be under a microscope and if you had done anything out of the norm your life would change and seldom for the better. Monty parked his car in the staff car park and entered thinking he had a friend in house.

The entrance was modest a single glass door with the initials IOPC etched into the glass leading to a reception area with a young lady in civilian dress seated at a free standing desk. A lift to the left and a closed door to the right. He walked up to her desk pre-empting her greeting.

"Assistant Chief Constable Brown to see Chief Superintendent Smith".

"Good afternoon sir, he is expecting you, please take the lift to the fourth floor".

He entered and noted there were only three floors marked; the ground, fourth and fifth, he wondered how you accessed the others. He pressed the button the lift door closed, the ascent was instant and rapid. The door slid open, stepping out into an empty corridor he waited a few seconds as the door closed behind him; no one came, annoyed at the apparent lack of courtesy, he turned left looking for a name on the doors to indicate where he needed to be; no sign; he turned to retrace his steps to be faced by Chief Superintendent Vernon Smith.

"This way Sir".

Vernon held open the unmarked door almost opposite and to the right of the lift. Monty stiffened and grunted as he stepped through into an office with a desk under a large window on the far side, filing cabinets to the left and right; in front was along table set with four chairs either side, a middle aged female police sergeant was seated on the left facing the window, a recorder and stenotype keypad by her side. With the woman sitting there he would have to be careful what he said in front of her. Vernon saw Monty's disquiet at seeing the set up.

"Come in Monty have a seat, Sergeant would you give us a moment, perhaps you could organise some tea".

"Yes sir".

Sergeant Mary Granger smiled and left, making tea was not something she would normally do, but her boss had explained, ACC Monty Brown was a bigot where women were concerned, so asked her to play along with this ruse where he would feel less threatened. When telling her of the plan he said, 'don't forget the biscuits' she replied, 'yes master' and did a curtsy; they both laughed.

"Well Smith what's this all about, that bugger Munroe has been hounding me about some dam pictures that had nothing to do with me. Some perv at a club I belong to has sent them to my computer without my knowing and is trying to make trouble for me in order to divert attention away from his grimy activities".

"Look Monty it's like this a complaint has been generated so I have to investigate in order to clear your name. You know how leaky police stations are and if the press finds out we brushed it under the carpet you will be forced to resign at the very least, you may even lose your pension".

"I don't like the sound of that what do you want me to do"?

"Well today a formal recorded interview with me my assistant DI Bonington and the stenographer. You can of course have a rep with you if you like and a more senior officer from another force present to ask the questions if you wish".

"No let's keep this with as few people as possible".

"Okay Monty the sooner we have this done the better eh"?

A knock on the door was followed by Mary Granger entering with a tray of refreshments, behind her Simon Bonington. Mary distributed the tea and some glasses of water to each position at he table; Mary to the left, Vernon next to her and

Simon to his right. Monty Brown sat alone with his back to the window.

"Sergeant please switch on the recorder".

They all remained silent while the recorder started, waiting for the beep indicating that it was active. Vernon opened the interview by asking those present to speak their names.

"Assistant Chief Constable Montague Brown you are here today to answer questions relating to images found on your personal computer. You are not under caution at this moment but have been offered an advisory police representative and an officer of more senior rank to be present, you have declined that offer and agree to answer questions put by myself and officer Bonington, is that correct".

"Yes that is true".

"Thank you, sir. Following investigations by Basingstoke police into a photographic club of which you are a member, images of young females in apparent distress, a copy of one such is before you, were found on your personal computer after you surrendered it voluntarily for examination. The images had been deleted prior to examination but were found present in residual memory of your hard drive. Can you explain how those images came to be there"?

"I did belong to that photo club where one of the members sent them to me without my knowledge".

"When did you discover them"?

"Only recently they must have been sent in an email as an attachment I should think; I'm not sure. I don't look at all incoming documents I just archive them to view later. I deleted them when I saw what they were".

"Who sent them"?

"I don't know, I didn't take any notice at the time I just binned the files".

"Reasonable I suppose, why did you not report this"?

"I thought the images couldn't be real, just made up to look shocking, I didn't see any point. Not an offence just offensive".

"Oh definitely offensive and more than that the girl depicted here apparently being strangled, was recently found dead. We await autopsy for cause of death my bet is strangulation and that is an offence".

"Now look here I didn't expect this, I thought we were going to clear up the fact that Palmer sent me some nasty pictures without me knowing; surely you don't think I had anything to do with her death"?

"So it was Earnest Palmer who sent you those pictures"?

"It must have been".

"You just told me you didn't know who sent them and now you say it was Palmer, you told Superintendent Munroe you had no idea they were there, now you are telling me you deleted them; all very inconsistent. How many times did you view them before they were deleted"?

"I don't know a couple I think".

"From the date they arrived as an attachment to an email, to your deletion three weeks later just hours before you surrendered your computer you opened those files a total of fifty seven times".

Monty Brown did not respond; it wasn't a question a statement of fact from Smith, one he knew to be true. His stomach was churning he felt bile rise in his throat the nausea made him sweat, he had to stop this before it went any further. Before he could think what to say, DI Bonington fired a question at him in a manner he would not normally tolerate from one of such a junior rank.

"When you went to George Grant's studio at Market Street, was that where you first saw the girls in your pictures; by the way the name of the girl we found was Karen Small. She was alive when you saw her at Market Street wasn't she; you said nothing and now she is dead"?

Images of the studio flashed before him; he had certainly been there but had taken pictures of only one girl for real, not the one in the picture, and she was alive when he left. The others where what Palmer had sent him. They wouldn't believe him. He had to get out of here now.

"Look when I went to that studio there were no girls or anyone except club members. I'm stopping this now; I want legal representation before we go any further".

"You are within your rights sir, but I must inform you we have many more questions related to this and other matters. If you want a break to think about your best options now would be a good time".

Monty nodded.

"Interview terminated".

Vernon indicated that Mary switch of the recording. She and Simon exited leaving Vernon and Monty alone.

Smith was not being the friend he expected, Monty felt isolated, his one saving thought was he had nothing to do with that girl s death but would they believe him. He had no idea whom he could call to help. Commander Blakewood would blow his top if he knew what he had done, he did have the power to help but Monty had already been warned not to make contact ever again. Calling in a legal rep and demanding more senior officers than Smith to ask the questions, would only make the whole thing top heavy and official; he needed to play this down as best he could.

"Look Vernon, you know I had nothing to do with that poor girl's death, and I admit I was foolish, an idiot even, to have looked at those images, I was fascinated and stupid I couldn't believe they were real. How can I make amends"?

"You realise your failure to report this was a major breach of conduct expected from a police officer. If we had known at the time you first received these images, we may have been able to prevent Karen Small from being killed. We believe Earnest

Palmer abducted and murdered at least two young girls and probably more, you may have been able to help us to arrest him sooner if only you had carried out your avowed duty".

Monty caught his breath, two girls dead maybe the one he saw was one of them. He saw a chasm open before him his vision blurred, what could he do. Admission would be his damnation, he was sorry, not for the girls but for himself for becoming involved.

"I am so sorry, none of this was intended, I don't want to escalate the situation by bringing in more people what do you want me to do".

"Go home now let us continue this tomorrow and see where it takes us. I have another interview to conduct, this time a real villain, you may remember him, it's Jake Snell the guy who escaped arrest when the corrupt officer Superintendent Vale and his lot were caught, well he has recently been apprehended and wants immunity, I have to debrief him first before they put him into witness protection; I'm given all the rotten jobs."

Vernon paused looking at Monty with his head in his hands saying nothing. He wasn't sure if he was even listening.

"Think about it tonight; you may know things that may help us with other matters and that will go a long way towards dealing with your current problem. Anyway you go home now Monty and have a good evening we can sort you out tomorrow".

Vernon exited the office leaving the door wide open; Monty rose slowly his mind almost vacant; the corridor was empty. He called the lift and left the building without seeing a soul. Dread crept into his heart as he walked to his car.

"Hello Colin. nice to hear from you is this a social call or something else"?

"Toni love all may calls to you are social, with the odd bit of business attached".

"Well, where's the party or is it to a slap up dinner I am invited"?

"To business first I think. Blakewood has been active, he's been accessing files concerning your investigation into the missing girls and has placed a security block on the Vale case files. All this was done very quietly he must have wind of something be careful".

"Interesting we found ACC Brown is involved up to his neck; Smith's officers have him now I don't think he can wriggle out of this one".

"Perhaps they have been in contact and that's why Blakewood is jittery".

"Thanks for the heads up; now where are you taking me and not chicken wings in the Shoes either"?

"Give me a call when all this is over then you and Nathan can come and stay with us for a weekend, will that do"?

"That will do nicely, I hope it will be soon".

"So do I. You can play with the kids while Nathan and I go for a drink".

"What! Taking on the role of a father figure by vetting my boyfriend are you"?

"Of course. No not really just need an excuse to go down the pub. Bye Toni".

"You don't need an excuse. Bye Colin".

Chapter 45

This room was different more comfortable, a large table with six chairs, the standard mirror and a recording machine with CCTV cameras in two corners. There were several glasses on the table alongside a jug of water, Jake was seated between two men both in plain clothes. He'd been introduced to them the man on his left was an officer who would be his liaison with witness protection name of John Jones; the other a lawyer Terrence Hardwick who was here to oversee the proceedings and check the documents related to the upcoming arrangement. Opposite was Chief Superintendent Vernon Smith alongside Chief Inspector Toni Webb, at the end of the table next to the recorder a uniformed officer Sergeant Derek Melbourne. Vernon Smith began.

"Right, we all know what we are here for, before we start recording and make this official we need to thrash out exactly what's at stake. Mr. Jacob Snell tells us he has information pertaining to an enquiry opened by us at the IOPC regarding two senior police officers. We know them to have been involved in criminal activities but require specific proof before we can proceed. He believes he is danger of his life from these officers and their possible associated gangland criminals. He believes he's particularly at risk if he were to be prosecuted and placed in custody in any state run prison. Three others of his group have been placed in custody with no recriminations, so I have some doubt these fears are justified although it is true they have not given any information to help our enquiries. Even so, I do however believe he could be in danger once he has helped us. Even if we secure the offenders there are others who will likely take revenge on Mr. Snell. We will now discuss if Mr. Snell be granted immunity from prosecution with regard to past offences he may have committed, yet to be determined, and be placed in a witness protection programme".

John Jones opened a folder and removed a pen from his pocket.

"Sergeant will you please start the recorder".

The machine whirred for a few second followed by its customary beep when recording was active. The Sergeant stated the time and date followed by everyone present stating their name and rank. Jones continued.

"I represent UKPPS, the Protected Persons Service, my role is to ensure that said person is placed in protective custody before during and after a trial when said person is a witness who may experience intimidation or retribution putting their life in danger. I accept Jacob Snell will meet these criteria if he decides to provide information leading to the arrest and prosecution of, at this time, certain unnamed persons. All present here are legally required to keep all that happens at this meeting to themselves. Any transgression will make them liable to arrest. It is not within my scope to grant immunity to Jacob Snell from prosecution".

The next person to speak was Terence Hardwick, Jake's legal representative.

"Thank you Mr. Jones, Jacob Snell accepts your offer subject to agreement with the police officers present here for immunity from prosecution with respect to certain activities to be stated later. In exchange he will provide information concerning individuals currently under investigation by Chief Superintendent Smith, the very persons who are now a threat to his life".

Smith was ready here is where things start to happen, the ground rules had be set out now the negotiation would begin.

"I am prepared to offer Jacob Snell immunity from prosecution from any criminal act he may have committed during the period of his activity whilst under the influence of DCI Vale and DI Branch. In detail the following activities; the abduction of children for the purpose of extracting their organs for sale to person conducting illegal transplants. Intimidation of others involved in the same activities. Transportation of persons overseas against their will. The unlawful killing of one Martin Reynolds. Does Mr Snell wish other activities to be added"?

Terrence Hardwick responded.

"Mr. Snell has provided me with a list of other items he could be charged with and wishes to add these. During his time under the influence of Vale and Branch he could be charged with control of prostitution in his local area and collection of illegal insurance payments from businesses, details of these and other minor offences are on the list, he would like this list to be added".

"Accepted. Is that all"?

Jake tugged his lawyers sleeve and whispered to him; Hardwick nodded. Jake then spoke.

"You mentioned Marty Reynolds but omitted his mother, I want her death included too".

Toni then butted in her voice showing surprise.

"You admit to killing Mrs. Reynolds"?

Hardwick held up his hands to stop Jake from responding.

"Remember once immunity has been agreed, there can be no prosecution. If he admits to this act immunity will be void, it is part of the blanket covering of his involvement with Vale".

"I know that Mr Hardwick but we were unsure how Mrs. Reynolds was killed. Was it the same gun you used to kill Martin"?

Her question pointed at Jake

"Hey, stop putting words in my mouth; I am not saying it was me but if I did kill them I would have used the same gun".

"Where did you buy your gun"?

"I can't remember I've had it years".

"Where is the gun now"?

"In the north sea somewhere; I dumped it overboard when I left two years ago".

Vernon interrupted.

"Sorry DI Webb you are digressing from our prime objective here. Mr. Hardwick I accept the killing of Mrs. Reynolds be included in the immunity document".

Jake smiled he thought Smith was trying to leave Ma Reynolds out on purpose to bite his arse with it later. His list was pretty comprehensive he could think of nothing else they may throw up at him, the lawyer bloke even included a clause for infringements forgotten to be included. He felt safe enough now to reveal all.

"I think that covers everything; I suggest we take a break whilst Sergeant Melbourne writes up the agreement. There will be only one original and two copies, the same with the recording. One for Mr. Snell and his lawyer, one for UKPPS, and one for IOPC. I'll organise refreshments if you want to wait here".

Sergeant Melbourne, Vernon and Toni left the room. Vernon use his phone to call for refreshments. Once the Sergeant had gone to carry out his typing duties Toni was able to relax.

"That went well, I mean you did well Toni, I hope he doesn't cotton on to what we were doing".

"I'm sure we are okay, did you see his smirk, he thought you were trying to exclude Mrs. Reynolds to catch him out so his mind was on making sure you included her. He's completely forgotten the gun was used to murder Lance Miller, five years ago, a witness against his mate Grimes charged with extortion. What next"?

"We obtain his information first, persuade him to go to a safe house pending trials of Brown and Blakewood where he will be our major witness".

"He won't do that he'll want to be gone to his new life".

"I know well go through the motions of trying to persuade him then spring a murder charge on him for Lance Miller; if he doesn't cooperate, instead of a safe house he'll be remanded in custody".

"I wouldn't fancy his chances there".

"Nor will he. He did not admit to killing either Reynolds but I don't believe he ditched the gun overboard either, when this is over ask Harrold to go back to his mate Lenny Bartram's house it could well be stashed there. Let's go back in we've a ways to go yet".

"Melbourne's not back yet I'll call Harold now, be good to have another nail for the coffin, eh".

"You do choose your words Toni".

Everyone sat in silence waiting on the return of Sergeant Melbourne, the tea and coffee had been consumed, on the plate where there had been a dozen biscuits, remained only a few crumbs. Ten minutes went by slowly, leaving each to their own thoughts, before Jake spoke.

"How long is this going to take"?

"Won't be too much longer quite a lot to put on paper. No electronic processing here we don't want any record going astray do we"?

Sergeant Derek Melbourne returned with three folders and a black and red typewriter spool. He switched on the recorder then handed one folder each to Jones Smith and Snell. These folders contain the agreement between Mr. Jake Snell and Mr. John Jones of the UKPPS and the agreement for immunity from Superintendent Vernon Smith of the IOPC.

"Gentlemen please read, sign and date each copy of the document where indicated and return them to me. I have the typewriter spool here which I will hand to Mr. Snell for him to destroy at his convenience. I will make copies of the recording one for each and hand over the files at the conclusion of these proceedings".

Vernon now took over.

"Thank you Sergeant most efficient. Now before this agreement is ratified it is up to Mr. Snell to fulfil his part of the bargain. The proof please Jake where is it"?

"Do you still have my old rucksack"?

"We do, it is the evidence locker downstairs".

"Please bring it here and also a computer of some kind".

"Bonington please fetch the bag and your laptop. Someone searched the rucksack, there was nothing there just the money, are you trying to play games with us here"?

"No. Wait and see".

Jake was glad the copper who took his bag from Davis had only looked inside he was not one of the SC officers who would have been more thorough, even then they may not have found anything. He couldn't resist a smile when he saw his rucksack untouched in Bonington's hand. He wasn't worried either way if they had found the disks they were protected, only he had the passwords.

"Has anyone got a pair of scissors or a knife"?

The lawyer reached into his pocket and brought out a small pipe smokers knife, he offered it to Jake.

"Will this do, I've never been able to give up". He said almost apologising to everyone for his habit.

Jake took the implement and used the pointed end to prise open the stitching in the bag's straps, it took longer than scissors or a sharp knife but Jake enjoyed the tension the wait created. He held out the two small memory devices in the palm of his hand for all to see. Bonington lifted the lid of his laptop and pressed the on button. Jake handed him the USB SanDisks. He inserted the first disk into the USB port and searched the contents. A warning message appeared.

'This disk is password and encryption protected. Incorrect entry or attempts to copy will result in complete deletion of all data'

Jake stood and reached over Simon's shoulder and quickly typed in a series of letters and numbers too fast for Simon to follow.

There were three folders; in the first ten numbered pdf files appeared, on trying to open the first file it demanded a password.

This file was a scan of a receipt from a Hotel in France paid by card. Jake explained.

"This Hotel is just five kilometres from the house where the abducted children had their organs removed. The card used to pay for this hotel is registered to Montague Brown".

Vernon was amazed this he did not expect.

"How on earth did you get hold of all this"?

"Not part of our agreement, albeit to say it took a long time and cost a few bob. Next".

It continued with a new password required for every file. They contained similar receipts for other Hotels in various parts of France where the illegal operations had taken place. Some were paid for in cash others with the same card. One in particular was paid for with a card where Jake did not know who it belonged to.

"It was Brown's job to collect the money from his French accomplices and distribute it amongst the accounts listed in the next folder".

Again Jake had to enter a password for each file before it could be read. These were .doc files, word processed account numbers, some French accounts some English and three for the Channel Islands. Toni thought, it would be easy enough to cross check these as Vale and Branch had banked in all these places; and if these files matched their already known account numbers it would be reasonable to assume the others were genuine and may lead to new suspects as yet undetected. The final folder had photographs of shots taken on a long range lens, not always clear as most were taken at night. Jake again explained.

"These are pictures of meetings between Brown and Grimes, Brown and Vale, Blakewood and Brown and one of all four. I know they are not clear but the images were taken on a high resolution so your techies should be able to enhance them to confirm identities. They are all date stamped for what it's worth".

The next disk was inserted. Just one video file again not of good quality with a sound-track leaving much to be desired. They played it twice without being able to understand what was being said apart from a few words. Two of those present whom Jake identified as being Blakewood and Grimes faced the camera the other two with their back to the lens could not be identified. Once more Jake added his commentary.

"If you enhance this you will find Blakewood is instructing the others to disband the operation and dispose of all evidence. Lip reading will help you confirm the audio where it is unclear, the still photographs will prove those with their back to the camera were Vale and Brown. I risked my life finding this stuff, so if you want the passwords I need you to agree now that this is sufficient for my immunity and protection to be ratified".

"I accept these files fall within the scope of our agreement however when we apprehend those suspects identified in these disks and if they go to trial we would require Jacob Snell to be a witness for the prosecution at said trial or trials".

At this point the lawyer Terence Hardwicke stopped Vernon before he could continue.

"Chief Superintendent Smith, from what I have heard here today it seems Mr. Snell has provided more than sufficient information to meet the required obligation for both immunity and protection. It could be many months before a trial and to keep my client in protective custody for what is likely to be a very long period would in fact put him in grave danger. He should be placed in a witness protection programme with a new identity as soon as possible. Unless this is agreed the passwords to the files will be withheld".

"I will need to verify the information is factual and not just made up, I do personally believe the files are genuine, but must check you understand, if valid I agree to Mr. Snell entering the witness protection programme without hinderance. I am disappointed he is not prepared to act as a witness at trial but hope he may change his mind later".

Terence Hardwicke reached into his briefcase and handed Vernon a hand-written sheet of A4 paper.

"In that case here are the passwords please proceed with care. I must remind you the wrong password will activate a wipe of all data as will attempting to make a copy of the disk".

"Thank you Mr Hardwicke, I will; in the mean-time Officer Jones please take Jacob to the safe house you previously designated and prepare him to enter the Witness Protection Programme. When the information he has given us is proved genuine I will come to release Mr. Snell into your custody for processing. This meeting is now closed. Sergeant please turn off the recording and make one copy each for Mr. Snell, Mr. Jones and me".

Toni wondered what was going on it seemed Vernon was conceding, letting Jake just disappear into the system without him having to testify or facing him with the murder charges. Nothing she could do about it now; she trusted Vernon but maybe he was so intent on getting to Brown and Blakewood he couldn't be bothered to pursue this evil bastard Jake Snell any further. What, she thought, had he in mind for Jake; would he soon attempt to bypass the now legal immunity and WP agreements; maybe he wasn't prepared to face the legal battle it would generate. The occupants of the room left in turn little being said except for curt departing comments leaving Vernon and Toni alone.

"What are you doing sir I thought you were going to pressure him into agreeing to be a trial witness".

"All in good time Toni, I wanted Jones and Hardwicke gone, the whole agreement is too fresh in their minds if I had sprung our trap now there would have been an uproar with little chance of success. I want to study the case file of Lance Miller's murder first and if Harrold finds the gun we'll have him for sure. I want Jake vulnerable and feeling safe when I spring this on him".

"Jake would not be a good witness you know; with his past, any good brief could discredit anything he may say and diminish this evidence we had to pay such a high price for; I'd much rather see him behind bars".

"I'm inclined to agree Toni, securing a murder charge outside the scope of the immunity contract, must be our aim, let's build a good case before we go ahead".

Chapter 46

"Hello, Debbie you've been quick have you been up all night"?

A call this early to her home from Debbie Taylor was unusual but Toni guessed her friend could not wait to carry out the autopsies of Karen Small and the unknown body found together in the same grave.

"Morning Toni, not quite, I did manage a couple of hours you know me, I can't leave things unfinished. The reports are on their way to Constable Busion as we speak. I thought you would be up by now so phoned to give you heads up on what we have".

"Kind of you, I've been wondering".

"First the girl Karen Small, her cause of death was strangulation. She died approximately ten days ago. The signs are of many ligatures being used over a period of time, the last one obviously too long. She had been sexually abused, old and new bruising confirms more than once. There were several drugs in her system and traces of others, I won't bore you with the names, they are in the report, some would have rendered her unconscious others awake but immobilised. If she suffered long term use there would almost certainly have been brain damage, had she remained alive that is. Bindings of arms and legs were present at the time of death and were removed post-mortem. She died in a sitting position; was wrapped in plastic sheeting and buried some hours later, certainly after rigour had subsided. A mixture of semen samples were found inside her, too contaminated for a positive match but two different semen samples were also present in her hair these were separate, only one profile was obtained. DNA shows this sample is a match to Palmer the other is too degraded to make a positive match, but some markers suggest George Grant. The minor details are in the report".

"So this is it, Earnest Palmer and one other, George most likely, assaulted and then killed her. I'll send a copy of your report to Detective Sergeant Linkman. What about the other body"?

"Yes much more difficult the body was wrapped in a blanket whereas Karen was in plastic. The decay was significantly more. A female of about fourteen or fifteen, dark hair, she died between ten and eighteen months ago, sorry I can't be more specific. Too much degradation from natural decay and insect infestation. No eyes and little flesh remains. Identification will be from dental records or from DNA, there is enough material if you have a known sample for comparison. Only a very small trace of one drug was found Raminadol Hydrochloride, one of the ones used on Karen. Compression marks around what is left of the skin on her neck indicate strangulation, not a positive cause of death but the situation of the bodies points in that direction. Find me a sample and I will confirm the ID".

"What about sexual assault and semen".

"Sorry Toni too long in damp ground, nothing doing".

"Thanks for letting me know Debbie, get together soon".

"I'd like that, by the way how's the HRT going; you did go to the quack didn't you"?

"He's not a quack, and yes I did, it's good, almost back to normal".

"Great call me when you have this lot wrapped up".

"Will do; bye Debs".

Her mood swings were still a concern so the white lie saying the HRT had done its job was just to stop her friend worrying. There was some improvement, or thought there was, she needed to give it time that's all. She dressed quickly skipped her coffee and toast and was on the road to the station in record time. She ignored her usual stop off at he squad room and went straight to Compton Busion's den. As per usual she found her sat in front of her beloved machine, this time downloading the very files Toni was interested in.

"Morning Ma'am thought you wouldn't be far behind the arrival of these".

She said pointing to the autopsy reports, that were spilling out of the printer behind her terminal.

"I've had a quick overview from Doctor Taylor, Compy, you know what I am wanting from you"?

"Missing girls from about twenty months I would think maybe a bit longer if I don't find anything quickly. I've already looked at anyone from Queen Marys ages ago up to two years back, like when Dawn was targeted and we knew of Karen. I'll do a general look in all adjacent Counties to start and whittle it down from there".

"I'll leave you to it. Look, I'm off to London, Vernon Smith, call me with anything that looks promising a name a date you know. Keep the Inspectors informed and have those autopsy reports distributed, I want everyone's mind on this".

Her next call was to Johnny or Keith whoever answered first. It was Keith who picked up.

"Where are you Keith"?

"Still at Welland Ma'am, the others have gone for a break and a change of clothes, Jonny and Mel will call at the station before they come back. It's been a bit muddy here, we'd a downpour at three this morning. I was lucky I was in the caravan the others were at the dig sites".

"That's good they will pick up the first autopsy findings, Doctor Taylor has been on it all night too. What's the news there"?

"The caravan tells it all Ma'am pictures of at least five different females in various states of........I'm not sure how to describe it Ma'am it's all weird, sexual but not explicit, torture too. Pain I think is the word I'm looking for, does it for me anyway Ma'am, some pictures were of Grants wife, even one of his lad; sick sadistic bastards. You remember those odd letters we couldn't understand on Grant's computer files, well it's simple, r is for ready, n for no, m for maybe and d for done, we found them written in full on the back of the photos here. Lots of other items, fingerprints everywhere Palmer's and Grant's for sure plus others probably the girls. There is a bundle of girls clothes too and some items of jewellery, which may help identify them. Cable ties, syringes and phials of several different pharmacy labelled drugs. By the way the first site has no more bodies, the second site has revealed nothing so far. SOCO are still working on it as there has been digging in that spot at some time".

"Thanks Keith, I'm off to see Vernon Smith in London, call me if you or Jonny need me".

ACC George Brown had not slept and it showed. He came reluctantly to the Conduct's office for the second time, he had nowhere to run to and was too cowardly to face up to what he had done. Smith had him over a barrel with the photos how could he convince him he had only looked at them and had not been involved with Palmer. He would show remorse and hope he would be able to salvage something from his dire situation. He had no idea if Smith knew about Blakewood and the French business; if he did he would try to make a deal with him. He knew very little of how things were organised he just did what Blakewood told him. His main job was as the collector from their French partners. Paying the cash into various bank accounts in different branches throughout the coastal towns of northern France. He kept his share in Euros in a safe deposit box at his own bank. He had never spent a penny he didn't have to. On reflection he wondered why he had fallen in with these people, he didn't need any of it. The excitement, the cheap thrills, the money, it was all crap and now it was going to destroy him.

The same room, the same recording machine, the same female sergeant stenographer, retired DCI Ronald Chambers an independent police representative; one he had not asked for, Chief Superintendent Smith and DI Bonington; all relative strangers who would soon know him for what he was.

"Sergeant please start the tape".

All those present spoke their names for the recording. Smith opened the file in front of him and began.

"ACC George Brown you are here to answer further questions following on from yesterdays interview. I took the liberty of bringing in ex DCI Chambers to ensure you are properly represented. I have accepted your request that a more senior officer than yourself not be called as you are prepared to answer questions from me and my associates. Are you satisfied with these conditions"?

Monty had little choice he just wanted it to be over with.

"Yes".

Toni sat by Simon Bonington in the next room the video link on the desk in front of them.

"He's going down this one Ma'am let's hope he drags a few with him. Snell's information should open him up he'll tell us anything if he thinks it will get him out of this".

"He's just a fool who follows orders its Blakewood we want, let's hope he tells enough for us to bring him in".

"Continuing from yesterday I accept your regret in acting foolishly by not reporting the images when they first appeared on your computer; I also believe you were not involved in any other way. By failing in your duty to report these circumstances you delayed our apprehension of the suspect Earnest Palmer. We will never know if we could have prevented the death of Karen Small whom we now know died at this man's hand but your lack of action cannot be discounted. An apparent minor infringement on your part but with serious consequences which I am sorry to say leaves me no choice. Montague Brown you are charged with misconduct in a public office. You do not have to say anything, but it may harm your defence if you do not mention when questioned something you later rely on in court. Anything you do say may be given in evidence. Do you understand"?

Monty turned to his rep.

"Can they do this, the stuff was private and I deleted it all, I had no idea it was real and that anyone was in danger"?

Chambers spoke to defend Brown.

"I hope a warrant was issued to search the computers of all who were members of the club including ACC Brown's; if not these charges are unlawful. I believe it is not the images themselves but ACC Brown's failure to report an unsolicited transfer of these that brings about the charge. He has explained his failure was because he considered them to be insignificant. He had no knowledge of the seriousness of the case you were following at the time, so his assertions of his failure to report were well within normal behaviour. I think you are stretching it to imply he was responsible for the girls death by an unproven delay".

"Your arguments are noted and can be presented at trial. A warrant for a legal search of ACC Brown's computer was obtained. His position as Assistant Chief Constable for Hampshire made him party to all cases being investigated. The high profile of this investigation cannot have failed to have been noticed. We checked his work activity whereby he did access these particular case notes on three occasions. He had received the images many days before this time so he must have been aware of their significance, The charges remain. Montague Brown I ask again do you understand".

"Yes, what happens now"?

"Some more questions relating to another matter, more serious this time I'm afraid".

"Now what have I supposed to have done".

"When did you last see Jake Snell"?

"I have never met Jake Snell; I do know who he is of course from past case files".

"What was the purpose of your visits to France during the period March to November of two years ago".

"I used to take holidays there from time to time".

Vernon placed a sheet with a list of French towns against each the names of banks and bank account numbers along with dates.

"Do you recognise these towns"?

"I've heard of some of them I travelled a lot in France".

"Did you stay in these towns on the dates shown"?

"I can't remember it is possible".

"Did you go to the banks noted here"?

"No I never went to any banks when on holiday".

"I have hotel receipts showing they were paid for with your credit card and bank statements showing large sums of money being paid in on those same dates. How do you account for that"?

"I may have stayed there; I don't know about any banks".

"I have witness statements that says otherwise. We will leave that for now. Who gave the orders, Vale and Branch"?

"I don't know what you are talking about".

"You can't remember a major case of corruption of only two years ago where two senior police officers Vale and Branch were convicted of very serious crimes".

"Of course I do but I had nothing to do with them".

"I have images of you and one other person in conversation with both these officers. A recording of the conversation where either you or this other person instructs Vale to eliminate a certain male. Was it you"?

Monty looked at his rep for support but all he received was a contemptuous look and a signal to keep quiet.

"For the recording ACC Brown refused to reply".

Smith stayed silent, watching, letting the evidence laid before Monty Brown sink in; watching him sit with his head bent. The jumbled thoughts and memories of what had been dragged up by Smith left him a beaten man. No way out for him now unless he gave up Blakewood, even then his life was finished.

"I am afraid for my life if I answer your questions; I admit what I did was wrong; I was influenced by others and was too wrapped up in myself to see what was happening. It became impossible to change once I was involved there were more and more threats and demands, I couldn't stop even if I wanted to".

"So do you admit to collecting money from French organised crime members and paying it into the bank accounts listed"?

"I suppose so, although I didn't know where the money came from".

"Who are these people who you say influenced you"?

"Look if I say anything I'm as good as dead, you will have to protect me, even if you put them in prison I won't be safe".

"What are you saying Monty"?

"If I give up someone really high up, I will want to be entered into a witness protection programme".

"That will depend on what you know that we don't already have. It will also mean giving evidence at trial, are you willing to do that"?

Monty had taken the first step, if Blakewood knew he was here his life wouldn't be safe, he knew what happened to those that threatened Blakewood's position of power. The phone call he made earlier reminded him of the danger he faced. Brown's presence in this building would be perceived as a serious threat, so he had little to lose by giving in to Smith's questions; the chance to escape into obscurity was worth the risk.

"I will give you what I have but before I do I need assurance I will be protected".

"I can do that I will have an officer from UKPPS, the Protected Persons Service here if what you have warrants such a move. First you must give me something to prove your true intent".

"It was Commander Newton Blakewood who ordered Vale to illiminate Reynolds".

"Were you present at that meeting and did you hear the order".

"Yes, I was present along with Blakewood, Vale and Branch. I heard the order".

"Who killed Reynolds"?

"I don't know, Grimes or Snell I would think".

"Okay we will leave it there, Montague Brown you will be held in custody pending further questioning and checking your information concerning Commander Blakewood. I will look into setting up the possibility of protection for your safety. Sergeant please switch off the recording".

Vernon waited till everyone had left then went to the room where Toni and Simon waited.

"What a surprise he didn't question the accusations even when you were just guessing without any evidence, like when you said you had a witness to him being in the bank".

"He is guilty Toni; what he knows about himself he thinks we do too so tried the ploy of demanding protection; they all do, it's their only hope".

"What next; Blakewood"?

"Oh yes; I've been waiting for this for a very long time. I'm going to arrest him at his home and bring him in; even if he has a way to wriggle out of it I will make sure it is so public that the mud will stick. No witness protection for this one, prison is what he deserves, at the very least we have enough now to force his resignation".

"Are you going to charge him with misconduct in a public office"?

"No conspiracy to murder. Wait here with Bonington if you want Toni, I'm going to call a team together and go there now".

The road on which Newton Blakewood lived was exclusive and expensive even for a very senior officer. His salary would hardly put a dent in what this London mansion would cost to buy and run. The high walls and iron gates closed out all but those invited in. Vernon and the team of officers were surprised to find the tall wide gates fully open; Blakewood's car was parked on the drive. Vernon and three officers approached the door, it was shut tight; it was not yet fully dark outside so expectedly there were no sign of lights on from the front windows where the curtains were drawn back; looking through the windows revealed nothing. They rang the doorbell and banged on the door with no response. He left two officers at the front and went to the side; a tall iron gate to the left was locked, it had spikes on the top, he thought too dangerous, so moved to the right. A large multi-vehicle garage adjoined the main house with a covered walkway where another iron gate blocked the way through to the rear of the property. No spikes here as the gate almost touched the walkway roof. Vernon used gaps in the gate to gain a foothold and resting his other foot on the shoulder of his companion officer scrambled onto the roof of the walkway. He traversed the gently sloping roof and dropped down the other side onto a path leading to the rear.

A long orangery across the back of the house blocked the view into the rooms it covered. At the far end there was a light from a wide window, the bottom of which was at Vernon's head height. He looked for and found a garden chair to stand on. The room was the kitchen one window to which stood open. The kitchen was empty. He called on the radio.

"There is an open window to the kitchen I am going in".

He pulled it fully to one side and hitched himself up onto the sill spilling head-first onto the worktop knocking a jar onto the floor in the process. The crash as the jar hit the floor spread its unknown sticky contents before him, the impact shattering the silence. Vernon expected someone to come running but silence remained. He turned on his back and sat up pulling his feet through the window and slid to the floor feet first avoiding the mess on the floor. He stood and listened calling out.

"Police officer, coming through stay where you are".

He was aware Newton Blakewood could be waiting for him, the silence was making him nervous. He left the kitchen, continuing to avoid the dashed pot of jam, stepped into a hallway, his target the front door. The chain removed and the dead bolt drawn back enabled him to open the door seeing the relief on the faces of the three men in blue.

"Keep the radio channel open, you two upstairs, stay together, you with me".

They called the police warning as they entered each room, a quick search gave the radio response of 'clear' as they went through the house. Vernon was in the dining room when he heard the call.

"You'd better come up here sir, second room on the right at the top of the stairs".

Newton Blakewood lay sprawled across his desk the back of his head spewing its contents out over the chair and onto the wall behind; a gun still in his hand pointed ominously at the four officers who stared in a motionless time lock.

"Okay no one goes in till forensics have been".

"Shall I radio it in sir"?

"God no, too many nosey ears. Use your mobile phone call Bonington he will set things in motion. Go and check the other rooms, use gloves, touch nothing except door handles then leave by the front door ".

They backed off their eyes still taking in the terrible scene until forced to turn away by the tasks before them.

Chapter 47

Chief Superintendent Vernon Smith in full uniform left his car parked several houses from his destination, he walked with the uniformed constable towards the safe house where Jacob Palmer had been waiting not too patiently for this visit Vernon was unconcerned their presence in full police dress would compromise the security of this site. He stood outside used his phone to warn of his arrival prior to opening the front gate and moving to the front porch. Inside the three officers from Witness Protection were on edge whilst one of their number checked the images on screen. John Jones verified the visitors were those who were expected before he told his colleague to open the door to let Smith in. The two policemen entered the hallway to be greeted by a young man simply dressed in jeans and shirtsleeves. Smith noted the full holster strapped across his shoulder.

"Follow me please sir".

He opened the door at the end of the passage and stood back to allow Smith and the uniform officer to enter the room beyond; the door closed behind them. Jake was sitting in the centre of a three seat sofa a closed paperback in one hand; John Jones stood by the chair adjacent to a laptop on the small dining table where he had obviously been sitting. Jake did not move when he spoke.

"You took your bloody time Smith; you must have put that bastard inside before now; what kept you so long"?

"It took a while to verify the information you gave us and we wanted to check on certain legal positions before we came here".

Jones was shocked to see Smith with a uniformed officer.

"Why have you come dressed like this, we try to keep these houses secure, your bloody uniforms don't help for sure; too late now I hope you weren't seen. I take it the information has been verified and I can proceed with entering Mr. Snell into the programme".

"Thank you for your observation Mr. Jones; duly noted. It is true the information provided by Mr. Snell is as he said in good order, and the list of crimes for which we have agreed immunity has been accepted by the CPS".

Jake jumped up a big smile on his face.

"Lets get on with it then Jones, I've been cooped up in here too bloody long already".

"There is one more thing however before you can take up your new life" .

"What the fuck is that, I'm not testifying if that's what you mean"?

"No I don't need you as a witness Jake, you will however have to serve some time first before you enter Mr. Jones's programme".

"What do you mean I have immunity, I have it in writing I have a tape, I have a lawyer".

"Indeed you do but not for every dam thing you have ever done. Jacob John Snell I am arresting you for the murder of Lance Miller. You do not have to say anything, but it may harm your defence if you do not mention when questioned something you later rely on in court. Anything you do say may be given in evidence. Do you understand"?

"You can't do this you promised me immunity you promised me protection, I will fight this".

"Do you understand"?

"Of course I fucking do, you bastard you have stitched me up, you won't get away with this, I'll rip your dam heart out".

The constable had moved unnoticed behind Jake during the confrontation, he reach forward grabbed his arm and had the shackle on him before he could react, he pulled Jake back and had both arms handcuffed in less than a second.

"I'll take him out sir, the car will be outside by now I should think".

Jake did not struggle; the uniform Sergeant was twice his size and he didn't fancy having his balls accidently crushed or his shins kicked. The lawyers must be able to fight his case. 'Stupid bastard' he thought 'I'd completely forgotten about Lance Miller. How the hell did they find out about him; I bet it was that sod Grimes'.

John Jones looked at Vernon with a heavy frown not happy with what had just happened but well aware he had no authority to intervene.

"You might have warned us, you obviously had this planned all along, now all I've left is a pile of paperwork and a boss who'll give me a month of crap duties".

"Sorry John, by the way is that your real name"?

"No but it's the only name you will ever have from me. Glad he's off the streets though, he's one very nasty fellow I did not want to process".

"There you go then, we both have what we wanted; goodbye, John Jones and good luck".

Just before Jake was driven off Vernon couldn't resist his slightly sadistic desire so whispered in his ear.

"By the way, we have found your gun".

Jake Snell sat in the police car, being shipped off to some remand prison. His thinking he was in control evaporated with the words Smith had just spoken. That bloody gun, he'd left it with his friend Bartram to dispose of, now he knew he had no friends. He did not know yet of Brown's arrest and Blakewood's demise so expected they would arrange his life in prison be cut short. He would not sleep much for a while.

Back in his office Vernon Smith sat alone, the angle poise lamp bent low on his desk, the rest of the room shrouded by deep shadow. In her home Toni Webb lay alone the light off where the night sky, visible through the window, threw a different kind of shadow. Two minds full of thoughts all mixed up, some regrets, personal desires, evidence anomalies from unsolved cases; yearning for a normal life but sucked into a world of greed and grief. Dealing daily with human frailties and sick minds finding little joy even when closure beckons, the doubt that one could always have done more.

Earnest Palmer was now in pieces for all his shouting and bravado he had been charged with abduction. They knew about Welland and probably searched the caravan, enough evidence there to convict him for sure. He did not know what George had done with the girls or where he had left the blue van. The room filled again with the same officers Melanie, Palmer, his solicitor Jarvis, Constables Faye Tenison and Alan Faraday. He wondered what was coming next. The recorder was activated and everyone stated their names his brief, for what little he was worth sat next to him. Mel was ready.

"Earnest Palmer you are still under caution do you understand"?

"Yes, yes, yes, get on with it what now"?

"We have found the body of Karen Small and another girl buried at the place known as Welland, autopsy reveals they were murdered and samples taken from Karen show you had physical and sexual contact with her. We have not been able to identify the body of the second girl as yet; will you tell us who she is"?

"I have no idea what you are talking about; I didn't kill or bury anyone it was George Grant not me. I did help to photograph Karen but she was alive last time I saw her. I don't know any other girl; you've got this all wrong".

"Earnest Palmer please stand. You are under arrest for the murder of Karen Small. You do not have to say anything, but it may harm your defence if you do not mention when questioned something you later rely on in court. Anything you do say may be given in evidence. Do you understand"?

"It wasn't me it was George he did it all, I'm innocent".

"It doesn't matter, even if George Grant did the actual killing, which I doubt very much, you were complicit in every way and just as guilty; once the second girl is identified you will also be charged with her murder. Sergeant take him out of here".

Chapter 48

Toni and Simon Bonington stood next to the Chief Constable for Hampshire in the gallery of the Richmond Pathology unit. The post-mortem of Commander Newton Blakewood was the first being conducted that day; both Doctor Taylor and Doctor Hart were present. The forensic team had already taken samples at the scene as were samples on the surfaces of the torso, hair, from under the fingernails and every area of the clothing. The pathologists started by washing the almost athletic figure that had seen better days; sponging him down from head to his feet removing the blood congealed on the skin and in the hair. Debbie Taylor made the commentary.

"The body is of a male aged approximately fifty five years of age. In fairly good health but slightly overweight for his height of five feet eleven; dark brown hair grey in places, blue eyes. Death almost certainly from a single gunshot wound to the head. From photographs the position of the gun in the right hand conforms to the entry angle for self-infliction. Gunshot residue from the hands and around the mouth supports this reasoning. The bullet had exited the rear of the skull and was found embedded in the back of his chair. It was a point 38 calibre, a match to the weapon found in his hand.

An hour later all they had learnt was his demise was most likely suicide, DNA samples confirmed it was Newton Blakewood, although there was never a doubt it was him. Both Toni and Vernon thought he may have been assassinated but the autopsy said otherwise. There was a brief note, left on the desk, to his ex-wife, with the simple words.

"Remember me for the good times. Sorry. Newby".

A tiny nagging doubt remained in Toni's mind, the note however appeared too personal to be forged or forced so she may have to accept the official line. Chief Constable Martin

Cheadle was obviously glad for the suicide assessment, he took Toni to one side ignoring Bonington

"Dam awful business this Webb, still we can at least close the case now. Keep it in house as much as possible eh. Balance of his mind disturbed, overworked, you know suffering from depression. No point in making anything of the corruption charges, okay, I will leave it to you to smooth things over. I'll be off now, let me see your report before it goes to file. Press conference tomorrow afternoon, so as soon as you can, right".

"This is not our case sir, Blakewood was a senior officer in the Met and it is now under the jurisdiction of the IOPC it will be up to them".

"Nonsense, it was our investigation into Brown remember that identified Blakewood as possibly corrupt, that bloody Smith can't charge a dead man; it is still a case for the Hampshire Police, you send me that report tonight, I will put out our press release before Smith can muddy the waters".

"Sir".

Cheadle left without a word to Bonington or anyone.

"Are you going to write the repot like he says Ma'am".

"I'm not sure what I'm going to do Simon; nothing till I have spoken to his ex. I have to give her the note we found, at least let her read it. There will of course be an inquest, I imagine our friend Cheadle will insist it is behind closed doors, he will want to delay it as long as possible and suppress the corruption angle".

"I'll be leaving now; Chief Superintendent Smith will want my input; shall I tell him what Cheadle said".

Toni looked at him with a questioning frown.

"Yes Ma'am, I did hear all of it".

"You do what you have to Simon and tell Vernon whatever Cheadle does it won't affect what I think. Brown will go down they will not cover that one up".

340

Mrs. Monica Blakewood lived in a modest flat in between Kingston and the outskirts of South West London not too far from Richmond. The Blakewoods had been separated a few years ago but never divorced; Toni did not know their detailed history but was told they were still friendly. There being nowhere else, Toni parked in the surrounding courtyard; the only space free being obviously earmarked for one of the tenants, she put her 'On Police Business' sign in the car window knowing she would not be too long.

Monica opened the door within a few moments of Toni's ring. She opened the door wide inviting her in without a word, Toni's phone call of her imminent arrival being enough for her not to question who she was.

"Good afternoon Mrs. Blakewood I'm Detective Chief Inspector Webb, we spoke earlier".

"I know who you are; what do you want"?

"I'm sorry for your loss, I know this must be a difficult time but I thought I ought to inform you personally of the autopsy result before you heard it through the media".

"I know already, he was murdered".

"That seems not to be the case. The autopsy confirms he committed suicide; all the evidence points in that direction. He left you a note. You can't have the original I afraid, not until later anyway, however I have a photocopy for you".

She snatched at the note still standing but sat down slowly into one of the two chairs furnishing the small lounge.

"This proves it he was killed".

"What do you mean"?

"He didn't write this willingly look it is signed 'Newby' he would never have written a note like that unless he was forced. His family nickname is Newtby; he wouldn't have made a mistake with that".

"Is that his handwriting"?

"Oh yes, I can tell by the slope, but not his words".

"What do you mean by the slope"?

"He's left handed of course".

The ride back to Basingstoke was a time of reflection; was it a mistake, easily done when under stress and contemplating killing yourself or was it a deliberate sign, one he knew his former wife would spot. Did he change hand deliberately to confuse the suicide verdict? Perhaps they would never find out the truth, the powers that be would put it down as a simple slip of the pen and probably being ambidextrous, all due to him not being himself. Toni was certain he was murdered and there was still another fox hidden in the henhouse. She so wanted it to be over, she yearned for a quiet time, time with Nathan and normality. The pressure was too much, now almost willing to be seduced into following orders and write the report demanded. No one would blame her, no one would know, except her.

"Vernon sorry to wake you".

It was three in the morning and Toni had not slept working out what she could do. Bloody politics always wormed itself in the way and she was determined to not let Cheadle brush aside the efforts of her teams in bring these corrupt and evil people to book.

"You know the time I presume Toni; what's so important"?

"Simon told you about Cheadle"?

"Yes of course, did you expect anything different"?

"I suppose not, but here's the thing I don't think his death was suicide, there could be another one in our midst, I don't know who and no real evidence except Blakewood's wife questioned the note, and told me he was left handed. A press release from you this morning saying the apparent suicide of a senior officer who was under investigation by an independent police enquiry, is in doubt. New evidence to the contrary has come to light which will be presented at the inquest".

"My oh my, you have been thinking like a politician, you mean force Mrs. Blakewood to give evidence at the inquest"?

"Yes even if her evidence is rejected, the right questions from her brief will reveal the fact he was a corrupt officer".

"Will she go along with it"?

"Oh yes, his corruption ruined their marriage and her life. Revenge now he is gone will still be sweet for her. Look I sent a very sparse report stating the facts of the autopsy to Cheadle, he has a press conference set for the afternoon, if you act quickly it will bugger his plans to whitewash Blakewood as an overworked officer suffering from depression. It was and is your right to see this through; you are independent that's what the big 'I' stands for isn't it"?

"Okay, okay Toni, don't go all emotional on me consider it done. You realise the fallout will be on my head not yours".

"You are a tough cookie, water off a ducks back".

"I don't know about that. If all this is true and not just a way to prevent a cover up, will we ever be allowed to find out who killed Blakewood. Who the hell will want that job anyway; no one I know"?

"I'll worry about that another time Vernon, go back to sleep".

"Fat chance, goodbye Toni".

"Hmm".

Chief Constable Cheadle was fuming, his planned statement torn to pieces in his waste basket. His ambition to take on the UKs top job of Commander of the Met, in tatters. No one would want that job now Blakewood had tainted it. The Commissioner had just informed him of the press release made at ten am by the Independent Office for Police Conduct's press officer totally destroyed his intended afternoon speech to the Countries assembled newsmen. The new document before him was the opposite of what he intended to say; the admittance that corruption at the highest level had been active in London's Metropolitan force. Ever the politician he decided to change sides. His words would be of regret and a steadfast support of the IOPC for their sterling work in bringing the corrupt officers to justice. He knew the tirade of questions concerning the death of Blakewood will be more than difficult he wished he'd never put himself in this position. Bloody Smith had planned this and although DCI Webb warned him it was Smith's case he'd taken no notice; dam woman had done little to stop him making a fool of himself. As Chief Constable he had access to all the reports and case details, he should have spotted what was coming and chosen a different path. To save face he had to appear to have been supporting the IOPC investigation all along and heap praise on his Hampshire officers for their part in the multiple arrests. When the dust had settled maybe it would turn out okay after all.

Chapter 49

Compton Busion's search for missing persons was fruitless so far, using a time scale covering two years and locations along the Basingstoke Reading corridor had failed. There were several missing women but none of the right age. She spread her search to cover the whole of Hampshire and the border towns in Berkshire, Surrey, and Wiltshire; Dorset and West Sussex seemed too far from Basingstoke, so she left them out for now. The results here found seventeen possible subjects. Trawling through the case files revealed most of the girls had returned or been accounted for; there were two exceptions.

One girl Kerry Ward was a good candidate on the face of it; a fifteen year old who went missing thirteen months earlier from Newbury, never found. The other, Marina Fairfax fourteen, has been missing ten months, still unaccounted for, her home is in Marlborough. The digital files downloaded revealed Marina had gone to stay for a weekend with a friend from Basingstoke two weeks before she went missing. On the day of her disappearance she went to shop locally, a ten minute walk from her home. She never returned. No witnesses nothing since. The fact she had a link to Basingstoke rang a big bell for Compton.

Kerry Ward was less likely as she'd packed a bag and drawn all her funds from a savings account on the day she left. She was seen on CCTV at Newbury station on the platform for the London bound trains. Not abducted was the conclusion, she did not want to be found. Her home life was not good, a father who spent most of his time in the pub and a mother who brought clients home in the bedroom next to Kerry. Little was done to trace her beyond her probable arrival in London.

The officer who dealt with Marina Fairfax was based in Swindon was Detective Sergeant Scott Wilkinson. Her call to him found a man who couldn't wait to help. He promised to obtain a DNA sample and bring it himself whatever time of day and night it might be. She told him the police secure courier service in the morning would do fine as the laboratory would not process it any sooner even if it was in her hands this very moment.

Compton always arrived by six am passed by the night sergeants desk well before the change over to the day shift.

"Someone to see you Compy, I sent him to the canteen Name of Wilkinson been here almost half an hour".

"Thanks Sarge, I can't believe he came".

"What! Is it a problem"?

"No, no, I was talking to myself I'll explain later".

Compton went directly to the canteen; she knew everyone at the station so DS Wilkinson was easily picked out from the half dozen local officers who sat together. She went to the table where he was waiting and sat beside him.

"Hello DS Wilkinson, I'm Constable Busion, I can't believe you came here so early".

Scott Wilkinson who was almost dozing, became flustered at Compton's sudden presence.

"Oh....my goodness...sorry you're Busion....yes it's me. I phoned before I left, the night staff told me you always came in by six I hope you don't mind"?

"More than pleased to see you thanks for coming. Did you have any luck with the sample I asked for"?

"I have some stuff here, its hair from a comb she used and also her toothbrush, one of them should do for DNA. I also have her fingerprints and a dental record just in case. Have you found Marina"?

"Maybe, this should tell us one way or another".

"What about the file photo, its fairly recent"?

"Sorry not possible I'm afraid".

"That bad eh"?

"Unfortunately. Look give me the samples I'll have tech start processing. One of our detectives will want to speak to you,

Sergeant Melanie Frazer probably or her DI she'll be in first usually before eight; is that okay, you don't have to leave or anything"?

"No I'm here to see if it is Marina Fairfax, I won't go until I know".

"Good. Have yourself a coffee, if you're hungry the bacon rolls are worth a try; I'll be back soon".

Melanie was reading through her messages on screen prior to returning to Welland. Jonny had gone straight back to the site from home after a shower change of clothes and some breakfast. Two emails were of real interest. SOCO at Welland had found hard ground and rocks at the second site so it was concluded Palmer and Grant had intended it to be the original grave but when the going was too difficult had abandoned it in favour of the softer ground nearer to the Caravan. 'At least no more bodies' was her first thought. The second message was from Compton asking her to come down as soon as she arrived.

"What's up Compy"?

"Morning Mel, I think we have an ID on the second girl; not a hundred percent till we have the DNA results back. Her name is Marina Fairfax from Marlborough; the sergeant on her case came from Wiltshire this morning with samples. The dental records are very basic they seem to fit, however she never had any repair work done her last a check-up was at the age of twelve; she has grown a fair bit since, so the comparison is inconclusive". Fingerprints from the body are almost impossible with the decay, although they did recover a partial thumb print by expanding the skin over a type of balloon, apparently it can work sometimes, good enough for an ID but has not been approved for use as evidence in trial. Good chance it's her though as one of the prints found at the caravan were a partial match".

"Who's the copper"?

347

"DS Scott Wilkinson I left him in the canteen with a bacon butty. By the way the girl visited a friend in Basingstoke just a week or so before she went missing".

"What are you thinking, Palmer saw her here during the visit and followed her home"?

"Possible, with nutcases like those two you never know".

"Thanks Compy good work I'll go find him, see you later, let me know if anything comes back from the labs".

"Be two days or more for the DNA, to be certain it is her".

"I'm happy with the print from the caravan for now. I'll go and find this DS".

Scott Wilkinson was alone sipping his second coffee the bacon roll consumed and forgotten, he instinctively rose from the seat when Mel walked into the now empty canteen.

"Sergeant Wilkinson"?

"Yes Ma'am".

"No Ma'ams please, I'm Detective Sergeant Melanie Frazer".

"Sorry, I'm Scott is Melanie okay with you"?

"Just Mel will do fine Scott; let's sit. Tell me about Marina".

"Marina Fairfax was reported missing by he parents nine months and three weeks ago she went to the local shop bought a bar of chocolate, a pint of milk and a newspaper. Confirmed by the shopkeeper. She spent a few minutes browsing the magazines before she picked up the paper, it was for her dad, a regular habit they said. No one else was in the shop at the time, the shopkeeper noticed nothing out of the ordinary. Despite an extensive search and door to door the only thing of note was a blue van, seen hanging around, by two witnesses, in the layby fifty yards from the shop. No sighting of the driver or any clue as to the make or registration number. Over a week the search was expanded, to the waste grounds, fields and the nearby river. CCTV from the roads in and around the town were scanned for the vehicle; there's not much coverage, in the village. No sightings in fact she had just disappeared. Your constables call was my first clue to where she might be".

"I understand she visited a friend here in Basingstoke"?

"Yes that was two weekends before, her friend Josey Banks used to live in Marlborough and moved to Basingstoke when her dad changed jobs six months earlier. I spoke to her and her mother on the phone. They had no ideas and had not seen Marina since her visit, although she and Josey had spoken on the phone and texted each other. There was no boyfriend. I went to the school interviewed her teachers and classmates, no joy there either. With nothing to go on the case was toned down and put on the back burner, you know how it is the guvnor had other things for me to do. I've looked at it every week since checking possible reports or sightings from adjacent counties".

"Missing persons is tough and finding her like this only makes you wonder if you could have done more. We've one of the men who took her in custody; the other is dead. We found two young female bodies your Marina is probably one of them. I will find out how he took her, the only consolation is you can stop looking and it will give closure to her parents, even if it does destroy their hope of her being alive".

"Can I go and see her".

"I wouldn't advise it and especially not her parents, she has been buried for some months in an insect infested grave there is not a lot left. We are sure it is Marina but you will have to wait for DNA confirmation before you see the parents; when you do, play down her deteriorated condition but you must insist on a closed casket".

"I've never had to tell anyone their child is dead before Mel, I'm not sure if I can".

"She's been your case for a long while Scott it's not easy but you will find a way. Take the father to one side, explain that a long time has passed since his daughter died causing changes his wife should not see. Tell him she had been drugged so would not

349

have suffered. Emphasise that to see her now would spoil their memory of how she really was, leave him persuade her mother. Go home now and when we have DNA confirmation I will send you a full report".

"Thanks Mel I will. It feels strange, knowing she's been found I mean; don't forget me with the case details will you"?

"Don't worry Scott I won't leave you out; you will know everything I know".

Mel called Jonny to tell him of Wilkinson's visit and Marina Fairfax probably being the other girl.

"Thanks Mel we are nearly finished here there is no need for you to come over. Harrold has a possible lead on George's van, he found an address in the caravan for a garage rental in Basingstoke he's on his way there now".

There it was, another week gone by, their cases coming to an end with stories told, the missing truths discovered and separated from the mixed in lies, all done now. Jonny and Mel, Harrold, and Peter, Keith and June had finally caught up with their reports. Compton and her team took time from their screens to chat about the good looking new constable who had recently arrived at Basingstoke. The evidence logs had been filed all passed to the CPS. Only the trials to consider and evidence to be given if called. New crimes came in daily, a driving under the influence, as always, a break in at a local post office, the usual fodder to feed their constant need. No peace for these men and women, they will find no quiet until the quiet finds them.

Epilogue

Montague Brown was in custody at the IOPC awaiting trial on corruption charges. A reason for the delay in coming to trial was not forthcoming.

Jake Snell had been transferred to Serious Crime for further questioning. The CPS were proceeding with the Lance Miller murder charge so his immunity agreement was on hold; if found guilty it would not be implemented. Witness protection was no longer appropriate his antagonists being either dead or in prison. Rumour was he had helped S.C. with good intel and intended to plead guilty in exchange for his sentence to be carried out in an open prison. His friend Lenny Bartram was not charged with anything, he did not receive his two thousand pounds; it was deemed to be the proceeds of crime so was seized by the State.

Ernest Palmer had been transferred to Winchester, his trial in the Crown Court for abduction and the murders of Karen Small and Marina Fairfax was completed in record time. The finding of Palmer's van produced no evidence it had been cleaned from top to bottom using bleach. It made no difference to the charges as the evidence in the caravan and the two bodies were more than enough to convict. His solicitor advised Palmer to plead guilty, it would save his family having to endure him being totally exposed at trial. He was still blaming George Grant so at first refused. As the trial proceeded the overwhelming evidence and pressure from his lawyer caused him to change his plea to guilty on all counts. He made a statement saying although he was guilty by being present during the girls' ordeal and had helped to bury them, it was George who had actually killed the girls. He was sentenced to twenty years imprisonment on each count to run consecutively.

Thorough investigation of the photo club highlighted only two members to have been only marginally involved. They had been sent the suspect pictures by Palmer; which they deleted soon after. They were given police warnings concerning their failure to report the incident.

The charges against Mrs. Grant had been reduced to manslaughter her son Gabriel, similarly charged, was undergoing a psychiatric assessment prior to trial. Date under review.

Toni Webb sat on her bed not content but as close to relaxed as she had been in a while. The customary celebration drink with her teams, when a case closed, was not uppermost in her mind. The problem that still nagged at her was Blakewood's inconclusive inquest result; an 'Open Verdict'. Politics and powerful influences had been at work. The evidence concerning corruption had been toned right down, Vernon Smith was forced to recluse himself from giving evidence by the CPS fearing it may prejudice the trial of Montague Brown. The papers reported the inquest result but for the same reason the link from Brown to Blakewood had a 'D Notice' issued preventing that little gem from being published. She was glad suicide was not the result, thanks to Mrs. Blakewood's evidence. Unlawful Killing, which is what Toni knew it should have been, never achieved a mention. She settled for him being gone and would no longer be corrupting others to do his vile bidding. Blakewood's hidden money was never found; it was not in any of the accounts exposed by Palmer. Toni expected the big house would have been seized as an asset acquired through the proceeds of crime but because Blakewood had never been charged his ex-wife, as sole beneficiary was able to sell it and move to Spain. Toni wondered about her; she did not trust anyone who had been that close to him, was his hidden money, now her hidden money? The idea of all that suffering paving the way for Mrs. Blakewood to enjoy the lavish life hurt Toni deeply. Harrold and Compy could perhaps look into her later. There it was again her instinctive need to put thing right she could not let anything go if she felt she could do something about it.

'Enough of that for now' she thought, time was getting on and she had to be ready soon, Nathan was picking her up at eight and she only had ten minutes to tie her hair and put on her shoes, 'why do I always seem to be in a rush'.

The funerals of Karen Small and Marina Fairfax took place at last, giving the parents partial closure. When Palmer was convicted and sent to prison it left them finally able to grieve. The two officers Hamish Linkman and Scott Wilkinson could now continue with their careers and lives in relative peace, perhaps sleep a little better too.

"Hamish, hello".
"Mel that's you isn't it, good. Nice to hear your voice".
"The last time we saw each other was at Karen's funeral, I wanted to speak but it did not seem appropriate as you were so wrapped up with her dad".
"Yea, no chance that day. I spent a while with him, he's back at work now, I still keep in touch, the man's doing his best".
"Can we meet up, we seemed to get on eh"?
"You know what lass that's the best offer I've had in a very long time; when and where"?
"Tonight. the Four Horseshoes at eight okay"?
"I'll be there".
"Great, till later bye Hamish".
"Bye Mel".

Other Books by PW Lawrence

Looking on Darkness   Book 1 Detective Toni Webb

The Blind do See   Book 2 Detective Toni Webb

Then Begins a Journey   Book 3 Detective Toni Webb

The Eight   The life of an English boy
                       (Book in process)

Printed in Poland
by Amazon Fulfillment
Poland Sp. z o.o., Wrocław

62706987R00199